M000223644

What others are saying about *His Roses & Thorns*

"Wanda has a special gift for making spiritual truths come alive through her experiences with family and friends. *His Roses & Thorns* is warm, personal, biblically sound and inspirational."

Conrad Jacobsen, Founder and President of Teleios, a ministry for men

"There are hundreds of women and many men whose spiritual walk will be strengthened by her words....Wanda's talent for personable, warm expression is exactly what is needed for a devotional guide such as this."

Lynn Petroff, editor and teacher

"Wanda takes the risk to share her faith with stories that touch us right where we live. What a beautiful reminder of God's love in action!"

Pat Proud, Poet, Playwright, Peacemaker

"Even in the midst of life's valleys and deserts there always seems to flow a freshness in God's Word. Wanda reminds us of this as she reaches to the heart and challenges the soul to reflect in earnest over our own personal walk with Christ Jesus."

Candace Chambers-Belida, Inspirational speaker and author of *Dare to Stand*

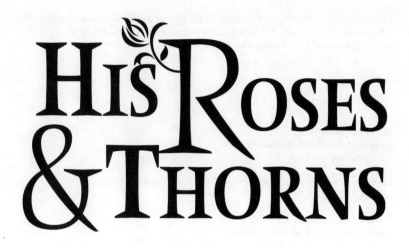

His Roses & Thorns

A Daily Devotional

WANDA SCOTT BLEDSOE

PRESS

ACW Press
Eugene, Oregon 97405

Scripture quotations are taken from the New King James Version, Copyright © 1979, 1980, 1982 by Thomas Nelson, Inc., Publishers. Used by permission.

I have made an honest attempt to contact each person named in this book for his or her permission to publish. If I inadvertently missed someone, please accept my apology. I hope you will feel honored when you read this book, as is my intent.

His Roses and Thorns
Copyright ©2003 Wanda Scott Bledsoe
All rights reserved

Front cover image by Janet Sannipoli of Wet Paint Graphic Design, www.wetpaintgraphics.com

Cover design by Alpha Advertising
Interior design by Pine Hill Graphics

Packaged by ACW Press
85334 Lorane Hwy
Eugene, Oregon 97405
www.acwpress.com
The views expressed or implied in this work do not necessarily reflect those of ACW Press. Ultimate design, content, and editorial accuracy of this work is the responsibility of the author(s).

Publisher's Cataloging-in-Publication Data
(Provided by Cassidy Cataloguing Services, Inc.)

Bledsoe, Wanda Scott.

   His roses & thorns / Wanda Scott Bledsoe. -- 1st ed. --
Eugene, OR : ACW Press, 2003.

      p. ; cm.

   ISBN: 1-932124-09-8

   1. Devotional calendars. 2. Devotional literature.
3. Meditations. 4. Spiritual exercises. 5. Spiritual life.
I. Title. II. His roses and thorns.

BV4832.3 .B54 2003

242/.2--dc22   0309

All rights reserved. No part of this book may be reproduced, stored in a retrieval system, or transmitted in any form or by any means—electronic, mechanical, photocopying, recording, or otherwise—without prior permission in writing from the copyright holder except as provided by USA copyright law.

Printed in the United States of America.

Dedicated to

My parents, Clovis and Ruby Scott

and

My maternal grandparents, Roy and Vannie Dulan

Acknowledgments

There are many family and friends who supported me in the writing of this book and I wish to express my appreciation, especially to

Ruby Scott   Bob and Karen
Milt Bledsoe   Sherri Kreissig
Lyle Peterson   Lynn Petroff
Janet Sannipoli   Denise Stewart
Robert Bergman

About the Author

Wanda Scott Bledsoe is an author and inspirational speaker. She has written daily devotions for her church and is the author of a faith-based job search manual. Wanda is Director of Women's Ministries at her church where she also fulfills her passion for music as church organist. Wanda enjoys being a spiritual mentor for women. She is the mother of two adult children and three grandchildren. Wanda and her husband of over thirty years reside in southern California. Visit Wanda's Web site www.hisrosesandthorns.com and e-mail: wanda@hisrosesandthorns.com to learn more about Wanda and how to contact her to speak at your next event.

A Note from the Author

Thank You, Family and Friends

Blessed is she who believed, for there will be a fulfillment of those things which were told her from the Lord. Luke 1:45

Planting the seed… A friend, Denise Stewart, had encouraged me to write a book of my own personal faith stories. Sherri Kreissig, another friend, said she had been led by the Holy Spirit to encourage me to develop a Web site, write daily devotions and do inspirational speaking.

Obedient to His will… I said yes! Then I called a very special friend, Janet Sannipoli, to see if she would design the Web site *and* the cover of this book. She said yes! Please visit our Web site at www.hisrosesandthorns.com. Mail me at wanda@hisrosesandthorns.com to share with me what this book has meant to you.

His *Roses & Thorns*, the name… *Roses & Thorns,* representing life's ups and downs, was to be the name of my book…until my son, Milton Scott, remarked, "How about adding the word 'His' to the title so people will know this is a book about God?"

Not on my own… I want to thank family and friends whose hard work, prayers and financial gifts made this book possible. I especially want to thank Lynn Petroff, who graciously agreed to do the first edits for me.

My prayer for you… That this book will be of help as you continue on your spiritual journey.

His *Roses & Thorns* to enjoy and *share*… Create your own bouquet of roses and thorns. And don't forget to tell family and friends so they can create a bouquet of their own.

"Now may the God of hope fill you with all joy and peace in believing, that you may abound in hope by the power of the Holy Spirit." Romans 15:13

Your sister in Christ,
Wanda Scott Bledsoe

"Cause for Joy"

A cause for joy
is in the silence
of daily devotions,
In the many stories
of other travelers'
inspiring words,
spoken to the soul,
in Holy moments,
where unworthiness
is replaced by love,
And the Lord
takes great pleasure,
not in what I've been,
but in what I'll be!

Robert Lee Larson
A gift for His Roses & Thorns

Introduction to January Devotions

Rules and Tools for a Great New Year

"Therefore, if anyone is in Christ, he is a new creation; the old has gone, the new has come." II Corinthians 5:18

Happy New Year! I decided to approach the New Year much like I used to approach a new sewing project. First, I would clean up the mess from the last project. All of the leftover scraps were thrown out and the area dusted. Then it was time to make sure the rules, the pattern pieces, were carefully folded and put away and the tools I needed were in their proper places.

Rules I like having guidelines to follow. It makes me feel more secure somehow. Why not get this New Year started off on the right foot. Open your Bible, your guide to life. See what His instructions are for you. Life is difficult enough without making it more so. In the New Testament Jesus gives us just two rules to live by, found in *Matthew 22:37* as He teaches us how we are to live Christ-like lives.

Tools This month you will read stories of His Rules and the tools I use to build my faith. I can't think of a better way to make sure I am ready for a great New Year. I hope you will agree.

Be prepared for a great New Year! I invite you to join me in daily devotions to see what God's instructions and faithful promises can mean for a great New Year for you.

Your sister in Christ,
Wanda Scott Bledsoe

January 1

I John 3:1-3

Someone Who Believes in Me

Behold what manner of love the Father has bestowed on us, that we should be called children of God! I John 3:1

Happy New Year…maybe! One day when our daughter was about 12 or 13, I found her in tears declaring she wasn't good at anything. As I held her, her brother came breezing through the house. He saw her crying, became concerned and of course demanded to know what was wrong. I gently explained. He quickly responded, "She's good at a lot of things!" His sister promptly countered with, "Name one!" There was this prolonged silence accompanied by her brother's facial contortions of intense thought. He was trying so hard to be supportive of his sister. It was just what his sister needed. "See, I told you," as she burst into laughter. I was glad Milton Scott loved his sister no matter what.

Want a fresh start? Done! Not only does God love us just the way we are, He paid a tremendous price to ensure that we are able to wake up each day to a clean slate, able to make a fresh start. What kind of fresh start would you like to make this year?

For your consideration God believes in you. He loves you unconditionally, just the way you are. Perhaps this New Year comes at the perfect time to establish a closer relationship with Him.

A question for the New Year What will I do with the fresh start God has given me today?

Prayers for our brothers and sisters in Christ Those who feel they are unworthy of a fresh start.

January 2

Developing Personal Relationships

*That is what is meant by the Scriptures which say that no mere
man has ever seen, heard or even imagined what wonderful things
God has ready for those who love the Lord.* I Corinthians 2:9

Put in the time Developing a personal relationship takes time.
Modern science has let us expand our world to include the moon
but we still haven't been able to expand our day beyond the twenty-
four hours that God has given us. The only option to overflowing
days is setting priorities. One of my priorities for each day is to
spend time with God.

Developing a personal relationship can be rewarding! Initially I
promised God that I would give Him ten minutes of my time the
first thing each morning. The wonderful discovery I made is that I
received more than the ten minutes I was giving. Have you ever volunteered to help someone only to discover you got much more out
of the encounter than you gave? That is what happened when I
started developing a personal relationship with God through reading His Word.

For your consideration What if we revisit how we spend our time? If
your list indicates you are spending time in areas that are not a priority for you, this may be a good opportunity to reprioritize your
days, starting with time for reading God's Word. Give it a thirty-day
trial and see what wonderful blessings God has in store for you.

A question for the New Year How can I make sure God directs and
guides me in the priorities I myself, or others, have set for this day?

Prayers for our brothers and sisters in Christ Those who feel overwhelmed by all they need to do today.

Committing to a Personal Relationship

Understand, therefore, that the Lord your God is the faithful God who for a thousand generations keeps His promises and constantly loves those who love Him and who obey His commands.
Deuteronomy 7:9

I promise! My father was 91 years old when he went to be with the Lord. He taught me many things in life, one I will never forget: "Your word is your bond. You have nothing that is more valuable than your good name." I think about my father's words when my plate is full to overflowing. It is at that time that I entertain the thought of going back on my promise. Who really expects anyone to keep a promise these days?

How can I trust you? Fortunately for us, we don't have to worry if God will keep His promises. Have you ever had someone break a promise they made to you? Have you ever broken a promise you made to someone else? How does it make you feel that God has made thirty thousand different promises and has never broken any of them?

For your consideration Why not set a goal that will help you establish a closer relationship with God? You may even want to have a partner with whom you can share daily devotional materials. It may just be the help you need, knowing your friend is having his or her daily devotions at the same time you are. How exciting to be able to share with a friend what the impact is on your daily lives.

A question for the New Year What can I do to deepen my personal relationship with God and my family?

Prayers for our brothers and sisters in Christ Those who have been hurt by a broken promise.

Revisiting Life's Instructions

"Teacher, which is the great commandment in the law?"
Matthew 22:36

"The Answer Is, Because He Loves You" I gave a message for children with this title. It was a message designed to help children view their parents and the Ten Commandments as a gift from God. The question; why did God give us parents and just ten rules to follow? The answer is, "Because He loves us, and He wants us to enjoy the world He created for us, He wants us to be safe in that world and He wants us to get along with others."

From a child's viewpoint I don't think God intended for life to be as complicated or burdensome as we have made it. What if we viewed God's rules for our lives as indications of His love? But what if ten rules are too many, maybe even too complex for today's "whatever makes you happy" way of living? Then take today's Scripture to heart. Two simple rules say it all: Love God with all your heart, soul and mind and love your neighbor as yourself. How simple and uncomplicated is that?

For your consideration Try the uncomplicated version. Then take some time to think about how these two rules can help you be safe, live happily and get along with others this year. Why is it important? The answer is, "Because God loves you."

A question for the New Year How can I improve my life by using God's two steps to Christ-like living?

Prayers for our brothers and sisters in Christ Those who are feeling angry, confused or trapped by the ever changing rules society imposes and the impact it has on their lives.

January 5

I Thessalonians 4:9-12

It Should Be Obvious

"But concerning brotherly love you have no need that I should write to you, for you yourselves are taught by God to love one another." I Thessalonians 4:9

Is it too much to expect? The last thing I expected or needed was a bill for four new SUV tires. It seems as if *real* SUV tires had not come with the SUV I had purchased two years ago. "Did you rotate your tires regularly? Did you check the air pressure? How often did you have your wheels aligned?" How I longed for the good old days when I could pull into a service station and actually receive service. A nice man would ask if I needed my oil or my tires checked. The people who worked at these service stations took a personal interest in letting their customers know if they noticed something that needed addressing...like tires showing abnormal wear. A sigh escaped my lips. Reality quickly intruded my fantasizing when the tire salesman asked how I wanted to pay for my new SUV tires.

For your consideration We are called to care for each other by showing love for one another. Perhaps we should take some time to analyze how our changing world has affected our ability to show and receive love. Does the ethnic background of someone influence whether or not we reach out in love? Maybe taking time to remember the good old days, when caring for our cars and showing love for one another seemed easier, is not such a bad idea.

A question for the New Year Who needs to feel my love and compassion today?

Prayers for our brothers and sisters in Christ Those whose ethnic background is different than mine.

Seeking Peace and Comfort?

And the peace of God, which transcends all understanding, will guard your hearts and your minds in Christ Jesus. Philippians 4:7

Like an old friend It was right after I had attended my first women's retreat. We had been encouraged to read our Bibles on a daily basis. I had written my own commitment to do this. Although I had been taught that books are not to be written in, it seemed crucial that I record my progress. I chose a yellow highlighter to mark Scriptures as I read them. Before long the devotions I was using had me rereading Scriptures I had read before. It was like returning to an old friend.

Unexpected miracles It was a year later and now there were lots of highlighted Scriptures that brought comfort and peace as I returned to them. It was as if God was reminding me of His love. Over the years, my Bible has become a record of faith, my faith in God as I read His Holy Word, and His love for me as He guides and comforts me through life's challenges.

For your consideration If people or things don't provide the comfort you are seeking, try the Bible. I find those small "Bible Promises Books" that list scriptures by topics (trouble, comfort, love, trust, worry, etc.) to be especially helpful when I am turning to the Bible for a specific need. Make a note of answered prayers and see the reassurance and hope it brings.

A question for the New Year How has God comforted you in the past? How would you like Him to comfort you today?

Prayers for our brothers and sisters in Christ Those who are experiencing family problems.

Luke 6:38,43-45

Something Worth Sharing

For if you give, you will get! Your gift will return to you in full and overflowing measure, pressed down, shaken together to make room for more, and running over. Whatever measure you use to give—large or small—will be used to measure what is given back to you. Luke 6:38

What is there to share? I scanned my e-mail. One caught my eye. It was supposedly a true story, about a large retail store that allegedly refused to refund a customer the $250 it had charged for a cookie recipe the customer thought cost $2.50. In revenge, the customer said they would e-mail the recipe to as many people as possible. So I forwarded the story to my e-mail list, only to discover the next day at church that it was just a joke.

Good news! In the job search workbook I wrote for people of faith I included a list of favorite Scriptures I had used through out the book. Shortly after it was published, I discovered that my former Sunday school teacher was dying of cancer. I sent her a copy of these Scriptures. Another friend was going through a challenging time in her marriage; she also received a copy. I started keeping them by my computer to add to a note, or to use when someone called needing some good news.

For your consideration Want to share some good news? Try a favorite Scripture. There is nothing like sharing life-tested Scriptures that have worked for you.

A question for the New Year Who do I know who would be uplifted by one of my life-tested Scriptures?

Prayers for our brothers and sisters in Christ Those who bring us the news.

January 8

John 20:24-29

It Sounds like Science Fiction

Then Jesus told him, "Thomas, you believe because you have seen me. But blessed are those who haven't seen me and believe anyway." John 20:29

I can explain Yuri was from Japan and studying at the University of Washington. She spent one weekend a month in our home. It was Good Friday of Holy Week and she said although she was Buddhist, she would love to go to church with our family. As we were driving home I could tell she had questions.

Our faith I began by explaining why Jesus died on the cross. Yuri looked at me in disbelief. I struggled on with the explanation of His resurrection. Her understanding of our faith hadn't improved one bit. I backtracked to the story of Jesus' conception and birth. As I tried to explain the conception part, I realized this was more difficult than I could have imagined.

A faith thing I felt like I had dropped into a science fiction movie. How was this young woman going to believe something as unscientific as a virgin birth, death, resurrection and the forgiveness of sin? She smiled at me politely as I quietly mumbled, "It doesn't make sense, I suppose, unless you believe and have faith."

For your consideration As we start a New Year, how can you benefit by believing in a faith that hasn't changed in over two thousand years? Do you like continuity, solid foundations, strong family ties? Then reexamine your beliefs and start this year off with a solid foundation in God.

A question for the New Year How will a firm foundation in my faith influence the kind of year I can expect?

Prayers for our brothers and sisters in Christ Those who have trouble believing in God.

January 9

John 6:30-35

Something More

Jesus replied. "I am the Bread of Life. No one coming to me will ever be hungry again. Those believing in me will never thirst."
John 6:35

The perfect plan When I was a child and didn't want to finish food that was on my plate, my mother reminded me of the starving children of the world. I have never had to go hungry due to lack of food, but there have been other hungers that I couldn't seem to satisfy.

A stress reducer It started during a period in my life when I was functioning as both the choir director and organist at my church. As the time for the Christmas program approached, choir members rushed to our pastor, concerned that I would self-destruct. My hunger to be seen as able to do everything was about to do me in. Miraculously, supported by their prayers, I experienced a "growth spurt" in my faith. I became so much calmer that the choir members now rushed to the pastor with, "What's wrong with Wanda? She is too calm." God gave me *more* while allowing me to do less.

For your consideration Perhaps it is time to ask yourself, "What more do I want from my faith?" Did you find yourself settling for less last year when actually you wanted *something more*? Can you feel the excitement and the possibilities of a New Year with a faith that promises you *more*?

A question for the New Year What more do I want from my faith?

Prayers for our brothers and sisters in Christ Those for whom going to bed hungry is a way of life.

John 8:3-12

I Never Did Like the Dark

"I am the Light of the world. He who follows Me shall not walk in darkness, but have the light of life." John 8:12

Not for me During my senior year I lived in a dormitory. Occasionally I would take a bus downtown and return just as it was beginning to get dark. As I walked the four or five blocks from the bus stop back to the dorm, I noticed the houses along the way ablaze with lights. Who were the owners waiting to welcome? Feeling alone in the gathering darkness, I rushed by, knowing the lights were not on for me.

The power in His light and yours I thank God for all of our brothers and sisters in Christ who work in the various fields of technology because if left up to my intelligence we would still be reading by candlelight. However, a candle can be a powerful source of light. When I think of the night that plunges us into total darkness and then visualize the impact of a single candle, I am reminded of our potential impact as candles of faith. Think about the impact of your faith like a candle of light leading others to Christ.

For your consideration Where does the light of God shine brightly in your life? In what areas do you seem to be stumbling around in the dark? And how does your faith provide light for someone else to see the light of God?

A question for the New Year How can I use God's amazing light to brighten my life and the lives of others?

Prayers for our brothers and sisters in Christ Those who restore power after a storm.

Someone to Watch over Me

Because the Lord is my Shepherd, I have everything I need.
Psalm 23:1

He was so wonderful It was a convention at Kansas State University for high school Latin students. During lunch we were entertained by a music major who sang, "Someone To Watch Over Me." I fell in love with his voice and dreamed about him for months. Although the song became one of my favorites, I never saw the music major again.

The words are so beautiful Throughout my life there have been many to whom I looked for love, support, protection and guidance. Sometimes they met my expectations and sometimes not. However when I read **Psalm 23,** "someone to watch over me" takes on a whole new meaning.

For your consideration If you are feeling the need to have someone special in your life, someone who will never let you down, someone who loves you unconditionally, then think about our Lord and Savior as the Good Shepherd in that role. Having our Lord and Savior as a role model we can respect and trust today, tomorrow and for all eternity is pretty awesome. My music major wasn't watching over me, he was just entertaining me. The sides of some police cars read, "To Protect and Serve." I think the Lord as our Shepherd adds a whole new dimension to those words, "protect and serve." What do you think?

A question for the New Year How can using the Lord as my Shepherd contribute to my feelings of security throughout the New Year?

Prayers for our brothers and sisters in Christ Those who are music majors; those who protect and serve.

Truth As You Interpret It

Jesus said to them, "You are truly my disciples if you live as I tell you to, and you will know the truth, and the truth will set you free." John 8:31-32

Good intentions Our dog Tiffany was a crotchety thing, snapping at you if you didn't honor her space. The children's friends, a brother and sister, had come to play. Gretchen had been warned about Tiffany's lack of manners but she decided to give Tiffany another chance. Tiffany snapped at Gretchen and we were off to the emergency room for a few stitches and lots of untruths.

The end justifies the means? I decided I could save Gretchen's grandparents a trip to the hospital by claiming Gretchen as my niece so I could sign for her medical care. "Just trust me on this," I told Gretchen. To support that untruth I had to tell another one. Then the emergency room staff started asking Gretchen questions. Gretchen reluctantly began telling untruths to support my untruths. Finally I called her grandparents who came immediately and signed for Gretchen's care. "Gretchen, I am so sorry. Telling untruths (lies) is not right no matter how good your intentions. Just trust me on this."

For your consideration As we head into a New Year, I am going to be on the lookout for interpretations of the truth: mine and others. Today's Scripture reminds us of the source of all truth. It doesn't need any interpretation by us nor does it allow for any justification for untruths.

A question for the New Year What part does truth play in my plans for a happy, healthy, and prosperous New Year?

Prayers for our brothers and sisters in Christ Those who feel betrayed by untruths.

"Just Reverse the Directions"

"And you know where I am going and how to get there." John 14:4

Lost My daughter and I were going to pick up some special makeup for her. The cosmetic specialist lived in one of those new developments with lots of twists and turns and dead-ends. I didn't have any trouble getting there. The problem came when I attempted to leave. "Just reverse the directions," she advised. I could not! Finally I asked a postman who said, "I know the way, just follow me."

Follow me I can be very naïve at times and so it is just a little scary when I feel lost and someone says, "I know the way, just follow me." While there have been many in my life who rightly or wrongly claimed they knew the way, only One claimed, "I am the way," and backed up His claim in irrefutable ways.

For your consideration Are you feeling lost? Have you started down a particular path only to discover that it is the wrong one for you? Do you need to reverse directions to get back to home base? God's Word provides direction for all of life's mazes. I may not know how to reverse directions to find my way out of a development, but I can always find my way in life when I read His Word. Maybe I am not as dense as I thought.

A question for the New Year Thomas Guides, telephone books, even our cars' global positioning systems are constantly being updated, but not the Guide to Life. What is God trying to tell us?

Prayers for our brothers and sisters in Christ Those who feel lost in life's confusing maze.

Use Plenty of Salt

"You are the world's seasoning, to make it tolerable. If you lose your flavor, what will happen to the world?" Matthew 5:13

An essential ingredient As I observed my daughter Shelly and her friends, I came to some interesting conclusions. The group always sought her out. What was it that seemed to make Shelly special?

Enhanced It was almost as if her friends realized that if they stayed close to Shelly, their strengths would be enhanced. In the course of their conversations and activities, Shelly had a presence that seem to bring out the best in them.

Every ten people I always knew Shelly was special to me, but now I believed others knew she was special. What if Shelly were interspersed in every ten people throughout the earth? What a kinder, gentler human race we would be. Isn't that what God calls each of us to do as the "salt" of the earth? Just as seasoning brings out the flavor in food, don't we as believers have a responsibility to bring out the best in the world around us? If not us, then who?

For your consideration Why not take some time to look again at your part of the world? Spend some quiet time with God in His Word and in prayer. Listen for His message to you. My brothers and sisters in Christ, you are the salt of the earth. God has plans for you.

A question for the New Year How can I use the love of Christ to bring out the best in those around me?

Prayers for our brothers and sisters in Christ Those who work for social justice.

January 15

Ezekiel 34:25-27

Counting to Ten

And there shall be showers, showers of blessing. Ezekiel 34:26

Math! Mathematical calculations have always been a mystery to me. I vividly remember trying to understand fractions. My father and my Uncle Art carefully drew a "pie" and then divided it in to eight slices. "If we remove four slices, Wanda, what part is left?" As I pondered this newest mathematical mystery, my little sister Pat, who was four grades behind me, piped up with the correct answer as she played nearby."

Counting to ten As I grew up, my lifelong challenges with math were soon joined by other even more significant challenges. By the end of one particularly taxing day, I found myself going to bed feeling overwhelmed. I wondered, "How can I pray? All I would do tonight is complain." One of my mother's "sermons of life" came to me. When as a dramatic, emotional child, I would claim to be depressed, Mother would say, "Think happy thoughts." I decided to try her advice. My goal was ten blessings for the day. The first two or three took some effort and then the floodgates opened! When I reached thirteen, I sighed contentedly and drifted off to sleep.

For your consideration Try finding a quiet spot at the end of your day and go on a treasure hunt. Start from the beginning of your day and count the ways God has blessed you.

A question for the New Year How would I feel if I gave someone I love a gift and they didn't even say thank you?

Prayers for our brothers and sisters in Christ Those who fail to recognize the way God blesses them on a daily basis.

January 16

Choosing One or the Other

Look at the birds! They don't worry about what to eat, they don't need to sow or reap or store up food for your heavenly Father feeds them. And you are far more valuable to Him than they are.
Matthew 6:26

Pray or worry? I have always been a worrywart. Something had to be done! As I pondered my dilemma, I thought of the Israelites in their journey to the promised land. What could *I* learn from the way God cared for the Israelites?

Pray! I began praying for the things I felt I needed that day. Then I asked God to Divinely Order my day. It wasn't long before I noticed several things: 1) at night when I checked my list against my blessings of the day, a lot of them matched, 2) I fell asleep feeling I didn't have to worry about tomorrow because God had taken such good care of me today, and 3) when my carefully scheduled day didn't go as planned, I was able to say, "I'll just have to trust You on this one."

For your consideration Try it for yourself. The first thing in the morning get your Bible and pencil and paper. Make a list of all the things you need for the day. Open your Bible to a favorite Scripture. Pray for God's Divine Order and that His will be done. Have faith and then at the end of the day count the ways God has blessed you.

A question for the New Year How might my day be different if I asked God for what I thought I needed and then trusted Him to arrange it?

Prayers for our brothers and sisters in Christ Those worry too much.

January 17

I John 3:18-23

The Answer Is, Yes, No, I'll Think about It

And we are sure of this, that He will listen to us whenever we ask Him for anything in line with His will. And if we really know He is listening when we talk to Him and make our requests, then we can be sure that He will answer us. I John 5:14-15

Yes or no? The immediate yes or no answers were the easiest because then I knew the issue had been decided. Sometimes I liked my mother's decision and sometimes I didn't, but once she handed it down, that was that and I moved on. It was the "I'll think about it" answer that was so frustrating for me. The questions usually involved life-threatening issues near and dear to any teenager's heart. While I might have questioned her answer in my mind, somewhere in my heart I knew she loved me. And remembering her love made it easier to accept her answer.

History repeats itself As a mother who only through God's grace survived raising two teenagers, I now know what my mother meant by "I'll think about it." She really meant, "WAIT! I need to pray about it because I love you so much and I don't want to make a mistake.

For your consideration God promises an answer to our prayers: yes, no, wait. *Psalm 40:1* calls us to wait patiently on God. It is at these times that I need to remember other instances when I waited on the Lord and His answer and timing were perfect.

A question for the New Year How can I wait more patiently on the Lord?

Prayers for our brothers and sisters in Christ Those who are mothers of teenage daughters.

January 18

Matthew 28:16-20

Let's Play Black Jack

"And be sure of this—that I am with you always, even to the end of the world." Matthew 28:20

A father's love Mother had said a resounding NO! Daddy didn't understand that my sister and I wanted her to say no. So he sat us down on this Saturday night to entertain us by playing blackjack with us. My sister Pat and I schemed together. When we got tired, we executed our plan. It worked beautifully. We gradually lost all of our matches to Daddy. He was happy thinking he had helped us through a difficult evening and we were happy because we knew he loved us!

Through it all It was easy to turn to my father when I scraped a knee or suffered some disappointment. But perhaps one of the greatest lessons I learned was to turn to him seeking his love and comfort when he said yes to my request and when his answer was NO!

For your consideration God promises to be with us even when His answer to our prayers is "No." We are the ones who move away in our anger, disappointment, hurt and sorrow. I can always find God as I sit in my office and write to Him in my prayer journal, pouring out my heart and then turning to His Word for His assurance, comfort and guidance. Find your special place with God no matter what the circumstances happen to be. HE has promised to always be there for you! Even when His answer is "No."

A question for the New Year What do I need to do to stay even closer to God?

Prayers for our brothers and sisters in Christ Those who are fathers of teenage girls.

January 19

He Talks to Me

I will instruct you says the Lord and guide you along the best pathway for your life; I will advise you and watch your progress.
Psalm 32:8

The answer is Ronald Reagan The message light was blinking when I opened the door to my hotel room. The call was from one of my organization's attorneys. About four years ago, an employee from another division who had been suspended called to ask my advice. I directed her to our human resources department. After experiencing continuing disciplinary action, she brought a discrimination suit against the organization. During her deposition, she had been forced to name the manager she had consulted with. I knew it was just a matter of time before I was "summoned."

God promises us wisdom. I stared at the ceiling and called to God for help. I heard a voice say, "Remember Ronald Reagan?" I replied, "Lord, what has Ronald Reagan got to do with this?" "Wanda, if President Reagan can't remember specifics of the recent Iran Contra incident, even aided by all his advisors and records, how can you remember details of an incident that occurred four years ago?" A perfect calm overtook me and I closed my eyes and went blissfully to sleep.

For your consideration God has promised to guide us through the challenges we face in our everyday lives. If you are having trouble hearing His voice, it could be a loose connection, static from outside interference, or maybe you are on a totally different wavelength. Try spending time with Him and see if that doesn't clear up the connection.

A question for the New Year Whose voice do I usually listen to when I need advice?

Prayers for our brothers and sisters in Christ Those who are attorneys.

Prayer Formula

But when you pray, go away by yourself, all alone, and shut the door behind you and pray to your Father secretly, and your Father, who knows your secrets, will reward you. Matthew 6:6

What? I was sitting in the congregation listening to my husband, Milton, bring the message on Effective Prayer. My mind was so busy being upset that my husband was telling us how to pray that I almost missed what he was saying about ACTS.

ACTS! Milton was talking about a formula for prayer. Like a recalcitrant two-year-old, my immediate reaction was, "Who needs a formula to pray?" But wait! This was starting to get interesting. I might like this!

How should I pray? Milton explained that the ACTS method of praying began with A for Adoration, C for Confession, T for Thanksgiving, and S for Supplication. Cool! This is where I get to ask God for everything I think I need for just today. Kind of like a To Do list that has been prayed over. Last but not least I added my prayers for others, sometimes called intercessory prayers. They include family and friends. They also include people I don't know, like those falsely imprisoned, or abandoned and abused children. I pray for them a lot!

For your consideration Pray! God hears us any way we chose to speak to Him, spontaneously or using a formula like ACTS. Speak from your heart. HE hears, He knows, He answers.

A question for the New Year How can I pray more effectively?

Prayers for our brothers and sisters in Christ Children who have no one to pray for them.

The Kindergarteners' Ecumenical View

"Then he took the children into His arms and placed His hands on their heads and He blessed them." Mark 10:16

Let's say grace We lived in the suburbs of Dayton, Ohio at the time and there were lots of *at home* moms. We moms decided to car pool and as an extra bonus, to provide lunch on the day we took the children to school.

An ecumenical discussion Rocky's parents were Baptist, Patrick's parents were atheists, Kathy's parents were Catholic and we were Presbyterian. I had placed the children's lunch on the table. Before I got out of earshot I heard Rocky inform everyone that they needed to say grace before they began eating. All of the children except Patrick began reciting prayers their families said at mealtime. Patrick chimed in with why his family didn't say grace, adding that he felt it was all right to give thanks for the food, he just didn't know to whom. The discussion continued until a compromise was reached, grace was said and these wonderful children began eating their lunch.

For your consideration What interesting answers might you get if you asked your children, of any age, what problems they face, and if they prayed to God about them? Yesterday's ACTS formula for praying can easily be adapted for children. This could be a project you work on as a family. God hears our children when they speak to Him. Teach them to speak from their hearts. Assure them that He hears, He knows, He answers.

A question for the New Year How would helping my children pray influence their everyday lives?

Prayers for our brothers and sisters in Christ Those children whose parents do not believe in God.

Acts 2:46-47

Always Be with Family

And they continued steadfastly in the apostles' doctrine and fellowship, in the breaking of bread, and in prayers. Acts 2:42

Free at last! My mother had to be the strictest mom in the whole wide world. There were rules and more rules to protect my sister and me. I always knew the rules were for my own good. They made me feel special. I carry my maiden name, Scott, as a testimony to my loving parents. However, I was looking forward to the freedom of going away to college.

Whatever you do Mother was now telling me that no matter where I was, the first order of business was to find a church home, join and then make myself useful. She called it being under the protection of God's family.

Stay with family During over thirty years of marriage, we have belonged to five church families in Kansas, Missouri, Ohio, Washington and California. Those church families saw me through the death of a child, challenges in my marriage and my career, and rearing two children. Sunday worship was an oasis in the midst of life's desert that refreshed me for the coming week.

For your consideration Whether you are new to an area or have lived there for years, if you don't have a church home maybe it is time you did. Reach out with a handshake and a smile. Then be ready to experience all of the blessings and love that comes with being a member of the Family of God.

A question for the New Year What am I missing by not being an active participant in a church family?

Prayers for our brothers and sisters in Christ Those who are looking for a warm and wonderful extended family.

Running Away from Family to Family

Two are better than one, because they have a good reward for their labor. For if they fall, one will lift up his companion. But woe to him who is alone when he falls, for he has no one to help him up. Ecclesiastes 4:9-10

Running away! When I announced to my two small children that I was running away, they knew I would be back. They calmly asked that I tell them where I was going so they wouldn't worry. My husband just shook his head.

My church family I knocked on Jean and Gerry's door. When they opened it, surprised to see me, I announced that I had run away…for awhile. They smiled and invited me in. Coffee was soon poured and for the next hour I chatted with this part of my church family. After a refreshing visit I returned home to the family I loved. Oh, how important it was for me that year to be able to run away to the loving and protecting arms of my church family.

For your consideration Most of us would admit that on any given day, life can seem pretty overwhelming. If you need to run away for awhile, and your extended family lives too far away, try turning to someone from your church family. A smile, a cup of coffee and a time of shared laughter could be just the "pick me up" God has in mind for you.

A question for the New Year Why should I ever feel there is no one to turn to when I am a part of the family of God?

Prayers for our brothers and sisters in Christ Those who lend a helping hand to new and or overwhelmed mothers.

January 24

Psalm 122:1,6-9

A Special Place

"I was glad when they said to me, Let us go into the house of the Lord." Psalm 122:1

Something to look forward to I have always loved light, airy places, yet this church with its walls covered with polished dark paneling felt peaceful to me. I eagerly looked forward to Sunday morning worship services.

I made it The peacefulness of that church took on a whole new meaning a few years later, after I had two babies fourteen months apart. Leaving my children in the nursery with the loving attendant, I raced up the stairs to the peaceful and refreshing presence of God that awaited me. I would slip quickly into a pew and bow my head. I was in God's House and He would restore me and make me whole again.

For your consideration If you are looking for a sense of peace in your hectic life, an oasis available to you to help bring definition into you life, then God's house of worship is just where you might want to be on Sunday morning. Might I suggest you (1) attend twenty-one straight Sundays (psychologists say it takes twenty-one days to establish a new behavior) (2) reach out and introduce yourself to at least five new people each Sunday; don't wait for them to come to you, and (3) get involved; sign up for special events. After the twenty-first Sunday, look around and see the smiling faces of your new church family.

A question for the New Year How can I use Sunday morning worship to help me cope with Monday through Saturday?

Prayers for our brothers and sisters in Christ Those who are looking for a church home.

January 25

Psalm 112:5-10

Kids from a Rich Family with Holes in Their Jeans

"He gives generously to those in need. His deeds will never be forgotten. He shall have influence and honor." Psalm 112:9

A special lady One of my daddy's favorite sayings is, "Put your money where your mouth is." This was a special family who did just that. She happened to be the mother of the two little blond boys who wore jeans with holes in them to church. Her clothes reflected the look of many washings. What a rich person she turned out to be. How blessed I was when she reached out to help me.

Her sermon I had given birth prematurely to twins. Michael Spencer died shortly after birth. Milton Scott, weighing 2 lbs 13 oz was fighting for his life in an incubator. I walked out of the hospital with empty arms. That rich lady, the mother of the two boys with holes in their jeans, called right away. "I know you would like to visit your son. I can pick you up and take you." And she did, coming to take me to the hospital day after day in her well-loved and much-used station wagon. What a sermon she delivered in His Name.

For your consideration If you feel the need to be more connected, more loved, more secure, then perhaps one of the best things you can do for yourself and your family this year is to nestle them safely and securely in the family of God.

A question for the New Year How could I benefit from having a loving Family of God in whatever place I might find myself? What contribution could I make?

Prayers for our brothers and sisters in Christ Those with children in hospitals.

January 26

II Corinthians 9:6-8

Why Me, Lord?

"So let each one give as he purposes in his heart, not grudgingly or of necessity; for God loves a cheerful giver." II Corinthians 9:7

Grumble One of my new neighbors had invited me to her church, emphasizing that next Sunday was Advent and the service would be a special one. I could hardly wait! The phone rang and it was a pastor from a church in my old neighborhood. There was such hope in his voice as he asked if I would play for their services the following Sunday (the first Sunday in Advent) because their organist was in the hospital with pneumonia. What could I say since I was between organist positions except, "Yes, of course"? As soon as I hung up, I started grumbling. I grumbled so much that my sister said she would go with me.

What joy! With a smile on my face but martyred resignation in my heart, I took my place at the organ. The service began with the prelude sung by a guest choir of Tongans, Pacific Islanders. My mouth fell open. Growing up in the Midwest, I had never experienced the richness of the Pacific Islander culture. My heart filled anew with the wonder of the Christ Child and these people so different from me that He also came to love and to save.

For your consideration When asked to serve, I encourage you to think about saying yes with a cheerful heart and then be open to God's blessing for you.

A question for the New Year How can I be better at responding with a cheerful heart?

Prayers for our brothers and sisters in Christ Those who are part of a music ministry.

January 27

I Corinthians 11:23-26

Good-bye Ocean

"For every time you eat this bread and drink this cup you are re-telling the message of the Lord's death, that He has died for you. Do this until He comes again." I Corinthians 11:26

Awe! Our five-year-old grandson, Jay, and his mother were visiting us from Germany. We had spent a glorious day at the ocean. It was our grandson's first experience at the ocean and we thoroughly enjoyed watching him explore the beach. Our cameras clicked almost constantly as we tried to capture the wonder in his eyes. But the best was yet to come. As the sun began to set, Jay assumed a somber stance and watched quietly as the sun made its timeless journey beyond the horizon to signal the end of yet another day. We called to Jay to come; it was time to go home. He turned to acknowledge our summons and then slowly turned back to face the ocean. His little hand came up and slowly he waved good-bye.

The awesomeness of nature I thought of those people who claim they would rather worship God by themselves, surrounded by nature, rather than in a church. I reflected on how important the sacraments were for me and how much I appreciated the opportunity to participate in this sacred celebration along with other believers.

For your consideration Of course we should enjoy nature. But if you want to really feel close to God, come into His House and commune with Him and fellow believers. The best sunset cannot even come close.

A question for the New Year How does partaking of the bread and wine make me special?

Prayers for our brothers and sisters in Christ Those who will receive communion for the first time this Sunday.

Where Are the Blinders?

"Choose for yourselves this day whom you will serve. But as for me and my house, we will serve the Lord." Joshua 24:15

Forging ahead. My husband and I differ dramatically in our shopping technique. When I am going through a store to purchase an object, I shop along the way. My eyes are roving for items that might be on sale. My hands are feeling anything of cloth as I pass. My ears are listening for exclamations of other shoppers that might lead me to a potential sale item too good to leave in the store. My husband's shopping technique is a different matter altogether. He doesn't shop. He knows what he wants to purchase before he enters the store. He then proceeds to that item looking neither to the right nor to the left. Once he finds the item, he immediately proceeds to the checkout counter.

His point? Maybe we need my husband's "look neither to the right nor to the left" approach in leading a Christ-like life. The secular world provides so many seductive distractions. The technological explosion has created all kinds of goodies for us to explore. The marketing of these areas is slick, sophisticated and insidious.

For your consideration The choice is yours. Take some time to review God's rules for Christian living. Then decide if following God can help blind you to the temptations, doubts, fears and pursuit of selfish interests that abound in our secular world. When our focus is on God, Christian values are clear and we are not easily distracted. It is a matter of choice.

A question for the New Year What Christian values are important to me?

Prayers for our brothers and sisters in Christ Those wanting to make new choices.

January 29

Job 1:13-22

Steadfast Faith

"The Lord gave, and the Lord has taken away; blessed be the name of the Lord." Job 1:21

In plenty and in want An operation in which Arthur Ashe had received a blood transfusion left him HIV positive. Reporters asked if he felt God had treated him unfairly. I can't remember Mr. Ashe's exact words but they were something to the effect that he hadn't questioned God's fairness when he won the U.S. Open Tennis Match, why should he question God's fairness now?

Am I exempt? I needed to think about Mr. Ashe's statement. Did I really believe that because I was a Christian, life would be easier for me? And if God should bless me with a carefree life, how could He then use me? Who would believe anything I had to say about adversity if I had not successfully weathered any of life's storms?

For your consideration How can your faith help you be supple and unbreakable in the midst of the storm so that you can emerge sturdy and victorious? If you are in the midst of adversity right now, whom can you ask to help you get through it? And who do you know that will benefit by hearing your story of victory? What can we say even though there are tears in our eyes, sorrow in our hearts and a quiver in our voice? We can cry out to God through the words of *Psalm 57:1...and in the shadow of Your wings I will make my refuge, until these calamities have passed by.*

A question for the New Year What can I do today to strengthen my faith?

Prayers for our brothers and sisters in Christ Those in the midst of life's adversity; those willing to help.

January 30

I John 2:15-17

The Perfect Ten

"And this world is fading away, and these evil, forbidden things will go with it, but whoever keeps doing the will of God will live forever." I John 2:17

'Fraidy Cat! From grade school on, I can remember liking rules. Clearly stated rules gave me a solid foundation from which to operate. They made me feel secure. I wanted to do the right thing, and if you told me the rules, then I could be fairly sure I could obey them. I don't remember questioning the whys of the rules. Take the rule in my elementary school: "Thou shall not be in the halls during recess." I took that rule at face value. I didn't stop to think maybe it was for my safety because all of the teachers were on the playground supervising the children. I just followed the rule. It made sense to me to want to please rather than have someone be upset with me. Unfortunately many of my classmates didn't see it that way and thus the label, "Fraidy Cat."

For your consideration. Have you ever wondered why God in His infinite power does not just make us follow His rules? Rather He gives us the freedom to choose. Sometime I make the right choice, but sometimes the choices I make hurt myself and others. What are the choices that are facing you today? How will you use God's Instruction Book of Life to help make sure the choices you make are the right ones?

A question for the New Year When has breaking God's instructions for life not only hurt me but others as well?

Prayers for our brothers and sisters in Christ Those whose are whistle-blowers.

January 31

I Peter 3:13-17

A Way to Share

"Quietly trust yourself to Christ your Lord and if anybody asks why you believe as you do, be ready to tell him, and do it in a gentle and respectful way." I Peter 3:15

A faith story I didn't feel comfortable approaching friends, relatives, or coworkers about God, but I did love telling stories about my family and me and God's impact on our lives. When an opportunity presented itself, I would just begin my story. "You won't believe what happened to Shelly (our daughter). She was riding her bike down that big hill by our house when her brakes failed. She prayed and a voice told her to steer her bike into the curb. She and her bike went flying into the air. 'Mom, I was not afraid,' she told me. A man working in his yard ran to see if he could help. He found a stunned little girl with no tears, no blood, no broken bones *and* a bike that was no longer functional. He looked at her in amazement and asked if she was all right. Her response to him was simply, 'Yes, I prayed.' She picked up her bike and pushed it home." I closed the story with, "God is good."

For your consideration As you have grown in your faith this month, praying, believing, and, reading His Word, I pray your own *roses and thorns* of faith have bloomed in such abundance that you will want to share some of them with others.

A question for the New Year How have I grown in my faith this month? How have I benefited? How have others benefited?

Prayers for our brothers and sisters in Christ Those who work in places where God is never mentioned.

My Journal
January: Rules and Tools for a Great New Year

Insights: What do I want to remember about rules and tools for Christ-like living?

Challenges: What do I need to do to incorporate the lessons I have learned into my everyday life? When will I start?

What are the ten top blessings I received from God this month?

1.

2.

3.

4.

5.

6.

7.

8.

9.

10.

Answered Prayers

Introduction to February Devotions

The Universal Language of God's Love

God is love! John 4:8,16

God's language of love My husband, Milton, and I traveled to Germany so we could participate in the first communion of our grandson, Jay. The outpouring of love to us from Jay's family and friends was extraordinary, especially when 99 percent of that love was felt, not spoken. I do not speak German, and they spoke little English. That wonderful experience made me think about other expressions of love that are felt rather than spoken.

Textbook on love What source could I use to describe the various meanings we associate with love? Would His Word tell me of *all* forms of love, including love between family members? What about love expressed as kindness toward those we love as well as those we would consider enemies? Could I find love expressed as desire for things that give us pleasure and satisfaction?

Love poems And since the month of February includes the celebration of February 14 as Valentine's Day, a day for lovers, could I also find in my Bible love expressed as passion? If I had any doubt I only had to read the Song of Solomon. One Bible commentator talked about an interpretation of this book as one that encourages true love and fidelity within the bonds of marriage.

Love stories The devotions for February are just stories of the many forms of God's love I have experienced. As you read them, see if *you* can find God's love for us expressed through the love of others. Join me in this month's devotions and experience God's love for us anew.

> *"And now abide faith, hope, love these three; but the greatest of these is love."* I Corinthians 13:13

Your sister in Christ,
Wanda Scott Bledsoe

February 1

John 15:11-15

Lending a Helping Hand

*Though I speak with the tongues of men and of angels, but
have not love, I have become sounding brass or a clanging cymbal.*
I Corinthians 13:1

Dirty dishes I watched as Susan, the mother of our grandson, Jay,
and granddaughter Danielle sat exhausted. My husband and I had
traveled to their home in Mainz, Germany to be a part of the celebration of our grandson's first communion. Susan had prepared a
meal for us and at the last minute we were joined by Susan's good
friend Pietra and her four children. We now totaled ten as we sat
down to dinner. The adults sat lingering over dinner. Susan had
gone outside to check on the children. I didn't say a word as I went
to the kitchen to start cleaning up.

Teaming up Susan's friend Pietra followed me into the kitchen.
During the next few minutes, I experienced the true concept of
teamwork. We communicated through gestures and lots of laughs.
Soon the kitchen was spick-and-span. When Susan returned and
saw her kitchen standing tall and Pietra and I looking pleased as
punch, she felt our love.

Love in action Pietra and I took action to show our love for Susan.
The fact that no words were spoken during our act of love was a
whole new experience for me. Just think! Love transcends language,
cultures and countries. For me that means that no matter where I
am, I can speak God's language of love.

A question of love How can I put my love into action today?

Prayers for our brothers and sisters in Christ Those who are visiting
family and friends in foreign countries; those whose neighbors
speak little English.

February 2

I John 3:18-23

The Gift He Gave on His Birthday

*And though I have the gift of prophecy, and understand all
mysteries and all knowledge, and though I have all faith, so
that I could remove mountains, but have not love, I am nothing.*
I Corinthians 13:2

…that others might enjoy the day Susan had planned a buffet for all
the guests following the church service. In order for everything to
be ready when the guests arrived, someone had to remain behind.
Rieger, the husband of Susan's good friend Pietra, volunteered.

Working in silence The noise level ebbed and flowed as children
noisily played, and friends and family laughed and talked. Most of
the conversation was in German and since I don't speak any
German, the words meant nothing to me. Every time I ventured
into the kitchen, Rieger was speaking few words but working hard.
Finally it was over. Now Rieger can rest, I thought.

Love in action Someone announced that tomorrow was Regier's
birthday…about the same time that Susan told us Rieger had volunteered to drive us to the airport at 6 A.M. that next morning. My
mouth flew open. He looked at us and smiled shyly. It was one of
the many times on that trip that I experienced love in action, love
in a language that was not my own…but one I understood and
greatly appreciated.

A question of love How can I show my love today without even saying a word?

Prayers for our brothers and sisters in Christ Those who volunteer
to work in soup kitchens.

February 3

All About Town

*And though I bestow all my goods to feed the poor, and though
I give my body to be burned, but have not love, it profits me
nothing.* I Corinthians 13:3

Welcome Susan, the mother of our grandson, Jay, and granddaughter, Danielle, had taken us to visit her parents. Her mother, Hilde, had a wonderful lunch all prepared. Even more wonderful was her English that she had been brushing up on in preparation for our visit. Since the birth of our grandson some eight years before, Hilde and I as grandmothers, (Oma in German) had become not only friends, but family. Throughout our visit, Hilde took her time to show us historical sites, including breathtaking churches.

Music in any language What fun we had exploring the sights and laughing with the sheer joy of experiencing another country, its culture and its people. Hilde and I both share a love and talent for music. When family and friends asked us to sing at the buffet celebrating Jay's first communion, we lifted our voices in a universal favorite, "Amazing Grace." Our voices swelled, filling the room with English words and German words of God's amazing grace and love.

Love in action "Amazing Grace," what a perfect song to remind us of God's love in action. What joy awaits us when we put His love into action.

A question of love How can I show love and experience love through hosting students from foreign countries?

Prayers for our brothers and sisters in Christ Families that open their homes and their hearts to students from foreign lands.

February 4

No Reflection on Him

*The parents have eaten sour grapes, and the children's teeth are
set on edge.* Ezekiel 18:2

What a difference My husband, Milton, brings his gifts of leadership
to each church we've belonged to. He is known as a laid-back
visionary. A peaceful aura surrounds my husband. I, on the other
hand, am a take-charge, emotion-packed, charismatic person.

What will they think? It was a committee meeting that both Milton
and I were to attend. At the last minute, he was called out of town
and so I went to the meeting alone. As we were walking out of the
meeting, a gentlemen said to me, "So, you are Milt's wife." There was
an amused look on his face. No doubt he was comparing my passionate participation in the meeting with the laid-back style he
associated with my husband. I smiled my best, warmest smile and
said, "Yes I am."

Love in action After sharing with Milton my encounter with the gentleman, he reassured me, as he always does, that I am my own person and should remain that way. We are each responsible for our
own actions and the way we choose to use our gifts for the Lord.
Thanks be to God that in His grace, love and mercy, we are forgiven
for those actions that fail to measure up to the Christ-like lives we
are called to lead. God's love in action means that He accepts us just
as we are.

A question of love Who have I prejudged or judged and how has it
influenced my relationship with him or her?

Prayers for our brothers and sisters in Christ Siblings who are
pre-judged based on a parent's reputation.

February 5

Philippians 4:14-19

Who Could Have Known?

Be anxious for nothing, but in everything by prayer and supplication, with thanksgiving, let your requests be made known to God. Philippians 4:6

Absolutely not! My husband had just called wanting to know if we could have overnight guests. I was in the process of packing for an emergency trip home to be with my eighty-six-year-old mother during her cardiac catheterization. I also had to make arrangements for someone to help get our grandson Jay to and from school. All of this flashed through my mind as I gave a resounding "No!" So when my husband sheepishly announced that he had told them my situation and invited them to come anyway, I couldn't believe it.

Help, Lord Bob and Karen arrived and the blessings began to flow. Bob took one look at our eight-year-old grandson and adopted Jay as his own. *And* instead of having to wake Jay up and take him with us to the airport, Bob and Karen offered to get him up at his regular time, get his breakfast and make sure he was ready for school.

Love in action And the blessings kept on flowing. Bob thought I would be a great candidate to speak at his church's women's retreat. It was the start of a new career for me, a new ministry of service. Pastor Bob and I had many conversations as I prepared for that retreat. It was during this time that I began to think of Bob as my pastor. Love works in mysterious and wondrous ways.

A question of love Who needs to hear faith stories of how God abundantly provides?

Prayers for our brothers and sisters in Christ Those who are looking for ways to share the Good News.

Stinky *and* Beautiful

Get rid of all bitterness, rage and anger, brawling and slander, along with every form of malice. Be kind and compassionate to one another, forgiving each other, just as in Christ God forgave you. Ephesians 4:31-32

The Ginko tree I was joining my friend Jean for an early morning walk. "Careful," she warned. I had almost stepped on what looked like large grapes. "When they are fully grown, they are the size of a small plum," my friend went on to explain. "The fruit grows on this Ginko tree. It stinks beyond belief!"

A delicacy Jean said the irony of it was that the core of the fruit contained a kernel about the size of a pumpkin seed that a gourmet chef sautéed and served in his restaurant. It is considered a delicacy. It seems as if this famous chef dons protective gear before gathering the fruit and transforming it into a delicacy.

Don't get too close! A few weeks later I was having lunch with a friend whose brother had hurt her deeply years ago. What if no one could *or* would do whatever it took to get past the "stinky" part to a person's good part? What if God saw me and decided I wasn't worth approaching, let alone saving? I quickly said a prayer of thanksgiving for God's unconditional love for someone...like *me*, who could be a real "stinker."

A question of love How can I put love into action by forgiving someone who has hurt me deeply?

Prayers for our brothers and sisters in Christ Those who need to perform the loving act of forgiveness.

February 7

In His House

I was glad when they said to me, "Let us go into the house of the Lord." Psalm 122:1

The right book My husband and I had traveled to Mainz, Germany to be a part of the celebration of our grandson Jay's first communion. The service had begun. I sat quietly with my Bible resting in my lap. I had decided to pack my Bible, hoping to get some work done on the book I was writing. Now I found God had another use in mind.

Family problems A few hours before I had called home to let family know we had arrived safely, only to be told of a problem a close family member was facing. I was too far away to do anything but pray. And so I sat reading favorite Scriptures. I didn't understand a word of the service but I was transformed by the love and comfort believers find in God's house. I just had never considered that it happens in God's house *and* in any language.

Love in action I left the services feeling rejuvenated and reassured that God would take care of my loved ones. The smiles on the faces of the parishioners made me feel welcome. How could I have known that in God's universal language of love, I understood German perfectly?

A question of love What form of love can I show to people attending worship services for the first time?

Prayers for our brothers and sisters in Christ Those who greet newcomers at Sunday morning worship services.

"Mmmmah!"

"Let the little children come to Me, and do not forbid them; for of such is the kingdom of God." Mark 10:14

I love you Our grandson Conner turned two this summer. Shelly, our daughter and his mother, decided that it was time for him to learn to *say* the word "love." Anytime anyone said, "I love you, Conner," he would throw a kiss followed by his own word, "Mmmmah!" said with much enthusiasm.

Yes! Shelly had been practicing with Conner. She patiently sounded out the word, 'love." Now it was Conner's turn. "Conner," Shelly said, "can you say the word, 'love'?" "Yes," Conner replied with a big smile. Then without another word, he ran to his mother and gave her a big hug.

Love in action Our daughter Shelly would have two-year-old Conner holding conversations any adult could understand. The rest of us who are privileged to have Conner speak his language of love are not the least bit concerned. We are too busy learning Conner's language, learning his way of expressing love without words, learning to radiate the love Christ has placed within us and role models for us on a daily basis. If the expression "And a child shall lead them" is an accurate one, then Conner is at the front of the line. He speaks so articulately. We can all understand his language of love.

A question of love What child do I know who speaks the universal language of God's love? What lessons can I learn from him or her?

Prayers for our brothers and sisters in Christ Children who remind us of the true meaning of God's love.

February 9

Old Dog, Shep

The Lord is my light and my salvation; whom shall I fear?
The Lord is the strength of my life; of whom shall I be afraid?
Psalm 27:1

An early love One of my earliest memories is of my protector, Old Dog Shep. Shep was one smart dog who understood the universal language of love. There undoubtedly were many times and many ways in which Shep showed his love for me, but this is the story I will never forget.

Time to explore It seems as if at the tender age of three I decided to explore our neighborhood. In the split second it took my mother to look away, I took off. My companion on this impromptu journey was Old Dog Shep. We had only passed two houses when my mother came tearing after us.

My protector Fortunately for me, Old Dog Shep spoke and understood the language of a scared *and* frustrated mother. So Old Dog Shep in his wisdom, positioned himself firmly between my mother and me, speaking to her of love through his eyes *and* his bark. Mother smiled and thanked him for watching out for me.

Love in action Old Dog Shep has long since passed away. Those of us with pets might agree that they speak love in any language their owners need to hear. What lessons of love we can learn from our pets. How great if we put those lessons into practice along with the lessons that Mother taught me about God as my protector—always present.

A question of love What lessons can I learn from pets and how can I apply it to those I love?

Prayers for our brothers and sisters in Christ Those who work in animal shelters.

February 10

By the Book

Train up a child in the way he should go, and when he is old he will not depart from it. Proverbs 22:6

One of a kind Mrs. Temple and her family lived across the street from us. Mrs. Temple was a tiny woman who wore rimless glasses and eyes that pierced to the core in love *and* correction. I believe my mother adopted her as a role model for rearing us by the book, the Holy Book, that is.

Lessons learned Many times throughout my childhood, I heard Mother relate how Mrs. Temple was disciplining this child of hers or that one in love. I listened as Mother shared the successes of the Temple children with me: Father Temple, the oldest, an Episcopal priest, Miss Alberta, head of the dietary department at a local hospital; Miss Jeannette, a professor of speech at a local university, and known for her poetry; and Dr. Temple, a university professor.

Love in action Mrs. Temple died many years ago. As an adult returning to visit my mother, we always went to visit Miss Alberta and Miss Jeannette in the assisted living center and the nursing home where they now resided. I remembered them with holiday greeting cards. I wanted Mrs. Temple to know how much I appreciated all that she had done to help Mother rear us. "Mrs. Temple, it isn't a lot, but your daughters will always know of my love. Thank you for loving us enough to help Mother rear us by the Book."

A question of love What mother needs your help in rearing her children by the Book?

Prayers for our brothers and sisters in Christ Faith-filled mothers who are role models for young mothers.

Philippians 1:3-7

A Work in Progress

*…being confident of this very thing, that He who has begun a
good work in you will complete it until the day of Jesus Christ.*
Philippians 1:6

More beautiful day by day For as long as I can remember, some
friends of ours have been remodeling their house. It was a work in
progress when we met them many years ago, and as far as I know, it
continues to be…a work in progress. The house itself didn't get any
bigger, but inside…WOW! I loved seeing how the rooms changed,
expanded, contracted and became oh so beautiful.

Just ask When I started writing the inspirational book, *His Roses &
Thorns*, I told God I had no idea where I would come up with 365
different stories of faith, so I asked Him to help me. HE answered
my prayers and I completed the book. Then I began to wonder
where I would find the money to publish it. God sent a wonderful
couple who wanted to support my work. Next I worried about how
I would share my book with others. God was listening, and after
conducting my first retreat, I felt God telling me He wanted me to
share my faith stories with others.

Love in action I returned from that retreat renewed. "Well, Lord," I
prayed, "I guess I am like our friends' house that is a work in
progress. Help me to trust You *completely*." Putting our love for God
in action means trusting Him completely and then *moving* out in
faith.

A question of love What is God trying to *move* me to do because He
loves me so?

Prayers for our brothers and sisters in Christ Those who are facing
new careers.

February 12

II Thessalonians 3:1-5

Big Mike and Happy Jack

But the Lord is faithful, who will establish you and guard you from the evil one. II Thessalonians 3:3

Not a pet Some of my fondest childhood memories are of visiting Uncle Art and Aunt Mayme and their dogs, Big Mike and Happy Jack. The dogs were bred and trained as bird dogs. I could never understand why they couldn't be my pets as well.

Watch out for the tails One day when we arrived at Uncle Art and Aunt Mayme's for a visit, Uncle Art was in the yard with Big Mike and Happy Jack, throwing sticks for them to retrieve. I raced from the car to join in the fun. The dogs' thick tails wagged back and forth excitedly as they tried to jump on me and lick my face. Tears came to my eyes as their tails hit me. Within seconds Uncle Art had placed himself between the dogs and me as my father rushed over and picked me up and carried me out of harm's way.

Love in action From then on, I looked at Big Mike and Happy Jack from a distance. They looked like so much fun, but if I got too close they could hurt me. Later in life, I wasn't always so quick to separate and protect myself from things in this world that looked good, but when I got close, hurt. I needed God, the perfect protector. If you don't have a protector, might I suggest mine?

A question of love In what areas of my life do I need the protection of a loving God?

Prayers for our brothers and sisters in Christ Those who suffer abuse from those they love.

The Activator

In the same way, faith by itself, if it is not accompanied by action is dead. James 2:17

Taking matters into my own hands When I decided my thirtieth birthday was just too much to bear, I took matters into my own hands and with the able assistance of Miss Clairol, went from a brunette to a strawberry blond!

Combining the two One of the mysteries of becoming and remaining a strawberry blonde was in the mixing of the two bottles. When the peroxide was poured into the bottle containing the color and then shaken, the color was immediately *activated* and ready for use.

Spiritual activators It took a wonderful spiritual activator named Janet Sannipoli to get this book written. The first segment in writing *His Roses & Thorns* was to write the devotions and put them on a Web site. I knew I could write with God's help, but I also knew I would need someone else to design and maintain the Web site and Janet came through. A year later a couple with a heart for the Lord and a generous heart in sharing their resources, gave me the ability to self-publish.

Love in action Our good works are the fruit of our faith. We are saved by faith...period. And since that salvation is free for the asking, why wouldn't we want to be spiritual activators and do good works in His name?

A question of love What do I need to do to activate my faith in new and exciting ways? How can I help activate the faith of others?

Prayers for our brothers and sisters in Christ Those who are in great demand as spiritual activators.

The Rosses and Team Teaching

*Do not let any unwholesome talk come out of your mouths, but
only what is helpful for building others up according to their
needs, that it may benefit those who listen.* Ephesians 4:29

Teaming up God sent a husband and wife team to help me one
school year when I needed them most. Merrill Ross was the vice
principal of Monroe Elementary School where I was in the third
grade. His wife, Barbara, was substituting for my teacher who was
out on an extended medical leave.

His wisdom I was the perfect target for kids looking for someone to
bully. I remember cautiously approaching Mr. Ross as he stood so
tall and regal, questioning him about the role I should adopt to protect myself. Mr. Ross looked at me with kindness and wisdom and
asked, "Do you really want to be like them?" Of course I didn't. Mr.
Ross had just reinforced my belief that I had to find another solution.

Her kindness Mrs. Ross was someone I could emulate. If she had
survived childhood to become the beautiful, gentle teacher I learned
from each day, then there was hope for me. She was the gentle spirit
I needed to validate my own gentle spirit. She nurtured and protected that spirit when it was most vulnerable. How grateful I was
then and still am today.

Love in action The Rosses continue to be a great team of educators,
encouraging and gently shaping young lives. Thanks be to God for
the Rosses, who used their gifts to build children up *according to
their needs.*

A question of love What child can I encourage today?

Prayers for our brothers and sisters in Christ Those who encourage
learning through the building of self-esteem.

February 15

Mrs. Garvin, Mathematician to the Rescue

*It shall come to pass that before they call, I will answer; and
while they are still speaking, I will hear.* Isaiah 65:24

A lot at stake My top grades in every other subject had my mother
believing I could go to college on a scholastic scholarship. Except it
looked as if my poor grades in math were going to keep her dream
from becoming a reality. My mother prayed and did something
extraordinary for the time—she found me a first-rate tutor.

What a role model Mrs. Ann Garvin was the first black person hired
to teach mathematics in our high school. Algebra, geometry,
trigonometry and calculus might as well have been foreign languages, *except*, I needed them to enter college *and* qualify for a
scholarship. Could tutoring by Mrs. Garvin be the answer? She was
the perfect answer. I entered Kansas University on a full academic
scholarship!

Love in action Mr. and Mrs. Garvin had invited us to their home for
dinner. Mother was quick to fill us in on the many accomplishments
and contributions Mrs. Garvin had made in the area of education
and as past president of Church Women United, a worldwide
women's organization. "Now about this book of yours," Mrs. Garvin
began. "I know it is a big task you have before you, but you can do
it. Just like you conquered algebra, you can conquer this. I can
hardly wait to see your book completed." Mrs. Ann Garvin, mathe-
matician, encourager, and a woman of faith, a teacher for all times.

A question of love Who needs my words of encouragement today as
an expression of God's love?

Prayers for our brothers and sisters in Christ Those who lack confidence.

February 16

Acts 18:24-28

Pastor Lyle, Honking like a Goose

And when he desired to cross to Achaia, the brethren wrote, exhorting the disciples to receive him; and when he arrived, he greatly helped those who had believed through grace. Acts 18:27

Honking Geese The devotion for the day spoke of geese as encouragers. It seems that while we as humans honk our horns in frustration at fellow drivers, geese flying at the back of a formation honk to encourage those flying at the front to maintain their speed and stay on course.

Can I help? Pastor Lyle had just finished a sermon that addressed the small number of people who read their Bibles based on a recent survey. He talked of finding Bibles adorning coffee tables much like travel books...but often dusty from lack of use. An idea began forming in my mind. How could I help ensure that Pastor Lyle's Sunday morning messages would be food for thought throughout the entire week?

Yes you can. "Pastor Lyle, what if I created thought provoking daily devotions based on your sermon title and the Scriptures of the day?" "That sounds like a great idea, Wanda." For the next year and a half, I wrote daily devotions that appeared in each week's Sunday bulletin.

Love in action Two years later when Denise, another encourager, told me she wanted me to write the Christian version of a popular inspirational devotion book, I knew I could do it. Pastor Lyle had already given me an opportunity to try out my wings. Honk! Honk! Thank you, Pastor Lyle, for your encouragement

A question of love If I support someone's idea or talent today, where might they be tomorrow?

Prayers for our brothers and sisters in Christ Pastors who encourage the gifts of their flock.

February 17

James 1:22-27

Home-Cooked Meals to Share

But be doers of the word, and not hearers only... Pure and unde-
filed religion before God and the Father is this: to visit orphans
and widows in their trouble, and to keep oneself unspotted from
the world. James 1:22,27

Doorbell It is hard living so far away from Mother I thought as I talked with her during one of our daily telephone calls. She is eighty-seven and lives alone in Topeka, Kansas. I live in southern California. Her doorbell pierced our conversation. Having recently allowed my sister and me to purchase a mobile phone for her, she was able to continue our conversation as she went to answer the door.

Home delivery Mother went on to tell me that our neighbor, Mrs. Mansker, had sent over a home-cooked meal for her dinner. As mother described one delicious dish after another topped off with a mouthwatering dessert, I gave thanks for Mrs. Mansker's outpouring of love.

Love in action Often Mother didn't feel like preparing a meal for just herself. And no restaurant could produce love, the one ingredient that Mrs. Mansker included in all the dishes. I felt Mrs. Mansker's love showered on an elderly neighbor. She kept an eye out for Mother to make sure she was all right. The newspaper was taken over every day for Mother to read. Mother was invited to family gatherings and Bible studies. So much faith, and so much love in the way Mrs. Mansker applied it.

A question of love What elderly person could benefit from applying my faith through my love in action?

Prayers for our brothers and sisters in Christ Faith-filled neighbors who look out for others in need.

February 18

Acts 8:26-39

Connie and Art's Divine Appointments

"Do you understand what you are reading?" And he said, "How can I, unless someone guides me?" And he asked Philip to come up and sit with him. Acts 8:30-31

What kind of preacher is that? After some twenty years having Connie pop in and out of our lives...or maybe we were the ones popping in and out of his, I decided it was time I understood just what it was that Connie did. "My ministry strategy is simple; be available to meet with men, anytime, anywhere and without an agenda." Connie had just *kind of* met with my husband, Milt, over lunch here and there and *voila!* My husband developed this huge love for men's ministry, and for the last nine years, men had been gathering around our big-screen television to watch a bit of football or basketball, share a meal, support each other and learn from God's Holy Word.

Love in action Months later my husband was packing gear with all the enthusiasm of a little boy getting ready for camp. He would be joining Connie, Art and other men with a heart for the Lord to travel to Tijuana, Mexico where they would build a house of love. Just a few days, just one house, just Connie and Art continuing their action plan of love: meet with men anytime, anywhere and with no agenda. Thanks, Connie and Art for keeping your Divine appointments with our brothers in Christ.

A question of love Who can I hang out with in hopes of sharing the message of salvation?

Prayers for our brothers and sisters in Christ Men like Connie and Art who hang out for the Lord and the men whose lives are changed as a result.

February 19

Lady Di

And let us consider one another in order to stir up love and good works. Hebrews 10:24

Something in common In my opening remarks I had disclosed that the "stories" I would be sharing that weekend were taken from the faith-based inspirational book I was writing, *His Roses & Thorns*. I talked about the challenge of writing a 365-day devotional and asked for their prayers as I struggled to finish it. Later Lady Di congratulated me on my goal. She told me about her dream of incorporating her photographs into a book. She continued, "The stories you have shared with us this weekend are great. Others will want to buy your book. What a powerful message you have." "Let's keep in touch and encourage each other to get our books finished," I responded. "I can hardly wait to see your book. Photographs speak volumes. Please hurry and finish it."

Love in action Bags were packed, e-mail addresses and phone numbers exchanged. "Here is a copy of my brother's book," she said as she thrust it into my hands. "It's a gift. I know it will help encourage you." A few days later as I unpacked from the trip, I opened the book she had given me. The words inscribed inside did just that, "God bless you. Go with God and let him continue to guide you in your spiritual journey. Good luck with your book." Today's Scriptures calls us to "consider one another in order to stir up good works and love."

A question of love Who do I turn to when I need encouragement? Who turns to me for encouragement? How do I respond?

Prayers for our brothers and sisters in Christ Those struggling to complete the project of their dreams.

The Unconditional Gift

For I am persuaded that neither death nor life, nor angels nor principalities nor powers, nor things present nor things to come, nor height nor depth, nor any other created things, shall be able to separate us from the love of God which is in Christ Jesus our Lord. Romans 8:38-39

A loving couple This couple was aware that I was writing a faith-based inspirational book. They had seen the daily devotions on my new Web site, www.hisrosesandthorns.com, "You are writing a book," they said. I nodded my head, yes. "First-time writers should self-publish. "I don't have the money to self-publish," I responded. "We want to fund the publishing of your book." I was speechless. Finally I composed myself enough to say, "Thank you." It was all I could manage. I was so overwhelmed with surprise and gratitude, confident that I really would be able to publish my book. And that my mother in Topeka, Kansas would be able to walk into a Christian bookstore and see her daughter's book on the shelves.

Love in action I wasn't sure what the conditions of the gift were. "Is this an interest-free loan?" my husband asked. "No, it is a gift," they replied. "And the gift is unconditional." "I'll write as fast as I can so I can get the book published as soon as possible," I assured them. "Take your time. Make sure your book is a product you feel good about. We won't be putting any pressure to hurry on you. Don't put it on yourself," they admonished. What unconditional love.

A question of love How can I express my unconditional love to family and friends?

Prayers for our brothers and sisters in Christ Philanthropists

Jay, the Choir Boy

Be anxious for nothing, but in everything by prayer and supplication, with thanksgiving, let your requests be made known to God. Philippians 4:6

He doesn't want to go His mother was pleading our grandson's case. Jay really didn't want to sing in the children's choir. He didn't even want to go to a rehearsal to see if he would like it. I gave in. Jay was visiting us from Germany, a long way from home.

Trusting God's Divine order and timing A little over a year later, his mother called me. It seems as though Jay's school had begun an after-school enrichment program and he was enrolled in...guess what? Choir! Jay fussed and fumed. However, on the first day of class, the choir director, a young man and famous singer renowned throughout Germany, greeted him. "Let me hear you sing something." When Jay finished, the young man declared that Jay had a great voice and would certainly be considered for solo parts. Jay stayed for practice and the rest is history.

Love in action This was a great lesson for me, one that I am slowly learning with my adult children as well. When my children, grandchildren and husband resist doing something that I am convinced will be of great benefit to them, I let go and let God. Knowing how wonderful God is allows me to relinquish my control.

A question of love How can I relax, let go and let God work in my life?

Prayers for our brothers and sisters in Christ Those who need to be in control.

February 22

A Book of Love

And He took bread, gave thanks and broke it, and gave it to them, saying, "This is My body which is given for you; do this in remembrance of Me." Luke 22:19

Not my forte Our grandson Jay would soon be returning to Germany. He had spent about five months with us so he could have a nice, long visit and experience American schools. I just knew I would at some point have to create a scrapbook for Jay to take home with him. I started by carefully saving memorabilia: pictures, awards, special projects from school, and brochures of places he had visited. After many, many hours, it was finished. I wrapped it carefully and packed it for the long trip home.

Thank you "Thank you so much, Wanda. I could tell Jay was having a good time every time I talked to him on the phone," his mother, Susan, said. "But it isn't the same as seeing the awards from school, the pictures from field trips, visits to theme parks and his extended family there in the States. Thank you so much."

Love in action What if we created a scrapbook that depicted not only the wonderful times in our lives that we associate with God, but the difficult times as well? Then we could refer to it when we needed faith to trust that He would see us through a difficult time. And when we closed it, we would be filled anew with the hope His love brings.

A question of love How could I use a scrapbook for God to strengthen my faith and increase my sense of hope for the future?

Prayers for our brothers and sisters in Christ Those who are a long way from home.

Teaming with Love

This service that you perform is not only supplying the needs of God's people but is also overflowing in many expressions of thanks to God. II Corinthians 9:12

Packing for...? The family room floor began to look like my husband, Milton was packing for a camping trip. Milton had signed up with an organization called Houses Without Boundaries. He would be traveling to Tijuana, Mexico with a group of men to build two homes. How excited he was as he assembled the items listed on his "what to bring" sheet.

The debriefing Milton returned Sunday night quietly proclaiming how great the trip had been. "Nineteen men from the Seattle area and Milton had traveled to Tijuana to build two 12x20 foot homes. One family of five lived in a lean-to with one bed, a cooking area, and blankets that served as the only walls. Tears flowed down my husband's face as he told of building a house, but more importantly the relationships that were built with the family.

Love in action No one in that group of men from all walks of life spoke much Spanish. And yet my husband told story after story of heartwarming experiences with people who spoke little English. The translator was "love": God's abiding love. Twenty men were ambassadors of Christ; they weren't there to preach the gospel, yet God's message was given in that universal language that is understood around the world, the language of God's love.

A question of love What action can I take for others so they can hear the universal language of God's love?

Prayers for our brothers and sisters in Christ Those who speak the language of God's love by building houses for and with others.

February 24

Philippians 1:3-6

Under Construction

Being confident of this very thing, that He who has begun a good work in you will complete it until the day of Jesus Christ.
Philippians 1:6

A change of plans My husband, Milton, had returned Sunday night from a five-day trip in which he and nineteen other men had traveled to Tijuana to build two homes. As I listened to him emotionally tell of his love-filled experiences, I knew others would want to hear these stories of love. Perhaps we could team up and both bring messages of stewardship the following Sunday when I was scheduled to speak.

Love in action After each of the three services, our brothers and sisters in Christ expressed how they had been moved by our message. I turned to my husband and said with a heart overflowing with love, "This is the best thirty-six wedding anniversary present I could ever have." It had taken thirty-six years of God *constructing* us to do His will to get us to this day. "And," I thought happily, "the best is yet to come because my husband and I are a work in progress."

A reminder I probably should read today's Scripture every day to help remind me that as a believer, I am a work in progress, I am still under construction and I am confident of this very thing, that He who has begun a good work in me will be faithful to complete it *Philippians 1:6.*

A question of love Who can I team with to speak God's universal language of love?

Prayers for our brothers and sisters in Christ Spouses working together in the service of the Lord.

When We Are Called

Each one should use whatever gift he has received to serve others, faithfully administering God's grace in its various forms. I Peter 4:10

Who would have thought? The devotion was about a man, Theodore Fliedner, who by the mid twentieth century was responsible for more than 35,000 women serving churches, schools, hospitals and prisons.

My prayer list As I began praying fervently for abused women and children worldwide and those falsely imprisoned, I experienced my usual feeling of helplessness. Then the work of Theodore Fliedner reminded me of the many people working individually and through social justice organizations to help these, our brothers and sisters in Christ. I added those workers to my prayer list and gave a sigh of relief.

When I am called But wait! "Dear Heavenly Father, what are you calling me to do today?" My schedule called for me to conduct a Bible study with mothers of infants and toddlers, travel thirty-five miles to have lunch with a friend who recently lost her mother and then another forty-five or fifty miles to spend some time with a friend who was ill.

Love in action I decided I needed to pray again that I give my whole heart to today's call. I would prepare for the Bible study prayerfully and earnestly and I would make my visits to my friends in love and compassion. Love in action for me today means to listen for God's voice and then respond with all the love He has given me.

A question of love How is God calling me to show His love for my brothers and sisters in Christ?

Prayers for our brothers and sisters in Christ Social justice advocates for women, children and those falsely imprisoned.

My Neighbor, Sebastian

Love does no harm to a neighbor; therefore love is the fulfillment of the law. Romans 13:10

Good grief! I had just returned from church and was in the kitchen preparing lunch when I noticed Mischief, our cat, standing at the screened slider to the patio. Her tail was bushy, indicating anger or fear. When I saw the huge Siberian husky on the other side of the screen door, I knew it was fear. Slowly I slid the heavy glass slider closed and then heaved a sigh of relief. Then I hurriedly called our next-door neighbor, and in a steely voice asked them to come get Sebastian.

Love thy neighbor Sebastian continued to appear at the patio door, having found new places to dig under the fence that separated the two yards. His wagging tail and soft brown eyes spoke of his friendship and so I caressed his head and then told him how beautiful he was as I led him back to his house.

Love in action If you are waiting for the part in the story where Sebastian saves me from an intruder or his owners pull me from harm's way, then you will be disappointed. No, I just came to love Sebastian for who he was. Love can sometimes be spectacular, associated with spectacular events...or not. I am glad Sebastian and I speak the same language. And I am grateful his owners and I came to speak the same language too, God's universal language of love.

A question of love How is God calling me to love my neighbors?

Prayers for our brothers and sisters in Christ Those blessed to have loving pets.

Matthew 19:13-15

The Human Touch

"Let the little children come to Me, and do not forbid them; for of such is the kingdom of heaven." Matthew 19:14

A special story My daughter and niece would have me tell you the story of their grandmother. "Grandmother said all the classes were to be a part of the school program. Everyone was wearing something special. Grandmother didn't think she had anything to wear that her classmates would consider special. They day of the program, Grandmother walked into her classroom, eyes brimming with tears. Her teacher, who was quite a dresser and wore beautiful scarves draped artfully over her shoulders, saw Grandmother's tears and came over to her. She asked Grandmother why she had such a sad face. Grandmother told her. Then that wonderful, compassionate teacher took her scarf from around her shoulders and draped it around Grandmother's shoulders. With a warm, loving smile on her face she said, 'Now you are wearing something special and you look so pretty.' Grandmother will never forget the love and compassion of that teacher…and neither will we!"

Love in action Love is powerful and sometimes it is most powerful in the quietest whisper and the smallest gesture. Other sayings come to mind, "It is the little things that count," and "A little can mean a lot." God calls us to love one another just as He loves us. Today's faith story reminds us that when we don't feel we have a lot of love to give, a little will do just fine.

A question of love Who needs just a *little* love from me? What will I give?

Prayers for our brothers and sisters in Christ Children who need someone to help them feel special.

February 28

Exodus 20:12, Leviticus 20:9

Mother Bruce

You shall rise before the gray headed. Leviticus 19:32

Promises made and kept Even though my visit with Mom was to be a short one, I told her we had to make time to visit Mother Bruce; I had promised. Mother agreed. Mother Bruce was now well into her nineties and for several years she had resided in an extended care facility. Her daughter Earlene told us that the timing had been perfect. She had just returned from getting her mother a hamburger from Mother Bruce's favorite fast-food restaurant, Burger King. Mother Bruce had a taste for a hamburger and the only hamburgers she liked came from Burger King. "What a loving daughter," I thought.

Love in action I basked in the love of Mother Bruce and felt so uplifted by her spirit. I gave thanks for Earlene and her husband Ted, who had died a few years ago. Ted had showered my parents with love *and* delicious meals he often prepared for them in addition to loving and caring for Mother Bruce. We as adult children are called to honor the elderly as well as our parents. Living so far away from my parents, I gave thanks for the love of Ted and Earlene Henderson toward their parents *and* mine. And I gave thanks for the love of a ninety-four-year-old-woman whose faith in God sustains her and me. Love in God's language is an endless cycle.

A question of love When I am considered elderly, how will I want my adult children to show their love?

Prayers for our brothers and sisters in Christ The elderly who are an inspiration to others; the adult children who care for them.

My Journal
February: The Universal Language of God's Love

Insights: What do I want to remember about how to give and receive love in any language?

Challenges: What do I need to do to incorporate the lessons I have learned into my everyday life? When will I start?

What are the ten top blessings I received from God this month?

1.

2.

3.

4.

5.

6.

7.

8.

9.

10.

Answered Prayers

Introduction to March Devotions

Special People Remind Me of God's Sonshine

"Finally, brethren, whatever things are true, whatever things are noble, whatever things are just, whatever things are pure, whatever things are lovely, whatever things are of good report, if there is any virtue and if there is anything praiseworthy, meditate on these things." Philippians 4:8

Happy thoughts As a melodramatic child, I would often sigh and tell my mother I was feeling sad and sorrowful. She encouraged me to "think happy thoughts." My mother's response was perfect for her young "drama princess" daughter. She also listened, acknowledged, encouraged, and prayed...and I made it through. This year as I impatiently waited for spring to arrive, I decided I would think happy thoughts.

Creating smiles makes the Sonshine One day while I reminisced about special people in my life, I decided to send them a devotion that remembered them in the form of a sunshine letter from me. My mother was overjoyed with hers and thought others would enjoy theirs just as much. I found the perfect paper at my favorite stationery store and copied the devotion on it. What a hit! The recipients called me; we reminisced and we laughed. The warm feeling lasted long after I hung up the phone. I felt God's Son shining on me.

Sonshine letters What better way to brush away winter doldrums as we wait for spring than to write letters to friends and family members about a special memory. Feel the Son shine through you, warming your heart and the heart of those blessed enough to receive your Sonshine letter. What a great way to let God's love shine through us to others.

Your sister in Christ,
Wanda Scott Bledsoe

March 1

Psalm 19:7-11

The Pastor and His Family

"Let the words of my mouth and the meditation of my heart be acceptable in thy sight, O Lord, my strength and my Redeemer."
Psalm 19:14

A singing family Reverend Pearson, his wife and five children came to our church when I was a junior in high school. They soon became like family. It wasn't long before I was calling our new pastor Daddy Gus.

He was there I remember Daddy Gus at my Uncle Art's funeral. I didn't know how I was going to get beyond the casket that held my beloved Uncle Art until I saw Daddy Gus standing on the other side. He looked me in the eye and his love drew me to him.

How does it go? I was playing at my home church. I was supposed to know this song that I had long forgotten. What was I to do? Suddenly my eyes were drawn to Mother Pearson, accomplished vocalist, pianist and organist. She quietly began singing the song nodding her head up and down as if to assure me that I remembered it. She was right. With her love and support, the hymn from my childhood came back to me and I played it.

For your contemplation I believe God puts many people in our lives to love us, encourage and support us. Who are the special people God has placed in your life to help you through life's ups and downs? Do they know how special they are? If not, why not tell them. If they do, what would happen if you told them again?

A question or two Who would appreciate hearing about their positive impact on my life?

Prayers for our brothers and sisters in Christ Pastors and their families.

March 2

True Value

Do not overwork to be rich; Because of your own understanding, cease! Will you set your eyes on that which is not? For riches certainly make themselves wings; They fly away like an eagle toward heaven. Proverbs 23:4,5

You can drive When I was growing up, Uncle Wilson had a new car every year. He offered to let me drive his latest new car, even though I could not have been more than twelve or thirteen. I felt so loved and so special! Years later when our son was driving, we almost had to take out a loan to make the automobile insurance premiums. I again realized how much Uncle Wilson must have loved me to let me drive his new cars. The experience was priceless.

You can do it Uncle Wilson's wife, Aunt Faye, is one of the strongest, most determined persons I have known. When she suffered a stroke, we wondered if she would ever walk or talk again. Little did I know the depth of her determination. It is her voice, though, that is priceless to me. As a wife and mother facing the challenges of life, I sometimes doubt myself. Aunt Faye is always quick to say with both love and conviction in her voice, "You can do it. I know you can." Her words of encouragement are priceless.

For your contemplation True value comes from people loving people. The memories we have of loved ones can be priceless. If you want to make the memory even more memorable, share it with those you love.

A question or two What childhood memory of loving aunts and uncles would I consider priceless?

Prayers for our brothers and sisters in Christ Loving aunts and uncles.

March 3

Jeremiah 17:5-8

Trust in the Lord

Blessed are those who trust in the Lord. Jeremiah 17:7

Trust has to be earned My mother entrusted my sister and me to Uncle Art and my father for a ride in their small fishing boat powered by an outboard motor. I wanted to steer the boat and my Uncle Art said OK. All I had to do was remember three things; keep the handle in the center to go straight, move it left to go right and move it right to go left. I was really good at going straight. It was when we were headed for the bank that I froze. My Uncle Art quietly said, "Wanda, you need to turn the boat either to the right or the left or we are going to end up in your mother and Aunt Mamie's lap." Still I stared straight ahead as we headed for the bank. Again Uncle Art quietly said, "Well, Wanda it's time to turn." Suddenly it clicked. I turned the boat and we headed back out to the middle of the lake. "I was starting to get a little worried," my Uncle Art calmly said. My father just shook his head.

For your contemplation Perhaps this is a good time to reflect on the reasons you put your trust in God. What has He done for you in the past that would cause you to trust Him with the present and the future? Whom do you trust? "Blessed are those who trust in the Lord."

A question or two Why would God consider me trustworthy?

Prayers for our brothers and sisters in Christ Those who are aunts and uncles and the children who put their trust in them.

March 4

Matthew 28:16-20

In Our Time of Need

"...And lo, I am with you always, even to the end of the age."
Matthew 28:20

Mr. And Mrs. LaRue, a special couple Mr. and Mrs. LaRue didn't have children, but you would almost need a computer to keep track of the numbers of young people they have helped down through the years. It was Mrs. LaRue who stepped in to plan and coordinate the entire wedding for Milton and me that included some 300 to 400 guests. We have now been married over thirty-six years.

Helping my mother out Where, you might ask, was my mother when all of these wedding plans and preparations were taking place? I had been making plans to go to graduate school. Now I wanted to get married. My mother was so disappointed, knowing how important an education is. The wedding plans overwhelmed my mother, who was still reeling from my news. Her good friend, Mrs. LaRue, came to the rescue. My mother and I will never forget Mrs. LaRue's kindness. The LaRues are a special couple who so graciously continue to share their home, their time and their possessions.

For your contemplation Life can present challenges that seem impossible to meet on our own. God provides comfort through His Word, through our prayers to Him, and through you and me reaching out to others in their time of need. Today God may call on you to reach out and help someone in need. Tomorrow He may send someone to help you in your time of need. HE is always with us.

A question or two Today do I need to reach out to help or accept the help of others?

Prayers for our brothers and sisters in Christ Those who are brides-to-be and their mothers.

Planning Ahead with Mom's Morning Fellowship

I will praise You, O Lord, with my whole heart; I will tell of your marvelous works. Psalm 9:1

Test case "What if I made a calendar with a Scripture for each day and space to write a blessing of the day? What if there was space to write the blessing of the week and of the month? I needed to test this idea. Could the moms in our "Mom's Morning Fellowship" Bible study be my test case?

We'll give it a try "What do you expect to happen?" I asked. Ah, I smiled as they began to talk of hope and faith when they could not see the way or they were looking for an answer. They also talked of being excited about one project of faith that they could share with their families. "And what about New Year's Eve and New Year's Day?" I asked as a final question. They responded with ideas for incorporating the blessings of the month into existing traditions. I could hardly wait to get started.

For your contemplation In our busy world it is sometimes difficult to remember the many ways God expresses His unconditional love for us. By recording just one blessing a day, we are thrice blessed: blessed when we receive it, blessed when we recall it, and blessed when we give Him thanks. "A blessing a day keeps despair away." Hmm. Praise God from whom *all* blessings flow!

A question or two Where could I record a blessing a day? How could I use my record of God's blessings to plan ahead for New Year's Eve and New Year's Day?

Prayers for our brothers and sisters in Christ Those who journal to praise God and to increase their faith.

March 6

I Samuel 16:6-13

Judging a Book by Its Cover

But the Lord said to Samuel, "Do not look at his appearance or at his physical stature, because I have refused him. For the Lord does not see as man sees; for man looks at the outward appearance but the Lord looks at the heart." I Samuel 16:7

Unfamiliar places The first hurdle in getting to my job interview was to finding parking at a reasonable price. The next hurdle was finding enough change to feed the parking meter. I looked across the street and saw a vendor selling cookies. That would do, buy a cookie, get change, and then feed the meter.

Unfamiliar people As I approached the vendor, I noticed a "street person" talking to the vendor. I paid for my cookie and quickly pocketed the change as I headed back to the parking meter.

Unfamiliar responses As I walked toward the car I noticed the "street person" walking just ahead of me. Oh no! He was waiting for the right opportunity to ask me for money. Before I could say anything, he smiled, reached in his pocket, withdrew a handful of quarters and began feeding my parking meter. "Have a nice day," he said when the meter indicator pointed to full.

For your contemplation God knows our hearts. HE is able to look beyond the tattered clothing, the punk hairstyle, complexions that are not like mine, and bodies that are not perfect, and see the heart. If we are to be more Christ-like, shouldn't we do the same?

A question or two How will today's message cause me to look at people differently? Who is God calling me to serve?

Prayers for our brothers and sisters in Christ Those who live on the streets.

March 7

II Corinthians 9:6-8

Cousins Betty and Leslie, Cheerful Givers

But this I say: He who sows sparingly will also reap sparingly, and he who sows bountifully will also reap bountifully. II Corinthians 9:6

My cousin Leslie He had married my cousin Betty many years ago. Now it seemed that as I talked to my mother on a daily basis, Cousin Leslie's name was frequently mentioned. The memory I treasure most is when Cousin Leslie came to check on my mother one cold and snowy January morning. Mother was very sick and it was Cousin Leslie's repeated knocking that got her to the door and later to her doctor. I think Cousin Leslie's faithful visit to my mother that day saved her life.

My cousin Betty Mother kept questioning Cousin Betty and me about how we were hanging the curtains, although we thought we were doing a good job. Finally Cousin Betty looked at Mother with love and concern and asked, "Aunt Ruby, when was the last time you ate?" Mother looked surprised and then answered, "I haven't had time." It was 2 P.M. and my eighty-six-year-old-mother and I had been working hard since 6 A.M. How grateful I was that Cousin Betty loved Mother enough to realize Mother's feverish behavior wasn't normal for her and that something must be wrong.

For your contemplation My cousins Betty and Leslie taught me that a cheerful giver first has to have a heart full of love. That must be why they are so faithful in visiting Mother, bringing her gifts and taking her to their church for special events. Their hearts are over-flowing with love.

A question or two Who needs me to be a cheerful giver today?

Prayers for our brothers and sisters in Christ Those who visit the sick and shut-in.

March 8

Romans 8:31-39

Clean or Dirty

*And we know that in all things God works for the good of those
who love Him, who have been called according to His purpose.*
Romans 8:28

Clean or Dirty Today's Scripture reminds me of a sermon I once
heard. Pastor Doug held up a crisp twenty-dollar bill in front of the
congregation and asked if anyone wanted it. All hands went up.
Then the pastor crumpled the new twenty-dollar bill in his hands
and again repeated his question. The answer was the same. This
time the pastor dropped the money on the floor and stepped on it
until it was no longer clean. Again he asked, "Does anyone still want
this money?" "Yes!" the congregation answered. Pastor Doug ended
the illustration saying, "No matter how crumpled, messed up and
dirty this bill gets, it doesn't lose its value. The same goes for us. No
matter how messed up or dirty our lives looks today, we still hold
our value to God. We are worth as much to Him today as we were
when He created us."

For your contemplation Isn't it amazing what we can do when we
accept the fact that God loves us unconditionally? When I forget to
accept the person Christ sees in me, I make it hard for Christ to use
me in serving others. If you are full of God's love, who will benefit?
How will they benefit? When will you start?

A question or two How can Pastor Doug's sermon about the twenty-
dollar bill make this a better day for me and those around me?

Prayers for our brothers and sisters in Christ Men and women in
prison and our brothers and sisters in Christ who minister to them.

March 9

The Power of Love

...Your people shall be my people, and your God, my God.
Ruth 1:16

Taking risks What could Rahab, who was a prostitute, have in common with Naomi, a widow and dutiful daughter-in-law? Love and "guts" would be my answer. Rahab believed in this God she had heard about. She loved her family and risked her life to protect them. Ruth loved her mother-in-law and risked her life to remain with her.

Linked together for all time Naomi and Rahab became linked together in that they both became a part of the family tree of Jesus Christ. Rahab had a son, Boaz, who married Ruth. Ruth had a son, Obed, who had a son, Jesse, whose son was David the King. After reading their stories, how could I doubt that God works in mysterious ways His wonders to perform?

For your contemplation Sometimes the challenges we face in our daily lives may seem insurmountable, given the resources we have at hand. Sometimes the love required may seem more than we have to give or even more than we *want* to give. Often it is so difficult to see past the present we can't even begin to understand the impact our actions might have in the future. God sometimes brings us the most remarkable blessings through people and situations that we would most likely avoid. The stores of Rahab and Naomi remind us of the wonders God can work through us and others when we love, trust and obey.

A question or two If I supply the love and trust, what great and mighty things might God accomplish through me today?

Prayers for our brothers and sisters in Christ Loving sons and daughters-in-laws.

Are You a Storyteller?

Quietly trust yourself to Christ your Lord and if anybody asks why you believe as you do, be ready to tell him, and do it in a gentle and respectful way. I Peter 3:15

A faith story I certainly didn't feel comfortable approaching friends, relatives, or co-workers about God, but I did love telling stories about family and friends. They were everyday stories of God's impact on my life. When an opportunity presented itself, I would begin my story. "You won't believe what happened to Shelly (our daughter). She was riding her bike down that long hill by our house when her brakes failed. She prayed and a voice told her to steer her bike into the curb. She obeyed. She and her bike went flying into the air."

No fear "Mom, I was not afraid. I knew God had sent my guardian angel to protect me." Shelly landed on the grass between the sidewalk and the street. A man working in his yard ran to see if he could help. He looked at Shelly in amazement and asked if she was all right. Her response to him was simply, "Yes, I prayed." She picked up her bike and pushed it home. I close all my stories with, "God is good."

A question or two What joy, sorrow, peace, miracle, or funny situation have you experienced in which you felt God's presence? Why not turn it into your faith story? As I grow day by day in my faith, I benefit. And as I share my stories of faith, I allow others to benefit as well.

For your contemplation Who needs to hear one of my faith stories?

Prayers for our brothers and sisters in Christ Children who ride bicycles without helmets.

From the Mouths of Babes

*Be anxious for nothing, but in everything by prayer and suppli-
cation, with thanksgiving, let your requests be make known to
God; and the peace of God which surpasses all understanding,
will guard your hearts and minds through Christ Jesus.*
Philippians 4:6

Not yet One day one of Shelly's best friends was going through a crisis and called Shelly to ask for prayer. Shelly's response was, "I will
have my mother pray for you." Her friend hesitated and then
replied, "Shelly, I know your mother can pray, but I kind of had your
grandmother in mind." It was then that I realized I still had some
work to do in my prayer life.

Finally! I am happy to say that eventually Shelly's friends, as they
became adults and as I grew in my prayer life, began to ask Shelly to
have her mother pray for them. I felt I had truly arrived.

For your contemplation My credibility as a prayer warrior came after
my commitment to (1) trust God in all things, (2) look to His word
on a daily basis for love, guidance, comfort and correction, (3) pray
without ceasing, and (4) give God the glory when my prayers were
answered. I don't know how Shelly's friends determined when it was
safe to entrust their problems to me for prayer. Perhaps they heard
words of faith, hope and love and decided I was ready. Thank God
for teenagers who reflect God's Sonshine.

A question or two What can I learn from the children around me?

Prayers for our brothers and sisters in Christ Teenagers who believe
in the power of prayer and the adults they ask to pray for them.

March 12

Isaiah 40:28-31

Daddy, Carry Me

The beloved of the Lord shall dwell in safety by Him, Who shelters him all the day long; And he shall dwell between His shoulders. Deuteronomy 33:12

Playing Possum As we pulled up to our house after an evening out, Mother whispered, "Girls, it is time to wake up." I quickly replied, "Daddy, I am so tired. Please carry me."

Safe in his arms My father scooped me up and with my arms wrapped securely about his neck, carried me into the house. He made me feel so safe and so loved. By monetary standards, we would have been classified as poor. I am glad no one told me, because I felt like the richest little girl on earth when my daddy carried me.

We will carry you Years later I called my sister to see how she was doing in the midst of a crisis she was facing. "Wanda, I am too tired to even pray." I lovingly assured her that Mother and I would pray for her. I knew she just needed us to carry her for a little while. I remembered other times when my little sister carried me and when our faith-filled mother carried both of us. My father, who now resides safe in the arms of Jesus, would have wanted it that way.

For your contemplation Today's Scriptures reassure us that we are never too heavy for our heavenly FATHER to carry. In His arms we find the love, comfort and protection we need until we are able to walk again on our own.

A question or two What would happen if I gave my burden to the Lord today?

Prayers for our brothers and sisters in Christ Those in the midst of a crisis.

March 13

Psalm 92:12-14

Aunt Betty and Aunt Mary Lou

They shall still bear fruit in old age; They shall be fresh and flourishing. Psalm 92:14

Talking fast and praying even faster Aunt Mary Lou and Aunt Betty were visiting Mother when I called. Aunt Mary Lou proceeded to tell me her feelings about my then eighty-five-year-old mother driving herself to the emergency room because of heart palpitations. My silence gave her the clue that this was new information to me. Aunt Mary Lou caught on *fast*. "Baby, let's pray." Before I could ask her any questions, she began praying. She finished with, "Amen! Here's your Aunt Betty."

When in trouble How I love being a part of a large family. "Aunt Betty, it sounds like Aunt Mary Lou spilled the beans and left you holding the bag." "That's about right, Darlin'," Aunt Betty laughingly replied. "My mother is all right now?" "She is just fine," Aunt Betty assured me.

For your contemplation I laugh when I think about how Aunt Mary Lou solved her dilemma. In actuality, it is a great solution. Think about it. When in trouble, pray first and pray fast! It worked for Aunt Mary Lou. I began thinking about the key words here: first and fast. I pray about situations, but do I pray first and fast? Do I immediately give the problem to God in prayer, or do I "mess around" with it for a while trying to fix it on my own? I think there is a lesson here for us. When in trouble, pray *first* and pray *fast!*

A question or two What challenge am I facing that needs the power of prayer?

Prayers for our brothers and sisters in Christ Aunts who are prayer warriors.

March 14

"I Know That Voice"

"The Lord is my Shepherd, I shall not want." Psalm 23:1

Who is this? I decided to place a long distance call to Aunt Mary Lou. "Hello, Aunt Mary Lou." "Hello, Baby, how are you doing?" Aunt Mary Lou went on to ask about my family and to tell me what was going on in her family. After a few minutes of wonderful conversation, Aunt Mary Lou suddenly stopped and asked, "Baby, who am I talking to?" Aunt Mary Lou has twelve children, in addition to her grandchildren and great-grandchildren. She and my mother come from a family of eight children so you can believe me when I say, I have a "cajillion" cousins. No wonder Aunt Mary Lou wasn't sure just which one of us she was talking to.

It's my good ear Uncle Ed, on the other hand, is never fooled when I call. After the incident with Aunt Mary Lou, I decided I would see who else I could fool. Uncle Ed quickly spoiled my fun. "I recognize that voice. This is Wanda." When I asked him how he did it, he said, "I would know your voice anywhere."

For your contemplation Out of all of the "cajillion" people God created, He always remembers our name and recognizes our voice when we call. We can then believe in new and refreshing ways as we claim the Lord as our Shepherd who lovingly provides for all our needs.

A question or two What family member living in another city or state would like to hear my voice today?

Prayers for our brothers and sisters in Christ Volunteers who read the Bible to those who cannot see.

March 15

James 2:17-26

"I'll Get the Ice Cream"

If a brother or sister is naked and destitute of daily food, and one of you says to them, "Depart in peace, be warmed and filled," but you do not give them the things which are needed for the body, what does it profit? James 2:15-16

What can I do? Uncle Dorman lived in Oklahoma City, a long way from my home in southern California. For many years he had driven a school bus and would entertain us with stories of the children's antics. Now Uncle Dorman was fighting cancer.

Who can I call? I couldn't be there with Uncle Dorman, but I could call. "The nurses want me to eat more, but nothing tastes good and nothing will stay down. I believe if I could just have a little ice cream." Who could I call? Aunt Helen!

I'll get it "Aunt Helen, this is Wanda. I just talked with Uncle Dorman and he thought a little ice cream might taste good." "I'll take care of it." And later…"Isn't this amazing, Helen? Would you believe I was just talking to Wanda? I told her I had a taste for some ice cream." Uncle Dorman related with a big grin on his face.

For your contemplation Sick people and those who care for them need our prayers *and* our actions. Faith *combined* with good works is sure to bring the biggest smiles that cast a ray of Sonshine in an otherwise gloomy day. I gave thanks that day for Aunt Helen, telephones and a loving uncle.

A question or two What sick person and or their caregiver need my faith *and* good works?

Prayers for our brothers and sisters in Christ Those who have life-threatening illnesses, their hospice workers and caregivers.

March 16

Isaiah 55:8-13

The Monnahans and Their Gift

"For you shall go out with joy, and be led out with peace; the mountains and the hills shall break forth into singing before you and all the trees of the field shall clap their hands." Isaiah 55:12

Feel the joy When our family joined Rainier Beach church, we noticed the Monnahans immediately. Bob and Marty seemed to fairly radiate God's love. They generously gave of their time and money. But even more importantly, their faith became an inspiration to all of us.

Talents Bob is a big guy with a gentle touch that he enjoyed using to raise champion canaries! Marty is petite with a big smile and a talented arm that transfers the images in her mind to canvases for all the world to enjoy.

A gift from the heart When our family was preparing to relocate to southern California, there was a two-month period when our house had sold and we were between homes. Were we ever surprised when the Monnahans asked us to stay in their home while they spent time in their winter home? What a blessing!

For your contemplation "Joy!" What if we made a list of people and things that give us joy, bring us peace, and make us want to sing and clap our hands. What if the lists made us think of something we could do to bring joy to someone else? Would we do it? I think we would. What a way to cast a ray of Sonshine and hasten the coming of spring.

A question or two What would it take for me to cause someone else to feel joyful?

Prayers for our brothers and sisters in Christ Those who share their homes with others.

March 17

A Patch of Snow to Pillow His Head

"The Lord shall preserve thy going out and thy coming in from this time forth, and even for evermore." Psalm 121:8

A special story I heard something mysterious and full of awe in her voice when our daughter called. "Oh, Mom," she began, "remember me telling you how much snow we had yesterday? Well, this morning it was all gone from the streets and driveways, with little patches here and there. Conner woke up a little fussy, so I decided to take him outside with me for awhile. I slipped on a paper-thin coating of black ice and fell. Knowing the severe injury to his head this kind of fall could produce, I waited to hear Conner's wail. Conner had a look of puzzlement in his eyes that slowly gave way to a huge smile. His head was resting on the only patch of snow on the driveway. Mom, that patch of snow was one of God's miracles and no one can convince me of anything different!"

For your contemplation Stop! Look! And Listen! We as believers know that when we stop, look and listen, we can recognize God's miracles in our lives and in the lives of others. What should we do when we recognize miracles both great and small? Share them, of course. I call it sharing "faith stories." What better way to brush off winter doldrums than to give God the praise and the glory for His divine intervention, then share your faith story with someone who may be in need of a lift?

A question or two What faith story could I share? Who needs a faith lift today?

Prayers for our brothers and sisters in Christ Children with head injuries.

March 18

John 12:44-47

An Old-Fashioned Remedy

"I have come as a light into the world, that whoever believes in Me should not abide in darkness." John 12:46

She is so sick It was our daughter Shelly's wedding day, and a glorious day it was. "Where is Mother?" I asked my sister. It seems as if Mother's stomach was so upset she was lying down in the women's lounge. I prayed for her as she reassured me that she would be ready to go in with the family when it was time for the wedding to start.

Try this There was a knock on Mother's door. It was Mrs. Williams, a woman from the neighborhood, collecting signatures. Mother was experiencing discomfort from the same problem that had plagued her at Shelly's wedding, and shared the experience with Mrs. Williams. Later that day, Mrs. Williams returned with an old-fashioned remedy. Mother tried it and it worked. She began telling everyone about this old-fashioned remedy.

For your contemplation If you have been trying, with little success, various modern-day remedies for the challenges life has given you, perhaps it is time for you to try for the first time, or try anew, a good old-fashioned remedy that has been available since the beginning of time: God. Read His Word on a daily basis, join in the fellowship with other believers, and share the talents He has given you. Then tell family, friends and even perfect strangers about the wonderful old-fashioned remedy you have found.

A question or two Have I really given God a chance to remedy what ails me?

Prayers for our brothers and sisters in Christ Those suffer from chronic stomach problems.

March 19

God Bless

Bless those who curse you, and pray for those who spitefully use you. Luke 6:28

Fired! I had gone to my boss's office expecting a great performance evaluation. I staggered back to my office trying to accept the fact that I had just been fired.

This isn't over! I went home vowing I would fight this wrongful termination. "Why would you want to fight to stay with an organization that does not appreciate nor respect your talent?" my husband asked.

The solution A peace settled over me. I called my boss and requested a meeting for the following morning. I began the meeting with, "You deserve to have the team you want. Perhaps there is a solution that would be a win-win for both of us." I ended the meeting with, "God bless." His response surprised me. "This isn't what I expected. What is your secret?" he asked. "I am trusting in God," I replied.

A win-win Some time later I was in a crosswalk and heard a horn blow. It was my former boss. He asked how the job search was going. I told him I had just landed a great job. "Good for you!" he responded with enthusiasm. A win for him, a win for me; God blessed us all!

For your contemplation I didn't have a choice about keeping my job, but I did have a choice about how I left. I chose love, and a sense of peace and well-being were God's response.

A question or two How can my faith help me respond to people in my life who are treating me unfairly and in ways that hurt me?

Prayers for our brothers and sisters in Christ Those who have been wrongfully terminated.

March 20

Exodus 34:29-35

A Radiant Glow

When Aaron and all the Israelites saw Moses, the skin of his face was shining, and they were afraid to come near him. Exodus 34:30

The color of honey Growing up, I thought my mother was the most beautiful woman in the whole wide world. She was tall and slender with auburn hair and ruby red lips. In fact, her name is Ruby. She was radiant.

Radiantly beautiful Some forty years later, young women at our church's women's retreat were discovering another kind of beauty in my mother. She stood before them as an eighty-five-year-old woman sharing her faith stories with them. Her face glowed with a brilliant radiance as she told them about God in her life as a child, a young married woman, a mother, grandmother, and great-grandmother. She talked to them about fasting and praying, love and forgiveness and even about chastity before marriage. And she talked to them about the trials and tribulations she had experienced in her life and how God had brought her through.

Grandmother Ruby The young women crowded around my mother. She reached out in love embracing them, giving them some of her favorite Scriptures and promising to pray for them. "Wanda," they said over and over during the remainder of the retreat, "your Mother is beautiful!"

For your contemplation God offers us the ability to become more beautiful every day of our lives, even if we live to be a hundred years old. We can all have a year-round radiant glow, no matter how little the sun shines where you live.

A question or two What can I do today to reflect God's radiance for all to see?

Prayers for our brothers and sisters in Christ Those who don't recognize their own beauty.

March 21

Mark 10:13-16

Interruptions or Opportunities

"Let the little children come to me, and do not hinder them, for the kingdom of heaven belongs to such as these." Mark 10:14

When unkind words are said "What do you do when someone is angry and wants to fight?" Pastor Skip asked during this children's message. "Walk away," piped up one little boy. It was a magnificent children's message. Pastor Skip made his closing point and dismissed the children to Sunday School. But wait! An interruption. Another little boy had listened to the message and taken it to heart. "I want to play with Joey but he won't play with me. I want to be his friend," the little boy's voice rang out over the congregation. Pastor Skip stopped and encouraged the little boy to keep trying. He also patiently responded to one or two more comments the little boy had about his own personal situation. The little boy was finally satisfied and ran off to Sunday School. We heard Pastor Skip breathe a sigh of relief as we went on with the service.

For your contemplation We never seem to factor in time for interruptions in our busy schedules, so when they come we may respond in frustration and grumbling. Is it truly an interruption *or* is it an opportunity to help others? If we agree that each day is one God gives us, then perhaps we can be open to interruptions as opportunities for God to bless others *and* ourselves in unplanned yet very special ways.

A question or two How can I turn today's interruptions in my schedule into opportunities for God to bless others through me?

Prayers for our brothers and sisters in Christ Those facing deadlines and tight turnaround schedules.

March 22

Sharing the Good News

"And go quickly and tell His disciples that He is risen from the dead, and indeed He is going before you into Galilee; there you will see Him. Behold, I have told you." Matthew 28:5-7

Providing support Our son, Milton Scott, and I both agreed the job being offered to him was a great opportunity. There was just one problem—Milton Scott didn't have a car. And so I began the arduous task of getting him to and from work—an extra two hours tacked onto my day.

Thanks, Mom Now he was calling me to say, "Mom, they are really giving me lots of opportunities to show what I can do. Sometimes during the day I just sit here smiling and thanking God that you were there for me. I am so grateful. I don't know how many ways I can say it. I love you, Mom."

Something to cherish and to share That was a conversation I will remember for the rest of my life. This wonderful experience was made even greater as I called my mother the next morning to share it with her. What a faith lift for her and for me!

For your contemplation I just love it when people share their faith stories with me. It gives me a sense of hope, my spirits are lifted, and the glow lasts even after I move on to something else. As God takes what we do in His name and provides the increase, our sharing and our witness may be just the invitation someone needs to reach out to God.

A question or two Who will I tell about God's love, grace and mercy?

Prayers for our brothers and sisters in Christ Those who lack transportation.

March 23

II Peter 1:3-8

Forever Fruitful

If these things are yours and abound, you will be neither barren nor unfruitful in the knowledge of our Lord Jesus Christ. II Peter 1:8

In the midnight hour As a young wife and mother, the midnight hour was those sometimes lonely hours between 2 A.M. and 5 A.M. when I couldn't sleep: when the challenges of my life lay heavy on my heart, when I didn't want to call and wake my mother, when the house was quiet while everyone else slept. Often during these times I called my Aunt Zelma.

I am praying for you I stopped apologizing for calling so early after the first few times when she assured me she was up sitting at her desk reading her Bible and praying for others. Although she never divulged just how many people were on that prayer list, I got the impression that it was extensive. How special, how loved I felt when she heard my concern and then said, "Wanda, let's pray." How I counted on those prayers.

The years passed but even when Aunt Zelma was confined to her bed, she could still utter those words that gave me such hope, such peace, "Wanda, let's pray."

For your contemplation As we approach retirement, or children leave home, or we experience health restrictions, or financial setbacks, we can feel less fruitful and even barren. Aunt Zelma's life of service for God reminds me that when we share our faith with others we can be forever fruitful.

A question or two How could I use the everyday skills God has given me to be fruitful?

Prayers for our brothers and sisters in Christ Those who need someone to pray with them in the midnight hour.

March 24

Luke 6:27-36

Hurting People Hurt People

And if you do good to those who are good to you, what credit is that to you? Even sinners do that. Be merciful, just as your Father is merciful. Luke 6:33, 36

No fair! She was the organist and I was the pianist. We would agree in what key we were going to play the hymns. Inevitably she would begin playing in a different key. There I would sit, my hands still, the piano quiet while I fussed and fumed in my heart.

A lost opportunity Pastor Skip told of a college professor who had received a scathing letter from one of his students. The professor went to the registrar's office and opened the student's folder. "Now I understand," he said quietly. The student had been in an accident recently that had left her paralyzed from the neck down. "If I were in her shoes, I could see myself writing a letter like this." Pastor Skip ended with, "Hurting people hurt people." I bowed my head in shame. Less than two years after I started playing with her, the organist at my old church died of cancer. I had missed an opportunity to be a friend.

For your contemplation Today's Scripture calls us to reach out in love to those who would do or say hurtful things. Maybe that means taking the time to try to understand them. We are called to do good to them. Maybe that means trying to meet their needs. We are called to lend to them, expecting nothing in return. Maybe that means serving them.

A question or two When hurting people hurt me, what can I do to help?

Prayers for our brothers and sisters in Christ Those who are hard to love.

March 25

Mr. Tice, an Unforgettable Teacher

"Still other seed fell on good soil. It came up, grew and produced a crop, multiplying thirty, sixty, or even a hundred times." Mark 4:8

What a teacher! Mr. Tice wore a crew cut and his eyes twinkled while his lips curled up in a scowl as he barked out "commands." He got this dreamy look when he played music from great composers for us during music appreciation. He would look around the class trying to see who else got it, this whole miracle of music which he seemed to love with all his being.

Play! Mr. Tice, my beloved chorus teacher would stand with one foot propped on the bench next to me. He directed the chorus from my music, helping me keep time and scowling if I slowed down when I happened to make a mistake. He taught me to play in ways that supported the chorus and made them look good.

I shall never forget you I worked hard to gain his approval and in the process I became an excellent accompanist for my classmates at our State Music Festivals and later for numerous church choirs.

For your contemplation Mr. Tice sowed the seeds of music appreciation and instruction freely, perhaps never knowing where they fell; He just planted seeds, watered and fed them. Second, Mr. Tice helped teach me to serve others as I set aside my need to be seen as an accomplished pianist so that I could become accomplished at helping others be great. Thank you, Mr. Tice.

A question or two What seeds would God have me sow today? Who needs me to set aside my needs to help support theirs?

Prayers for our brothers and sisters in Christ Those who are music teachers.

The Perfect Job

"Do you not say, 'Four months more and then the harvest'? I tell you, open your eyes and look at the fields! They are ripe for harvest." John 4:35

Entry-level position John landed a great job two years ago. He started out as a "Marketing Trainee." He latched on to that "Training Manual" and he just wouldn't let go. It wasn't long before his Boss promoted him to "Marketing Specialist" and then to "Marketing Manager" because, not only did John make good use of the product in his everyday life, he became very effective in getting others to use the product as well.

A great Boss How John loved his job. It didn't matter whether John had a good day or was struggling through one of his bad days health wise. Regardless of the situation, John was always happy with his job, his Boss and the product his Boss chose John to market.

A promise fulfilled It wasn't long before John's Boss, our Lord and Savior, promoted John one last time and called John up to meet Him in that great mansion He has prepared for us.

For your contemplation I wrote this tribute and read it at my good friend John's memorial service. The "Marketing Job" John held is open to all of us. The benefits package is unbeatable, the promotions endless, and the rewards unbelievable. And when we have done the job He calls us to do, wouldn't it be wonderful to hear Him say, "Well done, my good and faithful servant, well done!"

A question or two Who will I tell about God's plan of salvation today?

Prayers for our brothers and sisters in Christ Those who are bereavement counselors, and those who volunteer in crisis-intervention programs.

March 27

Deuteronomy 6:6-9

My Grandfather, a Remarkable Man

A good man leaves an inheritance to his children' children...
Proverbs 13:22

Tell me about my grandfather "Your grandfather Roy Dulan was a remarkable man. He taught us to respect our elders, to love others and to work hard. He was a loving father who hugged us and played games with us but he was also strict with us. We grew up in the depression but your grandfather found so many ways to let us know that we were special. I remember your grandfather buying apples for all of us. But the biggest apple he gave to our mother because she was extra special. We followed our father's example and treated our mother extra special too.

Doing for others "Grandfather taught us to share what we had and to love music. I remember my brothers and sisters gathering around your grandfather while he played hymns on his harmonica.

His love, his legacy "Mom, Grandfather taught you and you taught us. Remember how Pat (my sister) and I took some of our money to treat you and Daddy? Daddy went swimming with us, taught us to ride bicycles, roller skate and play cards. You and Daddy gathered around to hear Pat and me play hymns. Now I know where your work ethic came from and the one you taught us... 'Everyone works until all the work is done and then everyone sits down to rest.' My grandfather was indeed a special man."

For your contemplation We had little by the world's standards, but my grandfather's legacy ensured that we grew up rich beyond measure.

A question or two What legacy of love will I leave my children and grandchildren?

Prayers for our brothers and sisters in Christ Children and their grandparents.

March 28

I Peter 4:9-11

A Helping Hand

Each one should use whatever gift he has received to serve others, faithfully administering God's grace in its various forms. I Peter 4:10

No secret My husband, Milt decided a surprise fiftieth birthday party would be a great way to announce this milestone in my life. Our twenty-four-year-old daughter and he planned the event. I was so impressed with the unique touches. What a fabulous birthday party. Where did our daughter get such super party ideas?

Sharing and caring "Mom, your next-door neighbor, Marsha, is such a special person. She wanted to help but she didn't take over. She gave me suggestions and then helped me with the ones I wanted to use. I always felt like it was my party to plan. Marsha is wonderful. I will never forget her!"

For your contemplation God has given each and every one of us a gift to share. Sometimes we are not always sure what those gifts might be. Perhaps an equally challenging aspect to sharing our gifts is *how* to share. Maybe we can learn a lesson or two from my neighbor, Marsha. It was obvious that her goal was to help. Marsha listened to Shelly's needs, made suggestions, and then helped Shelly with the suggestions Shelly liked best. What a friend. What a gift. What a servant.

If you are having trouble identifying your special gifts, try asking family members and friends. Be prepared for answers that are sure to add a blessing while you wait for the arrival of spring.

A question or two How will I use the gifts God has given me to serve others?

Prayers for our brothers and sisters in Christ Those who have never had someone throw a birthday party for them.

March 29

Teaching Children To Share

...And remember the words of the Lord Jesus, that He said, "It is more blessed to give than to receive." Acts 20:35

Sunday evening treats How proud we were to show our parents the money we had earned. It was accompanied by a math lesson: if we are to give 10 percent to God, how much of your earnings will you put in the collection plate on Sunday? Of course some went into our banks to save, and then some went to buy food for our special Sunday evening treats. How exciting it was for my sister and me to plan the surprise treat for that Sunday.

Giving is such fun Our parents taught us the joy and excitement of giving. They made such a big fuss over our gifts at Christmas, birthdays and other occasions that we could hardly wait for our parents to unwrap them. To this day I get excited when I give surprise gifts. Many times the gifts are personal and sentimental with little monetary value. Those are the best kind.

For your contemplation Need some excitement as you anxiously await the arrival of spring? Today's Scriptures provide the perfect solution. Give! Give of yourself to family and friends. Set a five-dollar limit and see what huge personal gifts you can give from your heart. Be sure to wear sunglasses when giving your gift so you won't be blinded by the smile of the person who receives it.

A question or two What kind of excitement and joy can I bring to my day with a personal gift for a family member or friend?

Prayers for our brothers and sisters in Christ Those who are in need of a gift of Sonshine.

March 30

John 15:12-17

Friends For a Lifetime

"These things I command you, that you love one another."
John 15:17

A part of our lives Mr. and Mrs. Holland both taught Sunday School. Mrs. Holland gave me my first lessons and experience in speaking before a group of people. Mr. Holland was the principal at Monroe School, which I attended along with Linda Brown of "Brown vs Topeka Public Schools" the landmark case that integrated schools throughout the nation. A building has been named after Mr. and Mrs. Holland in tribute to their outstanding contributions in the field of education.

Life's challenges Now my father was in the beginning stages of Alzheimer's disease. My sister and I lived in Washington State, my parents in Kansas. We both called regularly, and when we asked how mother was doing, the answer was always, "Great."

Saturday morning calls Each Saturday I called, Mr. Holland was there playing dominoes with my father. Mr. Holland started taking time out of his hectic schedule to visit after my father became ill. I relaxed. I knew that our family friend wouldn't hesitate to call us if he saw that conditions warranted direct intervention by my sister and me. What a friend! What a great way to bring Sonshine on an otherwise gloomy day.

For your contemplation I believe it is up to us to be creative in the ways we reflect God's love for others. In a world that continually challenges us with uncertainty, loneliness, health issues, financial reverses, strained relationships and violence, there are unending opportunities for us to show our love by being a friend.

A question or two What can I do to be a great friend?

Prayers for our brothers and sisters in Christ Those who are great teachers and great friends.

March 31

What Brother?

Then He said to the disciple, "Behold your mother!" And from that hour that disciple took her to his own home. John 19:27

May I speak to Mother? I answered Mother's phone and heard a male voice say, "Hello Sis, it's good to have you home. May I speak to Mother?"

Who? I didn't have a brother and was about to hang up when he added, "This is Ted Henderson from church." Mother had mentored and prayed for him. He returned that spiritual mothering by adopting her and my father. Thereafter, he would bring over special dishes he had cooked, leaving them on the back porch until Mother finally gave him a key to the house. What a blessing it was for her and my father to walk into the house and find a home-cooked meal waiting.

Behold your mother My sister and I lived in different states, too far away to prepare a surprise birthday dinner for Mother, so our brother, Ted, did it. All the things that money can't buy, those things that are priceless, our brother, Ted, did for our folks. He was their son; he was our brother.

For your contemplation My husband and I, during thirty-six years of marriage and two children, have moved to eight different homes in four different states, far away from family. I rejoice in the Family of God that has allowed me to adopt, love and be loved by countless mothers, fathers, sisters, brothers, sons and daughters. I have a big family and I love it!

A question or two Who needs me to adopt them?

Prayers for our brothers and sisters in Christ Birth mothers and the adoptive parents they have chosen for their children.

My Journal
March: Special People Who
Remind Me Of God's Sonshine

Insights: Who are the special people in my life that remind me of God's love? How will I let them know?

Challenges: What lessons did I learn and how will I incorporate them into my everyday life? When will I start?

What are the ten top blessings I received from God this month?

1.

2.

3.

4.

5.

6.

7.

8.

9.

10.

Answered Prayers

Introduction to April Devotions

Sisters in the Faith

"But the angel answered and said to the women, 'Do not be afraid, for I know that you seek Jesus who was crucified. He is not here; for He is risen, as He said.'" Matthew 28:5-6

Dear Brothers and Sisters in Christ,

Who are these women? Over the years as I read my Bible, I have often admired the women I met there. Sometimes it was their commitment to their faith, sometimes it was their bravery, sometimes it was their intelligence, and sometimes it was their love and compassion for others. And sometimes my heart broke for the way they had been treated. I wondered why I hadn't heard about some of these women in the hundreds of sermons I had listened to down through the years. I believe they hold important lessons for young girls.

Mothers...Grandmothers...Queens...Judges....Advisors...Servants ...Construction Workers...Wives...Daughters There are so many interesting women from all walks of life; sisters in the faith with whom we can all relate. The best part is when we read about them in the Bible we see that they are not super women, they are just ordinary people like you and me. What a message. God created us, He loves us and He can use us to do His work wherever we are and whomever we might be.

It is my prayer that by getting to know some of our Biblical sisters in the faith, you will be inspired to examine anew the ways in which God may be calling you to help our young girls grow up in faith, and experience first hand the love that comes with being a part of the Family of God.

Your sister in the faith,
Wanda Scott Bledsoe

Our Sister Abigail, the Mediator

*So David received from her hand what she had brought him, and
said to her, "Go up in peace to your house. See, I have heeded
your voice and respected your person."* I Samuel 25:35

The plan The humility Abigail displayed in taking responsibility for
the disastrous actions of her husband did not diminish her; rather,
it significantly increased her status. First, Abigail took responsibility
for receiving David in the hospitable manner he deserved. Secondly,
she was sincere in her apology for her husband Nabal's insulting
behavior, and thirdly, she graciously presented gifts as she asked for
David's forgiveness. The plan worked! Not only did Abigail protect
her husband and his servants from harm, but also David, a future
king, who thanked her for keeping him from acting on his anger, an
act he would have later regretted.

For your reflection Abigail's story reminded me of the jockeying for
power, position and control we see too often. Titles become a way
of establishing a hierarchy of power. Chains of command can make
it difficult for those doing the work to communicate critical information to those making the decisions. What then can we tell our
daughters, our young girls, about power? I think we can read
Abigail's story with its surprising ending and tell them that Abigail
modeled Jesus' teachings about humility with powerful results.
When we would teach our young girls about power, let us teach
them not as the world teaches but as God teaches. "Blessed are the
meek, for they shall inherit the earth" *Matthew 5:5.*

A question for the ladies How can I gain more power and more status by being humble?

Prayers for our sisters in Christ Those who mediate in hostage situations.

April 2

Our Sister Elizabeth, an Older Woman

*"And Mary remained with her about three months, and returned
to her house."* Luke 1:56

The greeting Elizabeth greeted her cousin Mary with joy and
affirmed that Mary was indeed carrying Jesus, Son of God. How
wonderful it must have made Mary feel to have a woman who was
older, also carrying a child, and who just happened to be a family
member greet her with joy and affirmation. Just imagine the support Elizabeth must have been able to give her young cousin, Mary.

For your reflection When I read about Elizabeth, I am again
reminded how important an extended family is. Our daughter,
Shelly, still has letters her older cousin, Betty Leora sent her when
she was going through the challenges of being a teenager and Betty
Leora was a medical student. I still seek my mother's spiritual counsel, but I also sought the spiritual counsel of my Aunt Zelma, who
was much older than my mother. In a society that seems to value
youth over age and wisdom, Mary reminds us of the benefits of
seeking the counsel of older women. We can't prevent the challenges
life brings to our young girls, but we can use the story of Elizabeth
to teach them the value of seeking the counsel of older spiritual
women. Equally as important, we who are "older women" can continue to develop and strengthen our faith so that when we are
approached, we can give counsel based on the Scriptures and how
we applied them to help us meet the challenges life presented to us.

A question for the ladies What faith-filled older woman could I turn
to for spiritual counsel?

Prayers for our sisters in Christ The older women in our churches.

April 3

Our Sister Deborah, Here Comes the Judge

"And she would sit under the palm tree of Deborah between Ramah and Bethel in the mountains of Ephraim. And the children of Israel came up to her for judgment." Judges 4:5

War strategist Deborah called Barak, one of the Israelite commanders, and told him the strategy God had given her for Barak to defeat Sisera, the commander of the dreaded King Jabin's army. Barak was willing to take the risk if, and only if, Deborah would go with him. Deborah agreed, but told Barak that he would not claim any glory in the victory because Sisera, the commander of the enemy's army, would be taken and killed by a woman. Deborah's prophecy came true.

For your reflection When we teach our young girls faith in God, we open up endless possibilities for God to use them in small and great ways. They might have titles like those we could appropriately assign to Deborah: Counselor, Judge, Army Recruiter, War Advisor, and War Hero. As we read this amazing story to our young girls, we should also read it for the lessons it has for us. Nothing is impossible when God is with us. When He calls us to do scary things, we can trust that He has prepared us and will guide us to success, *or* we can be hesitant like Barak and miss the glory God has in store for us. We have a choice. How will you respond?

A question for the ladies How might I use Deborah's faith story to inspire our young girls to excellence?

Prayers for our sisters in Christ Those who are military commanders.

Our Sister Jael, Courage under Fire

However, Sisera had fled away on foot to the tent of Jael, the wife of Heber the Kenite; for there was peace between Jabin king of Hazor and the house of Heber the Kenite. Judges 4:17

Switching sides Jael and her husband, Heber, were of the Kenites, a semi-nomadic desert tribe who had been friendly with the Israelites since the time of Moses. Heber had left his own people and had become an ally of King Jabin, who had subjected the Israelites to tyranny for the past twenty years.

Whom will you serve? Sisera, commander of King Jabin's army, sought refuge in Jael's tent, where he assumed he would be safe. He asked her to stand guard, putting her life at risk to save his own. Was Jael afraid? One would think so! What did she do? I won't spoil the ending for you. You will want to read it in amazement for yourselves.

For your reflection Not many of us are called to put our lives on the line like Jael in order to make a statement about our faith. There are, however, opportunities every day in a society that has strayed so far from God's Word, to take a stand for social justice and God's Righteousness. What kind of support do you think God gave Jael in her hour of need? What kind of support do you think He will provide for us when it is our turn to declare our faith in a difficult situation?

A question for the ladies How will I use this story to teach a young girl about bravery and faith in God?

Prayers for our sisters in Christ Heroines in the fight against social injustice.

April 5

Our Sister Dorcas, the Celebrity

At Joppa there was a certain disciple named Tabitha, which is translated Dorcas. This woman was full of good works and charitable deeds which she did. Acts 9:36

A woman of distinction Dorcas sewed beautiful garments, which she gave to the many widows and orphans living in the city. After Dorcas' sudden death, her friends, as an expression of love, prepared her body for burial, then sent for the apostle Peter.

His mysterious ways No one had to tell Peter how important this disciple was; he could see for himself. Peter prayed and brought Dorcas back to life. When the people heard, the Scriptures say, "many believed on the Lord." God used a simple woman and her sewing skills to bring His message of salvation.

For your reflection When I was in the health-care field, the physicians who were specialists would sometimes debate which part of the body was the most essential in sustaining life. Was it the brain, the heart, the lungs or the kidneys? Today's Scripture answers the question, which talent is the most important? "But now God has set the members, each one of them, in the body just as He pleased. And if they were all one member, where would the body be?" *I Corinthians 12:18,19*. God calls all of us to spread His Word, using the "part" He has given us. Respect your talent, develop it, and then use it to the glory of the Lord.

A question for the ladies Have I developed and used the talents God has given me to my fullest ability?

Prayers for our sisters in Christ Those who sew quilts for the homeless.

April 6

Our Sister, a Woman of Great Faith

...If only I may touch His garment, I shall be made well.
Matthew 9:21

Chronically ill Scripture tells us that she "had a flow of blood for twelve years" (verse 20). We women who have had related problems can empathize with how debilitating, frustrating, and even depressing our sister in the faith's condition must have been. Twelve years is a long time to suffer from a chronic illness.

The risk of rejection How brave she had to be to even approach Jesus. Yet, in her faith, she touched the hem of His garment. Jesus immediately felt her touch. HE knew she needed His healing power. HE turned to her and told her that her faith had made her well.

For your reflection Sometimes as we try to encourage self-esteem and independence in our young girls, we may also give the impression that being strong and self-reliant means never needing to ask for help. Our young girls can learn from this sister in faith's story the importance of reaching out for help when they need it. Our older girls can learn from Jesus' response. No matter how successful, how important, how powerful they become, if they are to be Christ-like they must retain their ability to be seen as approachable, with compassion for all. Girls, ask for help when you need it and be compassionate when others ask you for help because they need it.

A question for the ladies How can I use my faith to respond to a young girl reaching out to me for help?

Prayers for our sisters in Christ Those suffering from chronic illnesses.

Our Sister Mary, at Risk for God

For He who is mighty has done great things for me, And holy is His name. Luke 1:49

Walk a mile in my shoes "I have always admired Wanda's talent," my friend Lynn told the group. "I have often thought it would be great if I could just trade places with her. Then I listened to a speaker talk about the challenges she faces as an African American woman. I asked myself if God offered me a chance to have Wanda's talent and her ethnicity, would I still want the talent? I am ashamed to say I would not."

My soul magnifies the Lord Mary, the mother of Jesus, will be remembered until the end of time, yet I would not want to trade places with her. Imagine being in a situation not of your doing that could cost you your life. However, when Mary heard the angel's message she immediately replied, "Behold the maidservant of the Lord! Let it be to me according to your word" (verse 38).

For your reflection God calls each of us to what may sometimes seem to be difficult, if not impossible, situations. Mary's faith story reminds us that when we step out in faith, singing God's praises, He provides in wonderful ways we cannot even begin to imagine. Today's Scripture helps us step out in faith, believe in His Word, trust in His Promises, sing His praises with your whole heart and receive His blessings!

A question for the ladies How can increasing my faith and my praise to God help me through a tough situation I am currently facing?

Prayers for our sisters in Christ Those who are looking for a way out of a difficult situation.

April 8

Our Sister Salome, The Price of Admission

And He said to her, "What do you wish?" She said to Him,
"Grant that these two sons of mine may sit, one on Your right
hand and the other on the left, in Your kingdom." Matthew 20:21

A steep price Salome wanted her sons to be in heaven seated on the right and left of Jesus. However, Jesus must have wondered if either Salome or her sons would want those positions if they knew the price.

Practice, practice, practice Perhaps it is human nature to want things to be easy, to wish we could do something great, without the motivation to do whatever it takes to get it. It is like the books that promise you can be playing the piano for family and friends in just a few lessons. That makes me smile when I remember the years of lessons and hours of practice it took for me to learn to play the piano.

For your reflection Perhaps we can use Salome's story to teach our young girls about the value of hard work and sacrifice in developing their faith and achieving their goals in life. So when we hear our young girls say, "I wish I could play like that, or be like that, or accomplish that, our answer could be, "You can be or do anything you like if you want it badly enough. How much time are you willing to devote? What are you willing to give up?"

A question for the ladies Am I a good role model for a young girl based on the time and effort I have used to become accomplished in a talent God has given me?

Prayers for our sisters in Christ Those who play a musical instrument.

Our Sister Rebekah, a Betraying Mother

"Whoever causes one of these little ones who believe in Me to sin, it would be better for him if a millstone were hung around his neck, and he were drowned in the depth of the sea." Matthew 18:6

Who will it hurt? My "little sister" was in her senior year of college. Graduation was very close, to be followed by an August wedding. I was surprised to get her phone call. She was in the midst of a terrible dilemma.

Who should I believe? My sister and her fiancée were struggling to manage their physical desires and their commitment to God. "What must I do?" my sister cried. I could not betray my sister with easy answers. How could I advise her to disregard beliefs we had held since we were young children?

Thank you "Thank you, Wanda. I needed you to be strong." Many years later our mother called me and said she had found a letter of "thanks" my sister had written to me long ago when I was a young married woman and she needed my strength.

For your reflection When our young girls come to us with hard questions, will we "betray" them with easy answers that make them vulnerable in a society that does not honor the commandments of our faith, or will we take the time to tell them in love, "Thus saith the Lord"?

A question for the ladies Who needs me to help them make choices that reflect our belief in God? How will we both benefit?

Prayers for our sisters in Christ Those who are facing peer pressure to do things that are against their beliefs.

April 10

Our Sister Jochebed, Acting in Faith

"But when she could no longer hide him, she took an ark of bul-rushes for him, daubed it with asphalt and pitch, put the child in it, and laid it in the reeds by the river's bank." Exodus 2:3

Trusting in God Acting on faith There is a saying, "Do your best and God will do the rest." It certainly seems to apply here. Jochebed (called by name in *Exodus 6:20*) had her daughter, Miriam, watch to see what would happen to her little brother after she had placed him in the river. Pharaoh's daughter came to bathe in the river and saw the basket. When she opened it, the baby cried and Pharaoh's daughter showed compassion. Miriam offered to get a Hebrew woman to nurse the child. The woman Miriam found was none other than the baby's mother, Jochebed. Pharaoh's daughter gave the baby to Jochebed to nurse *and* told her she would be paid! This baby grew up in Pharaoh's house to became the leader God chose to deliver the Israelites to the Promised Land. We know him as Moses.

For your reflection Our sister Jochebed's faith story teaches us first to trust God when a situation looks hopeless. Second, listen for His guidance, and mostly importantly, act in faith, even when you don't know, can't control, and could not even imagine the outcome. Then "Wait on the Lord, be of good courage and He will strengthen your heart. Wait, I say on the Lord" *Psalm 27:14.*

A question for the ladies How am I limiting God's ability to help me by not stepping out in faith?

Prayers for our sisters in Christ Those who look after younger brothers and sisters while their parents work.

April 11

Exodus 2:1-10

Our Sister Hannah, a Promise Keeper

Then she made a vow and said, "O lord of hosts, if You will indeed look on the affliction of Your maidservant and remember me, and not forget Your maidservant, but will give Your maidservant a male child, then I will give him to the Lord all the days of his life, and no razor shall come upon his head." I Samuel 1:11

Promises made and kept It is easy to make a promise. Keeping it is a different matter. How many times do we make a promise, but when it is time to follow through we tell ourselves, "I didn't realize it would be this hard to make this marriage work...to love and have patience with this child who seems to get into one scrape after another...to make payments on that car deal we just shook hands on because we are friends...to let you ride my bike to school for one whole week like I promised if you would help me with my math homework. By the way, I aced the test."

For your reflection Our sister Hannah's faith story has some critical lessons for us and our young daughters and sisters in Christ. Hannah reminds us that a promise is a promise no matter what. Imagine the moral integrity, the spiritual depth, the influence, the self-esteem, the servants of God our young daughters and sisters in Christ can become if we can teach them Hannah's lesson and role model her commitment to...a promise made is a promise kept, no matter what.

A question for the ladies Who needs me to be a role model for Hannah's lesson in promises made and kept?

Prayers for our sisters in Christ Mothers and fathers who give their newborns up for adoption.

April 12

Our Sister Rhoda—She Knew His Voice

When she recognized Peter's voice, because of her gladness she did not open the gate, but ran in and announced that Peter stood before the gate. Acts 12:14

I didn't have to see him When Peter knocked at the door, Rhoda recognized his voice and in her excitement ran back to tell the others without opening the door. The group of gathered Christians did not believe Rhoda. She kept insisting until, hearing the continued knocking, they went to the door and opened it.

For your reflection Rhoda, our sister in faith, must have heard Peter's voice so much that she didn't have to see him with her eyes to know it was he who was knocking at the door. "God with us" is a hard concept to teach because we can't *see* Him with our eyes. Yet if we can help our young girls learn to *know* Him in a personal way through reading their Children's Bible with them, if we can help them *learn* about Him by taking them to Sunday School, if we can be good role models so that they see us read our Bibles, hear us pray and listen as we give thanks for answered prayer, then we can help our young girls *recognize* God's voice. Our children's teachers will readily admit that even the youngest students face challenges on a daily basis. Is it ever too early to help them know God, to call upon Him in their time of need and to recognize His voice when He speaks to them?

A question for the ladies How can I help our young girls learn to know God's voice?

Prayers for our sisters in Christ Those who teach the hearing impaired.

April 13

Our Sister, Lot's Disobedient Wife

When the morning dawned, the angels urged Lot to hurry, saying, "Arise, take your wife and your two daughters who are here, lest you be consumed in the punishment of the city." Genesis 19:15

Ignoring the warning Lot's wife was headed for safety. All she had to do was look ahead to the new place God had provided. What was it that made Lot's wife ignore the threat of destruction and turn around for one last look at her old life? Scripture doesn't say, but it is clear about the price she paid for ignoring the warning. She was turned into a pillar of salt permanently!

For your reflection Our sister, Lot's wife, has some sobering lessons we can pass on to our young girls. The pull of a society that glorifies alcohol, drugs, guns, promiscuous and perverted sex, violence, and gambling is a strong one. The lessons we can teach our young girls and remember ourselves are basic ones. When we act in ways that are against God's laws, He sometimes gives us a second chance by warning us. When we ignore the warning, we suffer the consequences. And sometimes when we ignore the warning, others who are innocent suffer the consequences...sometimes along with us...and sometimes instead of us. Perhaps we can explain the importance of keeping God's rules to our young girls in another way. God created us and He gave us rules to keep us safe, happy and to help us get along with others. When we ignore the rules, there are consequences; sometimes delayed, but rest assured, there are always consequences.

A question for the ladies Which of God's rules have I been breaking?

Prayers for our sisters in Christ Substance abuse counselors that work with our youth.

April 14

II Kings 5:1-6

Our Sister, Namaan's Maidservant, and Her Forgiving Heart

Then she said to her mistress, "If only my master were with the prophet who is in Samaria! For he would heal him of his leprosy."
II Kings 5:3

Enslaved Naaman was the commander of the army of the king of Syria. He had contracted leprosy, a highly contagious and ultimately fatal disease. During a raid, a young girl from the land of Israel was brought back as a captive and given to Namaan's wife as her maidservant.

A forgiving Namaan's maidservant felt compassion for her captor and believed if he could only go to the prophet (Elisha) in Samaria, the prophet would heal him of his leprosy. Namaan was healed, and as a result he became convinced that *Yahweh* was the one true God. A young girl's forgiving heart led her captor to believe in God.

For your reflection I recently read a devotion that encouraged readers who wanted to or needed to forgive to try these three requests. "First, ask God to enable you to forgive the person; it's too hard to do this on your own. Second, ask God to bless that person, making the request every day. Finally, ask God to give you an opportunity to show kindness to him or her." God is love and calls us to love one another. How much better is it then for our young girls *and* for our society if we teach them early in life the importance of having a "forgiving heart"?

A question for the ladies Who must I forgive, bless, and show kindness to before I can teach forgiveness to others?

Prayers for our sisters in Christ Victims and families of violent crimes who are able to forgive the perpetrators.

April 15

Genesis 34:1-12

Our Sister Dinah,
When Bad Things Happen to Good People

And when Shechem the son of Hamor the Hivite, prince of the country saw her, (Dinah) he took her and lay with her, and violated her. Genesis 34:2

Who is good? In our imperfect world bad things happen. So where is God? HE is with us. His compassion sustains us through the tragedies in our lives…if we let Him. The Bible is full of verses that can soothe, comfort and give us peace. I believe God sends people to help us and uphold us in time of trouble. I delivered twins in my sixth month of pregnancy. Shortly after birth, one twin died and the other twin was not expected to live. There was a wonderful nurse who lovingly helped me with the most basic personal functions because in my desolation I could not help myself.

For your reflection Dinah, our sister in the faith, has lessons for all of us. First, we must not raise our young girls to think they are "entitled" to a sorrow-free life if they become Christians. Second, we must protect our young girls and teach them how to protect themselves. Third, we must assure them that rape is never the victim's fault. Fourth, we must join with their fathers to help teach our sons to respect girls of all ages. And most importantly, we can assure them that no matter what life dishes out, God loves them; He is with them through His Word and through faithful, compassionate people—like you and like me.

A question for the ladies What young girl needs my compassion and support today?

Prayers for our sisters in Christ Victims of rape and those who counsel them.

Our Sister Naomi, a Spiritual Mother and Mentor

And she said to her, "All that you say to me I will do." Ruth 3:5

Opportunities to mentor Naomi had two sons who died and left her with two daughters-in-law. At first Naomi, who had also lost her husband, was very bitter. The story of Naomi and Ruth remind us that being a mother is not necessarily the same thing as being a spiritual mentor. Spiritual mentoring is so much more. The Bible calls older women to be spiritual mentors to younger women. We as older women have been through many of the challenges that await them, and we can share our experiences, teaching them the lessons we have learned. We can love them, pray for them and support them. Many of our young women have not had a Christian upbringing. Many of them carry insecurities, hurts and questions about their self-worth. We can help them walk as God intended, knowledgeable about His Word and secure in His love.

For your reflection Naomi teaches us some simple lessons. Focusing outward to love others heals the hurts within. When we give unselfishly of ourselves, it sometimes feels as if we are the ones who benefit the most. Just ask those who teach our children. And what Great blessings await us and our young girls when we accept the role as spiritual mentors.

A question for the ladies Who needs me to be a spiritual mother and mentor?

Prayers for our sisters in Christ Young women who would like to know more about incorporating Christ into their everyday lives and the older women willing to mentor them.

April 17

Our Sister Eve, Giving In to Temptation

"And the Lord God said to the woman, 'What is this you have done?' The woman said, 'The serpent deceived me, and I ate.'"
Genesis 3:13

If it looks good and feels good, it must be good I didn't need the shoes, yet there was that voice again, hissssssssssing in my ear. "You have to play for the Christmas Eve service. What a sacrifice you are making. You deserve those shoes." I bought the shoes. After getting dressed, I decided to prepare a dish for Christmas dinner. The fire under the skillet was much too high. Pop! Splatter! Grease spots covered the toes of my new shoes. They were ruined!

For your reflection What shall we teach our young girls about not giving in to temptation? For starters we can encourage them to surround themselves with friends who exercise self-discipline. Think what a difference it would have made if Adam could have exercised self-discipline when Eve offered him the apple and just said, "No!" I realized that when I lose a battle with temptation and feel farther away from God than I would like to be, it is not God who distances Himself from me, it is I who distance myself from God. No matter what my transgression, be it little or huge, God stands ready to forgive. As I move toward Him in repentance, asking forgiveness, I am restored to that wonderful relationship with God that makes me feel whole again.

A question for the ladies What changes should I make in my personal life that would help me avoid temptation?

Prayers for our sisters in Christ Teenagers whose choice of friends puts them at risk.

Our Sister Achsah, a Team Player

Now it was so, when she came to him, that she persuaded him to ask her father for a field. Joshua 15:18

A loving father My father gave generously of his love, his time and his money to his family. Just one of many memories comes to mind. I had asked my father for a specific amount of money. He opened his wallet, pulled out the bills and then said, "Are you sure that's enough?" His generosity always caused me to smile and say, "No, thanks Daddy, this is a gracious plenty." Caleb had given his daughter, Achsah, land as a wedding present. She must have known that the land without a source of water wasn't worth much because Achsah went to her father with a request for land with water. We might assume that Achsah was loved by her father because he responded by giving her both the upper springs and the lower springs" (verse 16).

For your reflection This devotion was supposed to be about teaching our young girls how to work as teammates with their spouses. But my heart was captured by the love between Caleb and his daughter Achsah. So perhaps the true lesson is the importance of a loving father. Our Father, who art in heaven, assures us that our daughters and sisters in Christ will always have a loving father no matter what the circumstances might be here on earth. "Yes, Jesus loves me." How do I know? "The Bible tells me so."

A question for the ladies How can I help a young woman rely upon God's love to help her through a tough situation she is currently facing?

Prayers for our sisters in Christ Those who did not have a loving father.

Our Sister Martha, a Need for Balance

And Jesus answered and said to her, "Martha, Martha, you are worried and troubled about many things." Luke 10:41

A frequent visitor From the three separate accounts of Jesus visiting in their home, we see Martha in the role of hostess. We also get a glimpse of her sister, Mary. In today's Scripture, Martha is busy serving and Mary is seated at Jesus' feet listening to Him speak. Martha's response is one that many if not all of us would have, "This is her house too. Shouldn't she be helping with the work of serving our guests instead of sitting around like she *is* a guest?"

For your reflection I can certainly identify with Martha. Our sister in Christ's story reinforced a message I have been trying to listen to most of my adult life. Take a look at your priorities. Make sure there is a balance. I have always loved having people in our home. Unfortunately I had a habit of carrying the preparation and cleaning to such extremes that it tended to make my husband and children want to "head for the hills." And it often left me too tired to enjoy our guests as much as I would have liked. Jesus might have been speaking to me, cautioning me to reexamine my priorities and make sure there is a balance to my efforts when I open our home to guests. Our sister Martha's story helps remind us that we shouldn't forget to teach our young girls an important lesson: People first!

A question for the ladies How can I make sure my priorities reflect the love of Christ?

Prayers for our sisters in Christ Those who share their homes with visiting missionaries.

April 20

Exodus 2:1-10

Our Sister Miriam, a Very Smart Girl

Then his sister said to Pharaoh's daughter, "Shall I go and call a nurse for you from the Hebrew women, that she may nurse the child for you?" Exodus 2:7

Making the most of an opportunity Miriam's mother made a basket, waterproofed it with pitch and placed her son inside. Then she took the basket, laid it at the water's edge, and told Miriam, her young daughter to stay close by. Pharaoh's daughter came to bathe at the river. When she opened the basket and heard the baby cry, she had compassion. Miriam spoke up, offering to find a Hebrew woman to nurse the infant. That woman was Jochebed, the baby's mother. Since I am a firm believer that God can meet our needs in ways we can't begin to imagine, it is no surprise to me that Pharaoh's daughter told Miriam the Hebrew woman would be paid for her services!

For your reflection Our young sister in Christ, Miriam, reminds us that we don't have to wait until we are adults to make a difference. There are children who are organizing whole communities in behalf of a cause that helps others. Let us encourage our young girls to read Miriam's story and use her as a role model in obedience to their parents. Her story also reminds them to look for opportunities to do more than they are asked, especially when it is an opportunity to help someone else.

A question for the ladies How can I let our young girls know that God has important work for them to do?

Prayers for our sisters in Christ Children who are making a difference in their communities.

Our Sisters Lois and Eunice, Just Doing Their Job

"...when I call to remembrance the genuine faith that is in you, which dwelt first in your grandmother Lois and your mother Eunice, and I am persuaded is in you also." II Timothy 1:5

Wouldn't it be grand if...? In the best of all possible worlds, children grow up strong in the faith because of the homes in which they are reared. Unfortunately our children are not growing up in the best of all possible worlds. Parents in our churches may lack time, commitment or knowledge to instruct their children in the faith. Our highly mobile society and global economy also mean the family unit is likely to move away from the support of loving grandparents. Does that also mean that our young girls have to go without? Absolutely not! We women of faith have important work to do.

Everyone can help We can teach Sunday school, lead or support our church's young people's Bible study programs and offer to transport children to youth group functions. If you need more ideas, just call your church office and I am sure they will be glad to supply you with lots of opportunities to help our young girls grow in their faith.

For your reflection Lois and Eunice started teaching Timothy about the Holy Scriptures from early childhood. If we made a list of all the challenges our young girls currently face, how could we could we do any less? What child do you know who deserves less?

A question for the ladies What child can I help ensure a successful future by helping her grow in faith? When will I start?

Prayers for our sisters in Christ Those who help teach our children about the Bible.

April 22

Our Sisters, Shallum's Daughters

And next to him was Shallum the son of Hallohesh, leader of half
the district of Jerusalem; he and his daughters made repairs.
Nehemiah 3:12

Construction workers The city of Jerusalem's wall was in a terrible
state of disrepair. The prophet Nehemiah prayed about this horrible
situation and God put it in his heart to rebuild the wall. Nehemiah
accomplished this daunting task by recruiting volunteers! Chapter
3 tells their names, their craft and what part they played in rebuilding the wall. And in verse 12, we read that a man and his daughters
made repairs.

For your reflection Just one verse without description, just one verse
to teach our daughters a valuable lesson. What lesson? That there
were women working on construction sites in biblical times? Or
that women in biblical times held what we call today either "non-
traditional" or "male-dominated" jobs? Yes, and even more importantly, that the Bible is a current source for guidance and
encouragement for our young girls, *including* career counseling. If
you haven't been following this month's devotions on "Lessons Our
Biblical Sisters Of Faith Can Teach Us," then I encourage you to start
from the beginning and decide which biblical sisters in faith have
important lessons to teach us and our young girls.

A question for the ladies What young girl growing up in faith do I
know with whom I can share this month's devotions?

Prayers for our sisters in Christ Those sisters in Christ who own
construction companies.

April 23

II Kings 4:1-7

Our Sister, the Prophet's Widow

Now it came to pass, when the vessels were full, that she said to her son, "Bring me another vessel." And he said to her, "There is not another vessel." So the oil ceased. II Kings 4:6

Following directions In faith, the prophet's widow went to the prophet Elisha and asked him for help. Elisha asked the widow what she had in her house. She told Elisha she just had a jar of oil. Elisha told the widow to go to all her neighbors and borrow as many empty vessels as she could. She was then to go into her house, and with the help of her sons, pour the small jar of oil she had into all the vessels. She could then sell the oil to pay off her debts.

For your reflection The widow followed Elisha's instructions. Many times we ask God for help and then question or discount His answer. Or maybe we follow directions like my husband. When he has to put something together, first he tries to do it using his own ingenuity. And then if that doesn't work, he grudgingly breaks down and reads the instructions. It makes me crazy. I wonder if it makes God crazy when He provides the perfect instruction manual to help us enjoy the world He created for us and we respond by questioning, discounting or totally disregarding His instructions? Perhaps one of the great lessons we can model for our young daughters is to read His Word and then *follow the directions!*

A question for the ladies What personal faith story can I tell a young girl about following God's instructions?

Prayers for our sisters in Christ Those who write and edit technical manuals.

April 24

Luke 7:36-50

Our Sister Whose Actions Spoke Louder than Words

Then He said to the woman, "Your faith has saved you. Go in peace." Luke 7:50

You choose Imagine that you ran out of gas on a very hot day while traveling down a dusty country road. The person hosting the dinner party lives just a couple of miles ahead, so you decide to walk. After the first mile, your feet remind you that you are not wearing shoes designed for this kind of activity so you take them off. Finally you reach your destination. Nothing is said about you being barefoot and dusty, you are merely welcomed and invited to come to the table for the meal that has been prepared. Suddenly a woman enters. The guests blush because they know how she earns her living. Their mouths fly open in horror as she drops to her knees and begins to bathe your feet. She tenderly dries them, massages them with a soothing lotion and then slips your shoes back on. Who made you feel the most welcome: the ones who spoke or the one who acted?

For your reflection Our society puts a lot of value in words, titles and status symbols. Our young girls probably would get the message if we shared this faith story with them. I think they would tell us that what we do speaks louder than what we say or the titles we wear. How then can we help our young girls incorporate this faith lesson into their everyday lives? How do you think they will benefit?

A question for the ladies Do the title or titles I wear help or hinder how I respond to others?

Prayers for our sisters in Christ Podiatrists who treat the elderly.

April 25

Judges 9:50-55

Our Sister Who Used a Rock to Save Her People

So Abimelech came as far as the tower and fought against it; and he drew near the door of the tower to burn it with fire. But a certain woman dropped an upper millstone on Abimelech's head and crushed his skull. Judges 9:52,53

David and Goliath, the sequel Scripture tells us that a certain unnamed woman dropped a millstone, which she had been using to grind corn, on Abimelech's head. Like the story of David and Goliath, the stone did not kill Abimelech. Abimelech, having fallen with a severe head injury, called to his armor bearer, and said to him, "Draw your sword and kill me, lest men say of me, 'A woman killed him'" (verse 55). Hmm.

For your reflection Many times our young girl's response to a challenging situation is, "I am too young, or I don't have the brains or the training or the title or the money or the contacts or the right ethnic or social background." What we do have is God. We must encourage our young girls to step forward and with faith and determination, use what they have. Look up the following Scriptures for examples of other sisters in faith who delivered people and saved cities from destruction: *Judges 4:9, Judges 5:26, II Samuel 20:22, Joshua 2:12.*

A question for the ladies How can I encourage young girls to call upon their faith in God, their inner strength, and the resources at hand when they face a challenge, no matter how great the challenge might be?

Prayers for our sisters in Christ Children trying to survive in war-torn countries.

April 26

Our Sisters Euodia and Syntyche in Dispute

"I implore Euodia and I implore Syntyche to be of the same mind in the Lord." Philippians 4:2

Relationships and reconciliation Perhaps recognizing the importance of harmony in working relationships, Paul calls on these women to work it out!

Gentleness, prayer and peace Paul admonishes the group to let others see their gentleness, not to worry about anything, but through prayer, giving thanks to God, ask for what they need. The end result would be God's peace.

Focus on the good stuff Lastly Paul reminds them to focus on positive things: those things that are true, noble, just, pure, lovely, praiseworthy, and the God who is of peace would be with them. My friend Melanie Aamodt wrote a beautiful song that calls us to think on those very things. Focusing on such thoughts not only helps us have the right frame of mind for reconciliation, but also helps ensure ongoing harmony in our church relationships.

A peacemaker be Disputes compromise our effectiveness in doing God's work. Depending on how severe the dispute, sides may be taken and fellow members hurt. Churches may split. But the most horrible casualty of disputes within the church is the believer who turns away from God and no longer believes.

For your reflection God's work is too important to risk in disputes with fellow believers. Shouldn't we teach our young girls the principles and importance of reconciliation so they can use them in all aspects of their lives?

A question for the ladies With whom do I need to reconcile before I can be a role model for the young girls in my church?

Prayers for our sisters in Christ Children whose parents stop going to church because their feelings have been hurt in unreconciled disputes.

Our Sister Lydia, an Influential Business Woman

Now a certain woman named Lydia heard us. She was a seller of purple from the city of Thyatira, who worshiped God. Acts 16:14

Influential and hospitable Lydia was an influential woman, to say the least. We are told that while Lydia's name appears in Scripture only twice, she was apparently the first Gentile convert in Europe, the first Christian businesswoman, and the first believer to open her home as a place of worship for European Christians.

For your reflection Looking at the lifestyles and impact on society of some successful business people, we might come to the conclusion that being a businesswoman is not what we want for our young girls. However, Lydia, our sister in faith, provides a role model as a successful businesswoman who led her entire household to Christ and used her resources to support the early church. Using one's wealth and influence to spread and support God's work is a worthy ambition for our young girls. Lydia's story gives us another wonderful opportunity to show our young girls that the role models to help them learn about life, and how to live it happily and successfully, can be found in a best-seller—the Bible.

A question for the ladies How can I teach my daughter to use wealth and influence in a Christ-like manner?

Prayers for our sisters in Christ Children who come from homes of wealth and influence.

April 28

Our Sister the Psychic

Now it happened, as we went to prayer, that a certain slave girl possessed with a spirit of divination met us; who brought her master much profit by fortune-telling. Acts 16:16

"Do not turn to mediums or seek out spiritists, for you will be defiled by them. I am the Lord your God." Leviticus 19:31

Yesterday, today and tomorrow The story of our sister in faith, the psychic, reaffirms my belief yet again about how "right on" the Bible is for today's lifestyles. Take psychics for example. The attempt to contact supernatural powers to seek answers about the future or people who have died is widely practiced today. Psychics, and the practice of "divination," were also very common in the ancient Middle East.

What's the harm? Scripture tell us that Paul and Silas rid her of the special powers that possessed her. Why indeed is God so adamantly against turning to mediums and spiritists?" The answer seems pretty straightforward: God doesn't want us turning to anyone but Him for counsel, which He freely provides.

For your reflection The temptation to see into the future, to experience things that are "beyond our power" is great. How will our daughters know the dangers of participating in anything to do with spiritists and mediums if we do not tell them? The experience of our sister in faith, the psychic, can help us teach and protect those we love.

A question for the ladies What can I teach my children about God that will protect them from occultic practices?

Prayers for our sisters in Christ Those who are enslaved by occultic practices.

April 29

Our Sister Mary Magdalene, Devoted to the End

"Now when He rose early on the first day of the week He appeared first to Mary Magdalene, out of whom He had cast seven demons." Mark 16:9

Committed Mary Magdalene had a very personal relationship with Jesus, for He had freed her from seven evil spirits that controlled her life. From that point on, Mary Magdalene not only became a follower of Jesus, but a leader among the women who ministered to them. She remained with Jesus at the cross when most of His followers ran in fear after His arrest. And she remained faithful to Jesus' promise of resurrection, lingering at the tomb long after everyone else had given up hope and returned to their homes. Her commitment and conviction paid off. Jesus appeared first to this faithful woman when He arose. HE then commanded her to go and tell His disciples.

For your reflection Our society tends to be a "throw away" society in which we are given permission to walk away from commitments when they become too difficult. We want relationships in families, marriages, jobs, and even our relationship with Christ to be easy. We can share Mary Magdalene's faith story and teach our daughters the true meaning of commitment and devotion. What a way to help them grow in their faith and in their preparation for other important commitments they will make throughout life.

A question for the ladies What young girl needs to hear Mary Magdalene's faith story to help her learn about honoring commitments in good times and bad?

Prayers for our sisters in Christ Young women in premarital counseling and the pastors providing the counsel.

April 30

II Kings 22:13-23:3

Our Sister Huldah, Turned a Nation Back to God

Then the king stood by a pillar and made a covenant before the Lord, to follow the Lord and to keep His commandments and His testimonies and His statutes, with all his heart and all his soul, to perform the words of this covenant that were written in this book. And all the people took a stand for the covenant. II Kings 23:3

Delivering a hard message Which one of us would want to be the bearer of any kind of bad news to a powerful person? Yet Huldah spoke without hesitation, increasing the credibility and importance of the message by her preface, "Thus says the Lord." She delivered God's message, and a king and his people turned back to God.

For your reflection Whether to our daughters or young women we are mentoring, it is normal to want to say the things they want to hear that keep them liking us. When they come to us with hard questions about love, fidelity, faith, worship, truth, forgiveness, idols, premarital sex, adultery, alcohol and drugs, will we give them easy answers or the hard ones found in the Bible? When they ask what standards they should use in choosing friends, boyfriends and husbands, what part will God's Word play in our response? We want our young girls to grow up in the faith, but are we willing to open our Bibles and show them God's way?

A question for the ladies What hard messages from the Bible does a young girl in my life need to hear? Why is it important for me to step up to the plate and deliver?

Prayers for our sisters in Christ Children trying to decide right from wrong.

My Journal
April: Sisters in the Faith

Insights: What key lessons did I learn from my biblical sisters in the faith?

Challenges: How will I share the lessons I have learned with the young girls in my family and in my church? When will I start?

What are the ten top blessings I received from God this month?

1.

2.

3.

4.

5.

6.

7.

8.

9.

10.

Answered Prayers

Introduction to May Devotions

Living with the End in Mind

"To everything there is a season, a time for every purpose under heaven." Ecclesiastes 3:1

I was having trouble coming up with a clear-cut theme for the month of May. Since we celebrate Memorial Day during this month, I wanted to include faith stories about honoring our dead. But I also wanted to write about life and death and the hope we as believers cling to through the resurrection of Jesus Christ. And I wanted to write about choices we make in life that influence how we are remembered when we die. Suddenly a Scripture came to mind, *Ecclesiastes 3:1*. I turned to my Bible and as I read the first verse, my eyes continued on through verse 9. Those verses represent a lot of living before we die. No wonder I was having so much trouble coming up with a theme and basic outline.

Perhaps my difficulty in developing this month's topic is indicative of the difficult issues life embraces, issues that take courage to face like love and hate, war and peace, death and dying, illness and suffering, grief and sorrow.

I pray that as you read the Scriptures and the faith stories, you will gain a greater understanding—His understanding—about the mysteries of life and death. Perhaps you will be moved to live each day with the end in mind. Today we can choose to live Christ-like lives. We cannot count on what we will do tomorrow, for tomorrow is not promised to any of us. So supported by God's Holy Word and our brothers and sisters in Christ, let us do our loving, giving, mourning, and forgiving TODAY!

Your sister in Christ,
Wanda Scott Bledsoe

May 1

Faithful until Death

"Be faithful until death, and I will give you the crown of life."
Revelation 2:10

A touch of class The call came from my mother. Aunt Codie, at the age of ninety-five, had just died. As a child I think I was in awe of Aunt Codie. She seemed to live such a glamorous life. As an adult reflecting on her life, I realized it couldn't have been glamorous at all. She lived on a fixed income in a small older home where my father seemed to always be repairing something or the other. The skin on her hands was irritated by the mildest of soaps even though she wore rubber gloves whenever she washed dishes or did her laundry. She made frequent trips to the grocery store, some three to four blocks away, buying only that which she could carry in her arms as she walked home. She had health problems. Yet I never heard her complain, and I never heard her faith in God waver.

Practical applications for believers If I defined faith by the way Aunt Codie lived, I would have to say it is an unwavering belief that God loves us and is with us no matter what life dishes out. It is too late for me to talk with Aunt Codie about her faith, but perhaps not too late for you to talk with a special person in your life about their faith. What blessings there might be in store for both of you!

Something to pray about Who do I know whose faith seems to be unwavering in the midst of adversity? How could his or her faith story help me strengthen my faith?

Prayers for our brothers and sisters in Christ The elderly who live alone.

May 2

Matthew 11:28-30

He Lived with the End in Mind

"Come to Me, all you who labor and are heavy laden, and I will give you rest." Matthew 11:28

Godliness John Wong's life was to me a classic example of Christ-like living. John was such a gentle man. If you had asked me what John did for a living, I would probably have replied, "He works for Christ."

Goodness His commitment to God had a profound influence on my life. I shall always remember my shock when I heard John was letting a Young Life leader use his new van to take Seattle youth to a camp in California. My mouth was still hanging open when I heard him say, "This van doesn't belong to me. The Lord is just letting me use it to do His work." From that point on, I viewed my "possessions" in a different light, trying to make sure I used them as part of the resources God gave my husband and me to do His work. Not my house, not my car, not my money…but God's.

Practical applications for believers It was my privilege to play for John's memorial service. The most moving part was what his four grown children had to say about their father, his impact on their lives and their commitment to Christ. What a loud legacy for his family from such a quiet, gentle man. Perhaps my point about John's quiet, unassuming spirit is to live with the end in mind. John certainly did.

Something to pray about If my legacy needed to be finished by next week, how much work would I still have to do?

Prayers for our brothers and sisters in Christ Those who volunteer their time and possessions to help improve the living conditions of others.

May 3

In the Depths of Despair

"Why are you cast down, O my soul and why are you disquieted within me? Hope in God, for I shall yet praise Him For the help of His countenance." Psalm 42:5

A dark place Try as I might, I couldn't get out of bed. What was wrong with me? It was as if I had been thrust from a life in living, vibrant color to one of dull grays. As a church organist, I played the notes but the joy was gone. The diagnosis: a temporary depression related to menopause.

Walk a mile in my shoes What an awful time, but I wouldn't trade it for anything. I thought back to the people I had known in my life who had committed suicide and mourned anew at the despair that made them feel they could no longer deal with life. All were people of faith. There was a teenager, a young mother, a brilliant scholar and an elderly woman. Their deaths seemed to be an impulsive decision on a cloudy day. And yet we know better. We hear about the ongoing isolation and emotional pain that makes suicide seem like the only option left.

Practical applications for believers What can we do to support our friends and loved ones who may find themselves in a state of despair? I have no magic answers, only the old ones: love them, pray for them, acknowledge the pain they feel, be nonjudgmental and compassionate, keep them close, and encourage and support them in their medical regime. Life is precious.

Something to pray about Who do I know who is depressed and needs me to be a friend?

Prayers for our brothers and sisters in Christ Those who entertain thoughts of suicide.

May 4

Isaiah 30:19-21

I Can Do It Myself!

"Your ears shall hear a word behind thee, saying, 'This is the way, walk in it,' whenever you turn to the right hand, or whenever you turn to the left." Isaiah 30:21

"Nein!" Our granddaughter, Danielle, was visiting us from Germany. She had just turned three and spoke no English. We were unable to understand a word Danielle said, except "Nein!" meaning "No!" When we heard the word *nein*, we understood that she didn't want our help; she wanted to do it herself.

But I can't do it myself! I shook my head as Danielle determinedly worked at the seat belt until she got it fastened, and remembered some of the challenges and adversities in my life in which I had struggled, steadfastly refusing anyone's help.

I always planned to help you After reading a Bible devotion one day, I had this startling revelation! Many of the things I was trying to do on my own, God never intended for me to do by myself. Just as I became frustrated with the extra time it took for Danielle to fasten her seat belt before I could start the car, God must be equally frustrated with me when I refuse to let Him guide and direct my actions.

Practical applications for believers How do we balance a healthy work ethic with God's expectation that we depend on Him for our every need? Perhaps my mother's advice, "Have you prayed about this?" is the answer. We can't do life all by ourselves. With a Heavenly Father who loves us, why should we even try?

Something to pray about Where could I use God's help in my life?

Prayers for our brothers and sisters in Christ Those who make children's car seats.

May 5

Eyes Wide Open

"I will never leave you nor forsake you." Hebrews 13:5

"Come to Me, all you who labor and are heavy laden, and I will give you rest." Matthew 11:28

Sleepless I lay in bed, wide awake as my mind raced over the events of the day. Moans and groans escaped my lips as I thought of things I should have done and things I did but could have done better. Then I moved on to all the things that needed to be done tomorrow.

Relax Easier said than done *until* I decided to turn my bedtime prayers into counting sessions. What if I just counted all the good things that happened to me that day? There were blessings big and little. I soon fell fast asleep

A great discovery Reviewing my day to make sure I don't miss any of the ways God has blessed me is great! Even greater is looking at the things that didn't go well or events that could only be called horrible and then taking a deeper look to see how God was with me. Who did He send to help, to give an encouraging word, to give me strength, or show me the way out or around the problem?

Practical applications for believers God *is* with us. As we look for opportunities to thank Him, we become more aware of His presence and intervention in our daily lives. And when we are weary from the burdens of life, He calls us to lay all of those burdens at His feet so we can sleep in heavenly peace.

Something to pray about How can thanking God for today's blessings help me sleep better tonight?

Prayers for our brothers and sisters in Christ Those who suffer from insomnia.

Construction Crew or Demolition Crew?

Do not let any unwholesome talk come out of your mouths, but only what is helpful for building others up according to their needs, that it may benefit those who listen. Ephesians 4:29

The walls came tumbling down The commercial shows the demolition crew pushing a button and the giant skyscraper implodes in a soundless cloud of smoke. In a matter of seconds, what has taken months, even years, to build is destroyed. It occurred to me that relationships are like that. It takes years of love, time and trust to build a relationship and just a few harsh words to tear it down.

Not one of my finest moments I had set high expectations for myself and for my husband regarding an event we had planned for our children. I looked at my husband, furious that he had not held up his end…according to my expectations. Destructive words came tumbling from my lips, and the damage was immediately evident in the hurt I saw in his eyes. A childhood image flashed before my eyes of me throwing rocks into a lake. I couldn't gather in the ripples made by the rock hitting the water any more than I could gather in the words I had hurled at my husband.

Practical applications for believers God calls us to build each other up with encouraging words. And He calls us to seek the forgiveness of others when we fail. In His mercy and compassion He has wiped the slate clean so that we can begin each day anew as encouragers.

Something to pray about Would others say my words build them up or tear them down?

Prayers for our brothers and sisters in Christ Those who are grieving for demolished relationships.

May 7

What a Great Losing Streak!

"He who finds his life will lose it, and he who loses his life for My sake will find it." Matthew 10:39

Losing to win Think about it, you dominoes players. In order to win, you must give up your "bones." The first person to get rid of all his or her dominoes wins the game. In other words, you must give up to win, and in losing, you gain. Of course that depends on what you want to win. If it is life in our society, then this "loser" strategy won't work. Our society encourages us to get all we can, not give up all we can. However, if it is a life in Christ that you would like to win, then the domino strategy is the one for you.

A losing streak What must we lose to be Christ-like? Anything and everything that would keep us from being called "Blessed." Jesus calls us to a different way of life in Matthew 5:1-12, which He begins by saying, "Blessed are the poor in spirit, for theirs is the kingdom of heaven."

Practical applications for believers What part of yourself do you have to lose so that you might gain? When you give something away, who receives more, you or the person who is receiving your gift? It's crazy! The more we give, the more He gives to us. Try it. See if you can put together a great losing streak. What a way to live!

Something to pray about What part of me shall I lose today so that I can become more Christ-like?

Prayers for our brothers and sisters in Christ Those who have financial wealth but feel there is something missing.

Pleasure or Joy?

"These things I have spoken to you, that My joy may remain in you, and that your joy may be full." John 15:11

Not the same When I looked up the word *pleasure* in my Thesaurus, it lists *joy* as a word I can use for a substitute. However, the Bible doesn't agree. *Hebrews 11:25* refers to the "passing pleasures" of the world. While in *John 15:11*, we read of Jesus' offer of a joy that remains. Pleasures that pass…joy that remains.

The more you give In one of my many careers, I was a visiting nurse in a very poor section of the city. The idea was that I was well paid to provide nursing care in some very impoverished homes. Many times what I gave in nursing care could not begin to compare with the joy I received from my patients. They also taught me lessons about love, sacrifice, giving, family, happiness and forgiveness. They taught me the joy of the heart regardless of the circumstances of life.

Practical applications for believers Sometimes I lose my way, but when I remember to focus on giving of myself to others rather than obtaining things for myself, I am blessed with a joy that lasts. Which will you chose, the world's addictive and elusive pleasures, or lasting joy? Try the joy promised by Jesus for yourself. See if it makes a difference in your life and the life of your loved ones.

Something to pray about What can I do to bring lasting joy to myself and to others?

Prayers for our brothers and sisters in Christ Those who are overextended financially with credit card purchases.

May 9

What Time Is It?

And He rose from prayer, went to the disciples and found them slumbering from grief. Luke 22:45

A death of a child My husband just knew I was carrying the first member of the Bledsoe football dynasty. Twenty-four hours later, I delivered twin boys, 2 lbs 13oz and 2lbs 14oz. One twin survived and one twin didn't.

A hard decision We had some insurance but not the kind we needed to pay for the surviving twin's hospital stay. So when the hospital gave us the choice of taking care of the body of our twin son without charge or releasing his body to a mortuary, we chose the hospital.

I can't talk about it All my prayers and energies were focused on helping our remaining son survive...and surviving myself. I wouldn't talk about the twin's death, and I wouldn't let anyone else talk to me about it either.

Years of grief Nineteen years later I cautiously broached the idea of a memorial service with my family. The resulting memorial service was a glorious one. Afterwards the family gathered at our home for a meal and finally a chance to grieve, and to celebrate the short life of Michael Spencer Bledsoe who remains in our hearts forever.

Practical applications for believers Ecclesiastes 3:4 reminds us that there is "a time to mourn." If you are mourning, perhaps you will want to check the time. If you want to move on, then turn to Jesus and the compassion of family, church, and friends for support. It might help you avoid years of grief.

Something to pray about Who will I let help me work through my grief?

Prayers for our brothers and sisters in Christ Those who have lost children in their infancy.

May 10

The Sound of Silence

*For God so loved the world that He gave His only begotten Son,
that whoever believes in Him should not perish but have everlasting life.* John 3:16

Cutting peonies My mother cutting and arranging flowers for our
trip to the cemetery is part of Memorial Day memories from my
childhood. Later there would be fried chicken, potato salad and
baked beans to be eaten at a picnic with our family and Aunt
Mayme and Uncle Art and Aunt Fay and Uncle Wilson. But for now,
it was time to decorate the graves.

Silence As an adult, my mother began taking me to the cemetery
where my father was buried. Since these annual visits to my birth-
place didn't coincide with Memorial Day, Mother and I were the
only ones present. It was so quiet. Those who resided there could
tell me nothing of their lives. I looked at the graves and tried to
remember what those who rested there had meant to me and to
others. Some names flooded me with warm memories, others not
so many.

Practical applications for believers What a sobering reminder. There
is not enough room on a headstone to give any information about
how we lived. That information resides with the living whose lives
we have touched. I thought about what I would like family and
friends to remember about me long after I was dead. I wondered
what would Jesus have to say about how I had lived? It became blatantly obvious that I had some unfinished work to do.

Something to pray about If I died today, how long would I be
remembered, by whom, and for what?

Prayers for our brothers and sisters in Christ Those who work to
keep our cemeteries beautiful.

May 11

Ephesians 3:19-22

Who Am I?

"Now, therefore, you are no longer strangers and foreigners but fellow citizens with the saints and members of the household of God." Ephesians 3:19

You don't belong I remember as a child telling my precious little sister that she didn't really belong to our family. I told my sister that we had found her by the roadside and brought her home with us. She was devastated and went crying to our mother. Had she been left by the roadside as I said? Did mother really love her as much as she loved me? My poor sister was inconsolable.

You look like me! Mother called me from wherever I was hiding in anticipation of the punishment I was sure would follow. Mother then proceeded to point out the features my sister had in common with her. My sister slowly turned toward me with new questions in her eyes. My eyes and hair were a different color. Before my little sister could ask if I was the one who didn't belong, my mother pointed out that I had features in common with our father.

Practical applications for believers Those childhood memories made me think about my identity in Christ. I appreciated anew that I was a full-fledged child of God in His family. How could people really tell I was a legitimate member of the family of God? I could tell them I belonged or… I could act like I belonged. Who am I? I am a member of the family of God. Can you see the resemblance?

Something to pray about How will others recognize that I belong to the family of God?

Prayers for our brothers and sisters in Christ Those who feel estranged from their families.

May 12

I Corinthians 6:12-20

Forgiveness vs. Consequences

All things are lawful for me, but all things are not helpful. All things are lawful for me, but I will not be brought under the power of any. For you were bought at a price; therefore glorify God in your body and in your spirit, which are God's. I Corinthians 6:12,20

Take food, for example A friend and I had been talking about forgiveness. As mothers, we were also mindful of our children and the need to teach them about taking responsibility for their actions. "Take food for example," I said, "my weight counselors advise me to move on if I have a 'bad food' day. I am to cut my losses and start the next day fresh. So in effect I am to forgive myself when I give in to poor eating habits. But," I added, "I still am forced to accept the consequences of my actions when I step on the scale and see the resulting damage."

Practical applications for believers These Scriptures remind me that God's forgiveness, while unconditional, is separate from my need to accept responsibility for my actions *and* the resulting consequences. Is it possible that the some of the difficulties children of today are having are a result of us not teaching these lessons by example? A possible solution? Be responsible and take responsibility for our actions, realizing there are consequences even though there is forgiveness. These are some of life's lessons that may help us and those we love live with the end in mind.

Something to pray about What are some ways I show that I value my life and the lives of others?

Prayers for our brothers and sisters in Christ Those whose behavior has caused physical injury or death to others.

May 13

Isaiah 43:16-19

A Way through the Storm

"When you pass through the waters, I will be with you; and through the rivers, they shall not overflow you. When you walk through the fire, you shall not be burned; nor shall the flame scorch you." Isaiah 43:2

A storm is coming We were gathered at church for a youth convention. I was in the fourth grade and very excited about being there. Soon that excitement was replaced by the fear that comes from the anticipation of a tornado. The adults were giving us instructions about what to do in case the tornado really did appear, when suddenly I saw my father coming toward me.

Let's go home My father had come to take me home. I was afraid to leave the shelter of the church, knowing how deadly tornados could be. My father was very firm as he reassured me, "Don't worry. We will be alright." I trustingly took my father's hand and we headed for home.

Practical applications for believers Whoever we are, we will encounter storms. It is at that time that God commands from us total trust and obedience. Too often, I wanted to be in control. After God had rescued me yet again from myself, I declared, "Lord, I have got to do a better job of trusting you from the beginning. After all that is what faith is all about, me trusting You *before* seeing the rescue plan." It has certainly made it easier to get through the storms of my life.

Something to pray about How might I weather the storms of life better by choosing God's rescue plan over my own?

Prayers for our brothers and sisters in Christ Those who work in natural disaster rescue units.

May 14

Memory Verses

"The Lord is my light and my salvation; whom shall I fear?
The Lord is the strength of my life; of whom shall I be afraid?"
Psalm 27:1

Sunday School Mrs. Kendricks was one of my Sunday School teachers. She was always having us memorize the books of the Bible and Bible verses for prizes. I loved the challenge.

Hymn substitution As the years passed, my focus shifted from Bible verses and centered on music. I took pride in relating how I could sing a hymn for any situation in life that challenged me. Who needed Bible verses when you had these great hymns to play and sing?

Memory verses The television documentary featured some prisoners of war who had survived torture at the hands of their captors. When asked how they managed to live through such inhumane treatment, their response was, "The Bible." "They let you keep a Bible in your cells?" the commentator asked. "No, we wrote favorite Sriptures of the Bible from memory on bits of toilet paper and shared them with the other prisoners through a code we devised."

Practical applications for believers I shuddered to think what little contribution I would have made. The years have passed and my Bible has become an essential tool in helping me meet the challenges of life. The binding is falling apart, highlighted areas draw me to favorite Scriptures, and the notes scribbled next to them chronicle the joys and sorrows of my life. I think I could make a better contribution now.

Something to pray about If I could never open a Bible again, what verses would I want to have memorized?

Prayers for our brothers and sisters in Christ Those who have been and those who may still be prisoners of war.

May 15

A Burden Bearer

"Bear one another's burdens, and so fulfill the law of Christ."
Galatians 6:2

Her grief was overwhelming Carol was my friend and she had just lost her husband. Her grief seemed to engulf her. I had never witnessed such debilitating grief. I didn't know what to do. I felt helpless, useless, and even afraid. How could I help her cope?

Just be there The donkey that Jesus rode into Jerusalem amidst the flurry of palm branches was just there. He couldn't help Jesus with his knowledge that in just a few days, Jesus would not be in a parade, but on a cross. The donkey couldn't even commiserate with Jesus about the fickleness of the crowd. The donkey could just be there, bearing Jesus upon his back as Jesus entered Jerusalem.

Practical applications for believers Now I knew what to do. Scripture calls us to bear one another's burdens. The donkey that carried Jesus reminded me that it was enough for me to just be there for my friend. It wasn't a comfortable place to be, it was in actuality painful and emotionally draining. Yet, Scripture called me to be there, to help Carol bear this horrible burden. I lost some of my fear as I realized that God does not intend for us to bear life's heavy burdens by ourselves. He has promised to be our burden bearer and calls on us to do our part to be a burden bearer for others.

Something to pray about Who needs me to help bear their burden?

Prayers for our brothers and sisters in Christ Those who help others through their grief.

May 16

Romans 10:6-14

His Plan of Forgiveness

"This is the covenant that I will make with them after those days", says the Lord. "I will put My laws into their hearts, and in their minds I will write them." Then He adds, "Their sins and their lawless deeds I will remember no more." Hebrews 10:16-17

Setting the example It was one of those family things. I just couldn't get beyond the hurt. I prayed and I struggled. Then a quiet voice said, "If your mother can forgive, so can you." My mother indeed had set an example for me. I thought of all the ways in which I needed God's forgiveness and yet my heart was not softened.

His grace and mercy "Lord, you know my heart. You know I want to forgive. Lord, you know this anger is destroying me. Help me!" God in His everlasting mercy heard my cry and placed a child in my path that caused my heart to melt in ways that I would not have believed possible.

Free at last It felt like a weight had been lifted from my shoulders. I was free of the burden of anger. I wanted to dance and sing and shout for joy! I was free again to love and be loved.

Practical applications for believers God loves us and knows how destructive anger and hate can be. Perhaps that is why He talks so much about forgiveness in His Word. God offers us His plan of forgiveness and joy. We know it as God's Plan of Salvation.

Something to pray about How can God's grace, mercy and compassion help me forgive someone I haven't been able to forgive on my own?

Prayers for our brothers and sisters in Christ Families who are estranged.

May 17

Loved Sight Unseen

"For by grace you have been saved through faith, and that not of yourselves; it is the gift of God, not of works, lest anyone should boast." Ephesians 2:8-9

So wanted This grandchild was so wanted. His birth had been prayed for by our family and his family of God: the Lutherans, the Presbyterians, the Baptists, the Catholics and the Four Square Church. We could hardly wait for his arrival.

He's here I shall never forget the phone call from our daughter announcing Conner's birth. I couldn't wait to see him and to hold him in my arms. But for now, I just loved him sight unseen. Conner was here, healthy, and now an official part of our immediate family and our huge family of God. Of course when I first saw him, I fell in love with him all over again.

Sight unseen Still reveling in the wonder of the birth of our grandson, I thought, "Who have I accepted and loved sight unseen?" No one except my children and grandchildren. Love is pretty amazing.

Practical applications for believers God's grace is pretty amazing. HE loves us unconditionally and accepts us just as we are. I thought of the people in my life and the conditions I sometimes placed on them. Perhaps it is time for me to try loving them unconditionally as I love my grandson Conner, and as God loves me.

Something to pray about Who needs my unconditional love? From whom do I need unconditional love?

Prayers for our brothers and sisters in Christ Those who feel they must act in a certain way before their families will love them.

May 18

Love, War's Recurring Lesson

"Teacher, which is the great commandment in the law?" Jesus said to him, " 'You shall love the Lord your God with all your heart, with all your soul, and with all your mind.' This is the first and great commandment. And the second is like it: 'You shall love your neighbor as yourself.' On these two commandments hang all the Law and the Prophets." Matthew 22:36-40

The answer is love War is accompanied by human tragedies that we cannot begin to imagine. One person's life given so I might live is one life too many. Each war is supposed to be the last, yet it never is. If war doesn't fix our problems, maybe it is time to focus on another solution. God calls us to love one another and to promote peace. If all the children of God—that would be you and me—did what we could—that would be *pray in faith*—and then put that *faith in action*—that would be living our everyday lives in peaceful ways—*then* maybe in *love and peace*, we can *save a life*.

Practical applications for believers God's love is the answer. It is the starting point in building relationships, for forgiveness, reconciliation and healing. It is God's recurring message for all time. Love God with all our hearts, minds and souls and each other as we love ourselves *Matthew 22:40*. If we can get just these two commandments right, we can honor our dead heroes through love, peace and life.

Something to pray about What can I do to promote peace in my everyday life?

Prayers for our brothers and sisters in Christ Those who are currently serving in our armed forces, especially those in war-torn countries.

I Know Your Mother's Voice

And when he brings out his own sheep, he goes before them; and the sheep follow him, for they know his voice. John 10:4

Not on my block I became aware of two little boys about eight years old running alongside of a car taunting the occupants. The car stopped. A teenager got out and began chasing the young boys. One of the young boys stumbled and the teenager quickly caught up with him and began kicking him. I shouted, "Stop!" No response, so I took a deep breath and, using the highest notes in my soprano range and with all the power I could muster, I began calling, "Police!"

That's your mother's voice My daughter, Shelly, and a friend were inside visiting. "I hear your mother's voice. Something is wrong." As Shelly and her friend quickly came to see what was wrong, so did our neighbors. When the teenager saw all of the people, he got back in the car, and he and his friend drove away. Then the little boy got up and ran away. I rejoiced in the knowledge that my neighbors were the kind that would respond so quickly to see if help was needed.

Practical applications for believers When we are far from home we may be particularly vulnerable to those who would imitate God's voice and lure us into actions and behaviors that hurt us as well as others. The only way we can avoid these kinds of traps is by developing a relationship with God so that we know His voice.

Something to pray about Do I know God well enough to recognize His voice?

Prayers for our brothers and sisters in Christ Those who work in Veterans Administration Hospitals.

May 20

A Dumb Sheep

The Lord is my shepherd, I shall not want. Psalm 23:1

I am just like those dumb sheep It wasn't until I was an adult with children of my own that I really began to understand and appreciate the much-used Twenty-Third Psalm. I could relate to sheep that are often characterized as being extremely dumb and very much in need of someone to provide for all their needs. Yes, I had an education, but I still needed someone to guide me when I thought the "grass was greener on the other side of the fence." I certainly could relate to sheep's fear of turbulent waters because with my poor swimming skills, I had a healthy respect—if not fear—of water deeper than I was tall. And talk about needing someone to restore me and save me from the destructive paths I sometimes followed! Yes, I could certainly relate to dumb sheep. In fact, on any given day some of my actions would certainly qualify me as a "dumb sheep" very much in need of our Shepherd.

Practical applications for believers The Lord is our Shepherd, we shall not want. It is He who guides us, protects us and provides for us. If we but let Him, He leads us away from danger and worry to peace and safety. Now I know what the Psalmist meant when he wrote, "The Lord is my shepherd, I shall not want." It is more than just a verse to recite, it is the Lord's personal assurance to all of us.

Something to pray about How does God speak to me personally through the Twenty-Third Psalm?

Prayers for our brothers and sisters in Christ Those who are serving in peacekeeping missions far from home.

May 21

Stubborn or Sturdy?

Blessed is the man who trusts in the Lord, and whose hope is the Lord. Jeremiah 17:7

Morning glory As I gazed at some flowers growing in the backyard, I remarked to my neighbor about their beauty. "That's morning glory," she replied, "and its endless vines guarantee that you can never be totally free of it." I pulled the vines up easily, yet a few weeks later there were those stubborn vines again.

Tenacious vs. sturdy My faults seemed to be like that morning glory—stubborn. My desire was to be like the sturdy oak with deep roots that made it difficult to pull out of the ground even in the fiercest storm. I wanted to be viewed as a strong tree on which others could lean, not a pesky vine that no one could get rid of.

Practical applications for believers As we lean on God, He rids us of the pesky things in our lives and guides us as we grow spiritually so that our faith becomes sturdy, like the mighty oak tree, with deep roots to sustain us through the storms of life. As I have told my married daughter, with a child of her own, "Grow spiritually like the mighty oak so that when—not if—the storms of life come, you will be able to stand strong for yourself and for family and friends who might also need your spiritual strength.

Something to pray about Who needs me to be spiritually strong like a mighty oak? What pesky vines do I need to ask God to eradicate?

Prayers for our brothers and sisters in Christ Veterans who are dealing with war-related emotional and physical wounds.

May 22

Thank You, Alexander Graham Bell

"My little children, let us not love in word or in tongue, but in deed and in truth." I John 3:18

Running out of time It is a well-established family tradition. We send cards for special occasions. On one occasion, I just plain ran out of time. Why not try a telephone call, I thought. I did the math and figured that for the price of a card, three to five dollars, and a stamp, I could talk long distance to family and friends for several minutes. What a hit! They loved hearing my voice, especially those who were older; some without children, and some living alone.

He did his part In a month where we pay tribute to our loved ones who have died, I want to say a special thanks to Alexander Graham Bell, who received a patent from the U.S. Patent Office on March 7, 1876 for his invention of the telephone. Thank you, Alexander Graham Bell for getting us started with technology that allows us to communicate in ways that have forever changed the world in which we live.

Practical applications for believers Make a call, honor the living. Not a big thing perhaps, but when you listen to the sound of surprise, elation and appreciation on the other end, it is not such a little thing after all. This month as we pay tribute to those who have died, let us take advantage of Alexander Graham Bell's invention of the telephone and also pay tribute to friends and family who are still living.

Something to pray about Who would consider a telephone call from me a gift of love?

Prayers for our brothers and sisters in Christ Those who are alone and grieving for loved ones who have died.

May 23

Beyond My Control

Weeping may endure for a night, but joy comes in the morning.
Psalm 30:5

God knows just how much we can bear The recruiter looked like he wanted to say, "I know you must be in shock." How could this be happening? This wasn't in *my* plans for our son, and yet I had no control over the events as they rapidly unfolded.

The worst is yet to come The recruiter called to tell us where we should take our son to be inducted before he boarded a plane for basic training somewhere clear across the United States. I panicked when I realized that our son would not be going with a group of other new recruits, but traveling alone.

Weeping may endure for a night, but joy comes in the morning Anxiety about the safety of our son plagued me all day, but it was nothing compared to the nightmare I experienced when I went to sleep. I woke up gasping. I staggered to the chair in the living room and opened my Bible to **Psalm 30**. As I read the passages, I was reassured of God's love for me and for our son.

Practical applications for believers There continue to be numerous times when separated from my two adult children, I am forced to "let go and let God" care for and protect them. When I can't see the end, I reassure myself that God can. HE is and will always be the creator and guardian of all things—including an overly protective mother and her son.

Something to pray about How can I release my children to God's loving care and protection?

Prayers for our brothers and sisters in Christ Those with children serving in the armed forces abroad.

May 24

Isaiah 32:16-20

Teaching Our Children about Peace

Blessed are the peacemakers, for they shall be called sons of God.
Matthew 5:9

Which words look familiar? While Columbine is just the first of many schools where children shot and killed other children, we are still shocked. We haven't assimilated this behavior as "normal"...yet. What is your definition of violence? How do you think our children get from the wonderful little babies God gave us to children who are angry enough to take a life? They certainly weren't born violent. What behaviors do we as adults model when we solve problems—violent or peaceful?

The sanctity of life Some psychologists feel gang members take the lives of others because they no longer value their own lives. Would you agree or disagree with this theory? If God asked you to teach a gang member to value his or her life, how would you go about it? How do we go about teaching our own children about the sanctity of life?

Practical applications for believers God values all of us. Not just some of us, but all of us. In this month where we honor those who died fighting to protect our freedom, let us also honor them by living peacefully so no further human sacrifices are needed...anywhere. In the words of that well-known song, "Let there be peace on earth and let it begin with me"...and with you.

Something to pray about What can I do to end violence in my home, at school, at work, and at play?

Prayers for our brothers and sisters in Christ Those who are victims of gang-related violence. Those who have given their lives in peacekeeping missions.

May 25

The Price of Happiness

"I did not withhold my heart from any pleasure....All was vanity and grasping for the wind; nothing was gained under the sun."
Ecclesiastes 2:10-11

Happiness, free to all During a retreat for women, my mother at eighty-plus years of age, told her faith story. It was a story of joys and sorrows, laughter and tears, pleasures and pain. "Why aren't you angry or bitter over some of the disappointments and pain you have experienced in your life?" Mother looked at them with wonder as she replied, "It is God's love that sustains me and renews me so that regardless of the circumstances I can always have a song in my heart and a smile on my face."

Sounds like... The apostle Paul expressed similar beliefs when he said, "Not that I speak in regard to need, for I have learned in whatever state I am, to be content." *Philippians 4:12* Mother took the apostle Paul's declaration one step further. My mother was never just content, she was *happy*!

Practical applications for believers My mother's wisdom taught me (1) to learn to appreciate and be happy with the beauty of God's creations. (2) to get the most out of the "things" I do have, I need to share them with others. And (3) the best remedy for feeling down or sorry for myself, is to get out and help someone else.

Something to pray about How can the teachings of King Solomon and the apostle Paul help me find true and lasting happiness? How can I share it with others?

Prayers for our brothers and sisters in Christ Those who have an abundance of *things*, but are not happy. Veterans that are wheelchair bound.

May 26

Recycle Time?

Therefore God also has highly exalted Him and given Him the name which is above every name. Philippians 2:9

Killing time We can waste a lot of time using the excuse, "It's just a few minutes before I have to be there or start this, so I'll just kill some time." Instead of "killing time," who could I be encouraging? Who could I be praying for? Who could I be calling to say, "Hello"? What could I be doing that would touch the lives of others with a few minutes here and there? It is said that the mind is a precious thing to waste. The same can be said about time.

Practical applications for believers Jesus' ministry spanned just three short years and yet His teachings, His death and His resurrection touch all who came before us and all those who will come after us. As we strive to live our lives in a Christ-like manner, perhaps our focus should be on how we live and who we touch rather than how long we live. A few minutes here and there used to help others can make a difference in their lives and in ours. Can it really be that simple? Instead of killing time, could I *recycle* that time so that others could say, "She was a life saver for me today. It was just a three-minute phone call but it came at just the *right* time."

Something to pray about How can I recycle the time I had planned to kill to do something good for someone else?

Prayers for our brothers and sisters in Christ Those who use a few minutes here and there to help family, friends and others in their community.

May 27

Matthew 25:31-40

Something for Tennis Fans

Give, and it will be given to you: good measure, pressed down,
shaken together, and running over will be put into your bosom.
For with the same measure that you use, it will be measured back
to you. Luke 6:38

In order to win My husband loves to "share" with me the finer points
of the game of tennis. One basic concept made a lasting impression:
no matter how good you are at returning the ball, you can't win
without *serving well.*

Serve well That concept also applies to life. My mother loves the
story about a woman who lost her husband. Every month she
placed flowers on her husband's grave. Each time she arrived, she
saw that the flowers she had placed there the previous month were
gone. Seeing a caretaker nearby, she asked him if he knew about the
missing flowers. "Oh, lady, when you leave, I pick up those pretty
flowers and take them to the sick and shut-in, folks who can appreciate them." The next month, she arrived with two bouquets. She
placed one bouquet on her husband's grave, and gave one to the
caregiver who was working nearby. "Here, these are for your sick
and shut-ins. I am filling my days with volunteer work, and I have
never felt better!"

Practical applications for believers Life is like a game of tennis. You
can't win without serving well. Christ calls us to serve others: the
poor, the sick, the homeless, the disenfranchised, the dying and the
lonely. As we remember and honor our dead, let us also remember
and *serve well* the living.

Something to pray about What would Christ say about the quality
of my "service"?

Prayers for our brothers and sisters in Christ Grief support counselors.

May 28

Who Is a Hero?

*The commander took the young man by the hand, drew him
aside and asked, "What is it you have to tell me?"* Acts 23:19

Thank you! How do you possibly say thank you to someone who has
saved your life? Thank you is a start, but is it enough? This
Memorial Day could be a time to teach our children about the wars
we have fought, the sacrifices of the men and women who gave their
lives in them, and hopefully the lessons we have learned from those
wars. It could be a time to visit Veterans of Foreign Wars halls to
learn more about their work and to identify service projects we
could do with our families. Memorial Day is one day set aside to
honor our heroes. But it doesn't have to be the only day. Every day
can be a memorial day when we chose to promote peace by living
peaceably.

Practical applications for believers Life is precious. Life is sacred. We
can make a commitment to live and teach peace. While Jesus could
make a one-time sacrifice for all people, new human sacrifices are
called for each time our nation is unable to resolve a freedom-
threatening situation. Let us honor our brothers and sisters who
have given their lives in war. Let us live in Christ-like ways so that
no further sacrifices of lives are needed on foreign soil *or* on the
streets we call home.

Something to pray about How can I treat others who are different
from me so that those who lost their lives in the terrorists' acts of
September 11 are honored?

Prayers for our brothers and sisters in Christ For the victims of 9-
11 and their loved ones.

May 29

Romans 10:6-13

His Indiscriminate Love

There is no difference between Jew and Greek, for there is the same Lord over all, who is rich to all those calling upon him. For everyone who calls on the name of the Lord will be saved.
Romans 10:12-13

Indiscriminate love All wars are horrible because they start in the absence of love, take lives in the absence of love, and end in the absence of love. The Civil War was no exception. The story of the first Memorial Day is a story of indiscriminate love. On April 26, 1866, four Southern women from Columbus, Mississippi went to decorate the graves of the Confederate soldiers. Four years earlier, the Civil War battle of Shiloh had been fought here. It was now a cemetery, the Friendship Cemetery, where approximately 1,500 Confederate and 100 Union soldiers were buried. In their indiscriminate love, the women placed flowers over the graves of soldiers of *both* sides. The Grand Army of the Republic (GAR) a veterans' organization, heard of their acts of kindness and embraced the concept of honoring *all* the soldiers. They responded by organizing a Decoration Day service in Arlington National Cemetery on May 30, 1868 and the first Memorial Day, started by indiscriminate love, was born.

Practical applications for believers God's love is indiscriminate. If we are to be like Him we must strive to love indiscriminately. It is not easy, but with God, all things are possible *Matthew 19:26*. And He provides us with the strength to do all things *Philippians 4:13*.

Something to pray about How can God's love for me help me forgive and show love to those I would call my enemies?

Prayers for our brothers and sisters in Christ Those we would call our enemies.

May 30

Bitter or Better?

He who dwells in the secret place of the Most High shall abide under the shadow of the Almighty. Psalm 91:1

Protected My husband returned home in the middle of the day with the earth-shattering news that he had been *chosen* to be released from the company as part of its reorganization and downsizing plan. My first thought was, "Should I be bitter?" My husband had also been *chosen* to be transferred from the company's operation in Washington to the one here in California the previous year. We had *chosen* to leave our daughter, other family members and friends to move to a place we wouldn't have dreamed of living. We had also *chosen* a beautiful house with a big mortgage. But I decided to step out in faith, trusting that His provision would be *better*. And indeed it was! Within the year my husband was rehired in a new, wonderful position by his former employer. I was so glad I had decided not to be *bitter* because God had certainly made our situation *better*.

Practical applications for believers It is hard to trust that something *better* will come out of life's adversities because our perspective is so small. However, when we remember how much greater is God's perspective, how much more complex are His ways and, most of all, how much deeper is His love for us than even our love for ourselves, we can choose to step out in faith to reject *bitter* in exchange for the hope of something *better*.

Something to pray about How is my bitterness keeping me from receiving something better?

Prayers for our brothers and sisters in Christ Those who have been laid off and are having difficulty finding new jobs.

May 31

Proverbs 3:21-26

My Hero

When you lie down, you will not be afraid; Yes, you will lie down and your sleep will be sweet. Proverbs 3:24

I'm just afraid Our eight-year-old grandson, Jay, was spending some time with us and what a blessing he had been. I sat on his bed waiting for him to go to sleep. We were talking about the fears he experienced only at night. He couldn't name anything specific, he was just afraid. Suddenly he asked if the garage door was closed. It was now dark and his Opa (*grandfather* in German) was at a meeting. "Well, Jay," I said, "if the garage door *is* open, that could be a legitimate reason to be afraid. I'll go check." I got up to go downstairs and as I expected, Jay got up to go with me. He wouldn't want to be left alone, I thought.

Stepping out in faith What happened next truly surprised me. Jay skipped in front of me and said, "Oma, I had better go first. Just in case." My hero! Who would have imagined that this eight-year-old child, afraid to go to sleep even with the light on, would step in front of his grandmother to protect her from possible danger? What motivated this little boy to exhibit what I felt was extreme bravery? My guess is love.

Practical applications for believers God loves us and goes before us to guide and protect us. HE knows our fears and lights the way in the dark places in our lives.

Something to pray about Where do I need to step out in faith, believing that God is there to lead, guide and protect me?

Prayers for our brothers and sisters in Christ Those who live in fear.

My Journal
May: Living with the End in Mind

Insights: What do I want to remember about life and death as a believer?

Challenges: What do I need to do to incorporate the lessons I have learned into my everyday life? When will I start?

What are the ten top blessings I received from God this month?

1.

2.

3.

4.

5.

6.

7.

8.

9.

10.

Answered Prayers

Introduction to June Devotions

All the Right Tools for Loving Relationships

All Scripture is given by inspiration of God, and is profitable for doctrine, for reproof, for correction, for instruction in righteousness, that the man of God may be complete, thoroughly equipped for every good work. II Timothy 3:16,17

Because my sister and I live so far away, we try to do all the maintenance work we can when we come home to visit our mother. As we made a list of what we thought we could accomplish in the time we had left and shared it with our mother, she told us about the tools our father, now deceased, would have used to do each project *and* where we could find them. Our father was a skilled carpenter and took pride in having the right tools for the job.

One of my projects during my visit with Mother was to "thatch" the lawn. The handle of the thatcher I found in my father's toolshed was broken. I went to several stores in search of a lawn thatcher only to be told that they no longer carried such a tool.

Fortunately, we can be confident that all the tools we need for loving relationships can be found in the Bible, free to all and always in stock. And the best part is that in Jesus Christ, we have the perfect role model.

I pray that you will find the tools in this month's Scriptures and stories of faith helpful in building, nurturing and sustaining loving relationships with family, friends and God.

> *"And now these three remain: faith, hope and love. But the greatest of these is love."* I Corinthians 13:13

Your sister in Christ,
Wanda Scott Bledsoe

June 1

The Look of Love

Beloved, let us love one another, for love is of God; and everyone who loves is born of God and knows God. I John 4:7

So much love They had been married 50 years and now Alzheimer's disease was drastically changing their relationship. Over the next few years she began to do more and more for him: bathing and dressing him, cutting up his food and feeding him, and finally dealing with his incontinence. She took him everywhere—to church, shopping, and even on an airplane to spend holidays with their children and grandchildren. The tender look on her face as she cared for him was truly a look of love.

More than a good feeling I had come home to visit *and* to help. As I dried my father off after his bath I thought, "This can't be very romantic for mother." I remembered mother telling my daughter that she and my father had been so in love that they had gotten married after knowing each other for only three weeks! And now after fifty-plus years of marriage and a husband suffering from Alzheimer's disease, there was still the look of love.

Something to ponder Christ demonstrates a selfless love, concerned for the welfare of others. *Love from the heart,* unselfish and loyal, a perfect tool for a marriage that lasts through the physical attraction of newlyweds so that the look of love can still be seen shining brightly even in the midst of physical adversities.

Something else to consider What acts of love can I do to show love for my spouse?

Prayers for our brothers and sisters in Christ Those who are caregivers for spouses with Alzheimer's disease.

A Lifesaving Rope

A threefold cord is not quickly broken. Ecclesiastes 4:12

So many memories It was our daughter's wedding day. As I sat listening to Roger, our pastor and long-time friend, conduct the marriage ceremony, my mind drifted to a particularly difficult time in our marriage when our relationship had become so strained we sought marital counseling.

In His Hands I was concerned for my husband, and even in the midst of my own pain, I wanted to comfort him. Where would he turn for support? With a heavy heart, I turned to the Lord in prayer. "Help us!" I pleaded. As always, He heard my cry. How I rejoiced as my husband faithfully went to the men's prayer group every Saturday morning.

His lifeline My eyes swept over the scene at the altar and then upward to the wedding banner made by one of our church members and dear friend, Yvonne Johnson. The banner had three white and gold cords intertwined. Its message read, "A threefold cord is not quickly broken." When my husband and I stopped holding each other's hands, we still held on to the hand of Jesus Christ, He held on to us and the threefold cord held.

Something to ponder Jesus is not only an essential tool for loving relationships, His presence is an absolute necessity. When Christ is at the center of any relationship, that relationship is not easily torn apart. *Jesus Christ,* the most important tool for a loving relationship.

Something else to consider Where is Christ in the relationships that are important to me?

Prayers for our brothers and sisters in Christ Those whose marriages are troubled.

Limited Choices

Honor your father and your mother, that your days may be long upon the land which the Lord your God is giving you." Exodus 20:12

His choice Roger was a faithful member of our choir. What a wonderful voice he had. His love for God quietly emanated through his whole being as he sang. Yet, for the last few weeks he had been absent from choir rehearsal. I decided to call him and find out what was going on.

A spiritual discipline "My father is now in an extended care facility," he said. "Spending time with Dad is my priority now. Something had to give and unfortunately it was singing in the choir. You know how I love to sing. I miss it very much."

Love! Time! Work! Determination! I thought of other people I knew who were caring for aging parents. In each case, love, precious time, lots of work and unfailing determination characterized the commitment they had made. I never heard my friend profess his love for his father, not even at his father's memorial service. However no one could mistake Roger's profound love for his father in the commitment he chose to make *and* to keep.

Something to ponder Making a commitment to another person is a serious step. Today's Scripture is a clear message to all of us. Commitment is a necessary tool for any loving relationship. And God promised us a special blessing when we make that commitment to our parents, especially those who are aging.

Something else to consider What more can I do to honor my parents?

Prayers for our brothers and sisters in Christ Those who are caring for aging parents.

June 4

"More Than Just Beautiful"

"She was a woman of good understanding and beautiful appear-ance." I Samuel 25:3

Oh, to be beautiful She was so very beautiful, this classmate of mine. Everywhere she went, people commented on her beauty. Boys fell all over themselves trying to get a date. "How nice it must be to be so beautiful," I thought. My friend had another perspective, "Boys don't ask me out just because they think I am beautiful. They really like me." On one hand, I still envied her beauty and the attention it got her, but the sensitive side of me perceived her need to seek val-idation about her other gifts and talents.

Something to ponder My mother's old adage, "Beauty is only skin deep," is useful for us in today's beauty-oriented society. Physical beauty is enhanced when one is also gracious. Meanings for the word *gracious* include courteous, kind and merciful. Today's Scripture tells the wonderful story of Abigail, who was not only beautiful, but also acknowledged by her husband's servants as a leader, and by King David as "giving good advice." It was not her beauty, but her graciousness and wisdom that saved the males in her household from being slaughtered and King David from bloodshed. Those who are blessed with physical beauty will want to include graciousness, *mercy and wisdom* to their list of tools they use to ensure loving relationships.

Something else to consider How will being gracious, merciful and wise help complement the physical beauty God gave me?

Prayers for our brothers and sisters in Christ Those whom we con-sider to be beautiful.

June 5

Hebrews 12:7-11

"Not in Front of Oma!"

"Furthermore, we have had human fathers who corrected us, and we paid them respect. Hebrews 12:9

How precious I had gone next door to visit with Micah's mother about some activities we were considering for her son and my grandson, Jay. "Wanda, I have to tell you what Jay said about you. He was doing the latest dance and I asked if he had danced for you." Jay's eyes got really big. 'Oh, no. Not in front of Oma.' He struggled to come up with the English word he wanted. I suggested the word *strict.* 'No! My Oma is not strict. She tries very hard to be, what is the word, *beautiful.* She smiled. "I knew he meant he respected you and wasn't sure you would appreciate that style of dancing. He must love you very much."

Not what I say, but what I do I thought about an old adage, "Don't do as I do, do as I say to do!" I wondered if the times I had the greatest difficulty in getting my own children to do something, it might have been in part because they perceived I was telling them to do something I was not exactly practicing myself.

Something to ponder Scripture tells us how important children are to Jesus, in *Matthew 19:13-14.* His message to us might be restated, "Do as I say because it is exactly what I do." What perfect tools for loving relationships with our children…teaching them *and* earning their respect by loving example.

Something else to consider Are the standards I set for my children the same standards I apply to myself?

Prayers for our brothers and sisters in Christ Those who want better relationships with their children.

June 6

Time Tells All

But Ruth said, "Entreat me not to leave you, or to turn back from following after you; for wherever you go, I will go; and wherever you lodge, I will lodge; your people shall be my people, and your God, my God." Ruth 1:16

Relationships too Marlyn and I had worked together out of the company's San Diego office that Marlyn managed. I was a consultant and made the hour commute twice a week. The summer that my two children and my niece got married, I stopped consulting to help with the weddings. I assumed that was the end of my relationship with Marlyn. Thankfully she had other plans. Marlyn began by calling and suggesting we get together for lunch at a restaurant halfway between our homes.

What a friend Now it was some three years later and I was in Topeka with my eighty-six-year-old mother who was having a cardiac catheterization. The phone rang and it was Marlyn calling long distance to see how Mother was doing. It was so comforting to hear her voice. As I hung up, it suddenly occurred to me that after all of these lunches Marlyn had become a dear friend.

Something to ponder Today's Scripture reminds us that Ruth and Naomi were both rewarded for the time they put into their relationship. As we check our calendars, what does it tell us about who and what we value? Are there any surprises? Giving of our *time* is a wonderful tool to help us in building, nurturing and sustaining loving relationships.

Something else to consider What relationship could I improve by giving that person more of my time?

Prayers for our brothers and sisters in Christ Those who are striving to make family a priority.

June 7

Ephesians 3:14-20

A Chance to Talk

"Now to Him who is able to do exceedingly abundantly above all that we ask or think, according to the power that works in is, to Him be glory in the church by Christ Jesus to all generations, forever and ever. Amen." Ephesians 3:20-21

Why won't he talk? Our daughter, Shelly, had been a Head Start teacher prior to our grandson Conner's arrival, so she felt she was quite knowledgeable about our grandson's development. That was why she was concerned. The language development books she had been reading confirmed our grandson was not making the sounds that were mandatory for him to learn to speak. Everyone was supportive and also had advice to give. I decided I liked her friend Christi's advice best.

Give him a chance Christi's observation was that Shelly spent so much time talking to Conner and meeting his every need and desire that Conner was smart enough to know he didn't need to talk. How I laughed at Christi's accurate assessment.

Back and forth Conner was enjoying his mother enjoying him. Yet I knew that if Shelly waited just a bit, Conner would soon want to assert his independence and begin expressing his wants.

Something to ponder What if God thought Conner had the right idea? Trusting that his mother loved him and would abundantly provide for him, he had no need to tell her what he wanted. What if we trusted that our heavenly Father loved us so much that He would provide more abundantly than we could ever imagine. It might just render us speechless too.

Something else to consider What would happen if I waited silently for God to provide?

Prayers for our brothers and sisters in Christ Mothers and infants.

June 8

II Timothy 3:14-17

"Still Going Still Growing"

All Scripture is given by inspiration of God, and is profitable for doctrine, for reproof, for correction, for instruction in righteous.
II Timothy 3:16

A need to continue growing I have had three prayer and Bible study partners come into my life after the age of forty. Most recently as I increased the time I spent ministering to young women in faith, I came to a surprising discovery. In spending time with these prayer partners, my eyes were opened in new and deeper ways to the meaning of God's Word and the messages He has for me. I saw areas in my life that needed serious work, where before I felt I was doing an OK job in my spiritual walk. Thanks to loving Bible study and prayer partners, I am still *going and growing* in my attempt to lead a Christ-like life.

Something to ponder The apostle Paul reminded Timothy that "all Scripture is profitable for instruction in righteousness" *II Timothy 3:16*. We expect teachers, doctors, dentists, and even pastors to attend workshops, seminars and advanced classes to make sure they are up to date in their fields. They are still going about their jobs of providing service, and they are still growing in their knowledge. We too need to commit to continued spiritual growth as we keep going in our service to Christ. *Ongoing spiritual growth*—what a great tool to help us ensure loving relationships with Christ. Another observation: The closer I grow to Christ, the more loving I am in my relationships with my family and friends.

Something else to consider What have I done recently to help myself grow spiritually?

Prayers for our brothers and sisters in Christ Those who lead Bible study and prayer groups.

June 9

Philippians 2:1-4

Listening for the Harmony

Therefore if there is any consolation in Christ, if any comfort of love, if any fellowship of the Spirit, if any affection and mercy, fulfill my joy by being like-minded, having the same love, being of one accord, of one mind. Philippians 2:1-2

Rounds I love to sing. The beautiful harmony that occurred when our music teacher taught us to sing in rounds was wonderful. The trick is that not everyone starts singing at the same time. When we got it right, the sound was music to my ears. But when we came in too soon or if we came in late, we sounded awful. We really had to work together to make beautiful music.

Harmony As I grew older and sang with more advanced music groups, the harmonies also became more advanced. Sometimes we were divided into as many as eight different sections. The more complex the harmony, the more intensely we had to listen. If our section came in at the wrong time or sang the wrong notes, the discord was blatantly obvious to the director and the rest of the chorus.

Something to ponder Careful listening is probably one of the most important tools in achieving harmonious singing groups as well as harmonious and loving relationships. The more peaceful and harmonious we want the relationship to be, the more sophisticated our listening skills might need to be. The Scripture calls us to let harmony rule in our hearts. Listening intently to achieve harmony might be just the tool we need.

Something else to consider How can listening to achieve harmony help me with the people I encounter today?

Prayers for our brothers and sisters in Christ Those who conduct choral groups.

June 10

Ecclesiastes 3:1-8

Switching Gears

And we know that all things work together for good to those who love God, to those who are the called according to His purpose.
Romans 8:28

A working mother I balanced my own career with being the wife of a husband with a high-pressure career and the mother of two children fourteen months apart. I cooked many a meal in the suit and heels I had worn to work and would wear to their evening school event. I ran hither, thither and yon and I ran fast. I loved my hectic life.

Lying fallow Our children were now grown and married. I looked around in vain for the next project I could get passionate about. Finding none, I drifted, just going through the motions. A friend had these encouraging words. "Fertile ground goes through fallow periods where it rests before becoming fertile again."

Up and running The fallow period soon passed. My current projects were keeping me busy and fulfilled. I loved the role of being an "at home mom" as I listened when our children called long distance with the joys and challenges in their lives. I was back!

Something to ponder God is there to guide and support us as we transition from one period in our lives to the next. With God's support, we can use these times to grow personally and spiritually. As we experience God's loving support, we reach out to help support others. Loving support—what a great tool to help ensure loving relationships.

Something else to consider Who needs my enduring support to help them through a change point in his or her life?

Prayers for our brothers and sisters in Christ Those facing retirement or other life-altering changes.

June 11

After All These Years

Is the seed still in the barn? As yet the vine, the fig tree, the pomegranate, and the olive tree have not yielded fruit. But from this day I will bless you. Haggai 2:19

My godchild She was so tiny, this godchild of mine. Her mother and I had become close friends. In the next few months, my husband and I would be moving to Dayton, Ohio, but my friend and I promised we wouldn't lose touch. It seemed like no time at all had passed and our only contact was through the annual Christmas card.

Another chance Some thirty years later I happened to answer when my godchild's father called to talk with my husband. I asked about his wife and we exchanged telephone numbers. When I contacted my friend, she mentioned her daughter, my godchild, was in the process of conducting a job search. WOW! Here was my chance! As a career consultant with over ten years' experience, I could help.

Something to ponder I had been given a second chance. The fruit of the hard work my godchild and I put forth was a job that was a great fit for her. And in the process, we had developed a loving bond. God blesses us with endless second chances. Giving others a second chance and seizing the opportunity when a second chance is presented are two great tools to use when we want to develop and maintain loving relationships.

Something else to consider Who do I need to ask for a second chance?

Prayers for our brothers and sisters in Christ Those who are feeling guilty about lost opportunities.

June 12

Mark 10:35-45

Children First

But whoever desires to become great among you shall be your servant. Mark 10:43

Putting us first Being a child brought up in a strict family, which put a special emphasis on being respectful to adults, became worth it when it was time to eat at large family gatherings. The tables were turned. The adults put us first. They had us line up and made sure we filled our plates and were seated and then they got their own food. I can't even begin to describe the flaky, tender pie crusts, the moist, flavorful cakes, the hot cornbread dripping with butter, the home-grown green beans, well-seasoned with "bacon square" and of course the mouth-watering collard greens. How special I felt to have my aunts helping to make sure my plate had all my favorite foods on it. They served us before seeing to their own needs.

Something to ponder Years later when I was an adult with adult children of my own, I visited my aunts. The food was still wonderful, but this time I waited on them. What joy it gave me to make sure their plates had all their favorite foods. God loves us so much that He sent His only Son, Jesus Christ to serve us so that we might understand His plan of salvation, and to die for us so that it might be available to all of us. Serving others, what a great tool to use in nurturing and sustaining loving relationships.

Something else to consider How can I serve my family as a way of showing my love?

Prayers for our brothers and sisters in Christ Husbands who continually look for ways to serve their wives as Christ served His Church.

June 13

Matthew 13:3-9

Gardening Can Be Difficult

But others fell on good ground and yielded a crop: some a hundredfold, some sixty, some thirty. Matthew 13:8

Planning ahead Every few days my neighbor would drop by to give me advice on the garden I was planting. She said she liked to garden. I had to admit, the vegetables that she had shared with us from her garden had been wonderful. However, I decided my method would probably work just as well, so I listened politely and then proceeded to do it my way.

Not like hers A few weeks later I stood looking at the vegetables in my garden in dismay. They didn't resemble my neighbor's vegetables as all. What had happened? Where had I gone wrong?

Something to ponder In today's Scripture Jesus was offering the kingdom of God to nonbelievers. The parable was a warning that unless their minds and hearts were open to hearing and accepting the Word of God, the teaching of the parables would be useless. As it was with the seeds that fell on good ground and yielded a good crop, we must be open to hearing and accepting loving messages of help before we can benefit from them. *Hearing and accepting loving messages* given to help us by family and friends are great tools to use in growing loving relationships. Just think how different the vegetables in my garden might have turned out if only I had listened and *acted* on the loving messages I received from my neighbor.

Something else to consider How can I benefit from loving messages of help if I don't hear and accept them?

Prayers for our brothers and sisters in Christ Those who have difficulty accepting help.

June 14

Luke 23:1-12

A Soft Voice in an Age of Rage

A soft answer turns away wrath, but a harsh word stirs up anger.
Proverbs 15:1

A soft answer and a loving look "I don't ever remember raising my voice at my children," he said in a matter-of-fact tone. I had felt there was something special about this man from the beginning of the retreat. Now I knew God had a reason for placing us together in this prayer group. I leaned forward to hear his response as someone asked how he responded when his daughter was angry. "Sometimes I answer her in my quietest voice and sometimes I remain silent. But I always look at her with all the love and compassion I possibly can."

Something else to consider We live in an age of rage. Commuters experience road rage as they travel crowded freeways. Children are frustrated at school, and rage too often erupts with deadly consequences. Parents vent their rage at their children's sports coaches, fellow parents and sometimes the children themselves on the playing field. *Proverbs 15:1* calls us to try a soft answer. In *Luke 23:9* Herod was questioning Jesus "with many words, but Jesus answered him nothing." Whether we use a soft answer, or silence, let us also speak volumes with our eyes to convey Jesus' love, compassion and peace. *A soft voice, love, compassion and peace:* what effective tools to create loving, Christ-like responses in this age of rage.

Something else to consider How can I use soft, loving responses to diffuse angry outbursts directed toward me?

Prayers for our brothers and sisters in Christ Those who inflict their anger on others.

June 15

Acts 15:36-41

Agree to Disagree

They had such a sharp disagreement that they parted company.
Barnabas took Mark and sailed for Cyprus, but Paul chose Silas
and left. Acts 15:39,40

When Christians argue This couldn't be. Was I actually reading about a disagreement the apostle Paul was having over a fellow Christian? Paul and Barnabas were unable to resolve their conflict and so they went their separate ways. These great evangelists then formed two separate teams that resulted in two outreach missions instead of one.

Something to ponder I have a friend with whom I love to share the Scriptures. Sometimes our discussions start to become heated as we set forth in new ways our same deeply entrenched positions. It is then that we "agree to disagree" and move on. I have always thought that it stopped there, but maybe today's Scriptures offer another possibility. When we cannot resolve an issue and so agree to disagree, perhaps God has different ways in which He wants to use each of us to accomplish His purpose. The next time I agree to disagree with someone, I am going to try to follow my actions and the actions of the other person over time to see how God is able to work through both of us. What an awesome God! What a unique tool to help sustain loving relationships through disagreements: accept and respect that God can use opposing viewpoints for His good works.

Something else to consider How can God use me *and* the one with whom I disagree for His good?

Prayers for our brothers and sisters in Christ Those who disagree with each other about how God's work should be done.

June 16

John 14:19-31

Cleaning House

Jesus answered and said, "If anyone loves Me, he will keep My word; and My Father will love him and We will come to him and make Our home with him." John 14:23

YUK! I have always detested housework of any kind. Every Saturday morning as a child, mother awakened us at what seemed like the crack of dawn to begin cleaning house. By noon, our house was spotless.

Houseguest Houseguests, on the other hand, are wonderful! They make me not only clean house, but also do those extra things like throwing away other unnecessary articles that have accumulated over time. Anticipated houseguests also give me an excuse and the opportunity to buy special items that help give a room a "lift." There is nothing like the smell of a freshly cleaned house.

Something to ponder What if my houseguest were Jesus, come to spend some time in my heart? Oh dear! I would certainly have to clean the place up: throw away the junk that had accumulated *and* the smelly garbage. I would also need to make a trip to my favorite soul food store to buy a fruit basket like the one found in *Galatians 5:22* (but the fruits of the spirit are love, joy, peace, kindness, goodness, faithfulness, gentleness, self-control) that would add a special touch. *"Heart cleaning"* and a *replenishing of the "fruits of the spirit"* on a regular basis might be great tools to use in building, nurturing and sustaining loving relationships with family, friends, and God.

Something else to consider How would a good "heart cleaning" benefit my relationship with my loved ones and with God?

Prayers for our brothers and sisters in Christ Those who want a clean heart.

June 17

John 14:27-31

No Promises

My people will dwell in a peaceful habitation, in secure dwellings, and in quiet resting places. Isaiah 32:18

What a shock! It was the middle of our worship service when I noticed a commotion in the congregation. A man sat slightly slumped in the pew. People, including our pastors, began to gather around. We all gave thanks for the quick response of the emergency medical team even as we prayed for our brother in Christ and his understandably shaken wife.

What now? Pastor Skip did an excellent job of coming up with a new sermon on the spot one that gave hope and encouragement to the family of the ill gentleman and to the congregation at large. "I asked the Lord to comfort me, He said to me, I will comfort you, you only have to pray," I sang softly.

Silent but thinking After the service, my friend Chris said to me, "I know it's trivial, but I kept thinking what if that were my husband and remembering how I had fussed at him this morning because I didn't like what he chose to wear to church." I think her thoughts mirrored a lot of our thoughts. "What if it had been my loved one and our last words were spent arguing over some trivial matter?"

Something to ponder Living a life of peace in practical terms challenges us to strive for a peaceful environment in our homes. A peaceful, loving home: what a great tool on which to build, nurture and sustain loving relationships.

Something else to consider What can I do to create a more peaceful, loving environment in my home?

Prayers for our brothers and sisters in Christ Those who respond to emergency calls.

June 18

II Timothy 4:1-8

Blessed Assurance

I have fought the good fight, I have finished the race, I have kept the faith. II Timothy 4:7

Blessed assurance My father died at the age of ninety-one, with my mother and my daughter at his side praying and singing his favorite hymns. My daughter Shelly will never forget the smile on her grandfather's face and the light in his eyes when she and her grandmother sang *"Blessed Assurance"* moments before my father died. With diligence and determination, he had run the race of life set before him. I don't remember my father talking about a personal relationship with Jesus, I just remember how much he loved us and the way he lived. How reassuring to know that at the very end of his life, my father took with him the blessed assurance that Jesus was his Lord and Savior, and because of my father's life, Jesus is mine too. Well done, Dad!

Something to ponder Some of us are blessed to have fathers who love us unconditionally. Regardless of the kind of fathers we have or had, we can all make the commitment to run the race set before us as parents so that our children can have two tools on which to build loving relationships—the blessed assurance that Jesus Christ is their Lord and Savior, and the art of unconditional *love* as modeled by their parents. And perhaps when we have run life's race to its completion, our children will be able to say, "Well done, Mom and Dad!"

Something else to consider What assurances am I prepared to give my children?

Prayers for our brothers and sisters in Christ Children who have recently lost a parent or grandparent.

June 19

Matthew 18:21-35

Brighter Days Ahead

Then Peter came and said to him, "Lord, how often shall my brother sin against me, and I forgive him? Up to seven times?" Jesus said to him, "I do not say to you, up to seven times, but up to seventy times seven." Matthew 18:21-22

Sisters I felt like I was in some dark place and couldn't see the way out. I had always prided myself in being her big sister, being there for her, leading the way. Now I had lost my way.

Wanda? We were having yet another stilted conversation on the phone. Suddenly the line went dead. Had she hung up on me? My heart ached. Soon the phone rang. I could hear her voice quiver. "Wanda?" That was all she needed to say. I immediately responded, "I'm here. We will get through this together. We are sisters."

I'm sorry It must have been a year later that we met for lunch and some shopping in Palm Springs. As she tried on a size eight that fit her beautifully she quietly said, "I am so sorry." I said that I too was sorry. The hot Palm Springs sun was a promise of the brighter days my sister and I would have as we asked and accepted each other's forgiveness.

Something to ponder How blessed I am to have my sister. I shudder to think of all I might have missed if my sister and I had not loved each other enough to forgive and forget. Forgiving *and* forgetting: what wonderful tools for building, nurturing and sustaining loving relationships.

Something else to consider What is keeping me from true reconciliation with someone I love?

Prayers for our brothers and sisters in Christ Sisters who are estranged.

II Corinthians 9:6-10

A Gift from the Bride

Give, and it will be given to you: good measure, pressed down,
shaken together, and running over will be put into your bosom.
For with the same measure that you use, it will be measured back
to you. Luke 6:38

What a surprise Our daughter's wedding was but a week away. In
the midst of all the last-minute preparations and telephone calls, we
received this most precious gift from the bride.

Dear Mom and Dad "It means a lot to me to have had you raise me
in the church so that I have a *home* to be married in. I believe that
God places us with the parents that we need; He has blessed me with
the two of you. Dad, you often talk about roots and wings. I feel
ready to soar, knowing that you raised me with deep Christian roots
to anchor me through the storms of life."

Your commitment to your marriage "Thank you for working so hard
on your marriage. It has left a lasting impression on me especially as
I anticipate taking my vows. God has blessed you for continuing to
commit to each other. I know that if I live by the example that you
have set, He will bless me too. Thank you again for everything. Love
always, Shelly"

Something to ponder Giving of oneself brings so many rewards and
giving back is a priceless gift. Just ask the parents of this bride. *A*
generous heart is a wonderful tool to help build, nurture and sustain
loving relationships with family, friends and with God.

Something else to consider How can I give more generously from
my heart?

Prayers for our brothers and sisters in Christ Parents of a soon-to-
be bride.

June 21

Mark 7:9-13

"You Can Count on Us"

*Honor your father and your mother, that your days may be long
upon the land which the Lord your God is giving you.* Exodus 20:12

Blessings Galore! "Don't worry, Mom," I assured her. "You can count
on us. We will be there." It was as if at that moment the blessings
began. The first airline I called had a round-trip special for $200, a
savings of close to $300. I first booked mine, then was able to book
a flight for my sister at that same price. I gave my concerns about
Mother's upcoming cardiac catheterization to God in prayer and
then began to joyously anticipate the time together with my mother
and sister.

A special family gathering The morning of the procedure, we were
met by our pastor and our cousins, Betty and Leslie. We prayed and
assured Mother of our love. An hour later, the cardiologist
approached us with his eyes twinkling and a lilt in his voice. Mother
was fine. He couldn't believe he had been looking at the heart of an
eighty-six-year-old woman. We rejoiced, giving thanks to God!
Mother had called, we had come, and God had blessed us all.

Something to ponder God calls us to honor our parents. My sister
and I wanted to reassure our mother that she could count on us. I
thought about other relationships. Did people feel that they could
count on me, no matter what? What great tools to build, nurture,
and sustain loving relationships: *promises made and promises kept.*

Something else to consider Who is counting on me to keep a promise I made?

Prayers for our brothers and sisters in Christ Adult children who
live far from aging parents.

June 22

Matthew 24:36-42

Expect versus Know

But of that day and hour no one knows, not even the angels of heaven, but My Father only. Matthew 24:36

Not today College was certainly different. There was no handholding and few reminders about things that were my responsibility to remember. One Wednesday when I walked into my Spanish class, I was vividly reminded that I was in college, not high school. My eyes were drawn to the blackboard where the message "Test Today" was written in Spanish. "It can't be today!" I blurted out, panic-stricken. "I thought it was Friday. Can't I take it later?" I begged the professor. She said no, of course, and then added that surely I had begun studying for the test I thought would be given Friday and so I should be all right. HA! Did I ever learn a valuable lesson that day about not waiting until the last minute.

Something to ponder Some were not prepared when Jesus came the first time. We rejoice in His assurance that He will come again. How is our preparation for His coming influenced by whether or not we know the exact date? Some of us prepare in advance for scheduled tests, others of us cram. Perhaps that is why some teachers give pop quizzes. I am reminded of the stories I hear about people who put off healing a relationship, visiting a friend or relative, giving a special gift…until it is too late. Perhaps this is a good time to eliminate the word *procrastinate* from our relationships with our loved ones…and with God.

Something else to consider What part does procrastination play in the quality of my relationships?

Prayers for our brothers and sisters in Christ Those who have recently lost a loved one.

June 23

Matthew 16:24-27

"He Loves Me, He Loves Me Not"

For I am persuaded that neither death nor life, nor angels nor principalities nor powers, nor things present nor things to come, nor height nor depth, nor any other created thing, shall be able to separate us from the love of God which is in Christ Jesus our Lord. Romans 8:38,39

Plucking daisy petals It was a children's message with an added twist. Most of us at some time or another have picked the petals off a flower, reciting, "He (or she) loves me, he (or she) loves me not."

The twist Pastor Skip took another flower and started the litany again, only this time he intoned, "He loves me, He loves me, He loves me," until the last petal was picked. I thought the message would be about using such a meaningless method to determine a person's love. Surprise! The message was, "When we know God, we can be assured of the outcome, secure in the knowledge that God loves us no matter what!"

Something to ponder Romans 8:38-39 is one of my favorite Scriptures, perhaps my very favorite. It brings me so much comfort and assurance to know that in a world where people are afraid to make commitments, Jesus will not let anything, nor anyone, separate me from His love. And it is no surprise that when I feel loved, it is easier for me to love others. *Security in God's love* provides us with great tools to use in building, nurturing and sustaining solid, loving relationships.

Something else to consider How will feeling secure in God's love influence how I respond to those I love?

Prayers for our brothers and sisters in Christ Those who are afraid to accept love.

June 24

I'm Sorry

Now I rejoice, not that you were made sorry, but that your sorrow led to repentance. II Corinthians 7:9

Admitting I am wrong Sometimes I find myself going through various defensive moves to avoid saying two words, "I'm sorry." And sometimes those defensive moves hurt the one I've wronged more than my initial act. Why can't I get it through my head that the conflict cannot possibly be resolved until I say, "I'm sorry"?

Accepting responsibility A friend had shared an incident with me involving a mutual friend. I related the conversation to our mutual friend, thinking she would find it supportive, but she didn't. A few days later, as I was talking with the friend who had related the incident, I told her what had happened. She was upset, claiming she thought she had told me in confidence. My first thought was to debate the aspect of implied confidentiality but then I thought I just need to say I'm sorry. "I'm so sorry. I didn't mean to betray your confidence. Please forgive me." "It's all right," she said. "I probably should have made it clear that I didn't want the incident repeated."

Something to ponder Saying "I'm sorry" is the first step toward repentance that must be taken before we can ask forgiveness and experience that wonderful feeling of a fully restored relationship. Scripture calls us to admit when we've done wrong, and then repent or turn away from the wrongdoing. *Being able to say, "I'm sorry,"* from the heart is a wonderful tool for nurturing and sustaining loving relationships.

Something else to consider Who needs to hear the words, "I'm sorry?"

Prayers for our brothers and sisters in Christ Those who have difficulty admitting they are wrong.

June 25

Matthew 16:24-27

Time to Pray

Be anxious for nothing, but in everything by prayer and supplication, with thanksgiving, let your requests be made known to God; and the peace of God, which surpasses all understanding, will guard your hearts and minds through Christ Jesus.
Philippians 4:6-7

Long distance protection We had moved to southern California but our daughter had remained in Seattle, Washington. Her little car had bit the dust. She had called to tell me that she had a second job to help her save enough for a down payment on another car. "How will you get to this job?" I asked cautiously, fearing the answer. "Oh, I'll take the bus. I will only have three blocks to walk and at 10:30 at night there is still lots going on and lots of people out and about so I'll feel safe," she replied casually.

Prayers and peace of mind The anxiety attacks about our daughter's safety would come at odd times. I felt so helpless. Only through intense, heart-wrenching prayer could I find peace during those times when I couldn't care for and protect my beloved daughter as she struggled to make her way. I also found peace in knowing that the Holy Spirit knew just what she needed and could intercede for me. What a blessing for an anxious mom.

Something to ponder When we feel anxious about situations over which we have little or no control, it is comforting to know that in prayer we can find peace of mind. *Prayer* that brings peace of mind: a wonderful tool to support us in loving relationships.

Something else to consider How can I use prayer to bring me peace of mind?

Prayers for our brothers and sisters in Christ Those who are anxious about loved ones.

June 26

II Corinthians 2:14-17

Pastor Larry's Fragrance

For we are to God the fragrance of Christ among those who are being saved and among those who are perishing. II Corinthians 2:15

What is that fragrance? I had pulled into a gas station on my way home from work. As I filled the tank, making a face as the gas fumes filled my nostrils, I heard a man's voice, "Lady, what is that fragrance you are wearing? I sure would like to get that perfume for my wife." I told him the name of the perfume I was wearing, amazed that he could smell it some ten hours after I had sprayed it on and in the midst of what I felt to be overpowering gas fumes.

A subtle aroma I thought about our new pastor, Pastor Larry. He, with his quiet demeanor in expressing and living his faith, is like the subtle aroma of the perfume I was wearing. He helps us develop our own Christ-like fragrance so that it pierces through the odors of the world around us with love and compassion. How blessed I am to have a pastor with a Christ-like fragrance in the midst of an un-Christ-like world.

Something to ponder Today's Scripture reminds us that we are to be the perfume of Christ. I found myself challenged anew to make sure my actions toward others reminded them of Christ and would cause others who didn't know Christ to want to get to know Him in a personal way.

A question or two What actions can I take to make sure I am giving off the aroma of Christ?

Prayers for our brothers and sisters in Christ Those who witness to others through their Christ-like aroma.

June 27

Proverbs 3:5-6

Winging It With God

I will bring the blind by a way they did not know; I will lead them in paths they have not known. I will make darkness light before them, and crooked places straight. These things I will do for them, and not forsake them. Isaiah 42:16

Where others lead As a child, did you ever play a game where one person closed their eyes and the other person led them around the playground? I recently tried this experience at a retreat. My partner was a young man in his late teens. After he led me around the field the first time, I grew bold. "Let's run!" I said. He smiled, linked his arm in mine and off we went. While others walked cautiously, my partner and I careened in and out among them, enjoying the freedom from fear our mutual trust gave us.

Something to ponder Turning loose and winging it with God can be like letting go of someone's hand who is leading you through a dark, unfamiliar room. It was easier for me to trust my partner because we had spent time together in Bible study, prayer, and fellowship. Does it then stand to reason that the more time we spend with God, the easier it is to turn loose, trust Him and just wing it with Him. And what about my relationship with family and friends? What part does trust play in the quality of those relationships? Is there mutual trust in the relationships I hold dear? *Trust*, what a great tool to build, nurture and sustain loving relationships.

Something else to consider What would others say makes me trustworthy?

Prayers for our brothers and sisters in Christ Those who train seeing-eye dogs.

June 28

Their Heritage

We will not hide them from their children; we will tell the next generation the praiseworthy deeds of the Lord, His power and the wonder He has done. Psalm 78:4

Children at church I remember enjoying Pastor Roger's children's message at our church in Seattle...until my children were old enough to participate. Like the year our son, Milton Scott, had to tell the entire church that he didn't have any Christmas gifts, not one. That was the year that Christmas gifts were literally assembled, wrapped and put under the tree minutes before the children got to open them.

Their heritage I also remember Shelly as an adult, telling me how special it was to have our family friend, Marty Monnahan, as her secret pal during a time when she really needed to feel special. And Milton Scott finding solace during his teenage years from one of my brothers in Christ, George Nichols, who affectionately referred to me as "The War Department." And there were countless others. Only God could have provided such a wonderful, loving Christian family to help me rear my children in the practical applications of our faith.

Something to ponder Perhaps this is a good time to revisit our commitment to children as God commands. Listening to reports of child abuse, parents killing children, children killing children, and children killing parents, it is blatantly and terrifyingly obvious that we aren't coming even close to loving, protecting and educating our children as God intended. How about using our *Christian heritage* as a tool for building and sustaining loving relationships with children?

Something else to consider What am I doing to provide a Christian heritage for my children?

Prayers for our brothers and sisters in Christ Children with a parent serving a prison term.

June 29

Matthew 9:35-38

My Compassion, His Forgiveness

"Through the Lord's mercies we are not consumed, because His compassions fail not. They are new every morning; Great is Your faithfulness." Lamentations 3:22-23

Not a good day His head was down as he walked slowly through the classroom door. My heart went out to him. I put an arm around his shoulder and drew him close. "How was your day?" I asked. Tears ran down his face as he related what he had done that had gotten him into trouble. This is a wonderful opportunity for me to teach him about God's love, I thought.

A clean slate I asked Jay if he was sorry and he said he was. Next I asked him if he would try not to make that same mistake again. He agreed he would try. Then I told him God had forgiven him and not only that, but He loved him so much that God had wiped the slate clean just like the chalkboards in his classroom. So, I said, "Jay, God has forgiven you, your teacher has forgiven you, and I have forgiven you. Tomorrow is a brand new day and, thanks to God's love, you get to start it with a clean slate!" I will never forget the look of wonder in his face as he eagerly listened. Jay didn't say a word, but the smile on his face said it all.

Something to ponder In His ministry, Jesus dealt with people using compassion and forgiveness. What great tools for us to use in nurturing and sustaining loving relationships: *compassion and forgiveness.*

Something else to consider Who needs my compassion and forgiveness today?

Prayers for our brothers and sisters in Christ Children who are feeling distraught over mistakes they have made.

June 30

Titus 2:1-4

An Old-Fashioned Grandmother

The older women likewise, that they be reverent in behavior,
not slanderers, not given to much wine; teachers of good things.
Titus 2:3

Retreat speaker at eighty-plus My mother shared this faith story at our women's retreat. "I met a wonderful young man. On our second date he asked me to marry him. We were so much in love. He wanted to become intimate and couldn't understand why I refused since we were planning on getting married in the future. Oh, the pressure I felt from him and from myself, but I held fast to the Bible teachings I had grown up with. I was afraid of losing him if I kept saying no, but I was more afraid of how I would feel about myself as a Christian woman if I said yes. I prayed fervently. After some intense discussions with my uncle and aunt, with whom I was staying, we were married one month later on December 29, 1934. This marriage lasted fifty-nine and a half years until my husband, and Wanda's father, Clovis, went to be with the Lord." The women of the retreat flocked around Mother to hear more.

Something to ponder The message my old-fashioned mother gave is a strong one. Maybe it is past time to turn to the older spiritual women in our lives and listen to their stories of faith to help us through the spiritual challenges of life. *Faith-filled grandmothers and other older women*: wonderful tools to provide guidance and support in loving relationships.

Something else to consider What faith-filled older woman should I be listening to?

Prayers for our brothers and sisters in Christ Those who are spiritual grandmothers reaching out to young women.

My Journal
June: Tools for Loving Relationships

Insights: What do I want to remember about the tools I need to develop, nurture and sustain loving relationships?

Challenges: What do I need to do to incorporate the lessons I have learned into my everyday life? When will I start?

What are the ten top blessings I received from God this month?

1.

2.

3.

4.

5.

6.

7.

8.

9.

10.

Answered Prayers

Introduction to July Devotions

Freedom to Choose

I always assumed I was free if not equal I attended an all black elementary school until the fifth grade. Linda Brown of Brown vs the Topeka Board of Education, the landmark case that integrated schools, was a classmate of mine. My mother's response to segregation was to encourage, no, demand that I study as hard as I could and conduct myself in ways that would dispel the stereotypes that helped divide the races.

Perhaps I was a slave As an adult, I encountered other experiences that caused me to feel enslaved, in addition to the racial discrimination I experienced. Whatever the situation, whether I was being held captive by my own actions or the actions of others, I felt anything but free.

...to the wrong master Fortunately I came to realize that God was available and willing to set me free again and again. I had to remind myself that in fact I was already free. Jesus had paid the price for my freedom, forgiven me, and wiped the incident from His memory. We are free to put on the bonds of slavery, *and* we are free to take them off at any time. God's actions of love give us the *freedom to choose.*

I pray that you will find this month's Scriptures and faith stories helpful in identifying the things in life which enslave and the freeing power of Jesus Christ. What will you do with your freedom? You are *free to choose.*

The promise of His everlasting love for you and for me... "Therefore, if anyone is in Christ, he is a new creation; old things have passed away; behold, all things have become new" *II Corinthians 5:17.*

Your sister in Christ,
Wanda Scott Bledsoe

July 1

Freedom to Follow His Rules

And this world is fading away, and these evil, forbidden things will go with it, but whoever keeps doing the will of God will live forever. I John 2:17

Freedom to choose God gave us rules for Christ-like living to help us live happily, safely and in harmony with others. Have you ever wondered why God in His infinite power does not just make us follow His rules? But no, He gives us the freedom to choose. And sometimes the choices I make hurt myself and or others.

Choices and consequences My first boyfriend shared his philosophy with me on breaking rules. According to him, he first tried to think of all of the consequences if he got caught. Next he tried to imagine what it would be like to face those consequences. Finally if his desire to break the rule was stronger than his fear of the consequences, he went ahead and did it. The last part, I felt, said volumes about taking responsibility for one's actions. He finished with, "If I get away with it, great! If I get caught, I don't complain about the punishment, I just accept it. It was my choice."

For your consideration What choices are you facing today? How do you feel about the way you make decisions? What do you think children and others learn from watching you deal with the consequences? How long has it been since you seriously considered God's rules for Christ-like living when making important choices in your life?

A time to reflect Who influences the choices I make in my everyday life?

Prayers for our brothers and sisters in Christ Those who are living with the consequences of wrong choices.

July 2

Freedom to Be a Role Model

Be careful, however, that the exercise of your freedom does not become a stumbling block to the weak. I Corinthians 8:9

Selma, Alabama During the early '60s when the Civil Rights spotlight was focused on protests in Selma, Alabama, I was a freshman at Kansas University. In the midst of my confusing thoughts about the injustice of it all and my role as a black woman, my mother's voice rang loud and clear. "You are a role model for our race. Remember, someone is watching." Down through the years, trying to be a positive role model for my faith and my race has often caused me to choose paths I would not otherwise have chosen, paths that called for love, forgiveness and self-discipline.

For your consideration When is the last time we stopped to think of ourselves as role models? Just because we might not want to be a role model doesn't matter. The person watching us may admire us and want to follow our example. They like the decisions we make and the way we lead our lives. The next time we make a decision, let us stop and think, "Who might be influenced by my decision, and how?" We are called to be *ambassadors* for Christ, II Corinthians 5:20. Another word for ambassador is *representative*. How would we rate as a faithful representative of Christ? Want to improve the score? We have the freedom to choose.

A time to reflect What do others learn by watching me?

Prayers for our brothers and sisters in Christ The athletes our children choose as role models.

July 3

James 1:5-8

Freedom to Say No

If any of you lacks wisdom, let him ask of God, who gives totally, liberally and without reproach, and it will be given to him. James 1:5

They couldn't say no He was an authority figure for my daughter and her best friend, two girls in their teens. He made choices that immediately removed him from that position and from his marriage. Alone and lonely, he reached out to my daughter's friend for company. I think her friend wanted to say no, but couldn't, so she begged my daughter to go with her for an evening of movies at his house. Because they were best friends, my daughter couldn't say no, but I could and I did!

Another way I prayed for wisdom as I tried to help my daughter's friend see why the man's request was inappropriate. Then I suggested that her mother and I, as strong Christian women, would be glad to spend an evening watching movies and *praying* with this young man. He didn't take her up on my offer but it did get her off the hook.

For your consideration When we feel pressured to make or support choices that cause us to feel uncomfortable, and we sense we are not strong enough to say no, we can look for support in a brother or sister in Christ who is stronger in their faith than we are at that moment. Then listen for God to show us another way, *and* provide the strength to say NO!

A time to reflect Who do I know who is strong enough in their faith to help me say no?

Prayers for our brothers and sisters in Christ Children who want to say no to inappropriate requests by adult authority figures.

July 4

Freedom to Live Peaceably

Now the fruit of righteousness is sown in peace by those who make peace. James 3:18

What if? Fourth of July and Memorial Day celebrations always make me both grateful and sad. What a debt of gratitude we owe to the families who have lost loved ones in a war. And there is no amount of money that we could pay to compensate those who return from war forever wounded in mind, body and spirit. One life is too big a price to pay; hundreds of thousands of lives is unfathomable. How God must weep at the atrocities we heap upon each other. I am positive God did not intend for us to live in such a manner that makes us feel we have to resort to killing one another to settle our differences.

For your consideration On this Fourth of July, let us give thanks to God and to the many men and women who have made, and continue to make, our freedom possible. In a quiet moment, let us also think about the various ways we can promote peace through kind words, an understanding, compassionate and loving manner, and a gentle touch. We are all part of the family of God. As we teach our children to get along with others, let us work even harder to lead the way by example. Remember, God gave us the freedom to choose. Let us reject violence in any form. Let us this day and forevermore choose to live in peace.

A time to reflect How can I make sure that my actions this day and every day loudly proclaim my commitment to peace?

Prayers for our brothers and sisters in Christ Those who have lost loved ones through war.

July 5

Psalm 31:21-24

Freedom to Break Loose

"Jesus looked at them and said, "With man this is impossible, but with God all things are possible." Matthew 19:26

Their Christmas present My mother and sister were so worried. I could hear it in their voices as they expressed their unconditional love for me, and their concern about the danger the diet pills I was taking posed to my health. They begged me to stop taking them. I had a choice. I did not want to give up the diet pills and the support they gave me in losing weight, but my love for my mother and my sister won out. I decided that weaning myself off these powerful diet pills would be my Christmas gift to them. Over the years I have given my mother and sister many gifts, but I will never forget their expressions of joy that year when they opened the box with the note inside that said, "I quit! Merry Christmas!"

For your consideration What does God's unconditional love free you to do or not do? How does the Scripture, "Lo, I am with you always" *Matthew 28:20*, support you in making hard decisions? How can the Scripture, "I can do all things through Christ who strengthens me" *Philippians 4:13*, give you the courage to free yourself from habits that are destructive? It was not easy for me to stop taking the diet pills, but these Scriptures, along with the love and support of my family, gave me the strength to be free!

A time to reflect How could I use today's Scriptures to help free me from destructive behavior or habits? Who can I turn to for support?

Prayers for our brothers and sisters in Christ Those fighting substance abuse.

July 6

Proverbs 3:5-8

Freedom to Follow...Or Not

In all your ways acknowledge Him, and He shall direct your paths. Proverbs 3:6

I can't see There was plenty of music, food and laughter at the staff Christmas party. Content and slightly sleepy from a wonderful evening, I buckled my seatbelt and settled in for the two-hour ride home. My husband had his favorite jazz music softly playing and I yawned, ready to fall asleep. Suddenly I was wide awake. Our car was heading down the mountainside at a seemingly high rate of speed, given the fact that I couldn't see anything but thick fog all around me. Panic stricken, I cried out to my husband, "Slow down, I can't see where we are going!" He calmly replied, "You don't have to see, Dear. I am the one who is driving and I can see." He went on to explain that he was using the white lines that mark the lanes as a guide.

For your consideration It is easy to follow someone or something blindly. It is also easy to be persuaded to go along without knowing where or why. July is a month in which we can celebrate the freedom to choose how we will live, and whom we will follow. With God as our ultimate leader and His Book of Life as our guide, we have a fail-proof strategy that allows us to see through any "fog." It is your choice. What will you choose to do, follow Jesus and those who live Christ-like lives...or not?

A time to reflect What kind of leader am I and how is that influenced by the kind of leaders I follow?

Prayers for our brothers and sisters in Christ Those who hold political offices.

Freedom to Put on a Happy Face

They looked to Him and were radiant, and their faces were not ashamed. Psalm 34:5

So gracious My earliest memories of Aunt Codie were as a gracious lady with a wonderful sense of humor. At ninety-one-years old, she was sick, unable to care for herself, and treated unkindly by her caregiver. My mother and father came to take her home with them. As my father bundled her up in a blanket and carried her to the car, she smiled weakly and said, "Thank you for being so kind."

Put on a happy face I thought about other people I knew who were going through difficult times. How could they be so positive, when I knew their hearts had to be heavy? I asked my mother, who also is positive and giving even in the midst of adversity. She replied with a gentle smile, "I may not be able to control the circumstances, but I can control my attitude. I choose to help others as a way of helping myself. I choose to accept God's love and trust in His goodness and mercy. No one can take away my ability to be happy. That is my choice!"

For your consideration A smiling face seems like a great way to bring people closer. They just might be the help and support God has waiting for you. A frown or a smile— God gave us the freedom to choose.

A time to reflect How can I use a smiling face and a cheerful attitude to help me deal with the problems I am facing today?

Prayers for our brothers and sisters in Christ Those whose spirits are broken and those who respond to their need for help.

July 8

Freedom to Champion Impossible Causes

*Then I said to them, "...Come and let us build the wall of
Jerusalem, that we may no longer be a reproach."* Nehemiah 2:17

Somebody ought to Nehemiah was just a man who loved God, saw
a huge problem that needed fixing, and waded in to fix it. He didn't
complain about the horrible conditions, nor did he try to establish
blame. He just prayed and then took action to get the job done!

Not by himself Nehemiah used his talents as a visionary and leader
to inspire others. He prayed; he communicated his vision to others;
he elicited the help of those with the skills that were needed to do
the job; he kept focused on the goal; he worked alongside the volunteers; and he never lost faith in God and His ability to get the job
done. One man who believed in God, working through others, successfully accomplished God's work and rebuilt the wall of
Jerusalem.

For your consideration What needs building or fixing in your community? Is it the need for better schools, more jobs, social justice for
an underserved group of people, or a solution to gangs and racial
strife? What can we do as one person? Probably not much. But God
working through us, and others, can accomplish anything and
everything. God always gives us the talent and the resources to do
the work He calls us to do, no matter how impossible the task might
seem. *God with us* is an unbeatable combination. We are free to
make a difference.

A time to reflect What seemingly impossible task does God have for
me?

Prayers for our brothers and sisters in Christ Those who work with
gangs.

July 9

Philippians 4:4-8

Freedom to Count to Ten

Rejoice in the Lord always; again I will say, Rejoice. Philippians 4:4

A textbook solution One of the many lessons I learned in my life as a medical center administrator was about maintaining high morale. We could see twenty patients in a day who were either neutral in their response to the care we provided or even appreciative. However, it was the one unhappy patient we tended to focus on, putting a damper on our day. The solution?

Focus! We learned to celebrate the great experiences we had with our patients each day. We tried it and it worked! Staff morale improved significantly. Had the disgruntled patient changed? No, but *we* had.

At home too I decided to apply that concept to my prayer life as well. What would happen if, when I was in the midst of a challenge or problem, I stopped to first *thank* God for all the blessings, great and small He had provided, and *then* ask for His help? AHA! Giving thanks first lifted my spirits and I was then able to remember that God provides for me abundantly. What a concept. When in need, first give thanks.

For your consideration If you are having a string of what seems like horrible days, try counting to ten…ten blessings, that is. Then ask God to help you with that negative situation that has been spoiling your days. Look for His response while you continue to focus on the lovely things in your life and *give thanks!*

A time to reflect What are ten ways that God has blessed me today?

Prayers for our brothers and sisters in Christ Those who have trouble getting past the bad stuff to the good stuff in their day.

July 10

Hebrews 4:14-16

Freedom to Ask for Help

*Let us therefore come boldly to the throne of grace, that we may
obtain mercy and find grace to help in time of need.* Hebrews 4:16

I had a dream My sister had called to ask me to pray for a coworker
who needed a kidney transplant. One of the coworker's siblings had
donated a kidney to her some years ago, but now that kidney had
failed. Her coworker had several brothers and sisters and she was
preparing to make calls to her family for another kidney. My sister
continued, "I dreamed you called and told me you needed a kidney
and asked if I would be willing to give you one of mine. I told you,
of course, I have two; you could certainly have one of them."

A hard call I thanked my sister with tears in my eyes. "That would
have been a hard call for me to make." My sister was surprised.
"Why would you have difficulty asking me for a kidney?" "I have a
hard time asking for and accepting help," I replied.

For your consideration Solving my own problems as well as the
problems of others makes me strong, and perhaps too independent.
God wants us to depend on Him, not ourselves. Today's Scriptures
remind us that we are free to ask for God's help through prayer,
reading His Word, and the friends and family with whom He has
surrounded us. Rejoice and give thanks! Feel free to ask for help!

A time to reflect What issues do I need to set aside in order to ask
for help?

Prayers for our brothers and sisters in Christ Those who need kidney transplants and the donors who respond.

July 11

Freedom to Tell Others

Go therefore and make disciples of all the nations, baptizing them in the name of the Father and of the Son and of the Holy Spirit. Matthew 28:19

I'm afraid! My friend Nancy's boss had seen the Bible daily devotional booklet she read at her desk before beginning work. He had also noticed the difference in the way she approached challenges and dealt with adversities. He wanted her to tell her coworkers how she used her faith to get through the challenges they were all experiencing at work. "How will I speak to my coworkers about my faith?" my friend lamented.

Tell them a story "Coming to God in prayer and in reading His Word to find comfort and direction is not the norm for many people. That is why I like to tell real stories about God in my everyday life. Why don't you tell them a story about a difficult day you had and how you believe God helped you handle it as a result of reading from your devotional booklet and praying?" I advised.

For your consideration The message of salvation is so wonderful, and the benefit in our daily lives so miraculous—how could we not seize every opportunity to tell His story and ours? So many of our brothers and sisters in Christ are searching for the story of salvation. Why not tell them yours? We are free to do just that here in America, as part of the freedom paid for with countless lives.

A time to reflect How can I share with others how God is working in my life?

Prayers for our brothers and sisters in Christ Those who want to hear about God and those who are afraid to tell them.

July 12

Freedom from Guilt or Shame

If we confess our sins, He is faithful and just to forgive us our sins and to cleanse us from all unrighteousness. I John 2:9-10

Guilt vs. shame According to the dictionary, guilt is the act or state of having done a wrong or committed an offense. Shame is a painful feeling of having lost the respect of others because of the improper behavior. I was confused.

Help! I called my mother, my spiritual mentor, first. Then I called my pastor. I also called my very good friend, Marlyn, who happens to be Jewish. Lastly I brought the subject up during the birthday luncheon I had for my Uncle Ed.

My thoughts Here is what my family and friends decided. *Guilt* is the acknowledgement that I have done something wrong. The next step is the feeling of *remorse*. But if my family and or friends find out, then I am *ashamed* because now they might think less of me. Complicated? Yes and my heart goes out to children who are made to feel guilt and shame because of the actions of adults who take advantage of them. God can't be pleased by these heart-wrenching situations.

For your consideration What's the point? Feelings of guilt and shame are not only unhealthy, but unnecessary. Healing and reconciliation come from seeking and receiving forgiveness. How freeing to be able to seek God's forgiveness and know without a doubt it will be granted. We are forgiven! We are free!

A time to reflect What is the next step I need to take toward the freeing path of forgiveness?

Prayers for our brothers and sisters in Christ Children who are victims of sexual abuse and have been made to feel guilt and shame.

Freedom to Be a Magnet

And I, if I am lifted up from the earth, will draw all peoples to Myself. John 12:32

The power of the cross I like to think of the cross as a powerful magnet capable of drawing all peoples in all nations to Jesus. But if the cross is such a powerful magnet, why then are so many of us able to resist its pull? Let's consider free will. Although the plan of salvation is perfect, and Jesus' death on the cross the largest ransom ever paid, God still gives us the freedom to choose whether or not we resist the message. We are free to "demagnetize" ourselves. The good news is we are also free to be a magnet for Christ.

For your consideration If I envision myself as a magnet for Christ, how powerful a magnet am I? Do people seem to be drawn to me, wanting to hear how my faith works for me and how that faith might work for them? If I wanted to be a stronger magnet, how would I do that? The first things that comes to mind are the actions Jesus valued when He preached His sermon on the mount found in *Matthew 5:1-12.* The second step I might take to become a stronger magnet is to increase my willingness to tell others my faith stories. And the third step calls me to just do it! We can choose to be a powerful magnet for Him. God gives us the freedom to choose.

A time to reflect How can I act as a magnet to draw others to God?

Prayers for our brothers and sisters in Christ Those who are looking for someone to tell them a story about Christ.

July 14

Freedom to Be Rescued

"God is our refuge and strength, an ever-present help in trouble."
Psalm 46:1

Swimming away My heart ached as I watched the news story unfold on television. A young woman was treading water in the middle of the river. A helicopter overhead held her in its spotlight. A rowboat inched toward her with two would-be rescuers. I couldn't believe my eyes as I watched the young woman swim away from the boat again and again before finally disappearing beneath the murky water.

For your consideration When I look at my spiritual life, am I like the young woman who kept swimming away from her rescuers? My daughter knows how I love to "fix" things for people. Sometimes when she calls with what sounds like a problem I could fix, she will start the conversation by saying, "Mom I don't want you to fix this problem, I just want to be able to whine for awhile." Do I really want help in applying my faith to my problems or do I just want to whine? Am I in danger of compromising my relationship with God because I don't want to be rescued from activities or a lifestyle that separates me from a Christ-like life? The good news is that Jesus stands ready to rescue us through His Word and through other believers God has designated as rescuers. We are free to choose to be rescued or to swim away, to act in faith or to whine. Which will you choose?

A time to reflect What are some areas in my life that call for a spiritual rescue?

Prayers for our brothers and sisters in Christ Those who risk their lives in rescue missions.

July 15

Genesis 20:1-18

Freedom to Trust and Be Patient

Then to Sarah he said, "Behold, I have given your brother a thousand pieces of silver; indeed this vindicates you before all who are with you and before everybody." Genesis 20:16

Keep me safe When Abraham and Sarah entered King Abimelech's domain, Abraham was afraid that some man would kill him for his beautiful wife, Sarah. So Abraham asked Sarah to protect him by going along with story that they were brother and sister.

Trusting not in man but in God Sarah obeyed her husband and God protected Sarah. God did not allow Sarah to be touched while she was in Abimelech's household. God also protected Sarah's reputation as Abimelech announced to Sarah, before everyone, that she was blameless.

For your consideration Trust and patience. Sarah's story is about both. She trusted God, but it required patience. Can you think of a time when you were faced with a dilemma and you placed the situation in God's hands and waited and waited? And just when you thought He hadn't heard you or if He had, He wasn't going to deliver you, God did in ways you could not imagine? "But why does it sometimes take so long?" I often think. Trusting God and waiting patiently, produce results beyond our greatest imagination. Waiting on God isn't easy but trusting Him frees us to endure. We are free to choose to wait on the Lord. (Read about a time when Sarah didn't wait patiently for God and the disaster that resulted **Genesis 16**).

A time to reflect Do I really want to give up waiting for God to respond?

Prayers for our brothers and sisters in Christ Those who get impatient waiting for God to answer their prayers.

July 16

Psalm 15:1-5

Freedom to Recover from Acting like Frogs

Lord, who may abide in Your tabernacle? Who may dwell in Your holy hill? Psalm 15:1

Shell-shocked My career-consultant clients sat staring at me in disbelief as they told of designing some part or identifying some problem that saved their company hundreds of thousands of dollars. And yet they were being told their company no longer had a place for them. It was at the beginning of new terminology in the workplace: downsizing, reorganization, throw-away people and throw-away companies.

The water is fine Now almost a decade later, we as a working people seem to have adjusted. We continue to be updated about the unemployment rate, but it is no longer a headline item. I am reminded of the frog story. It seems that a frog accommodates itself so well that if placed in a pot of water over a fire, the frog will not jump out as the temperature rises, its internal system will just adjust.

For your consideration It's the little things that we look past on a daily basis that allow us to tolerate the fire being continually turned up, until we are compromising on the bigger issues. Jesus' unconditional love and forgiveness allow us to start each day with a fresh pot of water. It is never too late to jump out of the hot water into a cool, refreshing pond of Christ-like living. We don't have to act like frogs. God gave us the freedom to choose.

A time to reflect What am I finding more and more acceptable in today's society that is placing me in spiritual hot water?

Prayers for our brothers and sisters in Christ Those who are in spiritually hot water.

July 17

Freedom to Take Advantage of a Good Thing

I was glad when they said to me, Let us go into the house of the Lord. Psalm 122:1

A second home I recently returned to the place of my birth to be with my mother during a surgical procedure. As I sat in church that following Sunday with my mother and sister, memories of growing up there washed over me like a refreshing waterfall. I let my mind wander back in time to my childhood. How secure and happy I felt over the years I lived at home experiencing the Saturday preparation and Sunday morning routine.

Down on their knees I have images of my mother and father on their knees by their bedside, heads bowed in fervent prayer. Their love and the security they provided for me by raising me to love, worship, serve, and depend on God has not only sustained me down through the years as I faced my own challenges in life but has allowed me to retain an exuberance for life.

For your consideration Statistics given at a marriage-encounter weekend my husband and I attended, indicated that the divorce rate dropped significantly in couples that worshiped together. I am sure that there are also statistics about the health and well-being of families who worship together. God's love, comfort, protection, guidance, security and a loving church family are all there. God could make us go because He knows how much we would benefit, but He has given us a choice. We are free to choose.

A time to reflect What more could I be providing for my family through consistent worship with a church family?

Prayers for our brothers and sisters in Christ Families who are struggling spiritually.

July 18

Freedom to Succeed One Step at a Time

"Fear not, for I am with you; be not dismayed, for I am Your God. I will strengthen you. Yes, I will help you, I will uphold you with My righteous right hand." Isaiah 41:10

365 of them What was I thinking? I had just committed to writing daily devotions using my faith stories as the theme for my new Web site. Where would I get 365 stories about my life as a Christian? I remembered my son's warning, "Mom, time passes so quickly. Make sure you have at least two to three months of devotions ready before you start so you won't always be under the gun." Here I was with only one month's devotions ready, just 335 more to go. What was I going to do?

One by one "All right, Lord," I prayed fervently, "It's just You and me. I am going to calmly write at least one devotion per day until I can't possibly think of another thing to write." And so I began to write the devotions for the month of January. Now, I was writing devotions for July. Praise God from whom all blessings flow.

For your consideration How richly God has blessed me in this ministry of writing daily devotions based on my faith. Because of God's promises to be with us and support us, we are free to accomplish our goals according to His will…one step at a time.

A time to reflect What overwhelming goal do I need to let God direct me one step at a time?

Prayers for our brothers and sisters in Christ Those who are faced with a task that seems impossible.

July 19

I Corinthians 12:12-19

Freedom to Be Gifted

As each one has received a gift, minister it to one another, as good stewards of the manifold grace of God. 1 Peter 4:10

My gifts As I read the devotion from *I Peter 4:10*, I began to rethink the ways in which I was using the gifts God had given me, and the impact they had on others. I started with my profession as a career consultant. The words of the vice president of the company I consulted for came to mind, "Wanda, anytime we get an executive whose self-esteem has been crushed as a result of his being unemployed, we make sure we give that client to you." Maybe this was a special gift God had given me. Maybe my little part was important. My clients needed help. I am glad God chose me.

For your consideration Are you wondering how to identify your talents? Ask a friend, a family member, your pastor, your coworker, your classmate, your neighbor, "What would you say are my special talents?" Be sure to have a well-sharpened pencil and lots of paper. You might be amazed at their responses. Next, speak with God and ask Him for the wisdom, faith, love and direction so you can get busy really putting your special talents to work. Someone is waiting for the gifts you have to give. We can choose to recognize our gifts and to share them or sit by and marvel at the gifts of others. What will you choose?

A time to reflect How will I put to use the special gifts God has given me? When will I start?

Prayers for our brothers and sisters in Christ Those who feel they don't have any special gifts.

July 20

Freedom to Act like a Child

"Assuredly I say unto you, whoever does not receive the kingdom of God as a little child will by no means enter it." Mark 10:15

The contentment How excited we parents get, anticipating the look on our young children's faces as they open the gift we purchased at the toy store. We wait with cameras poised. We know that we had better get that first shot as the gift is unwrapped; soon the attention turns from the toy to the box it came in. If left to their own devices, young children would play contentedly with those things around them, the pots and pans, the spatulas and wooden spoons and, of course, the plastic containers found in most kitchen cabinets.

For your consideration If we could remember to act like children, we would then be free to receive God's Word with a child-like trust and put God's Word into action with a child's simple acceptance. We could be content while enjoying the ordinary things with which God surrounds us, like watching a brilliant sunset with a friend, experiencing God's love and constancy in the never-failing sunrise, reveling in the freshness of an afternoon shower, marveling at the majesty and power of Him who created the crash of the waves as the tide comes in…or the look of pure love and trust as a child lifts his or her arms to be picked up and held. In a society that offers us endless opportunities for "adult entertainment," we have the freedom to act like children and enjoy God's provisions.

A time to reflect When is the last time I enjoyed the nature God created?

Prayers for our brothers and sisters in Christ Children around the world.

July 21

James 1:19-25

Freedom to Be Voice Activated

But be doers of the word, and not hearers only, deceiving your-selves. James 1:22

Sitting around Since I am technologically challenged, the new voice-activated system sat in my office for weeks as I waited for the right time to tackle the installation. And then our daughter, son-in-law and grandson came to celebrate Easter with us. Our son-in-law is a computer whiz and loves figuring out programs, so he readily agreed to install the system for me. "At last!" I thought.

Do what you are told! The program had provided a lengthy section for the user to read so that the program could become accustomed to my voice. But no matter how fast or how slow I read, or whether I read with lots of expression or little expression, when I finished the section, the program still didn't do what I told it to do. After spending about an hour trying to get it to work, I set it aside with not-too- kind words for the designer.

For your consideration God, our spiritual voice activator, speaks to us, trying to tell us how to get through life. HE has carefully laid it out for us in His Word. My experience has been that the Bible never malfunctions. How much simpler and happier we would be if we just listened and did what God told us to do. But first we have to open the box— oops—Book, read it and follow the instructions...or not. God gives us the freedom to choose.

A time to reflect Would God rate me as a responsive, voice-activated believer or a malfunctioning one?

Prayers for our brothers and sisters in Christ Computer programmers.

Freedom to Soar

But those who wait on the Lord shall renew their strength; they shall mount up with wings like eagles, they shall run and not be weary, they shall walk and not faint. Isaiah 40:31

Rise above Some of the television talk shows feature adults who attribute their difficulties in life to a horrible childhood. Each time I watched one of those shows, I thought of my friend Laura. Her childhood would certainly have qualified her as a guest on one of those shows, yet her adult life makes her ineligible. Somehow my friend was able to rise above the less than loving environment in which she grew up.

Soaring The potbellied pig, rabbits, ducks, turtles, cats and dogs all found a haven in my friend's house. In the midst of raising a child as a single mom, teaching full-time at a local university, and getting her doctorate, she always found time to help others. People needing a place for the holidays were always welcome at her table filled to overflowing with food, love and laughter. My friend didn't just rise above her childhood environment, she soared!

For your consideration I don't know what makes one person rise, no, *soar* above negative circumstances while others struggle toward a happiness that seems forever destined to elude them. My friend is living proof that believing and acting on God's promise of support, no matter what our circumstances, provides the updraft that allows us to soar! God has set us free. We too can soar!

A time to reflect How can I use God's promises of love and support to soar above negative circumstances in my life?

Prayers for our brothers and sisters in Christ Adults dealing with the ravages of growing up in troubled homes.

Freedom to Reap

And let us not grow weary while doing good, for in due season we shall reap if we do not lose heart. Galatians 6:9

Ripples of kindness Pat was a New Yorker. She was introduced to us (medical center administrators of a west coast HMO) as an expert in preventive health programs for people who lived on the street. The culture gap was instantly apparent. Her personality intimidated me, but I had to try to help. I asked to have lunch with her to learn more about her program, which was already receiving rave reviews by the community. Slowly I began talking about the culture of our organization. I offered my assistance. She eagerly accepted.

Harvests of kindness It was now a year later. My severance package from an unjust termination was huge, but my self-esteem was almost nonexistent. Then I received a call from Pat. "Wanda, I am writing a grant to fund a job-readiness training program. I thought you would be the perfect person to develop and teach it." Who would have believed that I would reap infinitely more kindness from Pat than I had sown?

For your consideration In today's Scripture, the apostle Paul encouraged the Christians to persevere in their efforts to do good works. Sometimes we don't get to see the benefit of our efforts. However, sometimes we are blessed to see those we have helped go on to help others. And sometimes the help we have given them comes full circle in our time of need.

A time to reflect How can I reenergize myself spiritually so I can continue the good works God has called me to do?

Prayers for our brothers and sisters in Christ Unlikely friends.

Freedom to Enjoy God with Us

Behold, the virgin shall be with child, and bear a Son, and they shall call His name Immanuel, which is translated, "God with us." Matthew 1:23

Ups and Downs What would you say are the most exciting days of your life? The memory might be of college graduation, a wedding, the birth of a baby, a promotion, a dream house, the day you were baptized. How about those you would consider the absolute worst: the death of a loved one, a divorce, not getting accepted on the team, loss of a job, health problems? We may look back on our lives as a series of mountaintops and valleys. And generally speaking it is those times when we find it easiest to talk with God. "Please, God, help me out of this horrible situation." Or, "Thank you God, I am so happy!"

For your consideration How easy it is to think of our faith in relation to our mountaintop and valley experiences. In reality, most of our days are ordinary and indistinct in our memories. Yet God is with us during these ordinary days as well. So the question is, will we limit our close relationship to God to certain days or will we choose to seek a close relationship with Him everyday? The choice is ours.

A time to reflect What am I missing by limiting my relationship with God to the highs and lows in my life?

Prayers for our brothers and sisters in Christ Those who only spend time with God when there is a crisis in their lives.

Freedom to Be Passionate

"I know your works, that you are neither cold nor hot. I could wish you were cold or hot." Revelation 3:15

Joining in I marveled at the passion sporting events can bring out in people as my husband and I jumped up and down with friends cheering our favorite Super Bowl team to victory. And too often we watch in horror as spectators, team members and coaches become involved in shouting matches and even physical violence in the "passion" of the game.

How about us? What if God asked, " Where is your passion for Me?" We have no hesitation about passionately discussing our favorite team…anywhere. So what happens to all that passion as we sit quietly in our pews on Sunday morning? What happens to us when we are asked to pray out loud? What happens to us when our beliefs seem to be trampled by society's "live and let live" creed? Where is our passion for God?

For your consideration In today's Scripture, the apostle Paul was upset with the believers whose actions indicated they were neither hot nor cold regarding their Christianity. In *Matthew 28:18-20* Jesus spoke to His disciples calling us to make disciples of all the nations! How can we get others to join the kingdom of God if we aren't all that excited about being members ourselves? We can be passionate or we can be lukewarm. God may not like our choice, but He gives us the freedom to choose.

A time to reflect If I asked friends and family to name three things they see me being really passionate about, would my faith in God make the list?

Prayers for our brothers and sisters in Christ Sports figures who are passionate about God.

July 26

Psalm 51:1-2,10-12

Freedom to Enjoy a New Day

Through the Lord's mercies we are not consumed, because His compassions fail not. They are new every morning; great is Your faithfulness. Lamentations 3:22-23

I need a break The dark winter mornings remind me of the times I return to wallow in my own guilt. Yes, I had asked God to forgive me. Yes, I believed He not only forgave me but also forgot about my mistakes. Why then couldn't I forgive myself? Some of the mistakes I have made in my life resurface in my memory again and again.

I knew that! It dawned on me with the brightness of a summer morning. What does God say about confessing our sins? "If we confess our sins, He is faithful and just to forgive us our sins and to cleanse us from all unrighteousness" *I John 1:9.* How many Sundays had I not claimed that Scripture for myself because I automatically said the words without hearing the message? Perhaps we need to read this Scripture more often to keep reminding and reassuring ourselves that God has forgiven us and forgotten about it and therefore we should do the same?

For your consideration It is so easy to remain in the darkness of self-recrimination. And in doing so we lose precious time and energy we could be devoting to positive, fulfilling, Christ-centered thoughts and actions. *I John 1:9* is an ever-present reminder that we are free. Free to experience His forgiveness and enjoy the beautiful sunrise that heralds each new and wonderful day.

A time to reflect What does forgiving myself free me to do?

Prayers for our brothers and sisters in Christ Those who need help in forgiving themselves so they can move on.

July 27

Freedom to Make a Difference

And she said to them, 'Get to the mountain, lest the pursuers meet you. Hide there three days, until the pursuers have returned. Afterward you may go your way." Joshua 2:16

People who encourage Think of the people who have made a difference in your life, people whose influence or intervention has significantly changed your life. My thoughts go back to a gentleman who was an accomplished organist. He was seated in the congregation while I played a very difficult selection by Bach. After the service was over, he came up to give me support because I had not played the selection well. I will never forget his words, "Select an arrangement that is fairly easy for you to master note-wise and then focus on the fun stuff that turns it into music." His kind words had an extraordinary affect on the way I selected, practiced and played music from that moment on.

For your consideration Rahab is a good example of God using an ordinary person to accomplish extraordinary work. Joshua had sent two men to spy on the city of Jericho. They hid in the house of the prostitute Rahab. When the king heard about it, he sent word to Rahab to turn them over. Rahab decided to protect the spies. She chose to follow God and let Him turn her into someone extraordinary. God gives us a choice as well. We can choose to let God use us as ordinary people to accomplish extraordinary work. Which will you choose when God calls you: ordinary or extraordinary?

A time to reflect What keeps me from being extraordinary?

Prayers for our brothers and sisters in Christ Those who allow God to use them in extraordinary ways.

July 28

Deuteronomy 6:1-9

Freedom to Tell Our Children Faith Stories

"And these words which I command you today shall be in your heart. You shall teach them diligently to your children, and shall talk of them when you sit in your house, when you walk by the way, when you lie down, and when you rise up." Deuteronomy 6:6-7

Faith stories Telling "faith stories" helped me teach my children about their heritage as members of the family of God. My daughter was having a difficult time. It was the perfect opportunity for me to remind her of a faith story about how she ran out of gas. She had walked almost a mile toward a gas station when a man pulled alongside of her and offered to give her a ride. "Mom, I was so tired. I really wanted to get in that car. Just as I was about to open the door, I heard a voice saying, 'You don't need this ride. You can make it.' Suddenly my feet didn't hurt. I thanked the man and resumed walking. Mom, I know God sent my guardian angel to protect me then, and He will protect me and look out for me now."

For your consideration As believers, our lives are one continuous example of God's love. We are responsible for teaching our children God's Word from the Bible and its practical application in their lives. When we share our stories of faith with our children, we are making His Word come alive for them. It's your choice.

A time to reflect What will you tell your children about God's role in your everyday life?

Prayers for our brothers and sisters in Christ Homes in which God is mentioned only on Sunday *or* not at all.

July 29

Hebrews 5:12-14

Freedom to Grow Up!

For though by this time you ought to be teachers, you need some-
one to teach you again the first principles of the oracles of God;
and you have come to need milk and not solid food. Hebrews 5:12

Faith babies Can you imagine packing your first grader's lunch with jars of baby food? When, faith-wise, do we graduate from baby food to adult food? At what point should we be "old" enough in the faith to start spoon-feeding others? When should we be considered "adult believers"? I don't mean our chronological age, I mean our spiritual age. Is it when we can go to our Bible for answers to a challenge in our day rather than another person? Or perhaps when we can share the message of salvation with someone. Maybe it is when we are called in a crisis because it is known that we are strong in our faith?

For your consideration The people in today's Scripture had spent enough time being taught about living Christ-like lives that they should have been ready to teach others. Instead they were being scolded because the way in which they were living their lives indicated that they needed to "grow up!" We as believers have been freed to grow up spiritually through Bible study and meditation, prayer, and the practical application of our faith in our everyday lives. As we practice our faith, we gain the experience and the skills to graduate from "faith babies" to "faith adults." We are free to "grow up."

A time to reflect Would my brothers and sisters in Christ describe me as a "faith baby" or "faith adult"?

Prayers for our brothers and sisters in Christ Faith adults who are called in a crisis.

July 30

John 1:35-49

Freedom to Come and See

He said to them, "Come and see." John 1:39

You'd think I'd learn My eating habits are horrible. I know all about the healthy food groups I should include in my diet each day. I know the benefits my body derives from those brief episodes when I eat a balanced diet. And I have experienced time and time again the sensation of being literally "sick" of fast food and junk food.

So tantalizing As often as I venture into the fast food and junk food arena, I always return to a balanced diet because I know it is good for me. And yet even though I am well aware of the damage unhealthy diets can have on my body, I am lured time and time again by the tantalizing pictures, the graphic commercials, and remembered tastes.

For your consideration It continues to amaze and delight me when Jesus calls me to His Word time and time again, saying, "Come and see." And each time, I find new messages of love, comfort, direction, and hope in those old familiar Scriptures. His Word is always good, always personalized to our needs, and always available. Although we may turn to the world again and again for that which we know is harmful to us, Jesus stands permanently at the door to our hearts with His age-old message that is fresher than the news found in any morning newspaper, saying, "Come and see." What will you have today, the world or The Word? Come and see! You are free to choose.

A time to reflect What will I choose today, junk food or spiritual food?

Prayers for our brothers and sisters in Christ Those who suffer from eating disorders.

Freedom to Be a Pathfinder

But beware lest somehow this liberty of yours become a stumbling block to those who are weak." I Corinthians 8:9

Another option My husband and I invited a new couple to our traditional New Year's Eve party. After they had been offered the standard nonalcoholic beverages (including a nonalcoholic egg nog that never fails to elicit requests for my "secret" recipe), the husband said, "My wife is a recovering alcoholic and we debated whether we should come. We are sure glad we did. Everyone is having such a great time, including us!"

For your consideration Would you believe that in all the ways I have provided another path regarding alcohol, the responses have been positive? Many times we are reluctant to take another path against something in our society that hurts others. But what if someone who feels as we do, but is not quite as strong, is just waiting for us to take another path so they can join us? What do you see in your neighborhood, your school, the workplace or your home that is calling you to take another path in His Name? And then make sure there is plenty of room on your "path" for you to be joined by those who are just waiting for a Christ-like role model. We are free to offer another path when we know something has the ability to hurts others.

A time to reflect What are the risks involved if I take another path? What are the risks to me spiritually if I don't?

Prayers for our brothers and sisters in Christ Children and their families who are victims of alcohol-related deaths.

My Journal
July: Freedoms I Have Chosen

Insights: What freedoms do I want to claim?

Challenges: What do I need to do to incorporate the freedoms I have chosen into my everyday life? When will I start?

What are the ten top blessings I received from God this month?

1.

2.

3.

4.

5.

6.

7.

8.

9.

10.

Answered Prayers

Introduction to August Devotions

Job's Standards and our Sons

"There was a man in the land of Uz, whose name was Job; and that man was blameless and upright, and one who feared God and shunned evil. And seven sons and three daughters were born to him." Job 1:1

We have sons too In April, I focused on the women of the Bible and the lessons their faith stories could help us teach our daughters and other young girls in the faith. It occurred to me we could use some help from the men of the Bible in raising our sons and other young boys in the faith. I became excited about getting to know our biblical brothers in Christ through their faith stories.

Setting the standard The standards Job had set for himself seem appropriate standards for us to include in raising our young boys in Christ. Those standards would also help us to explore the faith stories of other brothers in Christ we find in the Bible and the lessons they have to teach our young boys.

These should work When I reread chapter 31, I found these standards within the Scriptures: Love Faith Commitment Trust Purity Justice Generosity Compassion Forgiveness Obedience Integrity Perseverance Courage Wisdom Respect Self-Control Peace Responsibility Accountability Loyalty Leadership. What a great list of attributes to instill in our young boys. What a challenging job! I am glad we can find help from our biblical brothers in Christ and their faith stories.

I pray that together we can explore faith stories of our biblical brothers in Christ that help us raise our young boys so they can grow up with a solid foundation in God and learn to apply their faith in their everyday lives.

Your sister in Christ,
Wanda Scott Bledsoe

Joseph's Lesson: "Do the Right Thing"

"Then Joseph her husband, being a just man, and not wanting to make her a public example, was minded to put her away secretly."
Matthew 1:19

Another law Everyone's sympathy would have been with Joseph. Yet even before an angel of the Lord appeared to Joseph to confirm the story Mary had told him, Scripture tells us Joseph acted with integrity. Joseph, as a just man, decided to divorce Mary quietly and secretly so as not to make a spectacle of her.

More than integrity As we reread the age-old story of Jesus' birth as told in Luke, chapters 1 and 2, Joseph's obedience to God is evident. He took Mary as his wife and named her son Jesus *Luke 2:21*. Joseph did that and more. He honored his commitment as a father when He protected the baby Jesus from King Herod *Matthew 2:13*, taught Jesus his carpentry trade, and saw to His religious upbringing *Luke 2:29-42*.

Joseph's message on integrity Joseph, our brother in Christ, has much to teach our young boys about quietly doing what is right even though it may cause them embarrassment by their peers. Joseph's story of faith would also remind them of the importance of obeying God. And lastly in a society where too often the message is, "Do just enough to get by," Joseph stands as a shining role model for doing more than we are asked to do and more than others expect of us.

A question for the guys How can I use Joseph's lesson on integrity to help a boy grow up to be a man of integrity?

Prayers for our brothers in Christ Those who are stepfathers.

"You Can Run but You Cannot Hide"

"Now the word of the Lord came to Jonah the son of Amittai, saying, 'Arise, go to Nineveh, that great city, and cry out against it; for their wickedness has come up before Me." Jonah 1:1

You must be kidding! God wanted Jonah to go to the city of Nineveh to give the people an important message. Jonah didn't want to go and boarded a ship going in the opposite direction. God wouldn't let Jonah escape. Jonah was tossed off the boat and ended up in the stomach of a whale. During this quality think-time that God had provided, Jonah decided he had better ask for God's forgiveness.

That did it! This time when God freed Jonah and told him to go to Nineveh, Jonah went. Jonah delivered God's message to repent or be destroyed. The people immediately obeyed so God decided to save them. Was Jonah ever upset! Jonah had wanted to see the people destroyed for their disobedience, yet God had forgiven them...as He had forgiven Jonah.

Jonah's message on obedience I think Jonah would tell our young boys to be obedient to their parents and to God; it is easier, saves time and is less painful. Jonah might also refer our them to the verse in the Lord's prayer that talks about forgiveness *Matthew 6:12.* What wonderful lessons on obedience and forgiveness our biblical brother Jonah has for our young boys.

A question for the guys If I read the story of Jonah with one of the young boys in my family, what lessons in life might he learn?

Prayers for our brothers in Christ Young boys who want to go their own way.

II Samuel 12:1-15

Nathan's Lesson: "You Are Wrong!"

"So David's anger was greatly aroused against the man. Then Nathan said to David, 'You are the man!'" II Samuel 12:5, 7

The verdict God had a harsh message for the prophet Nathan to deliver to King David. Nathan started by telling the King a story. It seems that there were two men, one rich and one poor. When the rich man begin preparing a meal for his guest, instead of killing one of the sheep from his extensive flock, he took the only sheep the poor man had. King David was outraged and declared that the rich man should die. Then the prophet Nathan delivered God's message, "You are the man!" What had King David done that God should be so angry with him? He had committed adultery with Bathsheba, now pregnant with his child, and he had Bathsheba's husband, a soldier, put in a position in battle that assured his death. God did not take David's life, but there were painful consequences.

Nathan's message on courage "When God places you in a position to speak out against someone because you know what they are doing is wrong, be courageous and speak out! When you encourage others to stop doing that which is wrong, you can make your community a better place to live. When you encourage others to stop doing that which is wrong and tell them of God's unconditional love…you just might gain a brother in Christ.

A question for the guys How could I use Nathan's message to teach a young boy about courage in pointing out wrongdoing, regardless of who is doing it?

Prayers for our brothers in Christ Young men who are courageous role models for Christ.

August 4

II Samuel 12:13-24

David's Lesson: "I Did It"

So David said to Nathan, "I have sinned against the Lord."
II Samuel 12:13

His response God was angry with King David and sent His prophet Nathan to tell him so. David's response was immediate, "I have sinned against the Lord" (verse 13). I can remember what I called the delayed response when I caught my son doing something wrong. Before he arrived at the "I was wrong" or "I'm sorry" part, he, with his smart, creative self, first tried other options: "When you look at it like this, it really isn't my fault." However, I knew that as a responsible parent, I had to help my son learn to admit when he was wrong, realize the consequences, and above all learn from his mistakes.

David's message on accountability David was a great King, made even greater in my mind each time I read his immediate response, "I have sinned against the Lord." David's lesson to our boys might be this: "We are human and we make mistakes. God is merciful and forgives us when we admit we are wrong and ask His forgiveness. If we lose our "attitude" and move on, God can help us do great things. But first we have to admit we are wrong. That is the first step and maybe the most important one." This is excellent advice from a great king to our young boys.

A question for the guys How can I use David's faith story to teach a young boy about taking responsibility for his actions and realizing that every action has a consequence?

Prayers for our brothers in Christ Young boys who tend to blame others for their mistakes.

Nehemiah's Lesson: "Show Some Respect"

"Then the king said to me (the queen also sitting beside him),
'How long will your journey be? And when will you return? So it
pleased the king to send me; and I set him a time.'" Nehemiah 2:6

May I have permission? While Nehemiah's vision was to rebuild the walls of Jerusalem to honor God, he also held a high position under King Artaxerxes. I was surprised as I read the account of how Nehemiah first prayed, and then humbly asked the king for permission to go and rebuild Jerusalem's city walls.

Just one more thing After Nehemiah had secured the king's permission, he asked for letters from the king to the governors of the different regions through which he would need to travel. The king granted that request as well. As a result, Nehemiah was assured that he would be able to leave with the king's full knowledge, approval and support. As an added benefit he also could travel safely and quickly through the regions without costly and potentially dangerous delays.

Nehemiah's message on leadership Nehemiah might have these words of advice for our young boys: "Showing respect for authority, asking permission, and giving those in authority an opportunity to help, goes a long way to ensuring the success of any project." In a society where lack of respect for those in charge seems commonplace, Nehemiah's leadership and respect for authority makes him an excellent role model for our young boys.

A question for the guys What would a young boy in my family gain by learning to work well under supervision?

Prayers for our brothers in Christ Young boys who have just been hired for their first jobs.

Nehemiah's Second Lesson:
"Making It Work by Working Together"

"Beyond the Horse Gate the priests made repairs, each in front of his own house." Nehemiah 3:28

A huge undertaking Nehemiah had been given permission by the king to rebuild the walls of Jerusalem. The problem was that Nehemiah had no idea how he was going to build a huge wall with no money, no skills and no labor force.

The group's interest Jerusalem was a large city with many gates that provided defense positions. Government business and merchant sales were conducted there as well. Rebuilding the city walls and gates was not only a security priority, but also important to the overall economy.

The individual's interest Nehemiah had the priests repair the wall in front of the temple and the citizens repair the wall in front of their own houses. Nehemiah knew that while working for the good of the group, individuals respond best to a project when their own interests are also being met.

Nehemiah's message Nehemiah might have these additional words of wisdom: "Young boys, I hope you are able to see what huge projects you can take on by using teamwork. It is important that you make sure each person sees the big picture…what it will mean for the group, as well as the little picture…how it will benefit him or her. And most importantly, pray to God first, just to make sure you are on the right track."

A question for the guys How can I make use of Nehemiah's lesson to help me teach a young boy to be an effective supervisor, project manager or volunteer coordinator?

Prayers for our brothers in Christ Young men who supervise others in volunteer operations.

Hosea's Lesson: "Try! Try! Try Again!"

"I will betroth you to Me forever; Yes, I will betroth you to Me in righteousness and justice, in loving kindness and mercy; I will betroth you to Me in faithfulness, and you shall know the Lord."
Hosea 2:19-20

Hurtful behavior God chose a wife for His prophet, Hosea, that He knew would be unfaithful in her marriage. We can see how upset God was with the Israelites and their unfaithful behavior in chapter 2:1-13. Yet even as God admonished Hosea to take his unfaithful wife back, so God in His compassion and mercy took the Israelites back. God proclaimed His willingness to try again and again to get His people to be faithful.

Hosea's message on perseverance Hosea's advice to our young boys might be: "In an age where anything that is too difficult is perhaps not worth doing, and anything or anyone that becomes uninteresting to us is often discarded in our ongoing pursuit of personal excitement and satisfaction, *don't give up!* God modeled perseverance for me and for you as He took the unfaithful Israelites back time and time again. Work hard on relationships that are important to you. And don't forget compassion. God is compassionate with us as we should be with others. If we don't want God to give up on us, we can't give up on others." Hosea's actions speak volumes, by which our young boys can learn about keeping the commitments they make.

A question for the guys How can I use Hosea's faith story to help a young boy develop lasting relationships?

Prayers for our brothers in Christ Young men who need encouragement to use compassion, forgiveness and perseverance in their marriages.

Jacob's Lesson: "The Boomerang!"

"Therefore, whatever you want men to do to you, do also to them, for this is the Law and the Prophets." Matthew 7:12

Full circle The boomerang is a curved piece of wood used as a weapon by Australian aborigines. Its design resembles that of the wings of an airplane. When it is properly thrown, it returns to the thrower.

Jacob's boomerang Esau hated his brother, Jacob, because of Jacob's deception that took away Esau's birthright and his father's blessing. Esau vowed to kill Jacob, so Jacob ran away. While Jacob was on this journey, he met Rachel, the daughter of Laban, and fell in love with her. Jacob had to work seven years for Rachel's father before he was allowed to marry her. When the seven years were up, Rachel's father consented to the marriage, but substituted Leah, Rachel's older sister. Jacob was distraught. He had been tricked!

Jacob's message on trustworthiness Perhaps Jacob would talk with our young boys about being trustworthy in a world full of deceit. He might use some common sayings to make his point, "What goes around, comes around." Or he might just refer them to their Bibles, Matthew 7:12, and advise them to do to others only that which they would want others to do to them. And then he might ask them, "How might my life have been different if I had been trustworthy instead of the mastermind of deceit?"

A question for the guys Who can I point to as a trustworthy male role model for a young boy in my family?

Prayers for our brothers in Christ Young boys who think they can get ahead using deception and trickery.

Jonathan's Lesson: "Friends Forever!"

Then Jonathan said to David, "Go in peace, since we have both sworn in the name of the Lord, saying, May the Lord be between you and me, and between your descendants and my descendants, forever." I Samuel 20:42

Choosing sides Jonathan had a big problem. His father, King Saul, had developed a paranoid distrust and hatred toward his best friend, David. It soon became evident to both David and Jonathan that King Saul was planning to kill David. David was worried. How could he trust his friend not to betray him to his father?

Loyal and wise Jonathan reassured David of his loyalty. God gave Jonathan the wisdom he needed to (1) try to convince his father that David was no threat to him, (2) keep David out of his father's sight, hoping that his father would change his mind about killing David, and (3) warn David by a prearranged signal to run when it became clear that nothing could be done to keep the king from seeking David's life.

Jonathan's message on loyalty The complexities of human relationships can sometimes present us with conflicting loyalties. Jonathan's message to our young boys seems to be, "When we focus first on our commitment to God then in His mercy He gives us the wisdom to know to whom we should be loyal as well as how we should express our loyalty," a great lesson for our young boys.

A question for the guys How can I help a young boy struggling with loyalty issues in his relationships with parents and friends?

Prayers for our brothers in Christ Young boys struggling to remain loyal to a friend who is unpopular with their parents.

August 10

Joshua's Lesson: "Your Choice, My Choice"

*"One man of you shall chase a thousand, for the Lord your God
is He who fights for you, as He promised you. Therefore take
careful heed to yourselves, that you love the Lord your God."*
Joshua 23:10,11

Amazing things Moses had chosen Joshua to take over and lead the
Israelites into the Promised Land. What could God do for Joshua to
help establish him as a leader? How about parting the waters, not of
the Red Sea as He did for Moses, but the Jordan River at flood stage.
God told Joshua He would part the waters so the priests carrying
the ark of the covenant and the twelve tribes of Israel could cross
safely over onto dry land. Joshua obeyed God and became known as
a brilliant military strategist (chapter 6).

Joshua's message on trust and obedience Joshua's message to our
young boys might be: "God gave you parents to help you learn to
love Him and to help you learn the important lessons in life. Listen
to your parents. Trust that they know what is best for you. Have
faith that when you obey them, things will go well for you." Joshua's
last message is an important one. Just before his death, he told the
people, "Choose for yourselves this day whom you will serve. But as
for me and my household, we will serve the Lord" *Joshua 24:15*.

A question for the guys What actions can I take as a parent that show
the young boys in my family that I am obedient to God and trustworthy?

Prayers for our brothers in Christ Young boys who feel they cannot
trust their parents.

August 11

Absalom's Lesson:
"My Father Let Me Get Away with Murder"

"Then Absalom sent spies throughout all the tribes of Israel, say-ing, As soon as you hear the sound of the trumpet, then you shall say, 'Absalom reigns in Hebron!'" II Samuel 15:10

No discipline! Absalom had it all: wealth, power and good looks. However, Absalom lacked self-discipline. Absalom plotted his revenge against his half-brother, Amnon, for raping their sister by arranging to have Amnon killed. When Absalom decided he should have his father King David's throne, he merely began using trickery and deceit to take it. When that didn't work, he plotted to have his father killed. The end was tragic. Everyone lost. Absalom was killed by his father's soldiers. David lost two sons and, for all intents and purposes, a daughter as well. No happy ending here.

Absalom's message on discipline Perhaps Absalom would tell our young boys who are chafing at the rules, structure and discipline meted out by their fathers with love and compassion, that they are indeed blessed. Perhaps he would wonder how his life might have turned out differently if only his father had helped him and his brothers develop some much needed self-control. Our young boys need loving fathers to set limits, hold them accountable for their actions, punish with love and compassion, and model a Christ-like life. Absalom and his father learned harsh lessons. Perhaps their story can help ensure that our young boys and their fathers profit from Absalom and David's mistakes.

A question for the guys How can I teach my son self-control?

Prayers for our brothers in Christ Young boys who want their fathers to say no when it is appropriate.

Moses' Lesson: "What My Pride and Temper Cost Me"

"Speak to that rock before their eyes and it will pour out its water." Numbers 20:8

Speak, not strike! God's instructions to Moses were clear. He was to speak to the rock and God would cause water to flow out of it so that the complaining Israelites might have water to drink. But Moses, in his frustration with the people, called them rebels and then struck the rock not once but twice! The Lord issued a punishment to Moses that was immediate and severe. Moses would not be allowed to lead the Israelites into the Promised Land.

Moses' message on anger Perhaps Moses would point to his disobedience in following God's specific directions and his display of temper and say, "My anger cost me a lot. For years and years I had done a great job of leading these people to the Promised Land. And now because of a few seconds of temper and failure to follow God's instructions to the letter, I will not be permitted to complete my mission." Perhaps Moses would add that nothing good comes from acting in anger and further that hitting is never an acceptable solution to a frustrating situation. In a society where our young boys encounter much that would anger them and provoke them to violence, Moses' lesson on anger is a critical one to share with them.

A question for the guys If a young boy looked to me as an example in dealing with frustration and anger in a Christ-like manner, would God think the young boy had made a good choice?

Prayers for our brothers in Christ Young boys who express their frustration through acts of violence.

Daniel's Lesson: "The Secret Is in the Action"

"Now when Daniel knew that the writing was signed, he went home. And in his upper room, with his windows open toward Jerusalem, he knelt down on his knees three times that day, and prayed and gave thanks before his God, as was his custom since early days." Daniel 6:10

Popularity and jealousy Daniel was admired by King Darius and as a result developed enemies. They persuaded King Darius to issue a law, forbidding anyone in his kingdom to pray to *any* god, punishable by death. They knew Daniel would ignore the king's law. Daniel kept praying and was thrown into the lions' den but an angel of the Lord kept him safe. The king was so overjoyed to see Daniel still alive that he ordered everyone in his kingdom to worship Daniel's God.

Daniel's message on leadership Perhaps Daniel would tell our young boys, "It is not so much what you *say* that leads others to God, but what you *do*." Daniel might encourage them to make sure their daily actions were heard loud and clear as a witness to their faith in God. Daniel was a disciple for the Lord by his actions. Our young boys can be disciples of God too. It all depends on their actions. How did Daniel convert a king and his kingdom to God? The answer is a lifetime of actions that spoke of Daniel's consistent and persevering faith.

A question for the guys What actions can I take as an adult Christian to help a young boy develop perseverance and consistency in his prayer life?

Prayers for our brothers in Christ Young boys who have never seen an adult family member pray.

August 14

Shadrach, Meshach, and Abednego's Lesson: "Garbage In...Garbage Out!"

"Or do you not know that your body is the temple of the Holy Spirit who is in you, whom you have from God, and you are not your own? For you were bought at a price; therefore glorify God in your body and in your spirit, which are God's." I Corinthians 6:19-20

This is a test! Daniel and his three friends, Shadrach, Meshach and Abednego, knew the important part a healthy diet played in their overall well-being. They knew they could not eat the rich food served in the king's palace. So Daniel went to the steward in charge and promised that if after ten days, Daniel and his three friends didn't look healthier and think smarter than the boys on the special diet, then they would begin eating the special diet as well.

A message from four friends about our bodies At the end of the trial period, the results were clear. The healthy diet resulted in healthy minds and bodies that were far superior to those on the king's special diet. Perhaps Daniel and his friends would remind our young boys that what they put into their bodies and minds affects how they look, think and act. They might even use the contemporary expression, "garbage in...garbage out," when our young boys are tempted to experiment with drugs, alcohol and sex.

A question for the guys How can I use today's message to help a young boy make Christ-like choices about what he puts into his mind and body?

Prayers for our brothers in Christ Young boys who are trying to decide whether or not to experiment with alcohol, drugs, or sex.

August 15

Meshach, Shadrach, and Abednego's Lesson No. 2: "No Ifs!"

"If that is the case, our God whom we serve is able to deliver us from the burning fiery furnace, and He will deliver us from you hand, O king." Daniel 3:17

Not so perfect King Nebuchadnezzar was furious after being told about Meshach, Shadrach, and Abednego's refusal to bow down and worship the golden idol the king had ordered made in his own image. His anger increased when the three friends told him they wouldn't bow down even though he threatened to throw them into a fiery furnace. And they said they would continue to worship their God, even if God didn't rescue them. The three friends didn't bow down *and* they didn't die in the fiery furnace. As a result the king accepted the God of Meshach and his friends for himself and for all who lived under the king's jurisdiction.

Meshach and his friends' message on faith Our society would have our boys believe that loyalty is conditional. *"If* you do this, *then* I will support you, love you, stand up for you, and be your friend." Meshach and his friends' faith was not based on God's performance. Just because we are Christians, professing a love for God, doesn't mean we are exempt from the pains we may find in life. Meshach's message might be, "Young boys, unconditional faith is believing in God, no matter what."

A question for the guys How can I use the challenges I have faced in life with God's help to reinforce today's lesson to a young boy in my family?

Prayers for our brothers in Christ Young boys who are trying to bargain with God.

August 16

King Nebuchadnezzar's Lesson: "You Work for Me!"

Nebuchadnezzar spoke, saying, "Blessed be the God of Shadrach, Meshach, and Abednego, who sent His Angel and delivered His servants who trusted in Him, and they have frustrated the king's word, and yielded their bodies, that they should not serve nor worship any god except their own God!" Daniel 3:28

Valued... *if* King Nebuchadnezzar valued his three Israelite captives: Shadrach, Meshach, and Abednego. Yet, when the king had a golden idol built in his image and ordered everyone to bow down and worship it, he expected the three Israelites to obey. They refused to worship anyone but God. The king then gave them an ultimatum: worship the idol or be thrown into a fiery furnace to die. The king also issued them a challenge: "Who is the god who will deliver you from my hands?" God answered the king's challenge and the three Israelites were saved.

King Nebuchadnezzar's message on choices Perhaps the king would say, "You can't win if you try to serve God *and* work for someone whose business practices are against God's laws!" There are too many people today who would lure our young boys to work for them with promises of "easy money." Perhaps the king would caution our young boys to carefully consider what their prospective employer stands for, and if he or she deserves their loyalty and respect before they say, "Yes, I will work for you."

A question for the guys What message does King Nebuchadnezzar have for our young boys about choosing the people they work for?

Prayers for our brothers in Christ Young boys who are being enticed to sell drugs.

August 17

Gideon's Lesson: "God's Power"

And the Lord said to Gideon, "The people who are with you are too many for Me to give the Midianites in to their hands, lest Israel claim glory for itself against Me, saying, 'My own hand has saved me.'" Judges 7:2

God's choice God chose Gideon, a most unlikely warrior, to defeat the mighty Midianites. First God had Gideon reduce his army from 32,000 to 300! Then God had Gideon equip his army with trumpets and jars with torches in them. Surrounding the camp, at Gideon's signal, they blew their trumpets, broke the pitchers, and held their torches high as they cried, "The sword of the Lord and of Gideon!" (verse 20). In the confusion, the enemy turned on itself. Not one blow was struck by Gideon's small army!

Cousin Leslie My cousin Leslie is also one of God's unlikely warriors. He has been retired for many years, yet Sunday mornings find him surrounded by rambunctious little boys who need and love having a male role model teach them about Christ and how to live Christ-like lives. Perhaps we would have chosen a youth minister for those young boys, but God chose Cousin Leslie. And Cousin Leslie was obedient to God's call.

Gideon's message on God-Power Perhaps Gideon's message to our young boys might be: "When the job is huge and God gives you less than enough to work with, don't worry. When you are successful, everyone will be reminded that God Reigns!"

A question for the guys How can I use today's message to help me teach a young boy about the power of God?

Prayers for our brothers in Christ Young boys who need a "Cousin Leslie."

August 18

Jeremiah's Lesson: "I Am Only A Child"

Then said I: "Ah, Lord God! Behold, I cannot speak, for I am a youth." Jeremiah 1:6

"I'm too young!" **"Not by MY standards"** When the Lord appointed Jeremiah to deliver a harsh message to a sinful nation, He wasn't concerned about Jeremiah's young age, or his inexperience as a public speaker. The Lord merely reassured Jeremiah not to be afraid, that He would be with him.

If you say so Jeremiah obviously decided to trust God and be obedient to His plan. Jeremiah did confront the nation's leaders and the people with God's message. Did they listen? No, but Jeremiah kept following God's orders. How discouraged he must have felt when his admonitions were ignored and the great city of Jerusalem fell. How frightened he must have been when his life was threatened because of his unpopular predictions. Yet Jeremiah remained faithful, serving God for over forty years.

Jeremiah's message on being used Perhaps Jeremiah's message to our young boys might be: "You are never too young to be used as God's messenger. When we are messengers for God, we may not get any thanks for the job we do. Just the opposite—we may be laughed at, left out, and even threatened. But if you are faithful, obedient and trusting, when God calls you to stand up for what is right and speak out against that which is wrong, say "Yes, Lord" even if you are just a little guy. Do your best and trust God to do the rest."

A question for the guys What job is God calling me to do today?

Prayers for our brothers in Christ Young boys trying to do the right thing.

The Younger Brother's Lesson: "Bright Lights"

"And he arose and came to his father. But when he was still a great way off, his father saw him and had compassion, and ran and fell on his neck and kissed him." Luke 15:20

Glitter and glamour "Boring! That's how I would describe my existence working the farm with my father and older brother. I needed some excitement in my life. I thought I could find it in the big city."

What happened? "Too soon my money ran out and with it, my friends. When I got a job feeding pigs so I could eat some of their food I knew I had hit rock bottom."

Admitting I was wrong "I had messed up big time. It was time for me to go back home, admit I was wrong, and ask my father to let me earn my keep."

Heartwarming love "I could hardly believe my eyes. My father was rushing to meet me and calling out for someone to start preparing a feast to celebrate my return."

My big brother "He couldn't understand how our father could celebrate my homecoming. I know I am difficult to love but if he could just forgive as our father had, then I knew with my brother's help, I could be the brother and son my family deserved."

The younger brother's message He might say, "If a family member or friend is hard to love, remember, they are the ones who need your love the most."

A question for the guys How can I be a role model in helping a young boy learn to show love when someone needs his forgiveness?

Prayers for our brothers in Christ Young boys who are estranged from their families.

August 20

The Older Brother's Lesson: "The Hard to Love"

And he said to him, "Son, you are always with me, and all that I have is yours. It was right that we should make merry and be glad, for your brother was dead and is alive again, and was lost and is found." Luke 15:31,32

Bitter love The older brother heard the loud celebration as he returned from working in the field. When he discovered his father was throwing a party for his wayward brother, he was bitter. The father acknowledged the older brother's faithfulness. However the father had been afraid he would never see his young son again. Having him safely back with the family was cause for celebration.

The older brother's message on love He might say, "I lost so much that day my little brother returned: the chance to step in and help my little brother start a new life, and a chance to support my father. And I missed a chance to *receive* the love of my little brother. We all need forgiveness at some time or another. Remember, God forgives us with compassionate love and welcomes us back to Him time and time again. How can we do anything less when someone asks the same of us? Giving and receiving love feels good; holding on to bitterness and anger does not. Trust me, I speak from experience."

A question for the guys How can I be a role model in helping a young boy learn about compassionate love?

Prayers for our brothers in Christ Young boys who have run away from home and would like to return.

The Father's Lesson:
"When You Have Sons of Your Own"

"And the son said to him, 'Father, I have sinned against heaven and in your sight, and am no longer worthy to be called your son.'" Luke 15:21

Against my better judgment "When my younger son told me he was going to leave this boring farm life and go to the city, I wasn't surprised."

As if he were dead "How I missed him as the days passed. While my older son worked by my side in the field as he had always done, I cried in my heart for the younger son, whom I thought I might never see again."

Lost and found "Only another father can imagine my joy as I saw my lost son in the distance. I was so grateful, I couldn't wait to show him how glad I was that he had returned home safe and sound."

A family reunion "Why didn't I see how the celebration would seem to my older son? Of course I could understand his resentment. Here he had never given me the slightest problem and yet the minute his troublesome younger brother returns, I throw a 'Welcome Home' party."

The father's message on unconditional love He might say: "An important part of being a father is to let your responsible children know they are appreciated. *I* certainly didn't take my older son for granted but without showing him my appreciation, it must have seemed that way."

A question for the guys How can I encourage a father to praise his responsible son?

Prayers for our brothers in Christ Young boys whose fathers forget to use words of encouragement, recognition and love.

Brother Joseph's Lesson: "Making Lemonade"

"But while Joseph was there in the prison, the Lord was with him; he showed him kindness and granted him favor in the eyes of the prison warden." Genesis 39:21

A sour deal Joseph's older brothers were so jealous of him that they sold him into slavery. One of Pharaoh's officials purchased him. The Lord blessed Joseph with success in everything he did for his new captor, who soon trusted him with everything he owned.

Made even worse His captor's wife found Joseph very attractive and tried to seduce him. When Joseph refused, the wife told her husband that Joseph had seduced her. Her husband had Joseph immediately thrown into jail.

May I help? While he was in prison, another prisoner had a disturbing dream. Joseph offered to ask God's help in interpreting the man's dream.

Lemonade anyone? Joseph's interpretation proved to be accurate. He requested that the man, upon his release, remember him to Pharaoh in hopes of obtaining his own release. Two years passed before the man followed through on his promise. Joseph was now free.

Joseph's message on attitude "Young boys, I could have been bitter, but I chose the positive route. With God's help you can take the biggest lemon the tree of life may drop on your head, add lots of your own sweet personality, some water, and what do you have? Lemonade you can share with others as a cool refreshing drink."

A question for the guys How can I help a young boy learn to make something good out of a bad situation?

Prayers for our brothers in Christ Young boys who feel betrayed by their families.

Reuben's Lesson: "Crumbling Under Pressure"

And Reuben said to them, "Shed no blood, but cast him into this pit which is in the wilderness, and do not lay a hand on him"— that he might deliver him out of their hands and bring him back to his father. Genesis 37:22

Being the oldest Reuben was the eldest of the ten brothers. They all found their little brother, Joseph, bothersome; he was their father's favorite. Joseph had further alienated himself from his brothers with his recent dream that seemed to place him above his brothers.

An opportunity to lead Joseph had been sent by his father to find his brothers. When his brothers saw him approaching, they decided they would kill him. Reuben, thinking to save Joseph, told his brothers to put him into a nearby well, but not to hurt him. Reuben left, planning to return later and rescue Joseph.

Preventing a disaster Before Reuben could return, his brothers saw traders on their way to Egypt. They decided to sell Joseph to the traders. Reuben returned only to find that Joseph had been sold into slavery.

Reuben's message on being a role model "What an opportunity to be a good role model and help my brothers deal with our pesky little brother in a loving way. But I was not strong enough. My message to you young boys is to be strong, and be courageous for what is right. You just might save your little brother or sister from being hurt."

A question for the guys How can I help a young boy who is jealous of his siblings?

Prayers for our brothers in Christ Young boys who are not accepted by their siblings.

Judah's Lesson: "A Promise Keeper"

Then Judah said, "For your servant became surety for the lad to my father, saying, 'If I do not bring him back to you, then I shall bear the blame before my father forever.'" Genesis 44:32

My promise Joseph's brothers appeared before Joseph (not knowing he was the brother they had sold into slavery years ago) to ask for grain so that they and their families would not starve. Joseph made one brother stay and told the others to go home and bring back Benjamin, the youngest brother. The brothers knew the loss of Joseph had nearly killed their father. So Reuben promised his father that he would keep Benjamin safe, literally swearing on the lives of his own two children.

Time to deliver Joseph continued to taunt his brothers by planting a silver cup in Benjamin's sack. When it was discovered, Joseph declared he would keep Benjamin as his slave. Reuben remained silent. His brother Judah came forward to say he had guaranteed Benjamin's safety to his father and begged Joseph to take him as his slave instead.

Reuben's message on promises "I didn't keep my promise to my father. It was Judah who put his life on the line so my promise to our father could be kept. Perhaps the message I would leave with you is this. Keep your promise even though it may be difficult. You may even be able to help someone else keep a difficult promise."

A question for the guys How can I recognize and encourage the efforts of a young boy who is a promise keeper?

Prayers for our brothers in Christ Boys who keep their word no matter how difficult the situation.

August 25

Brother Joseph's Lesson: "Payback Time"

Then he said: "I am Joseph your brother, whom you sold into Egypt. But now, do not therefore be grieved or angry with your-selves because you sold me here; for God sent me before you to preserve life." Genesis 45:4-5

Slave and ruler Pharaoh believed Joseph's interpretation of Pharaoh's dream of seven years of prosperity followed by seven years of famine and made him ruler so he could prepare for the famine, even though he was still a prisoner.

Caught! Joseph's father sent his brothers to Egypt to buy grain. The brothers did not recognize Joseph, but he recognized them. When Benjamin was caught with a silver cup Joseph had put in his sack of grain, Joseph declared he would keep Benjamin as a slave as his punishment for stealing. Judah begged to take his brother Benjamin's place, fearful that their father would die from grief should he lose yet another son. Joseph was moved to compassion and let his brothers know his true identity.

Family reunion Not only did Joseph forgive his brothers, he told them to return home and bring all the family to live with him so he could provide for them.

Joseph's message on generosity Joseph's message is about turning something meant to harm into something good: "If you find your-self in a difficult spot not of your own choosing, then trust God and just do the best you can where you are. You never know who God is preparing you to help or save."

A question for the guys How can I help a young boy be strong through a difficult time?

Prayers for our brothers in Christ Young boys who have triumphed in the midst of adversity.

August 26

Barnabas' Lesson: "Go and Glow"

"When he came and had seen the grace of God, he was glad, and encouraged them all that with purpose of heart they should continue with the Lord. For he was a good man, full of the Holy Spirit and of faith. And a great many people were added to the Lord." Acts 11:23-24

A special impact Joseph had such a reputation for being an encourager that he was renamed *Barnabas,* which means "Son of Encouragement." Pastor Skip gave a sermon recently on encouragement that made me think about Barnabas. Why can't all of our young boys be Sons of Encouragement? According to Pastor Skip, if we didn't grow up in a home filled with unconditional love where we received lots of encouragement from our parents or others, it becomes very hard to know how to encourage others. Perhaps Barnabas would borrow a few phrases Pastor Skip used in his sermon to help our young boys be better sons of encouragement. Phrases like "Good job," "Great effort," or "What an inspiration you are to me and to others."

Barnabas' message on words of encouragement Barnabas might have young boys note that when you put others in the limelight by expressing your encouragement, you carry a little of that light with you until everywhere you go, you glow. Who knows? You too could end up with a nickname that recognizes your important role as an encourager.

A question for the guys What young boy needs to hear words of encouragement from me? When will I start?

Prayers for our brothers in Christ Ministers and teachers who are encouragers.

August 27

Genesis 25:29-34, 27:30-41

Esau's Lesson: "Immediate Gratification Rules?"

And Esau said, "Look, I am about to die; so what is this birthright to me?" Genesis 25:32

Ongoing deceit Jacob betrayed his brother by deceiving their father, Isaac, into giving Jacob the blessing due Esau, the firstborn. It was a time when Esau's flagrant disregard for his birthright in handing it over to Jacob for a plate of food could have been reversed. When Esau discovered Jacob was now truly and unequivocally the rightful owner of his birthright, Esau became so angry that he decided to kill his brother.

Long-range implications When Jacob found out about his brother's anger and planned to kill him, Jacob was forced to run away from his home for his own safety. Esau, in his need for immediate gratification for food, had paid an enormous price without regard for the long-range implications.

Esau's message on self-control Esau might remind our young boys to stop and think about the long-term consequences of their actions. Perhaps Esau would advise them to reevaluate what is truly important and not worth sacrificing at *any* price. Esau might point to modern day examples where immediate gratification rules and the consequences may last a lifetime...like sexually transmitted diseases, marital infidelity and divorce, and prison sentences for shoplifting. "Hey, guys, exercising self-discipline and self-control helps you retain your self-respect and allows you to have a better life...now and in the future."

A question for the guys What are some ways I can demonstrate self-control to a young boy in my family?

Prayers for our brothers in Christ Young boys sentenced to juvenile detention centers for joy riding; young men sentenced to prison for hijacking cars.

August 28

Thomas' Lesson: "Doubting Is Good"

*So he said to them, "Unless I see in His hands the print of the
nails, and put my finger into the print of the nails, and put my
hand into His side, I will not believe." John 20:25b*

Give me a break Thomas' questioning attitude has earned him the
name, "Doubting Thomas." Down through the years, anyone
expressing doubts about what seems obvious to others may also be
referred to as a "Doubting Thomas." Sophisticated marketing
strategies target our young boys, enticing them to buy products and
embrace lifestyles that corrupt them morally and spiritually. In a
society where our young boys are at risk for betrayal by those we
would assume to be most trustworthy, a questioning attitude might
not only be wise, it might also be necessary.

Thomas' message on faith "God gave you an intelligent mind. Use it
to question for understanding. Taking things at face value may be
dangerous. Our faith does not mean exercising 'blind acceptance.' If
you question in a respectful manner, those who are trustworthy will
be glad to explain, as Christ responded to my doubts. Those who are
angered by your questions or respond with 'just trust me' may not
be trustworthy after all." It would be well for our young boys to
remember that questioning for understanding is a good thing.

A question for the guys How do I respond when young boys question my actions or edicts? Would it be easier to get the results I
desire if I take the time to explain my rationale?

Prayers for our brothers in Christ Those whose response to a young
boy's questions is, "Because I said so" or "Just trust me on this."

August 29

I Corinthians 15:1-7

James' Lesson: "A Guide to Christian Living"

"For even His brothers did not believe in Him." John 7:5

Too close James was the brother of Jesus. Can you imagine growing up with a sibling who claims that he is the real president not only of the United States, but of the whole world? James took the road some of us take today: denial.

Fast forward James now knows the truth, that his brother was indeed the Messiah. When we read the book of James written by him, we see that James chose to put his belief and the lessons he had learned from his brother's teachings into a written record. Now others could read, learn, believe and live in the way his brother Jesus had taught *and* lived.

James' message on responsibility "Guys, if you don't believe, you shouldn't pretend that you do. But once you know the truth about Jesus, don't just listen, act on your beliefs." He might add, "Once I accepted who my brother really was, I knew I had to try to leave something that would be a lasting record for others to read. In the book of James, written by yours truly, it tells you how to live like my brother, Jesus Christ...in only five short chapters. Check it out. I would like to think it is on my brother' 'must read' list for young boys."

A question for the guys What does helping a young boy read and understand the book of James say about my belief in Jesus Christ?

Prayers for our brothers in Christ Those who conduct Bible studies for our young boys.

August 30

Jesus' Lesson: "Be Strong in the Lord"

Jesus said to him, "Away from me, Satan! For it is written: 'Worship the Lord your God, and serve him only.'" Matthew 4:10

Setting the example As a child growing up in a loving but strict family, I was tempted more than a few times to experience aspects of life that my parents in their infinite love and wisdom had forbidden. "They just don't understand. They are adults; they've never gone through what I am going through," I fumed. And now each year as I struggle to meet the challenges of being a wife, mother and grandmother, I realize more and more that my parents knew exactly what I was going through because they had, at one time or another, been there themselves.

Jesus' message on temptation Perhaps Jesus would first have us redouble our efforts to start or strengthen our relationship with Him. Then we can better lead our young boys to an ever-deepening relationship with Christ. The temptations in our young boys' lives are plentiful, sophisticated, enticing…and potentially deadly. What is the answer? Ask them what would Jesus do? Know what He would do and then encourage them to just do it! Of course it helps to believe that He will not allow our young boys to be tempted beyond what they can manage, but will also make a way of escape *1 Corinthians 10:13*. Check it out, guys.

A question for the guys What can I do to help guide a young boy to a deeper relationship with Christ as a protection against the temptations of his world?

Prayers for our brothers in Christ Young boys facing temptations that put them in harm's way.

Another of Jesus' Lessons: "Say NO to Violence"

But Jesus said to him, "Put your sword in its place, for all who draw the sword will perish by the sword." Matthew 26:52

Not on my account Judas stepped forward to kiss Jesus on the cheek, a prearranged signal to make sure the soldiers arrested the right man. The soldiers drew their swords, no doubt anxious to make sure this important prisoner didn't get away. The disciples had to be very tense, fearing for Jesus' safety and their own as well. Simon Peter drew his sword and cut off the ear of one of the men *John 18:10*. In *Luke 22:51*, we read that Jesus showed compassion as he touched the man's ear and healed him.

Jesus' message on peace In an increasingly violent society, nation and world, Jesus reminds our young boys that when they pick up weapons of destruction and decide to use them, they are putting themselves in a position to be killed by those same weapons. Jesus, when attacked, not only refused to participate in the violence, but healed the wound of one of the men anxious to arrest Him. Perhaps this is a very important lesson to share with our young boys. Look at Jesus' example and then say NO to violence. Do as Jesus did, promote peace, not violence. And whenever possible, heal rather than harm. In a war-weary world, this message may need to be a top priority for our young boys…and for us.

A question for the guys How can I help a young boy say no to violence? How can I help him put the phrase, "heal rather than harm" into practice?

Prayers for our brothers in Christ Boys who think carrying weapons to school is cool.

My Journal
August: Job's Standards and Our Young Boys

Insights: What are some lessons I learned from my biblical brothers in Christ that I would like to share with young boys in my family and those in my church?

Challenges: What do I need to do to share the lessons I have learned? When will I start?

What are the ten top blessings I received from God this month?

1.

2.

3.

4.

5.

6.

7.

8.

9.

10.

Answered Prayers

Introduction to September Devotions

Lessons on Living a Christ-like Life

All Scripture is given by inspiration of God, and is profitable for doctrine, for reproof, for correction, for instruction in righteousness, that the man of God may be complete, thoroughly equipped for every good work. II Timothy 3:16-17

Higher education Even in kindergarten, I can remember my mother saying, "When you go to college…" Yet as important as she felt a college degree was, she knew that no college professor or college textbook would be able to teach me the lessons I needed to succeed in life. She knew I would also need lessons in living a Christ-like life. She provided a year-around education for me by taking me each Sunday to Sunday school and church for my *Christian* education.

How to books An online bookstore search indicated the availability of over 32,000 different "How To" book titles. WOW! I am certainly glad my mother taught me that I don't have to wade through 32,000 books to learn how to live a Christ-like life. The Bible is the ultimate sourcebook, *II Timothy 3:16-17*. The Bible provides comfort, *Psalm 46*, and guidance, *Proverbs 6:22-23*. In His Word we find strength, *Isaiah 40:31*. And most importantly, The Bible is the only true sourcebook on God's plan of salvation, *John 3:16-17*. This Scripture, found in the first chapter of *James, verse 22*, "But be doers of the Word, and not hearers only," might sum up this month's lessons on living a Christ-like life.

I pray that these faith-inspired and Scripture-based lessons on life will provide guidance and support for you in your faith journey.

Your sister in Christ,
Wanda Scott Bledsoe

September 1

Hebrews 4:14-16

Learning to Share God's Healing Touch

Let us therefore come boldly to the throne of grace, that we may obtain mercy and find grace to help in time of need. Hebrews 4:16

Peterson's Ointment I associate learning to ride a bike with Peterson's Ointment. When I fell, and in those early days of learning I fell a lot, my father would come outside to make sure I didn't have any broken bones. Then he would gently clean my "owie" and apply Peterson's Ointment with such love and tenderness. What healing powers Peterson's Ointment possessed, I thought.

Maybe not Years later as an adult, my sister was frantically trying to find more of that healing ointment. Finally she called the laboratory that made the product. She told the gentleman who answered that she was willing to pay almost anything to get more. The gentleman laughed and said, "There are so many new products on the market that have infinitely greater healing properties. I will send you what we have left in our lab, but I'm afraid the real healing powers lie in the touch of those who apply it."

Lessons learned in Christ-like living Our heavenly Father touches us with His love, grace and mercy and we too are miraculously healed. His healing touch provides us with forgiveness, consolation, unlimited joy and peace. When we reach out in a Christ-like manner to touch people with our love and compassion, then we too can have the healing properties found in my father's loving touch. It is all in the touch.

Applications of our faith Who needs my healing touch of love and compassion?

Prayers for our brothers and sisters in Christ Those who put bandaids on children's "owies."

September 2

Learning to Recognize His Divine Order

In the beginning God created the heavens and the earth. Genesis 1:1

Chance? Leslie, the youth pastor's wife, and I were talking about the April devotions. "I really need to use these devotions about women of the Bible in a Bible study with teenage girls," I glibly said, knowing I had no such intentions. Leslie chimed right in, "You should talk to Kari. What a bright young lady with such a love of the Lord." My mind started twirling. What an opportunity to work with young girls in such an exciting way.

Happenstance? A week later I was attending a fashion show. As I sat down, I noticed Kari with a few of her friends. I told her I was looking for a young lady to co-lead a special Bible study for teens. Her friends smiled and said, "And that would be *you*, Kari." That was the beginning of a wonderful new relationship with Kari and her unique ability to develop Bible study lessons geared to teens.

Lessons learned in Christ-like living If I didn't believe in Divine Order, my response to Leslie would have been, "I am just too busy." Instead, I agreed to pray about it. *And* when I attended that fashion show only to see Kari there, I recognized it as Divine Order so I said yes and Kari did too. I shudder to think of the special ministry Kari and I would have missed if I did not believed in God's Divine Order.

Applications of our faith How does God's Divine Order work in my life?

Prayers for our brothers and sisters in Christ Those who want to do a better job of recognizing God's place in their everyday lives.

September 3

Hebrews 10:19-25

Learning to Value Family Celebrations

Let us not give up meeting together, as some are in the habit of doing, but let us encourage one another—and the more as you see the Day approaching. Hebrews 10:25

No celebration It was the first time in over 30 years of marriage that we would be without any family for Thanksgiving. My husband talked me into not going to the trouble to cook our traditional Thanksgiving dinner. And why should we brave the crowds we were certain to find in a restaurant? So I reluctantly agreed to spend a quiet Thanksgiving at home.

Never again! When our daughter Shelly called from Seattle to wish us a happy Thanksgiving, she was shocked at the sound in my voice. "Mom, what's wrong?" "Shelly, this has been the worst Thanksgiving. Without family and friends to help us celebrate, I feel as if Thanksgiving Day just passed me by. I will never do this again!"

Lessons learned in Christ-like living As believers we have much to celebrate. When we assemble together each Sunday to sing His praises, read His Scriptures, take Holy Communion, and hear His message, we celebrate our life in Christ Jesus and His perfect love for us. When we come together in His Name to give thanks for His blessings and His forgiveness, our celebration brings us so much more joy and fulfillment than if we tried to celebrate alone…or not at all.

Applications of our faith How can I increase the joy I find in Christ through regular celebrations with His church, the body of Christ?

Prayers for our brothers and sisters in Christ Those who attend church infrequently or not at all.

September 4

Mark 12:41-44

Learning to Paint Pretty Pictures

…Many rich people threw in large amounts. But a poor widow came and put in two very small copper coins, worth only a fraction of a penny. Mark 12:41,42

You must be confused She was pulling a little red wagon, filled with food from her cupboards, through the low-income housing development where she lived. She told me she was giving the food to those she knew who were in need. I listened in disbelief as I remembered the bags of groceries I had dropped by her house a few days ago and the money I had slipped into her pocket for her to spend on herself.

An empty canvas That night I thought about my friend. What if God had given each of us a blank canvas that morning and said, "Paint me a pretty picture." Would my picture be as pretty as hers? Did my face look as radiant as hers? What if our paintings were placed side by side? Whose picture would claim the higher price? I thought I knew the answer.

Lessons learned in Christ-like living God gives us resources to use in caring for His people. Today's Scripture and the story of my friend remind us that it is not about how much we give but where the gifts come from. Some of us give *something* from our wallets and then there are those of us, like my friend, who gave *everything* from her heart.

Applications of our faith What are my motives when I give from the resources God has so abundantly given me?

Prayers for our brothers and sisters in Christ Those who are in need of food and shelter.

Learning to Apply Our Faith; A Wise Investment

"By faith Abraham obeyed when he was called to go out to the place which he would receive as an inheritance. And he went out, not knowing where he was going." Hebrews 11:8

A time for change It was a planning meeting for our upcoming women's retreat. "What will they say when I tell them we are downsizing and selling our house that everyone says is so beautiful we should turn it into a bed-and-breakfast?" Tears filled my eyes and joy flooded my heart as my sisters in Christ pledged their love, prayers and support. Somehow the abyss of not knowing what our next house would be like didn't look so dark and frightening. God provided further assurance as I read *Psalm 81:10*, "I *am* the Lord your God, Who brought you out of the land of Egypt; Open your mouth wide, and I will fill it." And fill it He did with a great new home and wonderful neighbors. Our family and friends think it is just perfect!

Lessons learned in Christ-like living Faith isn't easy to develop or to lean on. It takes time and work. It is an investment in our spiritual lives that has a tremendous return. I called on my faith in God and He provided my sisters in Christ who gave me the loving support I needed. Faith is a wise investment in living a Christ-like life, and it comes with tremendous returns.

Applications of our faith How can I use today's devotion to help me increase my faith?

Prayers for our brothers and sisters in Christ Those who are anxious about major changes they are facing in their lives.

Proverbs 30:1-6

Learning to Leave the Recipe Alone

Every word of God is pure; He is a shield to those who put their trust in Him. Do not add to His words, Lest He rebuke you, and you be found a liar. Proverbs 30:5-6

The recipe My dear Aunt Zelma had this wonderful dinner roll recipe that had been passed down through her family. When I asked her for her recipe, she smiled and gave it to me, happy that someone else in the family would be carrying on the tradition of serving these delectable morsels.

Improvising The first change I made was to use vegetable shortening instead of the lard the recipe called for. This saved a lot of time because I didn't have to heat the lard first and then wait until it was cool enough to keep from killing the yeast. Then...I decided to use the dough to make cinnamon rolls. Yum! Next I resolved to concoct my own glazes; one with concentrated orange juice and another using five different flavorings. Yum! Yum! Then I tried substituting whole-wheat flour for a healthier roll.

Lessons learned in Christ-like living God warns us about trying to "fiddle" with the Bible, His "recipe" for living a Christ-like life. Unlike my experimentations with Aunt Zelma's roll recipe, when we share God's Word with others, we don't have to worry about embellishing it or subtracting from it to make it more or less...anything. HE made His "recipe" for a Christ-like life straightforward, foolproof and perfect!

Applications of our faith How can reading God's Word for myself help ensure that I get the full benefit of His message?

Prayers for our brothers and sisters in Christ Those who translate the Bible into foreign languages.

September 7

Learning about Eyes That Are Bigger Than the Stomach

*Give me neither poverty nor riches—Feed me with the food
allotted to me.* Proverbs 30:8

Mother's point My mother was always teaching us lessons. This one
had to do with greed and discontent. When it came to food, my eyes
were always bigger than my stomach. Mother reminded us that God
provides, and that when we use His resources wisely there is more
than enough to meet our needs. It always amazes me that when I go
home to visit my mother, she puts such tiny portions of food on my
plate. Yet I always feel satisfied and the added bonus is I always lose
weight!

Lessons learned in Christ-like living My mother recognized that the
"eyes that are bigger than the stomach" syndrome could be a dangerous one. Her remedy, go to God's Word and apply it: (1)
Philippians 4:11-12 "I have learned the *secret of being content* in any
and every situation, whether well-fed or hungry, whether living in
plenty or in want." (2) *Philippians 4:6-7* "*Be anxious for nothing,* but
in everything by prayer and supplication, with *thanksgiving,* let your
requests be made known to God; and the *peace of God* which surpasses all understanding will guard your hearts and minds through
Christ Jesus." And finally, *believe His promises, Philippians 4:19* "*And
my God shall supply all your need* according to His riches in glory by
Christ Jesus." God's Word, the perfect remedy for this world's "eyes
that are bigger than the stomach" syndrome.

Applications of our faith What materialistic things of this world am
I overindulging in?

Prayers for our brothers and sisters in Christ Actors and actresses
struggling with substance abuse.

Learning to Leave the Lights of Love On

For I am persuaded that neither death nor life, nor angels nor principalities nor powers, nor things present nor things to come, nor height nor depth, nor any other created thing, shall be able to separate us from the love of God which is in Christ Jesus our Lord. Romans 8:38-39

Conserve, conserve, conserve! Energy crises have caused us who live in southern California to not only turn off our lights but to further conserve energy in other self-sacrificing ways. The penalty for not complying on a voluntary basis is that electricity will become twice as expensive and severely rationed!

God's extravagance Wow! Am I glad God doesn't ration His love *or* make us pay for it. Every once in a while a light bulb will burn out so that when I flip the light switch before entering a dark room in the house, nothing happens. What if God required us to flip a switch to access His love? What if the light of His love was conditional on whether or not I had paid my bill?

Lessons learned in Christ-like living Whenever I am feeling unlovable, I quickly turn to today's Scripture and am reassured that the light of God's love is always on for me...*and* for you. Do the people I love feel nothing can separate them from my love? My answer to that question is usually, "Lord, thank you for reminding me that I still have work to do."

Applications of our faith What do I need to do to show my loved ones that the light of my love is always on?

Prayers for our brothers and sisters in Christ Those who are without electricity because they could not pay their bill.

Learning to Live by Poetry

Then they cried out to the Lord in their trouble, And He delivered them out of their distresses. Psalm 107: 6

??? I don't seem to get the point of most poetry. But the book of Psalms is full of poetry that I *could* understand. This poetry spoke to the hills and valleys in my life and everything in between. In my joy I shouted, "O Lord, our Lord, How excellent is Your name in all the earth" *Psalm 8:1*. Tortured by guilt and longing for forgiveness, *Psalm 32:1* became a balm for my soul, "Blessed is he whose transgressions are forgiven, Whose sin is covered." And when I needed an invincible advocate, I was not disappointed, "Plead my cause, O Lord, with those who strive with me; Fight against those who fight against me" *Psalm 35:1*. As a wife and mother, I sometimes questioned my judgment and I cried out, "Teach me good judgment and knowledge, For I believe Your commandments" *Psalm 119:66*.

His Poetry The Psalmist's poetry became my lament in times of distress, "Be merciful to me, O God, be merciful to me! For my soul trusts in You; And in the shadow of Your wings I will make my refuge, Until these calamities have passed by" *Psalm 57:1*.

Lessons learned in Christ-like living Whether we as God's children express our emotions with a clanging of cymbals or as quiet tinkling brass, I have learned that the Psalms can be poetry for our souls to help us in Christ-like living.

Applications of our faith How can I use the Psalms to bring poetry to the challenges of life?

Prayers for our brothers and sisters in Christ Those who are feeling distressed.

September 10

Proverbs 2:3-12

Learning to Embrace Second Chances

When wisdom enters your heart, and knowledge is pleasant to your soul, Discretion will preserve you; Understanding will keep you... Proverbs 2:10-11

Can you wait? It seemed like I was always asking my precious little girl, Shelly, to "Hold on for a minute," "If you can just wait until…" Between advancing my career and trying to meet the needs of other family members, Shelly was often asked to wait. Her big bright eyes would look at me with such understanding, "It's okay, Mom," she would reply. But it wasn't okay.

That was then Some twenty years have passed and on this, her birthday, I thank her for a second chance…to be available and to give her my undivided attention. Now when she calls, interrupting the furious pounding of my keyboard as I try to meet yet another deadline, and asks as she did as a child, "Mom, are you busy?" I smile, thanking God and Shelly for a second chance. This time I get it right, "I am never too busy for you, sweetheart. It is so good to hear your voice."

Lessons learned in Christ-like living Today's Scripture reminds me that as I too have grown older, I should have become wiser. Learning to live a life in Christ is invigorating and enlightening, especially when it brings with it wisdom and joy. Happy birthday, Shelly. Thank you for giving me a second chance to "wise up to what is really important."

Applications of our faith Where do I need to wise up and embrace the second chance God is presenting to me?

Prayers for our brothers and sisters in Christ Those who want a second chance to repair relationships.

Learning to Live in His Comfort

Yea, though I walk through the valley of the shadow of death, I will fear no evil. For You are with me; Your rod and Your staff, they comfort me. Psalm 23:4

Nightmares Previously my nightmares had been scary but never life threatening. This nightmare was different. It was so real that I knew without a doubt that I was going to die a violent death. In what I thought were the last seconds of my life, I cried out in a loud voice over and over, "I love You, Lord!"

Lifetime comfort I used to think *Psalm 23* was only a psalm of comfort for the grieving. Upon closer examination, I would propose that this psalm be read at infant baptisms, First Communions and anytime in our lives when we feel unsure, afraid or lost. The Twenty-Third Psalm reminds us that in life and in death, God provides assurance, protection and *comfort*.

Lessons learned in Christ-like living Strangely enough, my nightmare had a positive impact. It was reassuring to know that I had come far enough in my Christian journey that at least in my dreams I could face death secure in God's love. My dream encouraged me to work even harder in my relationship with the God so that as I face life or death I can confidently proclaim, "The Lord is my Shepherd, I shall not want" (verse 1). What a comfort. What a blessed assurance.

Applications of our faith How can the Twenty-Third Psalm help me cope with issues regarding death and dying? How can this Scripture help me live in His comfort?

Prayers for our brothers and sisters in Christ Those who are victims of terrorism.

September 12

Judges 4:4-9

Learning to Lead Others

And Barak said to her, "If you will go with me, then I will go; but if you will not go with me, I will not go!"

Mrs. Norman, a natural leader a woman of vision Mrs. Norman, my Girl Scout leader, must have started planning when we began as Brownies in second grade how she would take our troop to Our Cabana, the Girl Scout Retreat in Cuernavaca, Mexico. Year after year we sold Girl Scout cookies and Christmas wrapping paper. I often wonder how she kept track of how much we needed to sell each year to realize our goal. However she did it, the summer before my senior year in college found Mrs. Norman, twelve girls, my mother and another assistant leader traveling from Topeka, Kansas to Mexico City. What a once-in-a-lifetime experience.

Lessons learned in Christ-like living I didn't truly understand Mrs. Norman's vision and commitment until I became a Girl Scout leader. Our troop was together for three years before we disbanded, nothing like the eleven-year commitment of time, money and energy Mrs. Norman made. My mother often said she would follow Mrs. Norman anywhere, places my mother would have never had the courage to go by herself. Mrs. Norman was a true leader who inspired confidence and trust. Thank you, Mrs. Norman. You taught me so many lessons in life. I will never forget you.

Applications of our faith How can I use my leadership skills to help others learn valuable lessons in life?

Prayers for our brothers and sisters in Christ Girl Scout leaders and their assistants.

Romans 9:14-21

Learning to Look in His Mirror

What shall we say then? Is there unrighteousness with God?
Certainly not!" Romans 9:14-15

A little apprehensive I was honored when my physician asked me to sing at her daughter's wedding, but a little apprehensive after hearing "Doc's" belief that the organist was prejudiced. After I finished singing the first selection, the organist gushed, "These selections of mine don't challenge your range one bit." Hmm "I too am an organist," I said. "I love classical music but every once in a while I like to 'pull out all the stops' with some black gospel music." "Oh how wonderful," she replied. "Please play something," she asked. The organist ran to get the pastor so he could listen too. I had been right after all. "Doc" had just imagined the prejudice.

A poor showing During the wedding rehearsal, both the organist and the pastor could be overheard making disparaging remarks against the wedding party that were directly related to their ethnicity. What a "poor showing" from these disciples for Christ *and* what a poor showing from me, for I said nothing. Yes, I was shocked, but I also passed up an opportunity to speak out against a grave injustice. Shame on them and shame on me!

Lessons learned in Christ-like living As an African American, it is easy for me to expect others to speak out against racial prejudice. How grateful I am that God looks at me and sees what I could be. I pray that He will help me do the same when I look at others.

Applications of our faith What incidences of racial discrimination do I need courage to speak out against?

Prayers for our brothers and sisters in Christ Those who work for racial equality.

September 14

John 15:9-17

Learning to Feel Special

You did not choose Me, but I chose you. John 15:16

Not on the playground Athletic prowess has never been a talent of mine. Consequently when teams were chosen for baseball or dodge ball, I was always one of the last to be chosen. There were certain things I did to show my classmates that it didn't matter when I was chosen—like looking bored. In reality, nothing kept me from feeling left out and overlooked. Perhaps it was a similar experience for Leah when Jacob chose her younger sister, Rachel, to marry instead of her.

Lessons learned in Christ-like living Love from our family and friends makes us feel special. And as each of us experience those feelings of being left out and overlooked at some point in our lives, let us remember those in our society for whom those feelings may have become a part of their everyday lives. In living a Christ-like life we are called to reach out and choose those whom society deems to be imperfect, as God reaches out to us in our imperfection. God blessed Leah with sons that made her special in her family. When we see those who are feeling unloved and unwanted, we have the ability to turn our love into actions that say, "You are special." Then they will know we are Christians not by what we say, but by what we do.

Applications of our faith What actions of love can I take to make someone feel special who seems to be left out?

Prayers for our brothers and sisters in Christ Those who need us to help them feel special.

September 15

Learning to Be in This Together

Rejoice with those who rejoice, and weep with those who weep.
Romans 12:15

A difficult time Who could I turn to during this difficult time I was experiencing with a loved one? In the past that could be summed up in one word, "Mother." But now, at eighty-six-plus years of age, wasn't it time for me to stop putting this kind of burden on her shoulders? My heart was heavy, yet I found a certain peace of mind as I cried out to the Lord, and a certain hope as I fervently read His Word.

Ask for help As I related with joy and thanksgiving how God had delivered me, my mother responded with, "Honey, I can appreciate your faith in trusting God to get you through this, but His Word also tells us to bear another's burdens *Galatians 6:2*. You are not meant to go through trials alone."

Lessons learned in Christ-like living When I read of others feeling all alone in the midst of a personal crisis, I wonder two things: (1) Did they know about the Scripture calling for us to bear one another's burdens, and if so (2) When they called out for help, did anyone respond? As Christians striving to live Christ-like lives, we are called to reach out when in need and respond when others are in need. Not sure you are strong enough to help carry another's burdens? Then reread *Philippians 4:13* and be reassured that you are.

Applications of our faith When I hear a cry for help, how will I respond?

Prayers for our brothers and sisters in Christ Those who are in need of a burden bearer.

Hebrews 6:13-20

Learning to Be Firmly Anchored

We have this hope as an anchor of the soul, both sure and steadfast. Hebrews 6:19

Dropping anchor We always enjoyed sailing with our friends Bob and Belva on their boat. Bob dropped anchor. We were surrounded by boats of all sizes and shapes as we settled in for an afternoon of entertainment on Lake Washington.

Drifting Were my eyes deceiving me? Bob had assured us that we had plenty of room to "swing" in the water without hitting or being hit by the surrounding boats that were "swinging" too. Yet, I was sure we were drifting.

Currents My own mind began to drift as I thought of the currents in my life that had the potential of pulling me off course. Sometimes I could see the currents of temptation, things that I knew were wrong or dangerous for me. Other times the current was less obvious, particularly when people I thought were my friends, or people I just knew I could trust, were pulling me along with them. It was at these times that I threw down the anchor of my Christian upbringing, confident that God would not allow me to drift.

Lessons learned in Christ-like living As this world becomes more and more sophisticated in packaging the temptations that continually bombard and threaten our Christ-like way of life, remember we have an anchor in Christ, a great strategy for successful Christ-like living.

Applications of our faith How do I need God to anchor me today?

Prayers for our brothers and sisters in Christ Those who participate in water rescue.

Learning to Do the Illogical

Then your light shall break forth like the morning, Your healing shall spring forth speedily, And your righteousness shall go before you." Isaiah 58:8

My mother's theory My mother must have read today's Scripture when she developed her theory on need. It goes something like this; if you are in need, give to others and that need will be filled. A friend of mine needed food so she shared what food she had with others. I needed a party-like atmosphere on New Year's Eve, so I gave a party that became a tradition we shared with our friends, our children and their friends. My 87-year-old-mother lives alone but is never lonely. She is too busy taking the elderly to their doctor's appointments, visiting the sick and attending elementary school programs that the neighborhood children invite her to. Whenever she feels lonely she finds a lonely person to visit—then she is no longer lonely. See how that works?

Lessons learned in Christ-like living Perhaps we should try putting today's Scripture into action. For example, the next time we are hungry, feed someone. If we are cold, provide warmth for someone. When we feel lonely, be a friend to someone who is alone. Not enough money at the end of the month? Try setting aside the money we return to God in thanks for His many blessings at the *beginning* of each month. When in need, try providing that need for someone else. Make it a strategy you use for successful Christ-like living.

Applications of our faith How will I meet my need by meeting the need in others?

Prayers for our brothers and sisters in Christ Those who share their food with the hungry.

September 18

I Kings 19:9-13

Learning to Communicate

...but the Lord was not in the wind; and after the wind an earthquake, but the Lord was not in the earthquake; and after the earthquake a fire, but the Lord was not in the fire; and after the fire a still small voice. I Kings 19:11b-12

Trying to talk My cell phone needed recharging and it made me think of its predecessor, the CB radio. It was all so awkward. Between the noise and static that made it difficult to hear the other person, and all the hoops I had to go through just to establish a two-way communication, it wasn't very long until I deposited the whole contraption in the trash.

Lessons learned in Christ-like living How glad I am that I can be technologically challenged, yet have no difficulty whatsoever in communicating with God. There is one major hurdle that I still have to overcome. I am struggling to become comfortable with silence, a difficult task given the noisy world in which we live. *Noise, noise, noise, and not a place to think.* Therein lies the challenge. When and where do we go to find the necessary silence needed so we can hear the Lord speak? How frightening to think about all the messages of comfort, guidance, love, correction and assurances from God we may be missing because we cannot find a time and place to be silent so we can hear "a still small voice" **(verse 12)**.

Applications of our faith If God needed fifteen minutes of silence so He could tell me something very important, would He be able to deliver the message?

Prayers for our brothers and sisters in Christ Those who have cell phones and pagers on 24/7.

September 19

I Corinthians 9:24-27

Learning to Have a Purpose, a Plan and a Prize

And everyone who competes for the prize is temperate in all things. Now they do it to obtain a perishable crown, but we for an imperishable crown. I Corinthians 9:25

Cracker Jacks I haven't purchased a box of Cracker Jacks in twenty or thirty years, yet I remember the excitement of anticipating the prize waiting for me at the bottom of the box. I had to eat the whole box of Cracker Jacks first. My plan was a simple one; get somebody to help me eat the Cracker Jacks until nothing was left...but the prize!

Goals and objectives Later in life, I discovered other "prizes" that also required a plan to achieve them. As an administrator of a large medical center, I was required to develop goals and objectives. My performance, which determined raises and promotions, was evaluated based on how well I implemented my plan.

Lessons learned in Christ-like living In today's Scripture, the apostle Paul reminds us that if we are going to be successful in living Christ-like lives, we must have a purpose and a plan. The prize that awaits us is a special *gift* from God. A *purpose* gives us focus, a *plan* provides direction, and the promised *prize* helps us persevere. The Scriptures provide us with all we need to develop our own customized purpose and plan for Christ-like living. The *prize* is waiting there for all of us.

Applications of our faith How will I live my life today so that everyone sees I have my eye on the *prize*?

Prayers for our brothers and sisters in Christ Those who are unaware of God's plan of salvation.

September 20

I Corinthians 9:24-27

Learning to Believe There Is More Than Enough

But his servant said, "What? Shall I set this before one hundred men?" He said again, "Give it to the people, that they may eat; for thus says the Lord: 'They shall eat and have some left over.'"
II Kings 4:43

A blessed event Family reunions are wonderful. My sister and I sat relaxing at long last. Mother chose that moment to plan the meal we would serve when all the relatives stopped by after church before making the five-hour trip home. My sister and I looked at each other in disbelief. The thought of going out Saturday night to purchase more food was too overwhelming to even consider.

More than enough Mother was not a bit worried. "We'll put out the leftovers and it will be more than enough." Later somebody asked my Aunt Helen's granddaughter if she weren't taking a big chance by waiting until near the end to fill her plate. "Aunt Ruby (my mother) said there would be more than enough and I believe her," she responded with conviction.

Lessons learned in Christ-like living When we are presented with an opportunity to serve God and sense that the necessary resources to complete the task are grossly inadequate, remember the faith of an eighty-seven-year-old great-grandmother who fed a multitude of relatives with a few leftovers. She was confident that having asked God's blessing, there would be more than enough.

Applications of our faith How does believing that God supplies us with more than we could ask or think, help me face today's challenges?

Prayers for our brothers and sisters in Christ Those who are afraid to trust God to provide what they need.

September 21

Learning to Work Cheerfully

And whatever you do, do it heartily, as to the Lord and not to men, knowing that from the Lord you will receive the reward of the inheritance; for you serve the Lord Christ. Colossians 3:23

Healing hands My shoulder hurt so much that nothing I did brought any relief. It was then that Pastor Lyle told me about Dr. Mary, the chiropractor with healing hands. She was wonderful! Soon I was claiming her as my California Mother. She giggled, knowing how much I loved my own eighty-eight-year-old mother. These two were cut from the same mold—God-fearing women with steel-like faith and a work ethic sure to leave the faint of heart in the dust.

Cheerful and determined Dr. Mary chattered away about this and that, some of it good and some of it not so good, always finishing with how she and the Lord got through it. At eighty-eight, she was still up at 4 A.M. four days a week preparing for the hour-and-a-half drive to her office. On Thursdays and Saturdays she sees grateful patients like me in her home office. What a woman of faith. What a wonderful Southern California Mother!

Lessons learned in Christ-like living In today's Scripture, Caleb appears as a strong, vibrant man who loves God and fully embraces life...at the magnificent age of eighty-five. How wonderful to be able to look to older Christ-like role models, standing firm in their faith, and leading cheerful, productive Christ-like lives.

Applications of our faith Who is the Dr. Mary in my life?

Prayers for our brothers and sisters in Christ Those who are over eighty years old and struggling with doubts of self-worth.

September 22

John 2:1-1

Learning to Let God Fix It

And when they ran out of wine, the mother of Jesus said to Him, "They have no wine." John 2:3

Stressful times Weddings can be so stressful. As I read today's Scripture, I thought about our daughter Shelly's wedding. It was beautiful in every sense of the word. If I had noticed a shortage of food for our guests, I would never have stopped with, "We have run out of food and half of your guests have not eaten." I would have offered at least two or three possible solutions to the dilemma.

Lessons learned in Christ-like living Instead of just telling our heavenly Father the situation and trusting Him to take care of it in His own way, too often we tell Him our problems and *then* proceed to tell Him how we think He should fix it. Scripture tells us in turning the water into wine, Jesus performed the first miracle of His public ministry. Mary exhibited her great trust in Jesus when she said to the servants, "Whatever He says to you, do it." Mary has an important lesson for us as believers. She tells us as His servants, "Whatever He says to you, do it." What great advice for Christ-like living, "Whatever Jesus says to us, just do it!"

Applications of our faith What would happen if I told Jesus about a current problem and then trusted Him to come up with the solution?

Prayers for our brothers and sisters in Christ Wedding planners and caterers.

Learning to Stick like Glue

Behold, I am coming quickly! Hold fast what you have, that no one may take your crown. Revelation 3:11

The Post-it generation It is almost as if Post-it notes were created for a generation that wants to stick just for awhile until we change our minds or choose something else. Church musicians are hard to find. Why? My best guess is that it takes years of persistent determination, discipline, sacrifice and hard work. My mother took me to my first piano lesson at the age of five. The newness soon wore off and the need to practice daily quickly became a bore. I wanted stop taking piano lessons and try the violin and maybe the flute and definitely ballet. My mother shook her head firmly, "I barely have enough money for piano lessons. You master playing the piano and then we will see about those other interests of yours." She was so wise.

Lessons learned in Christ-like living In today's Scripture, we as believers are encouraged to hold on to what we have...using persistent determination, discipline, sacrifice and hard work in our faith and our service to God. It is a model we can use in our everyday lives and to develop the talents God has given us. What a great model to help us lead a successful life of Christ-like living.

Applications of our faith What kind of glue am I using in my long-term commitments to develop and use the talents God has given me?

Prayers for our brothers and sisters in Christ Young music students who don't like to practice.

September 24

Learning How to Be Strong Enough

And not only that, but we also glory in tribulations, knowing that tribulation produces perseverance; and perseverance, character; and character, hope. Romans 5:3

Never alone My friend sat in our Bible study group softly sharing her personal experience of losing an infant at birth. She acknowledged that I too had lost a child at birth. Why was I so amazed at her story and her pain? Did I think I was the only one to endure this type of misfortune?

Maybe you *are* strong enough During the next few months, my friend began sharing other aspects of her life with me. Where did she get the idea that asking me to pray for her and with her could help lighten the load? Perhaps it was because she had heard me share my own tribulations, ask for prayer and relate how those prayers had been answered. I claimed to be strong in my faith, but it must have been my own trials that made her think, "Perhaps she *is* strong enough...."

Lessons learned in Christ-like living Today's Scripture tells us that tribulations build character. We can't help others be strong and grow stronger if we ourselves have not been made strong through the trials and tribulations of life. Putting our love into action by sharing how our faith helped us endure and grow stronger through our tribulations helps others endure and grow stronger through theirs.

Applications of our faith How can I use the faith of others in their tribulations to help me endure mine?

Prayers for our brothers and sisters in Christ Those in the midst of adversity and those who are willing to share their stories of faith and adversity with them.

September 25

Ephesians 4:29-32

Learning to Live a Life of Appreciation

Do not let any unwholesome talk come out of your mouths, but only what is helpful for building others up according to their needs, that it may benefit those who listen. Ephesians 4:29

Teaching children to appreciate others Seven-year-old Kendall had commented on how stinky garbage was. Our daughter Shelly, who was caring for Kendall and her two-year-old brother Elias, responded with, "Aren't we fortunate to have someone who will pick up our stinky garbage each week? What can we do to let our garbage collector know how much we appreciate him?" Kendall used colored construction paper to make an accordion-like fan to which she glued her drawing of a garbage truck. When the card was opened, the garbage truck popped out. She had then simply written, "Thank You!" Elias helped Shelly make muffins. Our thirteen-month-old grandson, Conner, was to be the taste tester. What a great time they had working on ways to say, "Thank you for doing such a great job."

Excitement and anticipation Shelly, Conner, Kendall and Elias were waiting eagerly at the curb when the garbage collector arrived. Kendall proudly presented the card she had made. Shelly helped Elias give the garbage collector the bag with their homemade muffins, and Conner waved. Everyone felt great! It was another banner day!

Lessons learned in Christ-like living Whether we are on a mountain-top experience or in one of life's valleys, sharing Christ'S love by appreciating others is always guaranteed to make us happy. What a great strategy for living a Christ-like life!

Applications of our faith How can I make this a wonderful day by letting someone know they are appreciated?

Prayers for our brothers and sisters in Christ Those who collect our garbage.

September 26

Hebrews 11:23-29

Learning to Recognize Faith Heroes

By faith they passed through the Red Sea as by dry land, whereas the Egyptians, attempting to do so, were drowned. Hebrews 11:29

What faith! Two of my faith heroes are seniors in high school. Dani is a vibrant young woman, committed to excellence in everything she does…including fighting cancer. Dani's unyielding faith was a source of inspiration for all of us. She showed us a dimpled smile and a firm commitment to her faith when the doctors thought they would be able to save her leg *and* when she found out they couldn't. That same smile and unyielding faith were evident as she sported her chemotherapy-influenced hairstyles, modeled her new prosthesis *and* spoke at our women's retreat!

What commitment! Kari and her family had prepared a gourmet meal for my husband and me when we first moved into the community some eight years ago. Now Kari was a senior in high school. "What a heart for the Lord. What talent," I heard people say of her. It wasn't until Kari and I started a girls' and women's Bible study program and I watched her develop and lead Bible studies, that I got a firsthand look at just how gifted and committed Kari is to her faith.

Lessons learned in Christ-like living The Bible is full of faith heroes, but so are our high schools. Our youth can be a spiritual inspiration for us, and a role model for our faith. Need great role models for Christ-like living? Take a good look among our youth.

Applications of our faith What young person do I know who could help me increase my faith?

Prayers for our brothers and sisters in Christ Teenagers living their faith.

II Corinthians 3:12-18

Learning to Be More Than a Look-Alike

But we all, with unveiled face, beholding as in a mirror the glory of the Lord, are being transformed into the same image from glory to glory, just as by the spirit of the Lord. II Corinthians 3:18

How can it be? We began to see a lot of my father's image and personality very early in our son's life. It wasn't the physical appearance that amazed us so much, for I look like my father too. It was some of the mannerisms that had us wondering, "How can it be?" It would have been easier to understand if our son was around his grandfather on a daily basis, but because we lived so far away, our children saw their grandparents only two or three times a year.

Lessons learned in Christ-like living Yes, our son looked like my father and had some of his mannerisms. However, our son would have had to spend considerable time with him to adopt his grandfather's most important mannerisms, those that made him Christlike. And so it is with us as believers. Yes, we are made in the image of our Lord, but it is only when we commit to spend considerable time in His Word learning about Him, and putting into practice what we have learned, that we come to look *and act* like Him. If we want to pass close inspection as followers of Christ, we have to be more than just "a look- alike."

Applications of our faith Who do I look like?

Prayers for our brothers and sisters in Christ Those who are falsely imprisoned based on mistaken identity.

September 28

Psalm 25:4-12

Learning to Heed the Stop Signs

Show me Your ways, O Lord; Teach me your paths. Psalm 25:4

Help me, please The lady and her seeing-eye dog walked briskly. I looked ahead and noticed the construction trailer and an obstruction that blocked the sidewalk. What would happen now? I slowed the car to watch. A few feet from a gaping hole in the sidewalk with a protective barrier, the seeing-eye dog stopped. She spoke to the dog for a few seconds then she began shouting, "I am blind, I need help?"

Now what? Hearing the loud construction noise, I realized she probably couldn't be heard. I made a quick U-turn and parked my car. I approached the lady, introduced myself and offered to help. After I explained the construction that was blocking the sidewalk and how we could get around it, the lady gave instructions to her seeing-eye dog. He immediately responded to her commands and they easily skirted the obstacle.

Lessons learned in Christ-like living We would do well to use the lady and her seeing-eye dog as models for us in Christ-like living. How wonderful it would be if when we saw an obstacle that God had clearly identified as a danger to Christ-like living, we came to a complete stop and had the patience to wait until it was safe to proceed! Obedience and patience in faith—a great guide for safe Christ-like living.

Applications of our faith What signals do I keep ignoring that could endanger my spiritual journey?

Prayers for our brothers and sisters in Christ Those who are visually impaired, those who train seeing-eye dogs.

September 29

II Corinthians 9:6-1

Learning to Live Abundantly

*But this I say: He who sows sparingly will also reap sparingly,
and he who sows bountifully will also reap bountifully.*
II Corinthians 9:6

Healthier than ever My mother and I had been talking about her health. At eighty-six years of age, I was telling her, it was time that she began to think of slowing down a bit. She had cut buckets and buckets of her peonies and placed them in her twenty-year-old station wagon. She kept this second car because it is big enough to accommodate the elderly with their canes and walkers when she took them to their doctors' appointments. She took the flowers to church and arranged them in vases on the church altar. "How beautiful they look" she said happily. "That's wonderful Mom," I replied. "Surely you have cut all your peonies and now you can rest." "Oh, no, dear, there will soon be even more. You see, cutting them keeps them healthy and sharing them with others keeps me both healthy *and* happy. Soon I will have even more flowers to share."

Lessons learned in Christ-like living During the downturns in the economy, we might have a tendency to hold on to resources as a way to keep them from dwindling so much. Today's Scripture gives us a better strategy. Just imagine God's blessings, like my mother's peonies, rapidly multiplying as we lovingly share them with others. What abundance, what joy, what fragrances abound in Christ-like living.

Applications of our faith How can I live more abundantly by sharing with others the resources God has so graciously given me?

Prayers for our brothers and sisters in Christ Those who visit the sick and shut-in with bouquets of flowers and love.

September 30

Daniel 6:10-2

Learning to Live by His Routine

Now when Daniel knew that the writing was signed, he went home. And in his upper room, with his windows open toward Jerusalem, he knelt down on his knees three times that day, and prayed and gave thanks before his God, as was his custom since early days. Daniel 6:10

Spontaneous living About a year ago I went through a period of "idleness" that seemed to last forever. In my previously busy, hectic schedule I had established a habit of starting my day with Scriptures, prayers of thanksgiving, prayer for others, and prayers for God to help me get ready for the day. During my recovery from surgery and from my "idle period," I depended more than ever on that spiritual routine.

Lessons learned in Christ-like living Without a routine that puts us on "automatic pilot" in doing our daily devotions, they can get bypassed. A friend told me that one morning Martin Luther said, "I have so much to do today, I don't know how I am going to get it all done." So he spent the next four hours in prayer. I can only imagine how productive his day must have been! We might learn a lesson from Martin Luther and make devoting time to God a priority in our day, just as we expect God to make us a priority in His.

Applications of our faith How might my day run more smoothly if I checked God's plans for me first thing each morning through meditation?

Prayers for our brothers and sisters in Christ Those who feel overwhelmed by life.

My Journal
September: Lessons in Christ-like Living

Insights: What are the most important lessons I learned about living a Christ-like life?

Challenges: What do I need to do to incorporate the lessons I have learned into my everyday life? When will I start?

What are the ten top blessings I received from God this month?

1.

2.

3.

4.

5.

6.

7.

8.

9.

10.

Answered Prayers

Introduction to October Devotions

Back to the Basics...
His Parables—Our Practical Application

Therefore I speak to them in parables, because seeing they do not see, and hearing they do not hear, nor do they understand.
Matthew 13:13

The ultimate teacher, Jesus, taught in parables that were designed to present short stories about everyday life that used the strategy of compare and contrast. Jesus wanted to motivate people to listen and think, then decide what implications the message had for them and, lastly, act on that message. In other words, incorporate that message into their everyday lives.

Keeping it surprisingly simple (KISS) The world, now run by high-tech gizmos that easily defy understanding by many of us, can cause us to feel that everything in our lives has to be complicated. " Not so," Jesus might say. If we want to go back to the basics of the kingdom of God, all we have to do is review Jesus' teachings. His use of parables provides us with surprisingly simple instructions on topics that include: Service and Obedience, Prayer, Neighbors, Humility, Wealth, God's Love, Thankfulness, Christ's Return, and God's Values.

Parables for you and for me We read a lot about the value in simplifying one's life. Perhaps you are feeling a need to simplify your life. If so, reading this month's daily devotions about Jesus' Parables on the kingdom of God and my faith stories might inspire you to use His teachings in new ways that simplify and enhance the quality of your spiritual life.

I pray that these faith-inspired and parable-based lessons on God's kingdom will provide guidance and support for you in your faith journey.

Your sister in Christ,
Wanda Scott Bledsoe

October 1

About the Kingdom of God:
All Kinds of Hearts

Still other seed fell on good soil. It came up and yielded a crop, a hundred times more than was sown. Luke 8:8

Parable of the soils As I sat in the audience at my first Mary Kay convention, I thought of today's parable. The women on stage obviously were fertile ground for the Mary Kay message and methodology. They wanted to hear, they understood, they acted based on their understanding and their reward was great. Others were not as serious about the message and so it was easy for them to quit. Still others were determined to do things their way; no firm Mary Kay foundation was laid and at the first disappointment, they too gave up. And others started out brilliantly but couldn't persevere and were choked out by other things that became more of a priority for them.

Parables and life applications My father used to say, "You can lead a horse to water but you can't make him drink." Jesus had an important message to give but He knew a person had to have an open heart to not only hear the message but let it sink deep roots so that the message couldn't be carried away, or die because it didn't get enough water, or choke to death by competing worldly cares and pleasures. The return of those who got it would be one hundred fold. That's putting it mildly when we consider the wondrous gift of salvation.

A question of application What kind of heart do I have for God's message and what kind of return do I expect?

Prayers for our brothers and sisters in Christ Those who install irrigation systems in third-world countries.

October 2

Matthew 13:24-30

About the Kingdom of God:
Weed and Feed

Let both grow together until the harvest. At that time I will tell
the harvesters: First collect the weeds and tie them in bundles to
be burned; then gather the wheat and bring it into my barn.
Matthew 13:30

Parable of the weeds Housing developments are "sprouting" up all around us. The landscaping and maintenance of the public areas amaze me. I watched as these areas were first cleared and then the shrubs, trees and ground cover planted. They grew rapidly but so did the weeds. "Why don't they pull those weeds," I wondered? Once the planted landscaping and the weeds grew to a certain height, the maintenance crew appeared and began weeding the area until it looked beautiful and pristine.

Parables and life applications A common weed in the Holy Land is called "Bearded Darnel." It is both poisonous and difficult to distinguish from the wheat in its early stages of growth. However, when full grown, it is very easy to tell the two apart and therefore easy to separate them. We are planted in the world. We must be careful not to be influenced by the "poisonous weeds" sprouting up all around us but rather sink deep roots of faithful application so that when Jesus Christ, the harvester, comes again we will be gathered to Him. Beware! Both the weeds and the wheat are growing side by side, but not for long.

A question of application How can I make sure I am growing like wheat and not like a weed?

Prayers for our brothers and sisters in Christ Those who work to keep our community landscapes beautiful. Believers facing peer pressure from nonbelievers.

October 3

About the Kingdom of God:
Miracle Grow

Again he said, "What shall we say the kingdom of God is like, or what parable shall we use to describe it? It is like a mustard seed, which is the smallest seed you plant in the ground." Mark 4:30-31

Parable of the mustard seed The message of Christ's love began to come through loud and clear in the new drama ministry and another exciting dimension to our church ministry opened up. Pastor Skip, its founder, was giving people of all ages and backgrounds a chance to present God's message in new and exciting ways. Over the next few years, the number of participants in the drama ministry grew—along with the age range, from four years of age to ninety-four. This tiny seed Pastor Skip planted some three years ago had grown into a wonderful "tree" where sturdy branches supported an ever-growing number of believers sharing their gifts with others in ways that are moving and exhilarating.

Parables and life applications How did Jesus know we would need to be reminded of the power and potential of a mustard seed as we struggle to grow the kingdom of God? How could He have known in the midst of modern-day sod that allows us to have instant lawns, we might need to be encouraged to start with just a seed, nourish it and then patiently watch it grow?

A question of application If Pastor Skip's drama ministry is like a mustard seed, what seed of faith do I need to plant for the Lord, believing it will grow to support others in their faith journey?

Prayers for our brothers and sisters in Christ Those starting new faith-based ministries.

October 4

Luke 13:20-21

About the Kingdom of God:
Little by Little

He told them still another parable: "The kingdom of heaven is like yeast that a woman took and mixed into a large amount of flour until it worked all through the dough." Matthew 13:33

Parable of the yeast My Aunt Zelma made the fluffiest, most delicious dinner rolls I have ever tasted. Each time I made Aunt Zelma's rolls, I looked in amazement at the tablespoon of yeast that would cause the dough to rise. I would make the rolls the night before and place the small mound of dough in the refrigerator. When it was time to make out the rolls, the dough had risen to the top of the bowl letting me know in advance just how light and fluffy these rolls were going to be. Yum!

Parables and life applications Jesus was warning the people of false teachings that would slowly infiltrate the kingdom of heaven. Leaven is always depicted as a type of evil in the Bible (*Exodus 12:15, Matthew 16:6,12, I Corinthians 5:6-8, Galatians 5:9*). It is much too easy to develop a taste for Aunt Zelma's dinner rolls and too easy to develop a taste for the false teachings and behaviors in our society. Today's parable warns us of how easy it is for "leavening agents" to permeate the "bread" of believers. I love Aunt Zelma's rolls and try to limit how many I eat, but when I am dieting, I can't eat them at all! Hmm.

A question of application What kind of "leavening agents" do I need to exclude if I am on a "spiritual diet"?

Prayers for our brothers and sisters in Christ Those who distribute bread to the hungry.

October 5

Matthew 13:44

About the Kingdom of God:
Hidden Treasure

"The kingdom of heaven is like treasure hidden in a field...
Matthew 13:44a

Parable of the treasure "We went on treasure hunts, my father and I. He told me that old empty cans sometimes contained treasure. I always searched for those cans and more often than not when I found them, they held money. Those were special times I shared with my father." Janet Sannipoli, my sister in Christ in our shared Internet ministry (www.hisrosesandthorns.com), tells of this special time with her father. In later years she realized that her father had planted the money in those old cans. The treasure for Janet was not in the old cans with money in them, but in the time spent with her father.

Parables and life applications We come to the kingdom of God in different ways. Perhaps Jesus was speaking about those of us who just stumble upon the Word of God and His wonderful plan of salvation. How frightening that we might have missed it. How amazing that when we do, we recognize the treasure for what it is...something worth giving up all that we are so that we might possess this treasure forever. How wondrous that the treasure becomes even greater when it is shared with others. Hidden treasure: God's gift of salvation available to all.

A question of application How valuable is the message of the gospel to me? What worldly part of me am I willing to give up for this treasure?

Prayers for our brothers and sisters in Christ Those who have stumbled onto the gospel but don't realize the treasure they have found.

October 6

Matthew 13:45,46

About the Kingdom of God:
Precious and Priceless

Again, the kingdom of heaven is like a merchant looking for fine pearls. Matthew 13:45

Parable of the pearl My husband Milton and I have celebrated over 37 years of marriage. I grew up in a Christian home with a loving mother and father and as I prepared to graduate from college, I could hardly wait to start a family of my own. And as my mother had been reminding me since I was in kindergarten, that family started first with a Christian husband. So I had my mother's admonitions in mind when I found a "pearl" of great value, my husband, Milton. I then gave everything that I had to him in exchange for a lifelong commitment together. That was over thirty-seven years ago. So far, so good! Thank you, Lord.

Parables and life applications Perhaps Jesus was talking about those of us who know that the message of salvation is a pearl of great value, and when we find it we are prepared to give everything we have for it. How blessed we are that while we have to spend a lot of money and travel great distances to find some pearls that are known to be priceless, the most priceless one of all is not only close at hand, it is also free for the asking. "Sirs, what must I do to be saved?" So they said, "Believe on the Lord Jesus Christ, and you will be saved" *Acts 17:30-31.*

A question of application How can reading God's Word help me know that the kingdom of God is the precious and priceless pearl I have been looking for?

Prayers for our brothers and sisters in Christ Those who harvest pearls.

October 7

Matthew 13:47-49

About the Kingdom of God:
Gone Fishing

"Once again, the kingdom of heaven is like a net that was let down into the lake and caught all kinds of fish." Matthew 13:47

Parable of the fishing net As a child, I had a few fishing experiences with my father. In one of his fishing lessons, he explained that we didn't use a net because we wanted to catch a certain kind of fish. He also explained that some fish were just not good to eat and we did not want them. As I watched my father throw some fish back and keep others I grew more and more confused. How could he tell which ones were good and which ones were not? They all looked pretty much the same to me. Was I ever glad that I did not have to decide which ones we threw back. Imagine the disappointment at the dinner table if I had kept the wrong fish.

Parables and life applications Perhaps Jesus is using today's parable to remind us of the sorting that will take place between believers and nonbelievers at the time of the Second Advent of Christ. Since I am a believer maybe I can sit back and relax...or maybe I need to start or redouble my efforts at sharing the message of the gospel with nonbelievers. I wouldn't want anyone, including me, to be left behind. How wonderful it is to benefit from believing in Christ now and at His second coming?

A question of application How wide am I willing to cast a net for the kingdom of God?

Prayers for our brothers and sisters in Christ Those who are fishers of men, women, and children.

About the Kingdom of God:
Growing Takes Time

He also said, "This is what the kingdom of God is like. A man scatters seed on the ground. Night and day, whether he sleeps or gets up, the seed sprouts and grows, though he does not know how." Mark 4:26-27

Parable of the wheat Every once in a while, my hair stylist will "misinterpret" my instructions and cut my hair too short. I am grateful that no matter how short my hair is, it always grows back. The question is, "How long will it take?" In the growth process there are growth spurts. We thought our son, Milton Scott, was going to take after his paternal grandfather and end up around 5'6" tall. It seemed like overnight Milton Scott started growing. When he finally stopped growing, he was 6'3" tall.

Parables and life applications We might use the parable of the growing wheat to illustrate our spiritual growth in the kingdom of God. It is a slow process as we learn new information, assimilate it, and then apply it. We may even go through dormant stages in which we seem to plateau, using what we already know but not gaining any new growth. When I look back on my personal spiritual journey I find it requires fertilizer. I would recommend one part Biblical knowledge, one part prayer, and one part faith mixed thoroughly and applied liberally. How goes your spiritual growth?

A question of application What kind of "fertilizer" am I using to enhance my spiritual growth?

Prayers for our brothers and sisters in Christ Those who feel they are stagnant in their faith.

October 9

Matthew 20:1-16

About Service and Obedience:
Not What I Deserve

These men who were hired last worked only one hour," they said,
"and you have made them equal to us who have borne the bur-
den of the work and the heat of the day." Matthew 20:12

Parable of the workers My Uncle Art was a special part of my childhood and I loved him dearly. He was a good man, just not a saved
man. As a child, no matter how much I cajoled, begged and pleaded,
I couldn't get Uncle Art to go to church much less accept Christ.
Part of the many wonderful memories surrounding my marriage
was that of my father and my Uncle Art all dressed up for my wedding. How handsome they looked. A year later, I was at my Uncle
Art's hospital bed. He was dying of cancer and had at last claimed
Christ as his personal Savior. It was then that the parable of the
workers in the vineyard took on a new and wonderful meaning for
me. I had worked faithfully in the vineyard all my life and my Uncle
Art had come at the end of the day, yet the landowner offered both
of us eternal life.

Parables and life applications I do not deserve a reward, I cannot
earn a fair wage and I certainly am not entitled to anything from
God no matter who I am. So what is service about? For me serving
and obeying is a response to our love for Jesus Christ and His love
for us.

A question of application What do my obedience and service say
about my love for God?

Prayers for our brothers and sisters in Christ Those who came to
believe late in life.

October 10

Matthew 25:14-30

About Service And Obedience:
A Good Return on His Investment

Again, it will be like a man going on a journey, who called his servants and entrusted his property to them. To one he gave five talents of money, to another two talents, and to another one talent, each according to his ability. Matthew 25:14-15

Parable of the loaned money I took music lessons from kindergarten through high school. I practiced every day and I applied what I learned by playing at church and accompanying school choirs. As a result, I believe I became skilled in some areas that I have used over the years to serve the Lord. It would be so easy for me to say, "I'll never play again, I'll never sing another note," when I hear master chorales sing great works, or when I play the CDs of talented organists and pianists. Instead of slinking off into the sunset, I remember today's parable and recommit myself to growing the talents God gave me according to the ability He created in me.

Parables and life applications Our job is to share the gospel, "This good news of the kingdom will be preached in all the inhabited earth for a witness to all the nations" *Matthew 24:14*. God has equipped us for this task, each of us according to our ability. Today's Scripture reminds us we need to use and develop that talent so that it produces more today than when we first received it.

A question of application How would God rate me today in terms of the return He expected on His investment?

Prayers for our brothers and sisters in Christ Those who are not using the talents God gave them.

About Service and Obedience:
Job-Readiness Skills

He replied, "I tell you that to everyone who has, more will be given, but as for the one who has nothing, even what he has will be taken away." Luke 19:26

Parable of the nobleman's servants One of the values I tried to instill in my children was that of working without supervision. How happy I was the day I received a phone call from one of my son's customers on his paper route. It seems that not only did he get himself out of bed very early in the morning to deliver the papers, he went above and beyond his job to place this person's paper close to his door so he could retrieve it easily in his wheelchair.

Parables and life applications Jesus has given us our assignments in building and expanding God's kingdom until He returns. No doubt we would be better motivated to complete our assignment and do it well if Jesus were standing over us telling us what to do. But that is not the case. HE gives us free will in our lives. Therefore, we need to work unsupervised, doing the very best job we can with the resources with which He has entrusted us. When He returns we will either (a) be glad to show Him what we have accomplished for Him or (b) hide, knowing our performance has been less than stellar.

A question of application Would God rate me as a worker who (a) needs constant supervision, (b) does only what he or she is told, or (c) works well without supervision, and goes beyond the assignment given?

Prayers for our brothers and sisters in Christ Youth who demonstrate a great work ethic.

About Service and Obedience:
In Order to Get a Raise...

So you also, when you have done everything you were told to do, should say, "We are unworthy servants; we have only done our duty." Luke 17:10

Parable of the servant's role I can't help it, I like praise. So when someone says, "Why do you expect thanks? You were just doing your job," I get a little cranky. Yet, the organization I worked for not only believed in that principle, they structured our raises based on that principle. If your performance met the expectations set forth in your job description, at your performance evaluation, you were marked "satisfactory." You kept your job, but your performance didn't warrant a raise. However, if you met any one of the previously set goal levels, pessimistic (doable with a lot of work) or optimistic (nearly impossible), then your raise was structured accordingly.

Parables and life applications Perhaps Jesus is using the parable today to remind us that we should not feel we are special or better than anyone else because of what we do or how much we do in service to Him. Perhaps today's parable is a message to those of us who stop working at church because we aren't being recognized, or stop helping our neighbor because they don't express their appreciation the way we think they should, or avoid those opportunities to serve that don't give us the visibility we need. Why should we expect any recognition? After all, at best "We have only done our duty" (verse 10).

A question of application How does my need for recognition affect the quality of service I give to the Lord?

Prayers for our brothers and sisters in Christ Those who are overworked but underpaid.

October 13

Luke 11:5-13

About Prayer:
Please say "Yes"

"I tell you, though he will not get up and give him the bread because he is his friend, yet because of the man's boldness he will get up and give him as much as he needs." Luke 11:8

Parable of the friend at midnight I was not allowed to date until my sixteenth birthday. Even when I turned sixteen and could date, my mother continued to shelter me and say "no" when appropriate. And she kept on sheltering me with her rules and regulations as I developed knowledge and wisdom about relationships, sex, love and the part my faith played in all of this. Through her persistence as a strong, loving Christian mom, I was protected until I gained the spiritual knowledge and wisdom I needed to say "yes" or "no" for myself.

Parables and life applications As we were preparing to move from Seattle, Washington to southern California, I persistently and fervently prayed for an opportunity to work full time in Christian ministry. It has taken over eight long years to realize my dream, yet the trials, the spiritual discipline, sometimes even the anguish I have gone through have taken me so much farther along in my spiritual journey. I have been persistent, and God has listened and given me opportunities to grow and prepare. I rejoice in the love and discipline of my mother and my heavenly FATHER. When they say "yes," I know I am truly ready.

A question of application What could God be offering to teach me while I wait for Him to say "yes"?

Prayers for our brothers and sisters in Christ Parents who are persistent with love.

October 14

Luke 18:1-8

About Prayer:
It's Not Fair!

And will not God bring about justice for his chosen ones, who cry out to him day and night? Will He keep putting them off?
Luke 18:7

Parable of the persistent widow I listened in fascination as my husband told about his mother teaching school. She was required to resign when she married. According to my husband, the school district had a rule: If a woman married, she no longer needed that salary to live on because her husband would provide. She was therefore forced to give up her job and her career to another single female teacher or another single or married male teacher. How unfair! I thought of other groups in our society who felt they were being treated unfairly and had persisted in presenting their cases before various courts until justice was achieved.

Parables and life applications The woman in today's parable was also persistent in taking her case to the judge day after day. Although he claimed to fear neither God nor man, the widow's persistence eventually wore him down and he granted her the relief she sought. Today's parable reminds us to persevere in our requests to God to right an injustice. Other Scriptures reinforce the message: "The eyes of the Lord are on the righteous, and His ears are open to their cry. The righteous cry out, and the Lord hears, and delivers them out of all their troubles" *Psalm 34:15-17*.

A question of application How does today's parable help me in my quest to address an injustice in my community?

Prayers for our brothers and sisters in Christ Those who are called to a ministry of social justice.

October 15

Luke 10:25-37

About Neighbors:
Is She My Neighbor?

Which of these three do you think was a neighbor to the man who fell into the hands of robbers? Luke 10:36

Parable of the Good Samaritan The mother of the bride called me the day before her daughter's wedding to say that the bridal salon had not finished the wedding dress and she and her daughter were beginning to panic. I offered to call my friend Velma, who designed and created wedding gowns, to see what she might recommend. The mother of the bride was hesitant. She and her daughter had talked with Velma but decided to use another bridal salon.

Whatever it takes "Wanda, I'll do whatever it takes to help them, including packing up my portable sewing machine and meeting them at the church." I wasn't surprised at Velma's response. The mother of the bride called a bit later to tell me that the dress was ready.

What should I do? The dress looked horrible! The owner of the salon called early the following Monday, wanting to settle the account. "What should I do?" my friend cried. I heard a voice say, "Reach out to her in love." I asked my friend, "How can you reach out in love?" My friend did just that and the owner, having heard all the details, apologized profusely and forgave the outstanding balance.

Parables and life applications The parable of the Good Samaritan had a neighbor in need and a good neighbor indeed. What role would you assign to the mother of the bride, the bridal salon owner and my friend Velma?

A question of application Who needs me to be a Good Samaritan?

Prayers for our brothers and sisters in Christ Those who work in bridal salons.

About Humility:
The Seating Chart

When someone invites you to a wedding feast, do not take the place of honor, for a person more distinguished than you may have been invited. Luke 14:8

Parable of the wedding feast Whenever I invite guests for dinner, I dream of living in a house with a large banquet hall and unlimited seating. Then I wouldn't have to worry about where I am going to seat everyone. Consider my dilemma. The dining room table seats eight. I can crowd two more in but that's it, a total of ten. When my guest list exceeds ten, then the challenge begins. I have a lovely folding table that seats six and a table in the breakfast room that also seats six. When I need all of this seating space I long for a seating chart.

Parables and life applications We jockey for seats at the banquet table for social position, career promotions, and financial status as evidenced by the names and numbers of our job titles, cars, houses, boats, jewelry, clothes, schools and even our churches. Part of our social-position needs can sometimes be reflected in whether or not our guest list is inclusive or exclusive. Jesus reminds us that the kingdom of God is open to everyone, and those who would be last shall be first...maybe not on an exclusive social register but definitely on God's. Which social register is a priority for you?

A question of application What status symbols are important to me? What does my guest list say about how I serve the Lord?

Prayers for our brothers and sisters in Christ Those whose dinner guests include the "haves" *and* the "have nots."

October 17

Luke 18:9-14

About Humility:
Exalted or Humbled

I tell you that this man, rather than the other, went home justi-
fied before God. For everyone who exalts himself will be hum-
bled, and he who humbles himself will be exalted. Luke 18:14

Parable of the proud Pharisee and the corrupt tax collector After
reading today's Scripture, I cautiously examined how I had gone
about serving God. How easy it is, I acknowledged, for my self-con-
fidence to creep into the area of arrogance. I could readily see why
God and others would choose the "humble" me instead of the
"arrogant" me.

Parables and life applications The contrast in the way the self-right-
eous Pharisee and the corrupt tax collector prayed allows us to see
a choice and make a choice about how we will live our lives for
Christ. When we try to serve without humility, our message con-
fuses and sometimes hurts others. I remember playing for a soloist
at a memorial service. We "served" in a small room apart from the
family and friends. "How strange," I thought "to be playing and
singing where no one can see us." What if all of my service for
CHIRST was done so that no one could see me? Hmm. What a big
dose of humbleness I received that day. Today's parable gives us an
opportunity to examine our relationship with God and with those
He has created. Are we serving God with humility or with arrogance?

A question of application How does my family see me, as the
Pharisee or the tax collector?

Prayers for our brothers and sisters in Christ Those who work for
the Internal Revenue Service.

October 18

Luke 12:16-21

About Wealth:
Aunt Betty's Heirlooms

"This is how it will be with anyone who stores up things for him-self but is not rich toward God." Luke 12:21

Parable of the rich fool One day while I was visiting my Aunt Betty, she presented me with a crystal cruet. Aunt Betty didn't say that the cruet was an heirloom, but I decided to make it so. When I told Aunt Betty of my plan, she just smiled in her quiet way and said, "Darlin' this cruet is for you to use, not to put on a shelf. And if it breaks, that is all right too."

True wealth One day I realized that the true heirloom Aunt Betty had passed on to me was not the breakable cruet but her unbreak-able faith: one that had been tried and tested down through the gen-erations of my mother's family. A faith that was worn from use yet shone with a brilliance reflected in the smile on Aunt Betty's face. A faith that only comes from loving and serving God in the hills and valleys of life.

Parables and life applications Jesus tells the parable of the rich man who had enough wealth to last a lifetime. There was only one prob-lem. The man was not going to live to enjoy even one more day of his accumulated wealth. Aunt Betty did not store her material goods. She shared them with others. And she gave me a true wealth. She gave me her unconditional love and her faith in God.

A question of application What would I do with all my possessions if I knew Christ was coming tomorrow?

Prayers for our brothers and sisters in Christ Those who measure their worth by their material possessions.

About Wealth:
She Didn't Come

A certain man was preparing a great banquet and invited many guests. At the time of the banquet he sent his servant to tell those who had been invited, "Come, for everything is now ready." Luke 14:16,17

Parable of the great feast I decided to call a friend I had invited to Thanksgiving dinner to see if perhaps she was on her way. She answered the phone and told me that although we had talked twice about what she was going to bring, because I hadn't called her to tell her the exact time, she had assumed I wasn't having Thanksgiving dinner. I apologized and, knowing that she lived only five minutes away, I asked her to come on over. She laughingly refused, saying she had already gone to the grocery store to buy the items she needed to prepare a Thanksgiving dinner for herself. I was stunned. We sat down to dinner but every once in a while, our guests would catch me starring off into space wondering why my friend had not called, why she had not come.

Parables and life applications I was very hurt that my friend didn't come to Thanksgiving dinner. Just imagine how God must feel when we ignore His invitation to come to His banquet table of salvation? Some of us just ignore the invitation altogether. And some of us accept the invitation but are too busy with the activities of the world to come when He calls.

A question of application What am I making more important than God's call to His banquet table?

Prayers for our brothers and sisters in Christ Those who are trying to decide whether to go to a sporting event or church on Sunday morning.

October 20

About Wealth:
Fraudulent Practices

Give an account of your management, because you cannot be manager any longer. Luke 16:2

Parable of the shrewd manager Our children were in the seventh or eight grade when they happened to see a newspaper article about fraudulent practices that had allegedly occurred at a institution where their father used to work. There was utter silence as they read the entire article and then looked at me, questions already forming. "Mom, Dad used to work there. Why wasn't his name mentioned in this article?" With tears of thanksgiving, I told our children that their father's name was missing because he was never associated with any of the alleged wrongdoing. He valued his reputation so much that he risked his position rather than compromise his integrity. There is not enough money in the world to pay for the light of love and respect my answer brought to our children's eyes.

Parables and life applications If we believe that all the resources are God's, then it gives us a clearer picture of how we are to use those resources. Whether God has given the resources to us directly or to others for us to manage and disperse, His expectation is the same: honesty and integrity. We can choose to use God's resources in ways that are pleasing to Him…or not. Perhaps today's parable helps us determine if the "or not" choices we make constitute fraudulent practices.

A question of application What am I doing with the resources with which God has entrusted me? Could God ever convict me of fraudulent practices?

Prayers for our brothers and sisters in Christ Those who have positions of power in large corporations.

October 21

About God's Love:
The Lost and Found

Suppose one of you has a hundred sheep and loses one of them. Does he not leave the ninety-nine in the open country and go after the lost sheep until he finds it? Luke 15:4

Parable of the lost sheep Our grandson Jay's third grade class was going on a field trip to Sea World. I was accompanying the class as one of three volunteer parents. Jay's teacher, "Mrs. C," informed the children they were not to leave their group for any reason without asking their group leader. When we emerged from an area where the lighting had been very dim, Mrs. C counted the children in her group, as we all did. "One of my children is missing," she stated. Admonishing the rest of her group to stay put, she whirled around to go search for the missing student. We waited anxiously as the minutes passed. Suddenly we spotted Mrs. C. We started cheering as Mrs. C and the student, lost but now found, rejoined us.

Parables and life applications God knows the dangers of our society and searches diligently for us when we stray from Him. God was so concerned for us that "He gave His only begotten Son, that whosoever believes in Him shall not perish but shall have everlasting life" *John 3:16*. We are assured that no matter how lost we become, we can always be found...*if* that is what we really want.

A question of application In what areas of my life have I strayed so far from God that I have become lost?

Prayers for our brothers and sisters in Christ Those who invite lost friends to church.

October 22

Luke 15:8-10

About God's Love:
The Homecoming Gift

And when she finds it, she calls her friends and neighbors
together and says, "Rejoice with me; I have found my lost coin."
Luke 15:9

Parable of the lost coin Our grandson Jay had a collection of cards that he treasured. When Jay discovered that one of the cards was missing, he was inconsolable. "It is just one card," I told him. "You have plenty more to play with." But Jay knew the exact card that was missing and began telling me through teary eyes why it was so important. I found myself down on my knees alongside Jay looking for the missing card. My effort was more than worth it when we found the lost card and Jay threw his arms around me. "Thank you, Oma. We found it!"

Parables and life applications The parable of the lost coin is one of three that Jesus tells one right after the other. Why does He need three very short parables on the same subject? Perhaps it is because the message is so important that it bears repeating and repeating until we get it. We can understand searching diligently for something of value that we have lost. If God is willing to go to such lengths to find us, we must be very valuable. How great is His joy when, though lost to the sins of the world, we present ourselves before Him seeking His forgiveness, grace and mercy. What a day of rejoicing!

A question of application In what areas of my life am I spiritually lost? Who can help me return to the fold?

Prayers for our brothers and sisters in Christ Those who are lost and want to be found.

About God's Love:
The Family Reunion

But while he was still a long way off, his father saw him and was filled with compassion for him; he ran to his son, threw his arms around him and kissed him. Luke 15:20

Parable of the lost son This man I knew, but did not like, was giving his life to Christ. "Who was he fooling?" I thought, "Certainly not me." Many, including our minister, knew this man and his tendency toward poor work habits, constant borrowing from friends to get by, and to add insult to injury, a penchant for believing it was his place to constantly remind his family members of their responsibilities while conveniently ignoring his own. I was incensed and yet there was the minister welcoming him with open arms.

Parables and life applications It wasn't until months later as I reread the parable of the prodigal son that I got the message. The father in the parable was fully aware of his son's shortcomings. Yet when his son returned remorseful and asking for forgiveness, his father welcomed him with open arms. Perhaps the older brother represented the Pharisees...and me. We resented God welcoming someone into His kingdom who was such a blatant sinner, unlike us who worked diligently to serve Him. But wait! I realized that some of my actions place me right alongside the prodigal son. And then I rejoiced that I only have to come before God with remorse and ask His forgiveness, and then I too will be welcomed back into His family with open arms.

A question of application How am I squandering the inheritance God has given me?

Prayers for our brothers and sisters in Christ Those whose self-righteousness makes them critical of others.

About Thankfulness:
He Cancelled My Debt

Two men owed money to a certain moneylender. One owed him five hundred denarii, and the other fifty. Neither of them had the money to pay him back, so he cancelled the debts of both. No which of them will love him more? Luke 7:41-42

Parable of the foreign debts During the children's growing up years, they squabbled like most siblings. And like most siblings, they were fiercely protective when one of them was hurt or in trouble. One could say Shelly was definitely in trouble. Her credit card debt seemed overwhelming to her. On one of Milton Scott's calls home he heard about his sister's financial troubles. "Dad, go into my account and pay off all of Shelly's debt." "Should I set up a payment plan so Shelly can pay you back?" my husband, the banker, asked. "No, Pops. It's not a loan, it's a gift," Milton Scott replied softly.

Parables and life applications Shelly was overwhelmed by her brother's expression of love. Today's parable is a reminder about our need to give the gift of forgiveness. Like that part of the Lord's prayer that says, "Forgive us our debts as we also have forgiven our debtors" *Matthew 6:12*. If I want God to forgive me, I need to always be ready to forgive others. I could always say, "Lord, hold off on forgiving me until I can bring myself to forgive…"—an interesting option when I am finding it difficult to forgive.

A question of application What debt do I need to forgive if I expect God to forgive an even larger one for me?

Prayers for our brothers and sisters in Christ Those who mail credit cards to teenagers.

October 25

Matthew 25:1-13

About Christ's Return:
Survival Kits

Later the others also came. "Sir! Sir!" they said. "Open the door for us!" But he replied, "I tell you the truth, I don't know you." Therefore keep watch, because you do not know the day or the hour. Matthew 25:11-13

Parable of the ten bridesmaids It was the third day after the terrorists' attacks on the Pentagon and the twin towers of the World Trade Center, and my husband was stuck in a hotel in Savanna, Georgia unsure when he would be able to get a flight back home to California. As I read a front-page article referring to people rushing to buy survival kits, I smiled, remembering the motto I had learned as a Girl Scout: Be Prepared. A peace settled over me because I knew I had a survival kit that sustained me through the little hassles of everyday living as well as the life-threatening catastrophes that can take us unawares.

Parables and life applications Two friends who were feeling overwhelmed by "9-11" approached our daughter. "What should I say, Mom?" "Tell them about God's security plan," I replied. Today's parable tells us of Christ's return. It would be nice if we knew when. Some of us buy survival kits in preparation for war, and some for the end of time. In the aftermath of catastrophic disasters, we as believers have a unique opportunity to witness to non-believers so they too can feel secure and be prepared when He comes. What a powerful response to a devastating time.

A question of application How might I use my faith as a survival kit during the challenges of life?

Prayers for our brothers and sisters in Christ Those who feel depressed and overwhelmed by the events of "9-11."

October 26

Luke 12:42-48

About Christ's Return:
He Expects More from Me

"From everyone who has been given much, much will be demanded; and from the one who has been entrusted with much, much more will be asked." Luke 12:48b

Parable of the wise and faithful servants Armed with her bachelor's degree in music and her faith, she enthusiastically described the goals she had set for herself should she be hired as our choir director. I smiled as I remembered her growing up in our church, singing and playing the piano. A young boy I know was composing simple but enchanting melodies at the age of five. His parents used every persuasion imaginable to get him to develop his talent. "How are you going to preserve your music for others to play and for you to remember as you create more and more music? If you learned to read music, that challenge would be solved," I suggested. He looked at me with his soft brown eyes and smiled.

Parables and life applications Not only are we to live Christ-live lives but we are to develop and use the talents He has given us. According to the parable, Christ might expect more from the young man who was born with an extraordinary talent than He would from our college graduate. Today's parable reminds us that God holds us accountable not for how much raw talent we have but for how we develop and use the talent He has given us. With our talent comes responsibility *and* accountability.

A question of application What more should I be doing to develop and use the talents God has given me?

Prayers for our brothers and sisters in Christ Those who are gifted musicians.

October 27

Mark 13:32-37

About Christ's Return:
When Can I Expect You?

Therefore keep watch because you do not know when the owner of the house will come back—whether in the evening, or at midnight, or when the rooster crows, or at dawn. Mark 13:35

Parable of the traveling owner of the house Selling our house was harder than I had expected. To show off our house to its best advantage, I needed to make sure lights were on in every room, soft music playing, and everything clean as a whistle. Wanting to conserve energy, I tried to turn the lights on at the very last minute along with pulling up the shades designed to keep out the bright sun and the tremendous amount of heat it generated. So when the realtors called asking permission to show our house, I would readily consent and then ask, "And about what time can I expect you?" Their two to three hour time range was not exactly what I had in mind.

Parables and life applications Scripture tells us that Jesus will return. The question is, "When?" The answer is, "We don't know." As believers there is a lot for us to do while we wait. We can feed the hungry, visit the sick, provide shelter for the homeless, invite nonbelievers to church, be a friend, lead Bible studies, work with our youth, volunteer in the church office, and pray unceasingly. Keeping busy serving the Lord is a good way to make sure we are awake and ready when He returns.

A question of application What can I do to keep busy serving the Lord until He returns?

Prayers for our brothers and sisters in Christ Those who are selling their house.

About God's Values:
Phony or the Real Deal?

What do you think? There was a man who had two sons. He went to the first and said, 'Son, go and work today in the vineyard." "I will not," he answered, but later he changed his mind and went." Matthew 21:28-29

Parable of the two sons We sat mesmerized as our classmate told us of her exciting life as the daughter of a high-ranking officer in the United States Army. She spoke of foreign countries, servants and exotic foods. Her little brother told us his sister was a phony. We only had to look at our teacher's face to know that there were no foreign countries, servants or exotic foods in her life. She was just a little girl who made up stories to help minimize the trauma of her frequent role as the new girl in class.

Parables and life applications The Israelites in Jesus' day claimed to want to do God's will but their actions indicated otherwise. They were "phonies." The son who at first said no, he wouldn't go work in the vineyard but later changed his mind and went, represented the people who were known to be sinners, but came to believe. Of what use are we to God when we say we will serve Him but instead we serve other gods…like wealth, social status, positional power, beauty and youth to name a few? Today's parable makes me think, "Am I a phony or am I the real deal?"

A question of application How can I make sure God does not see me as a "phony" believer?

Prayers for our brothers and sisters in Christ Those who help protect our country by serving in the military, and children who move frequently as a result.

October 29

Mark 12:1-11

About God's Values:
The Level

Have you not read this Scripture: "The stone which the builders rejected has become the chief cornerstone. This was the Lord's doing, and it is marvelous in our eyes" Mark 12:10

Parable of the wicked tenants I loved watching my father work. He was a carpenter, and the way he used the tools of his trade to build structures seemed almost magical to me. One of his tools fascinated me more than the others. It was his level. "What are you setting on that board, Daddy?" I asked one day as I watched him repairing a section of our garage. "It's a level, Honey. It helps me make sure the other boards I nail onto this board will be nice and straight," he replied. I remembered how hard it was for me to draw a straight line and when I tried to write on paper without lines, inevitably my sentences ran downhill. "What a marvelous tool," I thought.

Parables and life applications Perhaps we can use today's parable to help remind us how important the "Cornerstone" is in our spiritual lives. When we use Jesus and His Word as our Cornerstone, we can make sure our faith is straight and level. Then when the stresses of doubt, adversity, false teachings and life's temptations test our faith, we can remain strong, having built it on a solid foundation. My father used a level to make sure the structures he built were level and solid. We have the Chief Cornerstone, we have the Son of God.

A question of application How can I use my spiritual "level" to shore up my faith?

Prayers for our brothers and sisters in Christ Those who are carpenters.

About God's Values:
You Gotta Go!

So he said to the man who took care of the vineyard, "For three years now I've been coming to look for fruit on this fig tee and haven't found any. Cut it down! Why should it use up the soil?"
Luke 13:7

Parable of the unproductive fig tree I thought about the orange trees on our property. Some of them bore luscious, juicy fruit that my husband, having been born in Kansas and used to buying oranges from the grocery store, loved to pick and eat. However, the orange trees by the swimming pool were a different story. When they produced fruit, the oranges were small and the juice bitter. "You gotta go!" After a couple of seasons of their "poor performance" and low productivity, we had them...removed.

Parables and life applications Today's parable of the unproductive fig tree served as a wake-up call for me. Was God gently admonishing me to review my performance for Him? Was I really using the gifts, talents and resources He had given me to my full potential? How would God rate my productivity as one of His workers? Wait! Not yet, Lord! I know I can do a better job for you using the tools You have given me. Please give me one more chance! Yep! It is time for me to get to work helping to build, nurture and maintain God's kingdom. Hmm, the time for harvest is close at hand and I don't want to hear, "You gotta go!"

A question of application What is my spiritual productivity rating?

Prayers for our brothers and sisters in Christ Those whose jobs are in jeopardy through no fault of their own.

October 31

Matthew 18:21-35

About God's Values:
Mirror, Mirror

Then Peter came to Jesus and asked, "Lord, how many times shall I forgive my brother when he sins against me? Up to seven times?" Jesus answered, "I tell you, not seven times, but seventy-seven times." Matthew 18:21-22

Parable of the unforgiving servant The door slammed and my remorse was immediate. I had done it again; I had lost my temper. After thinking about my behavior, I tiptoed back into the family room. "I'm sorry I lost my temper," I whispered quietly. My husband looked up. "It's OK I understand," he answered softly. I knew I had been forgiven yet again.

Mirror, mirror on the wall My thoughts quickly turned to a person in my life who I felt had hurt me terribly. So many times had I forgiven this person in my heart that I had recently decided enough was enough! Yet Christ reminded me through today's parable that I can find the compassion in my heart to forgive once again as Christ and my husband have forgiven me. "Mirror, mirror on the wall, is there any hope for me at all?"

Parables and life applications Sometimes it seems to me that forgiveness surely must be easier for some than for others. Yet today's parable would remind us that none of us is exempt. The ability to forgive isn't something we inherit. The ability to forgive comes from a heart full of love, Christ's love for us and our love for Him.

A question of application If I were keeping score, would it show that I forgive others more or less than I need God to forgive me?

Prayers for our brothers and sisters in Christ Those who need to repeatedly forgive us.

My Journal
October: Lessons in Applying Parables

Insights: What are some of the parable lessons that seem most appropriate to my life?

Challenges: What do I need to do to incorporate these lessons of parables into my everyday life? When will I start?

What are the ten top blessings I received from God this month?

1.

2.

3.

4.

5.

6.

7.

8.

9.

10.

Answered Prayers

Introduction to November Devotions

Great Recipes for Giving Thanks

Oh, taste and see that the Lord is good; blessed are those who trust in Him. Psalm 34:8

Old traditions and new experiences We always had Thanksgiving dinner at Uncle Art and Aunt Mayme's house where all the traditional dishes were served. When I married Milton, I added Aunt Zelma's homemade rolls to the traditional dishes and oh, what a hit. Then our daughter Shelly added a stuffing recipe she concocted herself. "Taste this and see what you think, Mom," Shelly said as she lifted a spoonful of her dressing to my mouth. I could hardly finish swallowing before I was praising Shelly for her wonderful stuffing that has now been added to our list of "must have" traditional Thanksgiving dishes.

Thanksgiving is a time for remembering and sharing blessings. As I prayed about how to make this month's devotions really special, I thought, "This might be the perfect time to share Thanksgiving favorites: recipes of favorite Thanksgiving dinner dishes, traditions, songs, blessings and prayers. I pray that this will be a time when you remember and share faith stories of your own that help strengthen the relationship you and your family have with Christ *and* with each other. And that in the midst of the challenges that face our world, our nation and us individually, our praise and adoration to You, O Christ, will make this year the best Thanksgiving ever! Taste and see that the Lord is good! Who knows? You may enjoy yourselves so much that you decide to make every day a day of thanksgiving.

Your sister in Christ,
Wanda Scott Bledsoe

My Grandmother's 1-2-3-4 Cake

I will bless the Lord at all times; His praise shall continually be in my mouth. Psalm 34:1

Grandmother Vannie Dulan's 1-2-3-4 Cake

1 c. butter	3 tsp. baking powder
2 c. sugar	⅛ tsp. salt
3 c. flour	1 c. milk
4 eggs	2 tsp. vanilla extract
1 tsp. lemon extract	

Preheat oven to 350°. Cream butter and sugar. Add eggs one at a time. Mix well. Sift together flour, baking powder and salt. Add alternately with milk and flavorings to butter, sugar and egg mixture. Place in well-greased and floured cake or bundt pan. Bake for 45 minutes or until center is firm to touch.

Giving-thanks preparations What an unexpected surprise I received when I called Aunt Helen for a recipe to use in my book. "How about your grandmother's 1-2-3-4 cake recipe?" Aunt Helen responded. It seems as if all five of my aunts and my mother had made my grandmother's 1-2-3-4 cake over the years, passing the recipe down from the oldest sister, my mother, to the youngest, Aunt Helen. And now Aunt Helen had passed the recipe down to me.

"Taste and see that the Lord is good…" "Your grandmother would make this cake as a weekend treat. Your Uncle Curtis, cousin Billy and I got to make the homemade ice cream. I could feel the love in Aunt Helen's heart as she recounted wonderful memories of my grandmother and a childhood long past but never forgotten. It was another chance for me to *taste and see* how truly good God is.

A thought for Thanksgiving What wonderful memory of a deceased loved one can I share with my family?

Prayers of Thanksgiving For grandmothers.

The Appetizer

The poor shall eat and be satisfied; those who seek Him will praise the Lord. Let your heart live forever! Psalm 22:26

Romano Toasts

1 narrow loaf French bread	2 Tbsp. olive oil
1 8 oz pkg. cream cheese	1 c. grated Romano cheese
1 Tbsp. chopped red pepper	¼ tsp. ground cumin
1 can (4 ½ oz) chopped pitted ripe olives	
3 Tbsp. thinly sliced green onions	
¼ c. pimento strips	

Heat broiler. Cut 20 slices of bread, place on baking sheet. Brush bread with oil. Toast until golden, 2-3 minutes. Turn toasts and spread each with rest of ingredients (except pimento strips) that have been well mixed. Dot with pimento. Just before serving, broil until golden brown and bubbly, about 3-4 minutes.

"Taste and see that the Lord is good..." An appetizer is sometimes thought of as the "starter" course. I thought back to the "starter" courses that helped start me on my spiritual journey. My "starter" courses consisted of Shiloh Baptist Church with Sunday school teachers, Bible lessons, and baptism. There were choir directors and special songs, pastors and sermons that touched my heart and motivated me to live a Christ-like life. I thought of the wonderful people in that church who hugged me, and prayed for me, and encouraged me, *and* my mother and father who had made a commitment to get me "started" in God's church even before I was born. I developed quite an appetite from those early courses in God's banquet of life that have kept me eating at God's banquet table.

A thought for Thanksgiving Who needs me to get them started at God's banquet table?

Prayers of Thanksgiving Those who help children grow up in the faith.

Tart and Sweet

How sweet are Your words to my taste, Sweeter than honey to my mouth! Psalm 119:103

Cranberry Relish

16 oz. fresh cranberries	1 navel orange (peel too)
2 c. sugar	½ c. chopped pecans or walnuts

Grind cranberries, orange with peel, and nuts. Mix together with sugar. Chill. Will keep for up to one month. Can also be frozen.

Giving-thanks preparations Canned, jellied cranberry sauce had always been a part of our traditional Thanksgiving dinner. I looked at the recipe for cranberry relish and thought, "This might be different." I hesitantly took a bite of the cranberry relish recipe I had just prepared. A crisp texture was the first thing I noticed, quickly followed by the tartness of the cranberries, oranges and orange peel. My taste buds experienced a "sit up and take notice" call. I couldn't wait to see how our Thanksgiving dinner guests would respond.

"Taste and see that the Lord is good…" The surprise tartness of the cranberry relish made me wonder if *I* sometimes surprised people with a tart response? I stopped right then and there to give thanks for all the people in my life who respond even to my most ridiculous questions or suggestions with a smile. How blessed we are that Jesus' recipe for us is such a simple one: love God first and then others as you would love yourself *Matthew 22:37-39*. I really know I need to give thanks when my friends show that despite my "tartness," they love me anyway! Thanks be to God!

A thought for Thanksgiving Why might God expect me to give *extra* thanks to Him for the wonderful, loving people in my life?

Prayers of Thanksgiving For those who grow cranberries.

November 4

The Best Is Yet to Come

And we know that all things work together for good to those who love God... Romans 8:28

Pecan Cream Cheese Pie

8 oz. pkg. cream cheese
⅓ c. plus ¼ c. sugar
4 eggs
1 tsp. vanilla extract, 1 tsp. coconut extract
1 unbaked pastry shell, 9"

¼ tsp. salt
1¼ c. pecan halves
1 c. dark corn syrup

Beat cream cheese, ⅓ c. sugar, 1 egg, 1 tsp. vanilla extract and salt in small mixing bowl until thick and creamy. Spread mixture in bottom of pastry shell. Sprinkle with pecans. Beat 3 eggs in mixing bowl until blended. Add ¼ c. sugar, corn syrup and 1 tsp coconut extract; blend well. Gently pour mixture over pecans. Bake at 375° for 35-40 minutes until center is firm to the touch.

Giving-thanks preparations I was facing a difficult challenge in my life. Yes, there was a solution but it would require a lot of work, and a lot of emotional energy would need to be expended. And at my age, I just wasn't sure I *had* that much energy. "Oh, Lord. Help me!" I cried.

"Taste and see that the Lord is good..." The next morning I read today's Scripture as part of a devotional. It told me that if my hope was centered in Christ Jesus, then no matter where I was in life, the best was yet to come! Hope filled my heart and I felt wonderfully energized. With Christ's help, I believed the best was yet to come.

A thought for Thanksgiving What new challenges might I attempt if I believed through Christ the best is yet to come?

Prayers of Thanksgiving Those who support us as we make life-changing decisions.

Never Fail Pie Crust

What shall I render to the Lord for all His benefits toward me? I will take up the cup of salvation, and call upon the name of the Lord. Psalm 116:12-13

Never Fail Pie Crust

3 c. flour	1 egg slightly beaten
1½ c. shortening	1 Tbsp. vinegar
1 tsp. salt	5 Tbsp. cold water

Cut in shortening with sifted flour and salt until crumbly. Mix egg, vinegar and water together and add to flour mixture. Bake at 400° for 10 minutes. Makes enough for (2) 9" crusts (top and bottom) and 1 shell.

Giving-thanks preparations For me, the best part of any pie is the crust. It forms a perfect foundation for whatever is added. As you can imagine *or* know if you make piecrusts from scratch, it isn't easy to make the perfect crust. No wonder many of us just go to the freezer section in the grocery store and buy our piecrusts.

"Taste and see that the Lord is good…" Our daughter had asked for my advice. A friend of mine asked, "Does she believe in Christ?" How grateful I was to be able to respond with a resounding "Yes!" My friend nodded his head affirmatively and replied, "That sure makes it easier to support her." My mother makes the best piecrust ever, but she's even better in helping her family and others make Christ the foundation in their lives, a never-fail recipe for life.

A thought for Thanksgiving Am I struggling to create the perfect foundation for my life, or have I decided to use Christ as the best ever, most perfect foundation?

Prayers of Thanksgiving For mothers who lead family members and others to Christ.

I Corinthians 12

It Is All Good!

And the eye cannot say to the hand, "I have no need of you..."
I Corinthians 12:21

Turkey Giblet Gravy

Turkey neck, liver, gizzard, and heart
3 c. pan juices from cooked turkey
1 tsp. garlic powder

½ cup flour
Salt and pepper to taste
½ cup chopped onion

Place uncooked turkey neck and giblets in a saucepan. Add garlic powder, onion and enough water to cover. Boil for 1 hour or until giblets are tender. Remove meat from neck and cut giblets into small cubes. Measure 3 c. liquid from cooked turkey. Bring liquid to a rapid boil. Stir in flour and stock paste for thickening. Add giblets and cook slowly for about 5 minutes. Adjust seasoning and serve hot.

Giving-thanks preparations What would mashed potatoes and dressing be without a generous ladle of giblet gravy? Yes, the tender breast and tantalizing drumstick are important, but we know it takes all of our favorite dishes sharing the table with the turkey *and* the delicious giblet gravy to make the dinner a mouthwatering success.

"Taste and see that the Lord is good..." Today's Scripture reminds us that it also takes a variety of body parts each working together and in cooperation with each other to get the job done. When we take this message to heart, we benefit in three ways. We don't (1) put ourselves down, (2) or others and (3) we don't risk missing the important contributions that others make. Why not spend some time this month sharing with family members their special gifts that are also a blessing to us.

A thought for Thanksgiving What blessings am I missing by not recognizing and valuing gifts family members have to offer?

Prayers of Thanksgiving For loving family members.

November 7

II Corinthians 8:13-15

The Guest List

As it is written, "He who gathered much had nothing left over, and he who gathered little had no lack." II Corinthians 8:15

Mixed Greens

1½ quarts water	2 tsp. garlic powder
1 tsp. crushed red pepper	2 tsp. Lawry's Seasoning Salt
2-3 ham hocks	2 tsp. onion powder
4 lbs. mustard greens	4 lbs. turnip greens

Pour 1½ quarts water in a large pot. Add crushed red pepper and ham hocks and boil for about 1 hour while preparing the greens. Add remaining ingredients to ham hocks in boiling water. Put greens in last. Cover and cook rapidly for about 1 hour or until greens are tender. When done, cut greens with a knife and two-pronged fork while still in pot. Serve with sliced tomatoes, green onions and corn bread.

Giving-thanks preparations As I prepared the appetizer for our Thanksgiving dinner, I thought about my mother feeding extended family with the leftovers from the previous day's family reunion fare. I also thought about a friend in need I discovered wheeling a red wagon loaded with food she had been given, to share with her neighbors in need. And I thought of a coworker I had helped when she was new to our organization only to have her turn around and help me when I was fired by that same organization.

"Taste and see that the Lord is good…" I imagined all of us with our hands cupped to receive God's resources in our need but then tipped downward so those same resources flow uninterrupted to others in their need. I decided right then to invite someone in need for Thanksgiving. Taste and see that the Lord is good…and pass it on!

A thought for Thanksgiving Who can I share the blessing of loving family and friends with this Thanksgiving?

Prayers of Thanksgiving For those who invite others to Thanksgiving dinner.

Share and *Show*

,...when I call to remembrance the genuine faith that is in you, which dwelt first in your grandmother Lois and your mother Eunice, and I am persuaded is in you also. II Timothy 1:5

Lynn Petroff's Wonderful Serbian Dish

Giving-thanks preparations I was expecting to see a special recipe for a Serbian dish. Lynn had written, "The most important aspect of a recipe is in the memories. If there is a dish that needs to be made by showing the steps while working together, *that* recipe is the best. Cultural foods that have come down through the generations are learning experiences in many ways. The wonderful Serbian dish that my mother-in-law taught me to make, as her mother-in-law had taught her to make, is a challenging one. It took more than one try but my daughter-in-law and I worked together creating many priceless memories as we successfully made our wonderful Serbian dish one Father's Day. But of course there is no sense in giving you that recipe without the ability to show how it is done."

"Taste and see that the Lord is good..." My friend Lynn would remind us that perhaps we are missing the best part if we don't take time to *show* another family member how to make a favorite family recipe. Today's Scripture would also have us remember that it is not enough for us to develop and nurture our faith. We must take the time to share and *show* our faith to family members.

A thought for Thanksgiving With whom can I share *and* show a family favorite recipe this Thanksgiving?

Prayers of Thanksgiving For those who take the time to share *and* show a family member the family's faith.

Traditions

Therefore humble yourselves under the mighty hand of God, that He may exalt you in due time. I Peter 5:6

My Daughter Shelly's Mouthwatering Corn Bread Stuffing

8 c. corn bread broken into large pieces

1 c. chopped onion	1 c. chopped celery
2 Tbsp. chopped cilantro	1 c. chopped red pepper
½ tsp. Lawry's Seasoned Salt	1 c. chopped yellow pepper
1 tsp. ground black pepper	1 lb. spicy bulk sausage
½ c. sausage drippings	1 c. turkey broth

Brown sausage and drain. Add melted butter if necessary to make ½ cup sausage drippings. Sauté onion, celery, red and yellow pepper. Remove from heat while vegetables are still crisp. Add seasonings. Combine with corn bread crumbs and cilantro. Add browned sausage and turkey broth. Toss lightly with fork until well mixed. Put in baking dish and bake uncovered at 425° for approximately one hour.

Giving-thanks preparations Before our daughter married and there was another family's Christmas traditions to consider, gifts were opened *early* Christmas morning, even before breakfast, because we just couldn't wait!

"Taste and see that the Lord is good…" My husband and I patiently sat in Ken and Shelly's new home *late* Christmas morning along with Ken's family and watched as huge stockings were passed around. Sharon, Ken's mother, made sure my husband, Milton, and I each had one too! After lots of fun and laughter, Ken's family returned to their own homes to open gifts. Different traditions, yes, but oh so special. I gave thanks for Shelly's extended family *and* mine!

A thought for Thanksgiving What can I do to make the mixing of traditions with my extended family a true blessing for them *and* for me?

Prayers of Thanksgiving For extended families.

November 10

Psalm 37:3-6

The Desires of Her Heart

Delight yourself also in the Lord, and He shall give you the desires of your heart. Psalm 36:34

Candied Yams

6 large sweet potatoes	4 Tbsp. butter
½ tsp. salt	¼ tsp. cinnamon
1 tsp. grated lemon rind	¼ tsp. nutmeg
2 Tbsp. flour	½ c. brown sugar
½ c. white sugar	

1 c. frozen concentrated orange juice (undiluted)

Boil yams in their jackets until tender but firm. Cool, peel and cut into 1½ inch slices. Place in lightly buttered 9" x 13" baking dish. Mix salt, sugars, flour, spices, and lemon rind. Dot with butter and add undiluted orange juice. Bake at 300° about 1 hour or until sauce is bubbly. Add chopped nuts during last 15 minutes if desired.

Giving-thanks preparations "Why did I buy this ring?" I wailed. I offered to give the dinner ring to my mother but it didn't fit. "Mother, would you want to take it home and have it sized for you?" My mother's eyes lit up. "Yes! I have always wanted a dinner ring." "Why didn't you tell us, Mother? You know Pat [my sister] and I would have bought one for you." "I know. But the ring certainly wasn't something I needed so I just never asked."

"Taste and see that the Lord is good..." We both rejoiced at the awesomeness of God, capable of looking into our hearts and granting our desires *even* without us uttering a single word! Praise God from whom all blessings flow...and that is just what Mother and I did!

A thought for Thanksgiving What desires of my heart has God granted me? Did I remember to thank Him?

Prayers of Thanksgiving For mothers and daughters.

November 11

Romans 12:1-5

Square Watermelons

Do not be conformed to this world, but be transformed by the renewing of your mind. Romans 12:2

Aunt Zelma's Refrigerator Rolls

1 c. warm water	2 pkgs. dry yeast
1 c. tap water	3 eggs
1 c. vegetable oil	⅔ c. sugar
1 tsp salt	6 c. flour

Dissolve yeast in 1 c. *lukewarm* water. Mix together 1 c. tap water, vegetable oil, salt, eggs, and sugar. Add dissolved yeast. Mix well. Add flour gradually. Place in greased bowl and place in refrigerator overnight or for at least 4 hours. Let the dough sit at room temperature for one hour. Roll dough and cut into rounds with floured biscuit cutter. Brush tops of rolls with butter. Fold the rolls over and gently press the edges together. Brush tops with butter. Place rolls in rows on a ungreased baking sheet. Let rise in a warm place for one hour. Preheat oven to 325°. Bake for 25-30 minutes or until rolls are golden brown.

Giving-thanks preparations Some farmers in Zentsuji, Japan are growing *square* watermelons because they are much easier to store in the refrigerator! Placing them in tempered-glass cubes while they are still growing gives them their square shape.

"Taste and see that the Lord is good…" It is so easy for me to transform Aunt Zelma's dinner rolls into healthy whole wheat rolls or mouthwatering cinnamon rolls. Just call me "The Transformer." It is just as easy for our minds to conform to the shape of the world. The challenge is to make sure our actions reflect a commitment to living Christ-like lives so we can also be *transformers*.

A thought for Thanksgiving What shape would Christ have me take?

Prayers of Thanksgiving For those who bake bread for the hungry.

November 12

Matthew 22:37-40

Kindness Culprits

...You shall love your neighbor as yourself. Matthew 22:39

Berwin's (Ber's) Figs in Crème De Cacao
1 dozen fresh figs	1 c. sour cream
2 Tbsp. Crème de cacao	½ tsp. cocoa

Wash and drain figs. Peel with sharp knife. Combine sour cream and crème de cacao in mixing bowl. Mix well. Dip figs in mixture, coating them entirely. Set figs on end in serving bowl. Dust with cocoa or drizzle with chocolate syrup. Refrigerate until thoroughly chilled.

Saundra's Pecan French Toast
4 eggs	¼ tsp. vanilla extract
⅔ c. orange juice	½ loaf Italian bread cut in 1" slices
⅓ c. milk	⅓ c. butter
¼ c. sugar	½ c. pecan pieces
¼ tsp. nutmeg ground	2 Tbsp. grated orange peel

Preheat oven to 400°. Beat together eggs, orange juice, milk, sugar, nutmeg and vanilla. Place bread in a single layer in a flat dish. Pour milk mixture over bread, cover and refrigerate overnight. When ready to bake, cover a jellyroll pan evenly with melted butter. Arrange soaked bread slices in a single layer. Sprinkle with orange peel and pecans. Bake 20 to 25 minutes until golden brown.

Giving-thanks preparations When we moved into our new home, Ber and Saundra had a "Welcome Neighbors" party. Saundra offered to cat-sit Mischief whenever we traveled. During our two-year-old grandson Conner's visit, Ber became Conner's special friend. Every time Conner heard Ber's lawn mower, Conner would get *his* toy lawn mower and mow the lawn just like his friend Ber. And that was just the beginning!

"Taste and see that the Lord is good..." Experience God's goodness by kindness shown and received.

A thought for Thanksgiving What acts of kindness will I perform?

Prayers of Thanksgiving For great neighbors.

November 13

Psalm 103:1-5

Hmm, Hmm, Good!

Bless the Lord, O my soul, and forget not all His benefits.
Psalm 103:2

Cheese Grits Casserole for a Great Giving Thanks Breakfast

1 c. grits
4 c. boiling water
½ stick butter
3 eggs, separated

1 tsp. dry mustard
3 c. sharp cheddar cheese grated
1¼ tsp. salt

Add grits slowly to boiling salted water. Cook about 5 minutes until thick, stirring occasionally. Add egg yolks one at a time. Stir in dry mustard and 2 c. cheese. Set aside to cool. Beat egg whites until they form peaks. Fold into cooled mixture. Gently spoon mixture into 9" x 13" baking dish. Cover with 1 c. grated cheese. Bake at 350° for 30-40 minutes.

Giving-thanks preparations I first tasted Cheese Grits Casserole when I was in college. The old Campbell Soup commercial comes to mind. A woman is eating the soup with a smile on her face and we hear someone singing… "That's what Campbell's Soups are, hmm, hmm, good!" What would happen if after every blessing I received from God, I lifted my hands and sang, "That's what God's blessings are, hmm, hmm, good!"

"Taste and see that the Lord is good…" How delightful it would be if this whole month could be designated God Appreciation Month. What if we heard the roar of Christians throughout our communities lifting their voices in praise and thanksgiving? I wonder how it would change our Thanksgiving Day celebration? I wonder how it would change our everyday lives?

A thought for Thanksgiving What people, activities, and/or things do I express more appreciation for than I do God? What's wrong with my answer? How can I change it? Why would I want to?

Prayers of Thanksgiving For people who love to say, "Thanks!"

Bible Food for the Soul

Blessed are those who dwell in Your house. They will still be praising You! Psalm 84:4

Bible Food for All That Ails You
1 heaping cup of belief: John 3:16
2 pts. God's correction: Hebrews 12:10-11
A pinch of charity: Proverbs 22:9
3 c. courage: Psalm 27:14
A dash of comfort: Matthew 11:28
1 qt. forgiveness: Luke 6:35-38
A Tbsp. of contentment: Philippians 4:11
A heap of love: John 13:34-35

Shake well and take a tablespoon after each meal. Stores well; lasts a lifetime.

Giving-thanks preparations Soul food is a part of my ethnic background. My husband and I seize every opportunity to visit my cousin Adolf's soul food restaurant in Los Angeles. I love sitting in Cousin Adolf's restaurant and smelling the tantalizing aromas as I make the hard decision about what to order. Dining there is a special treat for my husband and me as well as the family and friends we invite to come along.

"Taste and see that the Lord is good..." There is another place I love to go where the absolute best soul food is served: the house of the Lord. I don't need a menu; I can have it all! I love not having to worry about overeating; it is impossible to get enough. The people are great, the ambience is uplifting and I always come away feeling satisfied. I especially like the "Giving Thanks" potluck dinner we have in our church the Sunday evening before Thanksgiving. What a great way to praise God for His blessings.

A thought for Thanksgiving What can I do to get my soul food?

Prayers of Thanksgiving For those who help clean up after Thanksgiving dinner.

November 15

I John 4:19-21

Someone to Fuss over Me

We love Him because He first loved us. I John 4:19

Fussed Over Green String Beans

2 lbs. fresh string beans with tips removed

3 slices thick sliced bacon   1 onion quartered

2 c. chicken broth   1 tsp. salt

1 tsp. garlic powder   2 tsp. black pepper

Dice bacon and sauté until slightly brown, not crisp. Add 2 c. water, onion and seasonings and bring to a boil. Add green beans and boil for 15-18 minutes. Adjust seasonings and serve using a slotted spoon.

Giving-thanks preparations My sister was lovingly "fussing" over her adult daughter. It was chilly and my sister wanted to make certain her daughter wore a sweater to work. Having recently moved into her apartment, my niece replied, "I am sure that's a good idea; however, I'm not sure where my beige sweater is." My sister immediately produced one she had brought with her. My niece smiled, rolled her eyes at me and said, "Mama might be returning home minus this sweater."

"Taste and see that the Lord is good..." It is hard to balance the need to "fuss" over our adult children with their need for independence. Perhaps God smiles as He watches us assert our independence. Yet, doesn't it feel good to have Him "fuss" over us, abundantly showering us with His blessings? I love the way my heavenly Father "fusses" over me, *and* I love the way my adult children and my adult niece allow my mother, my sister and me to "fuss" over them...every once in a while.

A thought for Thanksgiving How has God "fussed" over me today?

Prayers of Thanksgiving For loved ones who "fuss" over us, no matter how old we are.

November 16

Philippians 4:2-7

Thanksgiving Dinner at Aunt Mayme's

I implore Euodia and I implore Syntyche to be of the same mind in the Lord. Philippians 4:3

Buttermilk Pie

6 eggs

3 c. sugar

1 tsp. vanilla extract

1 large unbaked pie shell

1 c. buttermilk

2 sticks butter

Dash of nutmeg

Mix eggs, sugar and butter until light. Add vanilla, nutmeg and buttermilk. Pour into unbaked pie shell. Bake at 350° for 10 minutes. Reduce heat to 325° and bake 30 minutes or until firm to touch in the middle.

Giving-thanks preparations Thanksgiving dinner was always at Aunt Mayme and Uncle Art's. Aunt Mayme and Uncle Art didn't have any children…except my sister and me of course. So I am sure that it was assumed between the friends, who were more like sisters, that the children should be at home for Christmas. It never occurred to me that Aunt Mayme might like Christmas dinner at her house; it just seemed to be a quiet understanding between Mother and Aunt Mayme.

"Taste and see that the Lord is good…" Euodia and Syntyche could have learned lessons of love, cooperation and teamwork from Mother and Aunt Mayme. In today's Scripture, the apostle Paul pleads with them to "just get along." The love between my mother and Aunt Mayme allowed them to have quiet understandings. And oh how my sister and I benefited from that love. Aunt Mayme and Uncle Art were such a vital part of our lives: just a quiet understanding founded on their love for us and our love for them. What a blessing.

A thought for Thanksgiving How can a quiet understanding help enhance the relationship I have with my best friend?

Prayers of Thanksgiving For lifelong friends who are like family.

Room Enough

Even the sparrow has found a home, and the swallow a nest for herself, where she may lay her young... Psalm 84:3

Baked Macaroni and Cheese
1 (8 or 9 oz..) pkg. macaroni   1 Tbsp. salt
12 oz. sharp cheddar cheese, shredded
½ stick butter or margarine, melted
2 eggs, slightly beaten   2½ c. evaporated milk
¼ tsp. pepper   Paprika

Cook macaroni in water with salt. Drain and rinse in cold water. Lightly grease 2-quart casserole. Pour mixture of melted butter or margarine, 8 oz. of the cheese, eggs, evaporated milk and pepper on top. Sprinkle remaining 4 oz. cheese over top. Lightly sprinkle top with paprika. Bake in 350° preheated oven about 35 minutes or until bubbly and lightly browned.

Giving-thanks preparations I was stressing over where all of our overnight guests would sleep. I sighed deeply and relaxed as I remembered other wonderfully crowded family gatherings and how special they were. There was my parents' fiftieth wedding anniversary. Nine of us stayed at our parents' home that had two bedrooms and one bathroom. What fun we had. Yes, the message was coming loud and clear, "Where love abounds there is always enough room."

"Taste and see that the Lord is good..." Hotels are great but being all squished together with family and friends is even greater. There is always room in God's house. And I decided there would always be room in our house for as many family and friends as God blesses us with.

A thought for Thanksgiving What am I missing by focusing on having just the right conditions for visits from family and friends?

Prayers of Thanksgiving For family and friends who don't mind being squished together so they can *be* together.

November 18

Come Ye Thankful People Come

I will sing to the Lord as long as I live. I will sing praise to my God while I have my being. Psalm 104:33

Aunt Betty's Carrot Pie

2 c. cooked carrots	½ c. milk
¾ c. sugar	¼ tsp. salt
2 Tbsp. flour	2 eggs, beaten
¾ tsp. nutmeg	1 tsp. vanilla extract
4 Tbsp. butter	

Preheat oven to 350°. Puree carrots and milk in blender. Pour into bowl. Mix sugar, flour, and nutmeg together and add to pureed carrots and milk. Add eggs, vanilla and melted butter and mix well. Pour into 9-inch unbaked pie shell. Bake one hour or until center of pie is firm to the touch.

Giving-thanks preparations When I hear the Thanksgiving song, *"Come Ye Thankful People Come,"* I give thanks for God's abundance. I also give thanks for my Aunt Betty who is always thinking of the needs of others. When I asked Aunt Betty for a recipe to share, she immediately told me about the carrot pie recipe she had created for people who can't eat sweet potato pie. "My family and friends say they can't tell the difference." Now that Aunt Betty has shared her recipe with us, if we hear of family and friends who can't eat sweet potato pie, we can now provide a substitute that will taste just as good…if not better! Thanks, Aunt Betty.

"Taste and see that the Lord is good…" God abundantly provides for us. Whenever I hear this Thanksgiving song, I stop in awe of God's mighty love. Come, *we* thankful people, come.

A thought for Thanksgiving What blessings from God do I take for granted?

Prayers of Thanksgiving Those who prepare meals for people on special diets.

November 19

Psalm 36:7-9

God, Santa Claus, and Children

How precious is Your loving kindness, O God! Therefore the children of men put their trust under the shadow of Your wings. Psalm 36:7

My sister-in-law Milicent's Sock-It-To-Me Cake

1 pkg. Duncan Hines butter recipe cake mix	¼ c. sugar
1 c. sour cream (8oz. carton)	¼ c. water
½ c. Crisco vegetable oil	4 eggs

Preheat oven to 375°. Blend together cake mix, sour cream, oil, sugar, water and eggs. Pour half of the batter into a greased and floured pan; combine filling ingredients and sprinkle over batter. Pour remaining batter in pan. Bake 45 to 50 minutes.

Filling:
1 c. chopped pecans	2 tsp. cinnamon
2 Tbsp. brown sugar	

Frosting:
1 stick butter, softened	1 box confectioners' sugar
1 (8oz.) pkg. cream cheese	1 tsp. vanilla flavor
1 c. chopped nuts	

Cream together butter and cream cheese. Add confectioners' sugar. Stir in vanilla flavor and nuts. Spread on warm cake.

Giving-thanks preparations "How are Santa Claus and God different?" my sister-in-law, Milicent asked. She continued, "Santa Claus only brings gifts to good little girls and boys, but God loves us and blesses us unconditionally." Several years ago our niece Courtney and her mother Jackie were visiting for Christmas. Christmas morning found Courtney racing through the house ready to open her gifts, trusting that there would be something really good inside.

"Taste and see that the Lord is good..." Thanks to my sister-in-law Milicent's thought-provoking question, I will look for opportunities Thanksgiving Day to explain to children what God's unconditional love means to us *and* its benefit to them.

A thought for Thanksgiving How can my unconditional love help make this the best Thanksgiving ever?

Prayers of Thanksgiving For the wonder of children.

November 20

Psalm 103:11-14

Don't Look Back

As far as the east is from the west, so far has He removed our transgressions from us. Psalm 103:12

Louise Warren's Chess Pie Extraordinaire

1 cube butter	2 eggs
1 c. sugar	1 c. walnuts
1 c. raisins	1 tsp. vanilla extract
1 9" unbaked pie crust.	

Place crust in refrigerator for 30 minutes before filling.

Preheat oven to 350°. Cream together butter and sugar. Add eggs one at a time. Add vanilla and stir in raisins and nuts. Pour into unbaked, chilled pie crust and bake 45 minutes to one hour.

Giving-thanks preparations Louise brought her wonderful Chess Pie to a choir function. I tasted it and promptly decided I liked it much better than pecan pie, my usual Thanksgiving pie of choice. Louise's pie was not as sweet, yet it was brimming with flavor. I decided right there on the spot if Louise would share her recipe with me *and* "thee," I wouldn't look back. This Chess Pie Extraordinaire would be my new Thanksgiving pie of choice. Yum.

"Taste and see that the Lord is good…" My decision to look forward to having Louise' pie in the future reminded me of forgiveness. So often I catch myself reviewing something in my mind for which God forgave me years ago. The next time I start to feel guilty about a past misdeed for which I have already asked and received forgiveness, I am going to remember my response to Louise's Chess Pie and just refuse to look back. Praise God for His loving kindness.

A thought for Thanksgiving How can giving thanks for God's forgiveness brighten my day?

Prayers of Thanksgiving For family and friends with forgiving hearts.

November 21

Psalm 4:6-8

Silent Signals

I will both lie down in peace, and sleep; for You alone, O Lord, make me dwell in safety. Psalm 4:8

My Prayer Partner's Peanut Butter Pie

1 unbaked 9" pie shell	1 c. Karo dark syrup
1 c. sugar	3 eggs slightly beaten
½ tsp. vanilla	½ c. chunky style peanut butter

Preheat oven to 350°. Mix all ingredients together and pour into unbaked pie shell. Bake for about 30-35 minutes.

Giving-thanks preparations The fog was so thick I could barely see in front of me that morning as I began my 6:30 A.M. walk. Down the middle of the street came a boy, approximately nine or ten years of age, rollerblading. Headlights shining through the fog were rapidly approaching. Without thinking I lifted my left arm and pointed toward the young boy. He glanced my way immediately even though I had not uttered a sound. I then raised my right arm and pointed straight ahead. The boy waved in acknowledgement as he quickly skated to the side of the curb. The headlights sped past. No need for the warning blare of a horn. God has alerted His child with silent signals.

"Taste and see that the Lord is good…" I then began to wonder if I even came close to obeying God's silent signals to me with the same quickness as that young boy. Had I been living outside God's protection because I could not hear His signals *or* chose not to respond? A dear friend admonished me to stop, look, *and* listen…for God.

A thought for Thanksgiving What can I do to make it easier for God to alert and protect me today?

Prayers of Thanksgiving For people who drive cautiously when they see children playing.

November 22

Luke 10:39-42

Sisters in Unity and Diversity

She approached Him and said, "Lord, do You not care that my sister has left me to serve alone? Therefore tell her to help me."
Luke 10:40

My Sister's Salmon Log

1 large can salmon	1 tsp. prepared horseradish
1 8oz pkg. cream cheese	¼ tsp. Liquid Smoke
I Tbsp. lemon juice	2 tsp. grated onion
½ c. chopped pecans	½ c. snipped fresh parsley

Soften cream cheese; drain salmon well and remove any bones. Mix all ingredients except parsley and nuts. Cover and set in refrigerator for 1-2 hours. Chop pecans and add parsley. Form salmon mixture into log. Roll in nuts and parsley mixture. Refrigerate until ready to serve.

"Taste and see that the Lord is good…" Today's Scripture is about the conflict between Mary and Martha. If my sister Pat saw how important it was for me to be able to visit with Jesus, she would have said, "Go. I'll take care of this." My sister would have known that after dinner, I would have cleaned up the kitchen while she visited with Jesus. I guess it is a trust thing. We celebrate that we are different and alike, my sister and I. Families are so much richer when they celebrate and respect their unity *and* diversity.

A thought for Thanksgiving How can I celebrate and respect the ways in which my siblings and or family members are alike as well as unique?

Prayers of Thanksgiving For the unity of sisters.

November 23

"Gimme"

It is good to give thanks to the Lord, and to sing praises to Your name, O Most High. Psalm 91:1

Wanda's Prayer Praising Recipe

A Lots of ADORATION
"My soul magnifies the Lord, and my spirit has rejoiced in God my Savior." Luke 1:46

C Grateful CONFESSION
If we confess our sins, He is faithful and just to forgive us our sins and to cleanse us from all unrighteousness. I John 1:9

T Even more THANKSGIVING & Praise
Oh, give thanks to the Lord! Call upon His name. Make known His deeds among the peoples! Psalm 105

S All the SUPPLICATION you need
He shall call upon Me, and I will answer him. Psalm 91:15

Mix everything together and use liberally morning, noon, and night. Remember to add generous amounts of intercessory prayers…those you pray for family and friends.

Giving-thanks preparations One of my childhood memories is that of my father responding to the latest "thing" my sister and I wanted him to give us. "Gimme, gimme, gimme. How about saying 'thank you' for what you already have?"

"Taste and see that the Lord is good…" This Thanksgiving why not include a game of giving thanks? We could call it "Thank You Mania." Everyone would be given a certain number of minutes to list their top ten blessings for the year. An extra prize would go to those who could list twenty blessings in the same amount of time! Now *that* could be a Thanksgiving dinner that God might want to attend.

A thought for Thanksgiving What if I thanked God for my top ten blessings of the year *before* I began developing my Christmas wish list?

Prayers of Thanksgiving For those who create family-centered games.

November 24

Isaiah 41:17-20

The Absence of Fear in the Presence of God

Fear not, for I am with you; Be not dismayed, for I am your God. I will strengthen you, Yes, I will help you, I will uphold you with My righteous right hand. Isaiah 41:10

Cornbread with a Southwestern Flavor

1 can cream style corn	1 c. grated Cheddar cheese
1 pkg. Jiffy corn bread mix	3 eggs
1 onion finely chopped	
1 small can mild jalapeno peppers or green chilies	

Preheat oven to 400°. Mix all ingredients until well blended. Pour into a greased 8-inch baking dish. Bake for about 20-25 minutes.

Giving-thanks preparations Pastor Skip held the congregation spellbound as he told of helping one of his sons overcome his fear of water. With his son securely nestled in his arms, Pastor Skip ventured further and further into the family's swimming pool. "Hold your nose and we'll go under the water and then quick as a wink, I'll bring you back up," Pastor Skip promised. "Ready?" And with the faith of a child in a parent who had never let him down, the answer came, "Ready, Dad." Down he went, desperately afraid. Up he came, screaming in delight, safe in his father's arms.

"Taste and see that the Lord is good…" I remembered my father running behind me as I learned to ride a bicycle, ready to catch me if I fell. Our heavenly Father is ever present with outstretched hands, ready to help us overcome our deepest fears. What a blessed reassurance. What a reason to give thanks.

A thought for Thanksgiving What fears could I overcome if I chose to hold to God's ever-present hand?

Prayers of Thanksgiving For loving, trustworthy fathers.

November 25

Turkey Soup

For everyone who partakes only of milk is unskilled in the word of righteousness, for he is a babe. Hebrews 5:13

Turkey Soup

Turkey carcass

Salt and pepper to taste

2 large onions chopped

5 large celery stalks, including leaves

2 bay leaves

3 carrots sliced in rounds

Remove any remaining turkey from the carcass, dice and set aside. Place carcass in a large pot. Add water to cover, bring to a boil, and then lower heat. Add onions, bay leaves, and seasonings. Simmer for 2 hours. Remove large bones. Strain broth through a colander into a clean pot. Add carrots and celery. Continue cooking for 45 minutes. Remove celery stalks; purée in a blender. Stir purée into the soup to thicken. Add diced turkey, adjust seasoning, and simmer for 15 to 30 minutes.

Giving-thanks preparations Today's Scripture reminded me of my family's preferences for the soup's meat and vegetables over the broth. Just as we would be concerned if our five-year-old child could not tolerate solid foods, knowing that the child's growth would be stunted, we should also be concerned if we are not advancing from the milk of new believers to the solid food of older, more experienced believers.

"Taste and see that the Lord is good…" Knowing God's Word allows us to stand firm in our faith. As believers on solid food, we know without a doubt the difference between good and evil—we don't need anyone else to tell us their interpretation. Broth versus meat and vegetables is an acceptable preference in soup but not in our faith.

A thought for Thanksgiving How can I make sure I have grown in my faith from milk to solids?

Prayers of Thanksgiving For teachers of our faith.

November 26

The Power of Prayer

Now this is the confidence that we have in Him, that if we ask anything according to His will, He hears us. I John 5:14

Refrigerator Peanut Butter Pie
  6 oz. softened cream cheese
  1 c. chunky peanut butter
  14 oz. nondairy whipped topping
  1 can condensed milk (not evaporated)
  3 Tbsp. lemon juice
  1 9-inch prebaked deep-dish pie shell

Mix cream cheese and peanut butter in large bowl until well blended. Add condensed milk, lemon juice and nondairy whipped topping. Mix slowly until well blended. Pour into a cooled prebaked deep-dish pie shell. Refrigerate at least 2 hours before serving.

Giving-thanks preparations Fifteen-year-old Ryan's CD had become stuck in the rental car's CD player. I asked his mother if I might try to make it work. As I closed my eyes and placed my hand on the CD player, I felt Ryan's hand next to mine. I began with, "Dear Lord, if it be your will…" As I finished, my husband appeared and began issuing instructions. Seconds later, Ryan's favorite song boomed loudly for all to hear amidst our equally loud shouts of "Praise God!"

"Taste and see that the Lord is good…" I gave thanks for Ryan's faith that allowed him to place his hand next to mine while I prayed. Then I gave thanks that I could share with this teenager the message that if God loved us enough to hear and answer our little insignificant prayer, how much more confident we could be in believing He would hear and answer the really important ones.

A thought for Thanksgiving How can the power of prayer help me today?

Prayers of Thanksgiving For teenagers who believe in the power of prayer.

She Took *My* Place!

I had it in my heart to build a house of rest for the ark of the covenant of the Lord... I Chronicles 28:2

Pumpkin Bread

4 eggs, well beaten	3½ c. flour
3 c. sugar	1 tsp. cinnamon
1 c. vegetable oil	1½ tsp. salt
2 c. pumpkin	2 tsp. baking soda

Mixing together until smooth. Add:

1 tsp. Vanilla extract	1½ c. nuts
¾ c. water	1 tsp almond extract

Grease and flour two loaf pans. Bake at 325°

Giving-thanks preparations I was busy imagining how I would support the chorus for our Thanksgiving assembly and didn't quite hear what Mr. Tice, my favorite chorus teacher was saying to me. Did he really ask me, as the nineth-grade chorus accompanist to turn pages for the eighth-grade accompanist? "Wanda, I want you to help her all you can." Was I expected to share my copy of the music all marked up with my special notations? Could I even do that?

"Taste and see that the Lord is good..." Sometimes it appears we have done all the hard preliminary work and yet someone else is selected to do the job. I prayed for God's help as I sat next to the girl who would be taking my place. She was so appreciative of my help that before long, I was acting like the team leader Mr. Tice wanted me to be. She did a great job and thanks to answered prayers, so did I.

A thought for Thanksgiving What positive steps can I take to be helpful when God gives to someone else the project I was hoping to do?

Prayers of Thanksgiving For those who support the work of others.

November 28

Psalm 103:8-10

"Wow! I Don't Deserve This!"

He has not dealt with us according to our sins, nor punished us according to our iniquities. Psalm 103:10

Thanksgiving Potpourri

2 c. rose petals	2 whole cloves
2 c. rosemary	4 cinnamon sticks
2 c. mint	½ c. whole allspice

Mix all together and put in a large jar. Heat enough distilled white vinegar to cover and add it to the jar. Let the mixture stand for one week then use it in your electric simmering potpourri crock.

Giving-thanks preparations My sister and I love to shower our mother with gifts. Over the years, we have witnessed some spectacular responses when Mother opens her gifts like, "Oh, you girls. I don't deserve this!" When we see or hear the phrase, "I don't deserve this!" it is usually spoken by someone who feels they have gotten a raw deal. How often do we respond to something nice that happens with, "Oh gee. I don't deserve this!"

"Taste and see that the Lord is good…" *One* time an officer pulled me over for speeding and issued a warning citation instead of a traffic ticket. I gave the officer a big smile and thought "I don't deserve this…but thank you, Lord!" Too often I forget that I don't deserve *any* break from God. Somehow when I think about it like that, it makes me want to redouble my efforts to say, "Yes, thank you, Lord for blessing me. I don't deserve this!"

A thought for Thanksgiving What blessings did I receive today that I know I didn't deserve? How will I thank God for His mercy and His grace?

Prayers of Thanksgiving For those who protect and serve with justice *and* compassion.

November 29

Lightening the Load

The Lord is my Shepherd; I shall not want. Psalm 23:1

Breakfast Shake for the Health-conscious *or* the Dieter

8 oz. orange juice	8 to 10 fresh strawberries
1 medium banana	3 to 4 cubes of ice

Place all the above ingredients in a blender and blend at a high setting for approximately 30 seconds. If the shake is not the consistency you desire, blend it a little longer. Enjoy!

Giving-thanks preparations I was reading a devotion about standing on shoulders. The Scripture was from *Isaiah 49:22*. The image came to me of the Lord as my Shepherd with a lamb, not in His arms, but being carried across His shoulders. I remembered a pool party where my 280-pound husband climbed on my back. I took a deep breath anticipating that I would soon be pushed underwater by his weight. Much to my amazement, he felt light as a feather.

"Taste and see that the Lord is good…" When we trust in Jesus, He provides support, like the buoyancy of water, to help us carry loads that would be impossible for us to shoulder by ourselves. I made a mental note to myself. The next time I felt myself staggering under a heavy load, I would remember the support that allowed me to carry my husband, and the infinitely greater support available to me by the Lord, my Shepherd. What a blessing to be able to call on the name of the Lord whenever we need to lighten the load.

A thought for Thanksgiving What heavy load could I use my Shepherd's help in lightening?

Prayers of Thanksgiving For those who teach physically challenged children to swim.

Leftovers

No one puts a piece of unshrunk cloth on an old garment; for the patch pulls away from the garment, and the tear is made worse.
Matthew 9:16

Leftovers
Leftover
Leftove
Leftov
Lefto
Left
Lef
Le
L

Giving-thanks preparations Leftovers remind me of our grandson, Jay. Jay lives in Germany where he was born; English is a second language. When he was eight, he spent some time visiting us. Jay told me he liked macaroni and cheese. "Great," I thought. I made sure I prepared enough for two meals. Jay was delighted with the macaroni and cheese…the first night. When I attempted to serve it to him the second night, he pursed his lips, closed his eyes and said, "No, that is old." After a few questions I determined Jay was trying to tell me that he didn't eat leftovers. It seems Jay didn't believe in blending old food with the new.

"Taste and see that the Lord is good…" Today's Scripture is about the confusion that came about when Jesus tried to explain the difficulty in blending the laws and rituals of the Old Testament with the freedom of salvation and grace we find in the New Testament. Hmm. If during this month of giving thanks I have accumulated some leftovers—leftover thoughts and actions that are not consistent with who I want to be as a follower of Christ—maybe I should toss them out. Then free and unencumbered, I can enter the month of December ready to prepare for the gift of the Christ Child.

A thought for Thanksgiving What leftover thoughts and behaviors would keep me from a clean heart with which to welcome the Christ Child?

Prayers of Thanksgiving For the person who invented garbage disposals.

My Journal
November: Great Recipes for Giving Thanks

Insights: What are the most important lessons I learned about how to give thanks? How will they help me have the best Thanksgiving ever?

Challenges: What do I need to do to incorporate the lessons I have learned into my everyday life? When will I start?

What are the ten top blessings I received from God this month? How did they make this Thanksgiving special?

1.

2.

3.

4.

5.

6.

7.

8.

9.

10.

Answered Prayers

Introduction to December Devotions

Keeping Christ in Christmas!

"The virgin shall be with child, and bear a Son, and they shall call His name Immanuel. Matthew 1:23

MILLION DOLLAR CHRISTMAS GIFTS FOR UNDER $5!!!!! December is a time of preparing our hearts to celebrate the coming of the Christ Child. Yet the retail stores have been reminding us as early as September that it is a time to buy gifts, decorate, entertain, and flash credit cards.

For those of us who are so organized that all the gifts have been purchased and wrapped, this first week of devotions might have to be applied next year. But for the majority of us, these devotions and the ones for each day leading up to Christmas might be just what we need to *give* more while *spending* less. It might be the perfect opportunity to look at Christmas in a whole new and wonderful way. If you like the way this approach makes you feel, why not share it with family and friends?

The terrorist acts of September 11 caused us to think about "9-11" as more than a call for help. It has come to symbolize a loss of lives, security, and a way of life. The month of December comes at just the right time to help us refocus on the One who can bring comfort, peace and, yes, even joy. I invite you to experience all the love that God's gift brings. And I pray that these faith devotions help you keep Christ in Christmas, bringing you closer than ever to the One that created us and sustains us. "I am the light of the world. He who follows Me shall not walk in darkness, but have the light of life" *John 8:12.*

Your sister in Christ,
Wanda Scott Bledsoe

December 1

I Timothy 6:17-19

Enjoy Giving More While Spending Less

Command those who are rich in this present world not to be arrogant nor to put their hope in wealth, which is so uncertain, but to put their hope in God, who richly provides us with everything for our enjoyment. I Timothy 6:17

How? Several years ago I came to the realization that there is nothing I could afford to give my precious only sister that she didn't have at least two of already. So you can imagine my joy when she asked me if I would make a batch of rolls for her Christmas present. This was a special gift for her because the recipe had been handed down by our Aunt Zelma. What care and joy I took in making this Christmas gift for my sister. While I lovingly mixed the ingredients, I remembered and treasured those times our family had gathered around Aunt Zelma's table. It suddenly dawned on me that I was giving my sister so much *more* for Christmas while actually spending *less*.

Christmas deliberations Today's Scripture might be a reminder not to equate the amount of money we spend at Christmas with the amount of joy we hope to experience. Throughout the Bible, we find promises of God's provision for our wealth and happiness. As we turn to Christ anew this Christmas season to prepare our hearts for His coming, let us prayerfully consider how we might reflect His love through our gifts.

Christmas thought for today How is the "money issue" causing me stress during this Christmas season?

Prayers for our brothers and sisters in Christ Those receiving expensive gifts who would much rather receive a gift made by hand from the heart.

December 2

Isaiah 55:1-2

What Can't Money Buy?

*Come, all you who are thirsty, come to the waters; and you who
have no money, come, buy and eat! Come, buy wine and milk
without money and without cost.* Isaiah 55:1

What is in a price tag? What makes a gift priceless: ☑ its sentimental value, ☑ the love and understanding reflected in it, ☑ the effort
the giver put into it, ☑ the joy the giver seemed to feel in giving it,
☑ all of the above? How might your answer influence the kinds of
gifts you give this year?

So much love Our grandson Jay's maternal grandmother, Oma
Hilde, helps Jay make the gifts he sends to us at special times during
the year. The "custom made" calendar is one of our favorite gifts.
How hard and lovingly Jay and Oma Hilde must have worked to
gather the pictures and other treasures they pasted on the cover of
each month. That particular year has long passed, but we will keep
and treasure the Christmas gift forever.

Christmas deliberations How appropriate that the joy of giving and
receiving is as available to those without material wealth as it is to
the materially rich. This might be the perfect Christmas to give a
gift that is rich in sentimental value and packed full of love. Today's
Scripture is an invitation to God's table for all of us regardless of
position or wealth. The best Christmas gift of all is free to all!

Christmas thought for today What are some priceless gifts people on
my gift list would enjoy receiving from me?

Prayers for our brothers and sisters in Christ Grandparents who
want to give their grandchildren something more than money can
buy.

December 3

Money Can't Buy Everything, Right?

When Simon saw that the Spirit was given at the laying on of the apostles' hands, he offered them money and said, "Give me also this ability so that everyone on whom I lay my hands may receive the Holy Spirit." Acts 8:18,19

Right! Perhaps one reason we end up spending more than we want to at Christmas is the tendency to substitute money for time. One of my favorite Christmases was the year I made all of my gifts. I loved to sew. Mother, Daddy, my husband and our two children received robes; my sister, a hostess apron; my brother-in law, a down-filled vest; my niece, a hooded jacket and leggings to wear over the leotards she wore to dance class. The time I spent on each gift was enormous *and* well worth every minute when I heard the joy in their voices as they each thanked me. Our Christmas gift budget was low that year, but my family told me again and again that their gifts were priceless.

Christmas deliberations If you would like to get in touch with the true meaning of "Christmas" why not create a "Money Can't Buy This!" list. Ask family and friends to add to your list. Take a challenge and see if you can add an item each day between now and Christmas. Remember to stop and check how you are feeling about Christmas as your *priceless* list grows longer and longer.

Christmas thought for today What special gifts from God am I missing if I tend to look for dollar signs on my gifts?

Prayers for our brothers and sisters in Christ Children who are excited about the Christmas gifts they are making and those who will receive them.

December 4

Give What You Already Have

Well done, good and faithful servant! You have been faithful with a few things; I will put you in charge of many things.
Matthew 25:23

No money? What would you do if you had absolutely no money to spend for anything Christmas related? Make a list of "million dollar" gifts you could give for under five dollars. To get you started, barter your gifts and talents in exchange for those you would like that someone else possesses, or recycle those "special" gifts that you didn't use, which are stashed away in a drawer still in their original boxes. Get sentimental. Give family "heirlooms" you were planning to pass down at some point. Frame old family pictures, make a treasure recipe book, write a letter about a special memory. Commit to making visits, phone calls, or cookies. Prepare someone's favorite meal and take it to her or him. Promise to share your talents, especially those of you who get along very well with computers. Make a commitment to pray for or (even better) with someone.

Christmas deliberations Use your head, your heart and your hands. Give *more* of yourself. Spend *less* of your money. Sound good? Feel even better? Today's Scripture calls us to use the resources God has given us to the best of our ability. Why not apply it to Christmas giving?

Christmas thought for today What gifts can I give from my heart that are priceless?

Prayers for our brothers and sisters in Christ Those who are searching for work.

But Do You Lack Anything?

Then Jesus asked them, "When I sent you without purse, bag or sandals, did you lack anything?" Luke 22:35

Funny math My mother was anticipating a rather large dental bill at the first of the year. Our daughter decided to give her grandmother money for Christmas to help with the expense. When she told her husband how much they had given, he raised his eyebrows. He was looking at a check Mother had given *them* which was just $10 less than the check they had given her. I began explaining how God has moved His resources of money around in our family over the years so that we always have what we need. After my father died, my sister began sending money to supplement mother's income. My family sent money for plane tickets one year so our entire family could spend Christmas together. Mother sends money to the grandchildren and great-grandchildren. When they hear of a need, they send money to her. God provides!

Empty glass Just for fun, make a list of ten ways in which you feel God blessed you, guided you, and protected you today. Write "Thank you, Lord" on a Post-it note for each blessing and place it in a large glass. Wonder how quickly your glass will become full to overflowing? Try it and see.

Christmas deliberations Letting our children hear us say thank you to God on a regular basis just might be one way to teach our children how to keep Christ in Christmas.

Christmas thought for today How might saying, "Thank you for my blessings," help me keep Christ in Christmas?

Prayers for our brothers and sisters in Christ Families that share with each other.

December 6

I Timothy 6:6-10

Limited Funds?

For the love of money is a root of all kinds of evil. Some people, eager for money, have wandered from the faith and pierced themselves with many griefs. I Timothy 6:10

Low-budget shopping I had just been nominated for "Queen of Courts" at my high school. The honor would necessitate a new formal for the dance. Our budget was limited.

A designer dress! I remember the sales lady who showed us a dress saying, "I don't know if this will fit. It is a larger size but it is one of our designer dresses and it is on the clearance rack for $10." Wow! The alterations were done right in the store and for a few dollars more I had the most beautiful dress in the whole wide world!

Money problems? My daughter called, ecstatic. She and her husband had just paid off all their credit cards and had put themselves on a cash and carry plan. If credit cards had been available to my mother when we went shopping for my Queen of Courts formal, we would have spent money we didn't have on a dress that would have cost a lot more but couldn't have been any prettier than the designer dress we found.

Christmas deliberations Society would have us believe that if you have money you have everything. Can you remember a low-budget Christmas that was just about perfect? How do you think your answer will affect how much money you spend for Christmas gifts this year?

Christmas thought for today What part will the amount of money I have to spend play in how I measure the success of this Christmas?

Prayers for our brothers and sisters in Christ Those whose credit cards are maxed out.

December 7

What's a Christian to Do?

For I was hungry and you gave me something to eat, I was thirsty and you gave me something to drink, I was a stranger and you invited me in, I needed clothes and you clothed me, I was sick and you looked after me, I was in prison and you came to visit me. Matthew 25:35-36

I'm new here Early in our marriage when the children were very young, we moved to Dayton, Ohio. The first Sunday at College Hill was a little intimidating. My anxieties were soon put to rest as loving members of the family of God surrounded us and made us feel welcome. Before long my husband was using his voice in the choir and his leadership skills on the church council. The children made new friends in Sunday school and I was needed at the organ. That loving church family made a place for us.

Christmas deliberations Based on today's Scriptures, what activities might you want to make sure you include in this busy season? Ask family members to read this Scripture and then help add to your list. Then invite them to participate in those activities that help keep Christ in Christmas. And don't forget to look for the Christ Child in unusual places. You are sure to find Him there.

Christmas thought for today Where will I look for the Christ Child today? What will I do when I find Him?

Prayers for our brothers and sisters in Christ Those who are in prison and those who visit them.

December 8

Psalm 103:1-5

A Christmas Letter

Bless the Lord, O my soul; And all that is within me, bless His holy name! Bless the Lord, o my soul, and forget not all His benefits. Psalm 103:1,2

Something different One year I suggested that we write Christmas letters to each other instead of buying gifts. It was sort of like giving a gift from the heart rather than from the wallet. My gift from my daughter Shelly was priceless.

No price is too high "Dear Manamoo" (a term of endearment in the Greek language). She refers in the letter to something I purchased for her because I knew how vital it was to her well-being. "Mom, you then told me you would have paid anything. *No price was too high.* I will never fully be able to express my gratitude to God for blessing me with a mother like you. The sacrifices that you have made over the years have been enormous. I am truly grateful. You have set a wonderful example for me. I hope I can be the strong Christian woman and mother that you are. I will always love you. Merry Christmas! Love, Shelly"

Christmas deliberations I like to think of praise as "adoration from the heart" and gratitude as "a thankful heart." Too often we forget to tell our loved ones how wonderful they are and how much we appreciate all the ways, great and small, that they show their love for us. *Praise and gratitude*, what a wonderful way to keep Christ in Christmas!

Christmas thought for today What special person in my life is due an adoration and gratitude letter?

Prayers for our brothers and sisters in Christ Mothers and daughters.

"What *Do* I Know?"

And this gospel of the kingdom will be preached in all the world
as a witness to all the nations, and then the end will come.
Matthew 24:14

Sharing the good news Aunt Mary Lou's way Aunt Mary Lou wanted a young girl and relatively new Christian to share the good news with the occupants of her apartment building. "I can't do that," the young girl responded. "I don't know where to find the Scriptures I would need to answer their questions."

Start with what you know With conviction in her voice, Aunt Mary Lou said she told the young girl, "You know the Twenty-Third Psalm. You just raise your Bible and say, 'I will have to get someone to answer that question for you, *but this I do know*, The Lord is my Shepherd, I shall not want.'" It seems that the young woman who wanted to witness for Christ took Aunt Mary Lou's advice and shared the good news of the kingdom of God with her neighbors.

Christmas deliberations Not everyone wants to deliver God's message. Moses was concerned about his speech impediment, Jeremiah about his young age, and Jonah just didn't want to do it period. If you would like to share the Christmas story but you don't feel you know it well enough, remember Aunt Mary Lou's advice, "Just share what you *do* know."

Christmas thought for today What does the Christmas story mean to me personally, and how might I share it with others?

Prayers for our brothers and sisters in Christ Those who need to experience the Christmas story in a personal way.

December 10

His Code of Ethics

He has shown you, O man, what is good; And what does the Lord require of you But to do justly, To love mercy, And to walk humbly with your God? Micah 6:8

Surely it must be my math I was so uncertain of my own math skills that I hesitated for a second before I asked the cashier to recount the change. Then, I thought, "It won't be the first time I've looked stupid because I calculated something incorrectly. Here goes. 'Ma'am, I think you gave me too much change.'" She quickly recounted, and then slowly removed the ten-dollar bill in my open hand and replaced it with a one-dollar bill. The look in her eyes said more than the soft "thank you" that came from her lips. I thought to myself, "You're welcome. It is what Christ would have us do."

Christmas deliberations We are called to live Christ-like lives. But exactly what does that mean? The Bible admonishes us to love our neighbor as we love ourselves *Matthew 22:39*. We also know that the Golden Rule says we should do unto others as we would have them do unto us. Both rules apply in today's lesson. I would certainly want a clerk to call my attention to the fact that I had mistakenly overpaid for my purchase. The second greatest commandment and the Golden Rule—both great reminders to make sure we keep Christ in Christmas *and* all year long!

Christmas thought for today How will I apply the Scripture from *Matthew 22:39* during my holiday shopping?

Prayers for our brothers and sisters in Christ Cashiers who find their cash drawer short at the end of their day.

December 11

Proverbs 16:1-9

A Moral Commercial?

All the ways of a man are pure in his own eyes, But the Lord weighs the spirits. Proverbs 16:2

You're kidding! Imagine my surprise when I saw a commercial advertising beer in which the parents are in their pajamas facing a young couple and the father says, "I know you two are engaged to be married but our house, our rules." You then see the young couple go into separate bedrooms. I was shocked! I turned to my husband to ask when, if ever, he had seen such a message on a television commercial of any kind?

True or false... If our children assume that what they see and hear on television is how life is lived, what messages are they consistently getting? If you decided to make a list of the popular messages we receive from our televisions that are consistent with our desire to live Christ-centered lives, how long do you think that list would be?

Christmas deliberations How would we compare the amount of time we spend listening to messages from our televisions versus the amount of time we spend listening to messages about Christ-like living? Hmm. Why then are we surprised and upset when our children live their lives influenced by the messages they hear most, the messages we allow them to hear... the messages we listen to right along with them?

Christmas thought for today What adjustments do I need to make so that the majority of the messages my family and I listen to this Christmas season are Christ-centered?

Prayers for our brothers and sisters in Christ Children who spend several hours a day looking at television.

December 12

Psalm 119:105-112

Christmas Lights

And He will send His angels with a loud trumpet call, and they will gather His elect from the four winds, from one end of the heavens to the other. Matthew 24:31

My kind of neighbor Even though the last thing I wanted to do was tackle another box so soon after our move, I began rummaging through the area in the garage marked "Christmas decorations." Soon the outside of our new home was arrayed with bright lights. Our neighborhood became even more beautiful as night descended, illuminated by twinkling lights of all colors, shapes and sizes. Christmas lights through our community make everything seem more beautiful, more alive, and more special somehow. How sorry I am to see the lights come down after Christmas. How dull and drab everything looks. "Wouldn't it be wonderful if Christmas lights could remain throughout the year?"

Christmas deliberations The birth of the Christ Child brought light into a world of moral darkness and degradation that can never be extinguished. We can brighten our communities all through the year as we let the light of Christ shine through us. Our lamps are fueled with the light of His Word. "Thy Word is a lamp unto my feet and a light unto my path" *Psalm 119:105*. Just think, we can have— no we can *be*—Christmas lights every day of the year as we consistently read God's Word and then apply it in our everyday lives.

Christmas thought for today What dark corners of my community can I illuminate with the light of Christ?

Prayers for our brothers and sisters in Christ Those who distribute Bibles in foreign countries and here at home.

December 13

John 14:15-18, Romans 8:26-27

"Just You and Me, Lord"

And I will pray the Father, and He will give you another Helper,
that He may abide with you forever. John 14:16

The test The hurt remains vivid in my mind. What if God really wanted me to turn to Him for the comfort I so desperately sought? How would I find comfort in silence? I decided to test it by being totally dependent on God. In the stillness of the early morning, I read and reread today's Scripture. I was not alone, for God is always present through The Holy Spirit.

The peace It was as if I had embarked on a special spiritual journey. A peace slowly filled my heart as I felt God's reassurance that I was not alone and *together* we would get to the other side of my sorrow. It was a long week, but by the end of that week I had reached a new and wonderful place in my faith journey.

Christmas deliberations God sent His Holy Spirit to guide, comfort and correct. What a blessed gift. What a perfect gift made available to us all year long by God's unconditional love. How is the Holy Spirit evident in your life? If you were asked to explain the presence of the Holy Spirit to someone else, how would you go about it? Why would you want to?

Christmas thought for today How might turning to The Holy Spirit affect the way I react when I feel alone in the midst of a crowded Christmas season?

Prayers for our brothers and sisters in Christ People who feel lonely and alone during this time of year.

December 14

Luke 2:1-7

Receiving Blankets and Such

And she brought forth her firstborn Son, and wrapped Him in swaddling cloths, and laid Him in a manger, because there was no room for them in the inn. Luke 2:7

Pigs in a blanket My sister and I had taken our mother, aunts, and uncle out for breakfast. My sister, Pat, had decided she would have "pigs in a blanket." What on earth was it? "Just a pancake wrapped around a link sausage," my sister answered smiling. At the end of our breakfast, Aunt Helen pulled me aside and whispered, "I think you should write about these pigs in a blanket in that book you are writing."

Swaddling theory That episode made me think of the week I spent with our grandson Conner shortly after he was born. "Mom, if you swaddle him, he will feel more secure making it easier for him to fall asleep," my daughter instructed me. Mary the mother of Jesus wrapped her son in swaddling cloths used to keep a baby's limbs straight.

Christmas deliberations We sometimes chafe against those things that confine us. Yet the confining swaddling cloths were used to help ensure straight limbs for one infant and provide feelings of security for another. Both were wrapped in love. Perhaps we should take another look at those things in our spiritual lives that confine us. They just might be wrappings of love meant to keep us on straight secure paths.

Christmas thought for today How does the birth of the Christ Child and His love for me help me feel safe and secure in a security-conscious world?

Prayers for our brothers and sisters in Christ Drug-addicted mothers and their newborn babies.

December 15

Luke 3:1-6 and John 1:19-27

Who Wants to Be Different?

*As is written in the book of the words of Isaiah the prophet: A
voice of one calling in the desert, "Prepare the way for the Lord,
make straight paths for him."* Luke 3:4

Wanting to conform I sighed as I remembered that living in my parents' home and living out their faith, which became my faith, meant my sister and I were *different*. There seemed to be endless things my sister and I couldn't do or say because we were Christians. I remember the anxiety of being different in school. Butterflies invaded my stomach countless times over the years as I had to explain to my peers why I couldn't do something. Fortunately for my mother and for *me*, before I went away to college I finally caught on that being different was more than OK when being different was the result of living out one's faith.

Christmas deliberations John the Baptist was certainly different. That difference was reflected in his clothes, his diet and, most importantly, his message. Once we commit through baptism to a new life in Christ, we too are called to be different, to live a *different* message. In this Christmas season, the world bombards us with lots of messages about how we should spend our money and use our time. If we take a look at our Day-Timers, our Palm Pilots our checkbook registers and credit card receipts, would they indicate that we "got the message?"

Christmas thought for today What messages am I giving with the way I spend my time and my money during this Christmas season?

Prayers for our brothers and sisters in Christ Young people who need help in resisting peer pressure.

December 16

Isaiah 30:19-21

Security Checks

I will lead the blind by ways they have not known, along unfa-miliar paths I will guide them; I will turn the darkness into light before them and make the rough places smooth. These are the things I will do; I will not forsake them. Isaiah 42:16

Who would have thought As I began packing for our trip to Seattle to spend Christmas with our daughter and her family, I made a mental note to take my eyebrow tweezers out of the cosmetic bag I carried in my purse and place them in the bag I was checking. I shook my head, amazed at the long-range effects the terrorist attacks on the World Trade Center have had. My heart began to race as I thought of all of the calamities that might be waiting for our family in the New Year. I took a deep breath as I remembered the paths that God had led me on during the past year. We would be all right. I couldn't see what the New Year would bring, but that didn't matter because I knew God could.

Christmas deliberations We as believers can *seize this moment in time* when our nation remains focused on national and worldwide security checks. We can share our "security plan" with those seeking protection, guidance and comfort. "So we say with confidence, 'The Lord is my helper; I will not be afraid. What can man do to me?'" *Hebrews 13:6* As believers we know our security is in Jesus Christ and that He is infallible!

Christmas thought for today What am I doing to share my faith with those afraid of what the New Year might bring?

Prayers for our brothers and sisters in Christ Those who conduct security checks.

December 17

Romans 12:17-21

Forgiveness, a Special Gift

And whenever you stand praying, if you have anything against anyone, forgive him, that your Father in heaven may also forgive you your sins. Mark 11:25,26

Lashing out Right before my intense confrontation with a coworker, I received some wonderful news. No, make that spectacular news. Then bam! I thought I was being nice when I approached my coworker over what I considered a mixed signal between us. Boy, did he let me have it! I walked away in a daze. Soon I was planning how I would set the record straight with him. A quiet voice began whispering in my ear, "Forgive him so you can enjoy the good news I have just given you." "Yes, Lord," I replied, "but he had no right!"

Excuse me "Where is it?" I cried as I rifled through my folder looking for the item I needed for my presentation, just minutes away. My coworker's door was open. "What are you looking for?" he asked. When I told him, he reminded me that I had given him an advance copy, which he quickly retrieved from his files. What a special gift I had received…made possible by a forgiving heart *and* a restrained tongue.

Christmas deliberations Christmas is about giving. However, the birth of Jesus Christ was a gift that would be later used to *forgive* us for time eternal. What part could *forgiveness* play in helping you, your family, and friends experience Christmas as it was meant to be?

Christmas thought for today Who needs the gift of my for*giv*eness today?

Prayers for our brothers and sisters in Christ Those struggling to forgive people who have committed violent acts against them or their family.

December 18

Luke 3:11-14

Bumpy Roads

But do not forget to do good and to share, for with such sacrifices God is well pleased. Hebrews 13:16

Bumpy roads My chiropractor's office is located in "horse country" on a very bumpy road. Maybe bumpy is being too kind, for the bumps and ruts are quite deep. Most of the time I come barreling down the highway at 60 miles an hour, make a quick turn onto an access road, slowing down to 45 or 50 miles an hour for a block or two before making that final turn onto the bumpy road where, in protection of my car *and* my back, I cruise at a mere 5 to 10 miles an hour for the final two or three blocks to my destination.

A time to share The road leading to my chiropractor's office helps remind me to slow down. Maybe we could all use something as graphic as a bumpy road during our hectic Christmas schedule to help remind us to slow down. Then we might be able to see the opportunities to do good for those who are not a part of our family.

Christmas deliberations In a materialistic world that becomes even more so at Christmas, how could we use the experience of doing good for others to help balance the concept of "he or she who has the most presents under the tree wins"? Why might the Christ Child want us to explain the fallacy of this concept to children? How would you go about it? What child or children will you choose? When will you start?

Christmas thought for today What lessons could children learn about helping others during this Christmas season from observing me?

Prayers for our brothers and sisters in Christ Adults and children who gather toys at Christmas for underprivileged children.

December 19

I Timothy 6:8-12

Patience Is a Virtue

But you, O man of God, flee these things and pursue righteous-ness, godliness, faith, love, patience, gentleness. I Timothy 6:11

Random acts of patience I like to think that part of the Christmas spirit is taking the time to perform random acts of patience as we go about our even busier days. Unfortunately during the Christmas season we may experience more of those days when it seems as if no matter how many times you allow someone to cut in front of you at the checkout counter or on the freeway, your acts of kindness are not returned. I am told that parking lots are the most dangerous places to be during the holiday season as tired, frustrated people jockey for limited spaces. Parking lots, a great place for believers to exercise patience as a way of keeping Christ in Christmas.

Christmas deliberations Does it surprise you that in the midst of a season where we find ourselves rushing madly about from early morning to late at night, we need an extra measure of patience? Why not have a favorite Scripture close at hand? One of my favorites for trying times is *Philippians 4:13*, "I can do all things through Christ who strengthens me." What a thought, using Scripture to help us be patient with others so that they can see the kindness of the Christ Child shining brightly and lovingly through us.

Christmas thought for today How would Christ have me respond when others are impatient with me? How would He have me respond when I feel my patience is being tried?

Prayers for our brothers and sisters in Christ Impatient drivers looking for parking spaces in crowded parking lots.

December 20

Faith Toddler-Style

*Assuredly, I say to you, whoever does not receive the kingdom
of God as a little child will by no means enter it. And He took
them up in His arms, laid His hands on them, and blessed
them.* Mark 10:15,16

Full of radiance We were closing our "Mom's Morning Fellowship"
Bible study. "It is time to pray, children," we called. The toddlers
joined our circle standing next to their mommies, except for four-
year-old Alexis. She stood in the middle of the circle, clad in her
pretty green dress, minus her shoes and socks that she had removed
to make it easier to run around and play. At the end of the prayer
when I opened my eyes, Alexis still had her eyes closed, her face
turned up with the most beautiful countenance I have ever seen. I
stood spellbound, unwilling to be the one to intrude on the prayer
of a child.

Christmas deliberations What would happen if I brought the radiance displayed on Alexis' face to the Christmas season? What if I
replaced a countenance of frustration, impatience and exhaustion
with a countenance of radiance? And then what would happen, if
when people stopped to ask me why I looked so radiant, I told them
about the love the Christ Child brings to all of us? Yes! Christmas
gives us a chance to have the faith of a child.

Christmas thought for today What would it take for me celebrate the
birth of the Christ Child with the faith of a child?

Prayers for our brothers and sisters in Christ Little children whose
radiance warms our hearts.

December 21

Luke 2:1-21

"To Do" List Monsters!

But those who wait on the Lord shall renew their strength; They shall mount up with wings like eagles, they shall run and not be weary, they shall walk and not faint. Isaiah 40:31

Push and squeeze I sat checking off my "To Do" lists. There were gifts that still needed to be purchased, wrapped and mailed. And there were things to pack for our trip to Seattle where we would spend part of the Christmas holidays with our children. Panic started to build up inside as I realized I could never get it all done. Then I remembered the Scripture from Isaiah 40:31 I had read that very morning. Maybe that was the answer. Wait on the Lord to renew my strength. Hmmm, after an earnest prayer, I picked up my date book and started reprioritizing my "To Do" list. After all, my idea of a wonderful Christmas was the time and energy to enjoy celebrating the birth of the Christ Child with family and friends. And lest I forget, "Who controls my time? No one but me!" I began crossing out the "Nice But Not Necessary" items on my dreaded, "To Do" list. I felt better already.

Christmas deliberations What is sapping your strength during this Christmas season? How could these Scriptures be part of your unlimited source of strength? What can you do to make sure your priorities reflect the true meaning of Christmas?

Christmas thought for today How can reading and rereading the Christmas story help me prioritize my work so that I can experience the true joy of Christmas?

Prayers for our brothers and sisters in Christ Those required to put in extra hours at work preparing for Christmas sales.

December 22

Luke 2:8-12

"So, Who Is This God Person?"

Now when they had seen Him, they made widely known the saying which was told them concerning this Child. Luke 2:17

Good question A preschool teacher was reading the story of Jonah and the whale from the book of Jonah to a group of preschool children. One child raised his hand and with a puzzled look on his face asked, "So, who is this God person?"

Who knows the answer? Growing up in a family where the first outing of the newborn is to church, I could not imagine a child ready to enter kindergarten who didn't know about God. But how could he know if his parents didn't tell him? And if his parents didn't tell him, who would?

Christmas deliberations As we prepare to celebrate the birth of the Christ Child, there is a message we are called to give. *First,* Jesus came to live among us. And the Word became flesh and dwelt among us" *John 1:14. Secondly,* Jesus came for us. "God so loved the world that He gave His only begotten Son that whosoever believes in Him should not perish but have everlasting life" *John 3:16. Third,* He offers the gift of eternal life. "The wages of sin is death, but the gift of God is eternal life in Christ Jesus our Lord" *Romans 6:23*. It is the message of the true meaning and purpose of Christmas.

Christmas thought for today Why is the Christmas message more important than ever?

Prayers for our brothers and sisters in Christ Men, women and children waiting to hear the message that God still cares.

December 23

Matthew 2:1-12

O Christmas Tree

Go and search carefully for the young Child, and when you have found Him, bring back word to me, that I may come and worship Him also. Matthew 2:8

The makeover During the early years of our marriage when money was exceedingly tight, I chose our Christmas trees based on price rather than beauty. Dragging the poor tree home, I would place it in the Christmas tree stand and then the makeover began. When I had finished, I would step back to inspect my work, confident of the compliments I would receive for my beautifully *camouflaged* tree when family and friends came to visit.

Christmas deliberations Am I not like the misshapen Christmas trees I used to buy? Do I not work diligently to camouflage the ugly parts of me with makeup, clothes, and frequent trips to my hairstylist? Am I not capable of using words flowing from my mouth like honey that convey a false message? The wonder of it all is that God knows about the misshapen Christmas tree, King Herod, *and* me. As a believer, the only make-over I need is in my heart. It is the beauty that radiates from my heart as I strive to be more Christ-like that makes any camouflage efforts both useless and unnecessary.

Christmas thought for today What kind of makeover does my heart need before I am ready to celebrate the birth of the Christ Child?

Prayers for our brothers and sisters in Christ Those who suffer from low self-esteem.

December 24

"And a Child Shall Lead Them"

For to us a child is born, to us a son is given, and the government will be on his shoulders. And He will be called Wonderful Counselor, Mighty God, Everlasting Father, Prince of Peace
Isaiah 9:6

Pass the peace, please In some churches a part of their service involves passing the peace. "Peace be with you," says one member to another. I wonder how that greeting would work at home in the midst of family arguments, or on the soccer field as disgruntled parents charge each other, or in the workplace when tempers flare over missed deadlines and differences of opinions. What about in local governments when confronted with issues of how to deal with the hungry, the homeless and the disenfranchised? I wonder how passing the peace would work among the generals of nations and the soldiers they send to fight each other on scarred battlefields.

Christmas deliberations We celebrate the birth of the Prince of Peace this Holy Night. His promise of peace is not that our lives will always be peaceful, but that He comes to show us another way, a way to live our lives modeling His peace. Let us heed the angels' message and strive to live in peace while working for justice for all. Read and reread together with family and friends the greatest story ever told. It is a message that brings hope, joy, comfort, and peace yesterday, today, and forevermore.

Christmas thought for today How can I teach my children to resolve their differences peacefully? How can I show them by my example?

Prayers for our brothers and sisters in Christ Those who negotiate peace in foreign lands.

December 25

Christmas Day John 1:1-14

"He's Here!"

The light shines in the darkness, but the darkness has not under-stood it. John 1:5

Joy to the World the Lord Is Come!

They're here, they're here!...Perhaps Christmas morning should be like the wonder on our children's faces when they awoke to discover that their grandparents had arrived in the middle of the night from a "far-away" place. When we lived in Ohio, my parents would make the twelve-hour drive from Kansas to visit us, often arriving at one or two o'clock in the morning. There would be whispered greetings and then quietly and gratefully they would go to bed. Bright and early the next morning, as soon as our little ones opened their eyes and realized this was the day, they would run, peek in the room where their grandparents slept, and then begin shouting with joy, "They're here, they're here!"

Christmas proclamation: *The Lord is come!* What if we shouted His arrival with all the fervor and innocence of young children happy to see a loved one? The Christ Child, our Savior, *is* a loved one, come to save us in the midst of a morally depraved world. He comes promising peace in the midst of the endless wars we fight. He comes bringing hope for a desperate world. He comes to us to *each* one of us in our need. He is here! Let us all proclaim, "Joy to the World, the Lord is come!"

Christmas thought for this Holy Day How can I use the presence of the Christ Child within me to bring a message of hope and peace to myself, my family, and my community?

Prayers for our brothers and sisters in Christ Children waking up today in war-torn countries.

December 26

I John 4:7-12

That's the Spirit!

In all their distress He too was distressed and the angel of His presence saved them. In His love and mercy He redeemed them; He lifted them up and carried them all the days of old. Isaiah 63:9

My mother's friend Mrs. Cox lives by herself and she has health problems. One would think she had enough challenges in her life to make her less than a joyful person, yet just the opposite is true. When I travel to Kansas to visit my mother, we always visit Mrs. Cox. I watch her as she slowly walks to her kitchen to retrieve something she has made for us, a smile on her face. I marvel at her capacity to love.

Up and down It is all over: the buildup, the anticipation, the stress of the big day. Christmas is all over and for some that means a letdown.

After-Christmas deliberations Feeling down? Up you go. Share God's love. Take some of that leftover pumpkin pie to a friend in a nursing home. Bring pictures of the holiday festivities to share. Invite someone over for leftovers. Think of other things you can do that might brighten someone else's day. Reflect Christ's love for us by sharing our love with others. Get back into the true spirit of Christmas. Keep it all year long. Feeling down? Up you go!

After-Christmas thought for today What can I share with someone else that will help me keep the true spirit of Christmas alive all year long?

Prayers for our brothers and sisters in Christ People who experience a letdown after Christmas and the people who befriend them.

December 27

Just a Table

And my God shall supply all your need according to His riches in glory by Christ Jesus. Philippians 4:19

A fluke? Shelly, our daughter, was now calling me to tell me how good God is. Shelly had been asked to host her "Mommy and Me" Bible study group. Everyone was gathered around the dining room table. One of the mothers picked up one of the toddlers and gave him a pen to amuse himself. In a flash, the toddler had etched a scrawl in the table. Everyone gasped, including the mother with the toddler; she looked as if she might die right on the spot.

Don't worry "Mom, I about died too, but then a voice whispered to me, 'It is just a table.' So I asked God to give me the strength to be gracious. And I told the mother that I valued her friendship more than I valued that table."

Only God "Later I prayed that God would help me not be upset each time I saw the scratch. Then I went to the table and noticed that the scratch was on the table leaf. Mom, I have two leaves. I ran to the closet, got out the second leaf and switched it with the one that was scratched. God heard my prayer and answered it in ways I could not have imagined!"

After-Christmas deliberations Christmas celebrations are over for another year, but God's faithfulness to us remains with us throughout the entire year and the next...and the next...forevermore.

After-Christmas thought for the day Who needs my compassion and generosity because they have accidentally damaged some *thing* I value?

Prayers for our brothers and sisters in Christ Mommy and Me Bible study groups.

December 28

Exodus 14:19-20

Feeling My Way

*For this God is our God forever and ever; He will be our guide
even to the end.* Psalm 48:14

This old house In just a few weeks my sister and I will fly "home," the
place of our birth, to spend a week with our mother. We will sleep
in the same bedroom we had as children and recall childhood memories. Our bedroom has an old ceiling fixture that has to be an
antique. The light switch on the wall controls it as you enter the
bedroom. It is so comforting to know that when it is dark outside, I
can flip on the light switch before entering the room. I never have
to grope around in the dark.

After-Christmas deliberations Today's Scripture reassures me that
God is standing at the doorway to all of my life experiences, ready
to shed His light to keep me from stumbling in the dark. All I have
to do is flip the switch, which happens every time I read His Holy
Word and pray for His Divine guidance. So much of our world is
spiritually dark. As believers we have the power source to flood
those dark corners and rooms of our lives with His bright light that
shows us the Christ-like way. We never have to remain in spiritual
darkness. All we have to do is "flip the switch."

After-Christmas thought for today How might I use today's Scripture
to show me the way God would have me go?

Prayers for our brothers and sisters in Christ Those facing cataract
surgery and the surgeons who perform it.

December 29

Isaiah 64:1-8

Pie Dough

But now, O Lord, You are our Father; We are the clay, and You our potter; And all we are the work of Your hand. Isaiah 64:8

Starting over I called Annette, a young woman from our church, about a project I heard she was planning. I began sharing *my* mission and wondering how we could bring her project in line with my goals. Then I took a breath and let her talk. I discovered Annette was a one-woman army for the Lord. Desperate to think of ways I could support her vision, I made an attempt to reach out to *her* need. "What need do you have, Annette, that I might lift up to God?" She told me and I prayed earnestly and sincerely for her while silently asking God to forgive my steamroller mentality.

The power of prayer Annette looked at me in wonder as I approached her the following Sunday. "Your prayer for me was answered the very next morning," she said. "Let's have a prayer of thanksgiving," I said truly thankful that God had taken the mess I had made and molded it into something good.

After-Christmas deliberations When I was a little girl learning to work with pie crusts, the dough sometimes fell apart in my small hands while trying to transfer it into the pie pan. My mother would tell me I couldn't roll the pie dough out again, or it would become tough. Fortunately for me, God is able to mold and remold me as much as He needs to until He gets the results He wants.

After-Christmas thought for the day What is God trying to mold me into?

Prayers for our brothers and sisters in Christ Those who want to start over.

December 30

Philippians 4:6,7

Concerned for the Future?

He will be like a tree planted by the water that sends out its roots by the stream. It does not fear when heat comes; its leaves are always green. IT has no worries in a year of drought and never fails to bear fruit. Jeremiah 17:8

Getting ready for the New Year My husband and I had talked about leaving our home in sunny southern California when he retired to relocate to rainy Seattle to be near our daughter, son-in-law and precious grandson. I stood at the window one morning fretting about the idea of starting over again at our age. How would we survive without sunshine?

His Calendar of events Suddenly, I thought, why am I worrying about something that is four or five years away? This time last year I did not know that I would be traveling home to be with my eighty-six-year-old mother for her cardiac catheterization. And I had no idea that we would be putting our dream home on the market, or that I would consider our downsized new home to be the perfect dream home for our current needs. Or that God would provide the funds for me to self-publish this book. None of these events were on my calendar but they were evidently on God's. I sighed, content to let God's plan for my New Year unfold.

Christmas deliberations What a great way to start the New Year, believing and trusting in God's calendar of events. Perhaps this is a good time to review the major ways God blessed you last year. Why not write them down as an affirmation that He will also bless you in the coming year.

After-Christmas thought for today What fears do I have about the New Year and how can today's Scriptures help?

Prayers for our brothers and sisters in Christ Those who face an uncertain future.

December 31

Psalm 34:1-3

Tying Up Loose Ends

Oh, magnify the Lord with me, And let us exalt His name together.
Psalm 34:3

Thank-you notes The old year is almost gone. Time to tie up any loose ends...like the dreaded thank-you notes for all those Christmas presents we received. This message is really a reminder to myself. How I dislike writing thank-you notes.

Thank you, God It is a good thing God doesn't require me to write thank you notes in exchange for the many blessings I receive. How would we feel if we gave someone a very expensive gift and we never received a thank-you note? What if they never even mentioned the gift? And how frustrating if we would like to thank God for specific blessings that happened months ago but we just couldn't remember what they were?

Christmas deliberations Today's Scripture reminds us to give thanks and praise to the One who created us and provides for us. Here is one idea you might like to try. Start an ongoing list of memorable blessings. Add to it regularly. Pick a blessing of the month. Just think, at this time next year you will have a very special way to bring in the New Year by thanking God for His wonderful blessings of the past year. How affirming to be reminded yet again that God still cares.

NEW YEAR'S EVE thought for the day How does God's love help me joyfully anticipate a New Year full of hope and wonderful possibilities?

Prayers for our brothers and sisters in Christ Those who need hope rekindled.

My Journal
December: Help Me Keep Christ in Christmas

Insights: What are three things I can do to keep Christ in Christmas? When will I start?

Challenges: What are some million-dollar gifts for under five dollars that I can give using my hands and my heart?

What are the ten top blessings I received from God this month?

1.

2.

3.

4.

5.

6.

7.

8.

9.

10.

Answered Prayers

His Roses and Thorns
Order Form

Postal orders: 30520 Rancho California Rd
Suite 107 PMB #88
Temecula, CA 92591

E-mail orders: wanda@hisrosesandthorns.com

Website: www.hisrosesandthorns.com

Please send *His Roses and Thorns* to:

Name: _____

Address: _____

City: _____   State: _____

Zip: _____

Telephone: (_____) _____

Book Price: $14.95

Shipping: $3.00 for the first book and $1.00 for each additional book to
cover shipping and handling within US, Canada, and Mexico.
International orders add $6.00 for the first book and $2.00 for
each additional book.

Or order from:
ACW Press
85334 Lorane Hwy
Eugene, OR 97405

(800) 931-BOOK

or contact your local bookstore